Praise for
The Three Kingdoms Trilogy

SKY BOUND is a fantastic adventure and James Morris is a prince of an author. Family is who fights with and for you… and writes a book you want to reread. Props, Brother James!
— Nancy Holder, *New York Times* bestselling author of THE WICKED SAGA.

A world ripped into three kingdoms… A terrifying imbalance of power… A clever young adventurer with a streak of reluctant heroism… pure white-knuckle adventure at its very best.
— William H. McDonald, documentary film maker and author of *PURPLE HEARTS*, and *A SPIRITUAL WARRIOR'S JOURNEY*

Suit up, strap in, and hold on. *WATER TOWER* is dystopian Sci-Fi action at its heart-pounding, adrenaline-pumping best.
— Mike Hess, game concept designer and author of *SHATTERED EMPIRE*

Samuel Cutter and his artificially intelligent sidekick, Dac, take the reader on an adventure that will leave them hanging onto every word in sheer anticipation.
— Kerry Frey, author of *BURIED LIE*

…a masterful blend of action, intrigue, and edge-of-your-seat excitement that will keep you flipping the pages long into the night. James Morris combines the world-building ingenuity of Philip K. Dick with a raw-edged creativity that I've never seen in such a young author. Remember this kid's name, because you're going to be asking for his autograph.
— Jeff Edwards, award-winning author of *THE SEVENTH ANGEL*, and *SWORD OF SHIVA*

Books by James Morris

Three Kingdoms

Sky Bound
Water Tower
Surface

SKYBOUND

JAMES MORRIS

Rachel—
Words
create worlds

10/7/10

Edited by Natalie Fitzgerald
Character sketch of Sam by Rebecca Guay
Digital painting by Jonathan Nowinski

Sky Bound

ISBN 978-0-983-88440-8

Typography by James Morris
10 9 8 7 6 5 4 3

First Edition: Oct 2012

For everyone that has helped and supported
me through this crazy process

Prologue

It started, as always, with war. A war for land, a war for greed, a war, for power. Mankind tore itself apart for many years in constant struggle. Nearly one hundred years of fighting passed, and hope emerged.

A single man stepped forward and led his army through all the globe. Many describe this man as a savior, many as a merciless tyrant, and others as a lucky bumbling fool. This man conquered all the earth. After making the world leaders sign an agreement, he prevented many further struggles by spreading the earth into three nations. One remains on the Earth's surface as it always has been, another amongst the clouds, the third dwells beneath the waves.

For many years, the earth was ruled by the man; until the time of his three sons. The man loved his sons greatly, and wished each of them to rule one of his kingdoms. As they were all brothers, the man assumed the three nations would continue to coexist in harmony.

Among the man's fears was that his sons would be more enemy than friend. When his sons were a young age, the man assumed they would be each other's greatest allies, but as the years passed, the man learned he had been mistaken. The three sons became bitter rivals, each competing to rule the earth, none wanting to change from what they knew.

When the eldest of the boys turned nineteen years old, the man fell ill. A disease he thought had been expunged from his body at a young age returned to claim what fell from its grasp. In fear of his imminent demise, the man called his sons together to decide who would take each nation. The man then deemed each son a ruler and each with reason. The sky he gave to his youngest, for his free spirit and his yearning to do more than ever thought possible. The sea he gave to his middle child, for he usually preferred solitude and to see the world in his own way. Last, the man deemed the Surface for his eldest son. The man never gave a reason for why the eldest received the Surface. The man felt no ease of heart though, as he knew that none of his sons were yet ready to rule. The king knew how power hungry his sons could be at times. All three were grateful for the honors that had been bestowed upon them, and willingly accepted their roles as rulers.

Years passed as the king waited for death, all along training his sons to rule, and letting their ideas flourish for what would be their respective nations. When a decade had passed and the king saw that his sons were ready. He told them to go and gain the trust of those who would be their subjects and return to him. Over the next five years the man's sons did as they were told, making constant trips to see their father, and making many improvements to their original designs. When the five years had ended the three sons returned and told their father of what they had done.

Each in their own way had gained the trust of their subjects to be. Either with friendship, respect, or through fear, each son had done as they were told. The king told them then, that if they felt ready, each could take their thrones. In time, the three brothers accepted their responsibilities to rule. The king held onto a portion of each nation under his rule, just for emergencies.

While the two elder brothers set off to rule on their own, the youngest asked his father for aid and to share his knowledge. Soon, the third brother too took his role as a ruler. Shortly after, a cure of sorts for the king's illness was developed. It would extend his life to give him more time. The king's three sons agreed to take this "cure" with him, extending all their lives. With the thought of his life being extended, the king couldn't help but reminisce of what he's accomplished during his natural life, and wonder what he will do in the unnatural. He kept returning to his quest to reunite the world. One part specifically. One person. One night. As the king and his sons took the concoction to extend their lives, the king realized the truth that had been evading him. He had a fourth child. Who this child is, and what they will become, the king knows not.

"Sam, are you still awake?"

"No mommy," I say, hiding so that I look like nothing more than sheets. I think she will go for it.

"Are you sure?" Asks my mother. I don't respond, hoping it will help her think I was sleeping. "I think that you just might still be awake." My mother starts smothering me as she finishes speaking and gives me a big hug.

"How'd you know?" I ask as the sheets slide off my head.

"Just a hunch," replies my mother, smiling, "You do know it's time to go to bed mister."

"Aw, but mom—"

"No 'buts' Sam." I look at my mom with my best puppy dog eyes. She always says yes when I make these eyes and quiver my lip.

"Oh alright, you can stay up a bit longer, but only a few minutes." She makes a point to tell me only a few minutes, but I still won. I got my few extra minutes. With my mom sitting on my bed joining me, I opened up my holobook and it read to me with moving pictures.

The king looked until he could bear it no longer. As the king was begging for his death, his fourth child found him. He finally met his eldest *daughter*, which gave him the extra strength and hope he needed to keep living his life. The king's daughter appeared much older than she really was compared to his siblings. The king begged his daughter to take the potion that would extend her life, and stay with the king. The king begged for an opportunity to know his daughter. When the daughter agreed, the king cried tears of joy.

"Mamma?"

"Yes?"

"Why was the king crying?"

"Because he was happy. He found his child." When she saw some understanding, she thought I got what she said. "I think its time you go to bed."

"But mom, what about the adventure part of the story?" I already used puppy dog eyes, but I still have whining.

"Well," uh oh, my strategy isn't working, "we will just have to read that another night. Just because you're a big bad five year old doesn't mean you can stay up as late as you want." I knew it. I always know I've lost when she starts with 'well.'

"Alright mommy."

"Goodnight Sam," she gives me my goodnight kiss.

"Night night mommy." I throw the sheets back over me and turn my light off. I listen for my mom to leave the room. As soon as I hear my door close, I grab my holobook again and hide under the covers.

And so the daughter, being no ruler, did as her father dreamed. She explored the far reaches of the globe with her father and beyond. Still today, it is said that they are traveling to any place they can, working on better ways to see even more, possibly beyond earth.

When I wake up the next day, I go downstairs and see my mom crying. "Mommy, what's wrong?" she looks up at me; startled to see I'm awake.

"I'm proud and scared of that stupid idiot."

"That's mean!" I say. My mother laughs.

"I'm glad I taught you well. Why don't you go talk to your stupid father and see if you can talk some sense into him." She points out the window, wiping her eyes. I see my dad walking away with a bag over his shoulder.

"Daddy!" I start running after my dad, yelling for him all the way to get his attention. He turns around when he hears me.

"Hey kiddo." He says, perfectly happy.

"Daddy, where are you going?"

"I'm going to get us a better life," When I look confused he continues, "I'm going to get onto one of the transports up to the Sky Nation. Nathanael is supposed to be much kinder than; "*The King*" He says "The King" with as much venom as I know he can muster. "I'm trying to start a new life for us. As soon as your safety is guaranteed, I'm going to come back and get you guys."

"But what are you going to do daddy?"

"I'm going to make things better for us, all of us. Listen, bud, I need you to promise me something alright?"

"Alright daddy." I have no idea what he is talking about.

"Promise me that you will take care of your mother while I'm gone." Still not knowing entirely what he means, I agree.

"I promise." I hold out my pinky for him to shake. My dad laughs for a moment, and then shakes my pinky with his.

"Can I watch you go daddy?" I ask. He seems genuinely shocked by my request.

"Uh, ask your mother." Why does he always say that? I run back inside and ask my mom if I can. She says she would have to come and that there would be many rules. Apparently sneaking onto a transport is against the rules. My dad left for the transport's loading station where it trades supplies with us here on the Surface much earlier than my mom and I. We wait until it is dark out. My mom parks the car far away from the loading docks, and we go to hide somewhere where we can see.

When it is time to go, my dad comes by and kisses my mom and me, saying that he will see us soon. I watch my dad sling his bag over his shoulder. He manages to sneak his way onto the transport before something happens.

"Hey, what are you doing?" I heard one of the guards yell when they find my dad. He tries to fight them off, but there are too many and one soon hits my dad in the back of the head, knocking him out.

"Da—" my mom covers my mouth as I start to scream for my dad in panic. My dad turns enough for me to see something on his face. Terror? My mom drags me away as the rest of the people around turn their eyes towards us because of my outburst. We get back to the car without incident, but I watch the shuttle take off with my dad on it, looking as frightened as an animal caught in headlights. Gone, supposedly forever, but I plan to see him again someday

Chapter One

Ten years have passed since my dad was taken away from me, and I'm more determined than ever to get him back. Five months of planning. Much more time than my dad took, but I want to make sure that it works. When my best friend, John, found out what I was planning, he immediately jumped on board. No matter how much I warned him that it would be dangerous, he refused to let it go. I knew he would be this way, and I was ready for it. Only two things left to do, and I don't know which one scares me the most.

"You know you're going to have to tell her eventually, right?" John asks me.

"Can't we just leave? I think I'd rather fight off the enforcers than tell her."

"She's your mom, she has to know. It'd be wrong to just leave."

"Fine, but I think I should write my will out first." I'm not kidding, "Let's go. Just make sure I get a good coffin."

I stand up, getting off my bed. My bag is packed and I'm ready to go, but I still have to get past the most frightening part: telling my mother. I shrug my favorite backpack over my shoulders holding all I'm bringing with me; some cash, my phone charger, a spare pair of jeans, and a couple of my favorite shirts. I don't think there is much else I can bring. I have my bag packed, and John has his. Together I think we have enough for a while. I wonder what we will do for more money and supplies as I walk down the stairs to face my mother.

"Hey Mom?" I call. I don't know what to expect, but she was waiting at the table for me. "There's something I need tell you."

"You're going to sneak onto one of the transports." She says with a flat tone.

"Or you can tell me. How did you know?"

"Your father acted the same way." She starts to look sad.

"I'll be back as soon as I can," I argue, "I'm going to find Dad, and bring him home, or bring you up there if life's better."

"He said the same thing." She still has no tone to her voice. I don't know how to respond to that. Apparently my dad argued the same points I did, and look what happened to him. Hope I'm not going to end up the same way he did. I'm about to say why I'd be different when she starts speaking again, "and like him, I won't be able to change your mind, will I?" I finally notice what she has in her hands when she looks down. She is holding a necklace and a small metal container. When I look back up, she is smiling. "These are for you." She first passes me the metal container. "Here's some money for you; I hope it helps." This is going a lot different than I thought it would, "and this," she shows me the necklace that is a beautiful green gem embraced by wings on either side, "I want you to have it." She weakly smiles, "It's been passed down my mother's side of the family, and I thought it would give you luck." Shock doesn't even begin to describe it.

"Mom— I. Thank you." She stands up and gives me a hug. When she was finished she takes a step back and looks me over.

"I'll give you a ride and see you off. Just don't forget to wave before you go. Do you remember where we were for your father?"

"How could I forget?"

"I'll be right there again."

Nightfall, time to go. My mom, John, and I jump into the car. As we drive I start thinking—I know, rare anomaly—about all I'm going to miss, everything that I'm never going to get to do. I won't even get to finish high school! Sophomore year and I'm running off to one of the different nations. What the hell am I getting myself into? I don't even have a girlfriend. There was that one time I got close, but never *officially*. My life's going to change forever after this. Nothing will ever be normal again, but then again, it never was. Ever since my dad was taken, life's been different. I didn't join a gang or do drugs or anything like that, but it's all been different. I haven't done much of anything. John is one of my only friends, and all the others I don't see out of school or the factory.

I'm pretty sure everyone thinks I'm a freak, and they might be right. I don't even know anymore. Why am I even analyzing my life? I'm probably crazy. I like it though.

"We're here," says my mom. She still seems sad, but she's also focused now. She parks the car and we all jump out. "Good luck," my mom says to me. I can't help myself; I run over, give her a hug and tell her I love her. I swear, if John ever tells anyone about this I'm going to let hell loose on him. John and I separate from my mom, and I wonder if I will ever see her again. I just tell myself that I will, and that we will be back with my dad.

"Come on, we have to change," says John, thankfully interrupting my thoughts. "The shuttle should be arriving in a few minutes, and we have to be ready." About a month ago, we befriended two of the workers here, who load the transport, and got them to lend us their uniforms. I later explained to them what we were planning to do, and they helped us plan it out; they wanted to join us. They were old friends of my dad's. Fred and Rick are their names, and according to our uniform disguises, I'm also Fred, and John is also Rick. This'll be interesting.

12

We change into our dull, worn out cross between navy and denim blue button-down shirts, and stuffed our backpacks into a crate that I'd be carrying. I think about putting my mom's necklace into my backpack with the money she gave me, but I decide to wear it instead. We sit around for what must easily be over an hour, waiting for the transport to show up. Finally, it did.

"Let's go," I say to John as we start to move forward. The work field is different than I remember. It now has boxes piled high over our heads instead of many small piles spread out. I don't know if it is because of the new appearance, or because it's now me instead of my dad, but the labyrinth of crates is really freaking me out! John has to grab a box while we are walking so he can blend in. At first we have no idea where we are going, but as soon as we see someone, we follow him.

"John," I whisper to him, "it's not to late, you can still back out."

"Nah, I got this. Who else is going to cover your ass when you mess up?" I laugh.

"Ya, I'm sure that's exactly how it's going to happen."

"You know it." When I see the transport moments after our conversation I'm in awe once again. It is magnificent yet daunting, and it seems to have been upgraded since I last saw it. The first thing of note is it's even more massive than I remember. I remember it being big, but this is ridiculous. It must be five stories high! A massive steel hull, it is enclosed all the way around. This one isn't even smoking or anything like that. I also remember it used to be a little unstable, now it doesn't even waver. This beast must be a new ship. I can't believe I thought that they wouldn't update it for ten years.

"John," I nudge his arm, "we might have a problem. I've never seen this ship before."

"I thought you said that you saw it take your dad away when you were five."

"I did, but this is a new ship. They must've made a new model."

"Well that's just great. Can't we ask them to use the old one? Just for us?" I stifle a laugh because we have to cross a few other dockhands. I look around after they pass to make sure it is safe to keep talking.

"It's too late. We're just going to have to go through with it." I can see the worry on his face. I'm feeling it too. The rows of boxes are starting to look less like giant walls, but still very much so. The nerves only get worse as we get closer to the ship. I've wanted to do this for ten years now. Now that I am, I'm scared. Not enough that I don't want to go through with it, but butterflies don't even begin to describe it. When we come into the ship's shadow, it looks even bigger than it was before. I swallow the lump in my throat, and keep walking. There is a ramp to the ship, so I can't yet see inside. That probably is what makes me worry more.

14

I remember a promise that I'm going to keep. In one motion, I turn around, waved for a moment, turn again, and keep walking. I hear a rattling next to me and couldn't figure out what it was until I saw John shaking.

"Calm down. You're going to give us away." I tell him as much as I tell myself. "Everything's going to work out fine." I reassure John, and maybe myself. The first thing that hits me when we enter the hull is the smell. Imagine gym socks mixed with unwashed brother. The ship's interior itself is even bigger than I imagined. My five stories assumption is close though. The ship has six floors that I can see right now, most of it an empty mass in the center. People are moving all over it. I don't think there is one floor without activity. The only ones slacking off are John and I. We're not blending in all that well.

"Hey, yous twos," calls a heavier man who was in charge of the loading. I look around me, confused, before he continued, "Yes, you. Get over here. What's ya carryin'?" Well, we're really caring backpacks full of stowaway gear, but I don't think saying that would go over so well with this guy.

"Hey Ron," I heard someone yell over my shoulder, "they got what we got. Freddy and I'll show 'em where it goes." The coordinator, I guess Ron's his name, grunts and continues doing whatever it is he was doing before. I should start counting my blessings. Rick, you have perfect timing. Let's just hope Ron doesn't look too closely at our nametags. Fred comes up the ramp a moment later and he and Rick usher us off to some corner behind a bunch of the boxes.

"Thanks, I owe you one." I say to Rick.

"It was nothing. Now, hotshot, you got a plan?"

"John and I worked one out a while ago, but I don't know how well it's going to work out now. This ship's layout is different than I expected."

"Alright, so what was the original plan?"

"Well, we were going to hide in the boxes we brought in, but now I'm worried we'll get stuck." I say lamely. Fred and Rick just look at me as if expecting something more.

"That's your genius plan?" Fred asks me, sounding irritated. I looked from Fred, to Rick, to John, to my feet.

Looking at my feet and rubbing the back of my head, I respond, "Ya." There is a pause while Fred and Rick look at each other, then back at me, and back at each other.

"I like it," says Fred.

"Simple, easy." chimes in Rick

"Don't think anyone's tried it before even."

"And how are ya going to fit all of us in some crates?" And there's my issue.

"I don't know. We could try to fit two per crate, one of you with one of us, or we could take shifts." I'm expecting some complaints, or at least an opinion, but none come. "What do you guys think?"

"The shifts are more dangerous," interjects Rick. "As

much as I hate to say it, it looks like we're going to have to smell you guys. How long did you think the trip is? This ship only flies for a few minutes before it docks again."

"Depends on the dock. When I was doing some research, I read that most docks are only a few minutes away, half hour at most, but there's one or two that are a few hours away." I want to be ready for the worst.

"So we'll plan on going two per crate. Who gets to smell the coward over there?" I didn't notice John is still shaking. Man, what am I getting him into?

"Are you alright?" I ask, " You know it still isn't too late to turn back."

"Who-who's scared. I-I'm excited," he stutters. Note to self: hate self for rest of life.

"I don't want you to do anything you're not ready for," John looks like he's going to throw up.

"I've got to do this. I promised my sis that I'd find a better life for her. No way I'm letting," he swallows audibly, "The King get her." Fred gives him a pat on the back.

"That's the spirit," he says to John with a smile. I think I like Fred more now.

"We have to go load more crates, or Ron will get all suspicious. You two can hide out here. We'll be back as soon as we can. And so they leave. John and I are left behind the crates to wait. A couple minutes pass and I get antsy. I really hope it isn't the long flight; I'll end up cutting up a potato and naming it. Would a coconut be better? I'll save that discussion with myself for another time.

"Come on, let's get our stuff organized." I say to John. I need a distraction, I'm not meant to sit there and do nothing. My mom always said it'd be the death of me, but my dad would laugh and say that that and determination are what make the greatest of men. Thinking of my dad gives me mixed emotions. I'm sad that I haven't seen him for ten years, but I'm excited and happy and nervous to be doing what he did and to hopefully see him soon. While John and I sort our backpacks, I turn my head so he can't see that my cheeks are wet.

I work in silence, shaking. I understand why John was shaking; at least, I think I do. Why am I so unsure of this? I've wanted to do this for years, and now that it's happening, I don't know anymore. It's probably just the nerves talking. Just get the ball rolling and I'll be fine. Is this ship ever going to take off? The anticipation is killing me.

John and I continue to sit in silence, counting minutes. I lost track after ten. We made some noise, and small talk, but other than that, try to be as quiet as possible. Another few minutes pass and Fred and Rick come back. They're each carrying a large, heavy looking box. I assume they were just going to put them off to the side, but they don't. They come closer to us, turn around, and then put the boxes down. What are they trying to do? They must see the

18

confused look on my face because they explain.

"Extra insurance. It was Fred's idea."

"If we close ourselves in, there's less chance that they'll see us." It's brilliant.

"We have to get another load a crates to finish the wall though, so we'll be right back." A couple minutes later, I hear footsteps close by and assume it is the guys again, but no such luck. It's another crate carrier, and I don't know what this guy's track record is for squealing. I grab John and shove him down so that his head isn't over the crates Rick and Fred already put down.

"Hey, what the—" I clamp my hand over his mouth. We haven't even taken off and that could have been it. That was the first person to get close. I thought they would have more people looking. I peek up over the crates to see if the guy is gone. He is. I let go of John's head.

"What was that about?" he asks me, slightly indignantly.

"I just stopped you from getting caught is what that was for." He looks over the crates and sees the same guy I did walking away.

"Oh, thanks."

"Anytime buddy." I clapped him on the arm. More footsteps come by, but this time it really is Fred and Rick. They hop over the crates they put down, and place the ones they just carried over on top. They double-check their newly built wall before turning to us.

"Alright, that's the last of 'em," says Fred.

"We should be taking off in a few minutes," adds Rick. I hate waiting. I'm deciding now and forever more that I hate waiting around doing nothing. I already knew this, but now I really know. I was always told patience is a virtue, but it doesn't seem to be working that way. I have this feeling that I'm going to be waiting a lot in life. I'm going to go crazy. Well, if I'm not already. After another minute, someone goes over a loudspeaker.

"Clear the hull. Prepare for take off."

"Finally," I mumble, "Come on, we should get in the crates."

"Monitors, check for stowaways," the loudspeaker continues. Damn, that's why nobody was looking before. They were waiting until the workers left. "Anyone not permitted on board will be punished by alternative law." Fred, Rick, and John are staring at me. Little creepy.

"Hurry, get in," I say to them and they start shuffling into the boxes. "Fred, Rick, you first. John and I will have to work around you guys after you're in." Rick and Fred get in while John and I try to stay as quiet as possible.

"Sam," calls Rick from the crate I brought in, "here's your bag. It's hard to work around." He hands me my backpack and I sling it over my shoulder.

"Thanks, now hurry." While they situate themselves, I look through my bag to make sure that I still have everything in it. I see my clothes, and other supplies I brought. Then I see the tin my mom gave me. I check inside it and see all the money she gave me. There's a lot in there. How long has she been saving up? I promised her that I'd find a better life for us, and I will. Wait, where's the necklace she gave me? I start panicking and tearing my bag apart looking for it. I'm about ready to turn my bag inside out when something hits my chest. I grab what I felt and look at it. It's my necklace. Please tell me nobody saw my idiocy.

"Alright, come on in," and with that cue from Rick, I start to climb in. I see John do the same with Fred. As I get in, I pull the lid on over me.

The crate's dark. I take out the flashlight I had in my backpack and flick it on. I didn't know if two people would fit in each crate, but apparently, they do! I'm bigger than John, but Fred is bigger than Rick so that's why we arranged ourselves this way. The guy on the intercom comes on one more time.

"Preliminary sweep, clean. Prepare for take off. Monitors, please continue searching." The ship rumbles to life. I know it was already floating, which is impressive all on its own, but here's the noise I was expecting. There's a lot less noise than there was on the transport my dad was on. His sounded like it was going to fall apart. This one groans to get going, then quiets down again. The only real noises to be heard are the wind and the constant droning of the engines. I grab my necklace as I think of what lay ahead of me. Step one, find dad; step two, get him home; step three, get all of us back up here. That doesn't even make any sense! I didn't think this out all that well. What if he doesn't even want to see me?

"What's that?" whispers Rick. He points at my necklace with his chin.

"It's been in the family," I whisper back, "my mom gave it to me before I left saying it was rightfully mine now." I look down at the necklace and smile. All my fears and doubts, gone; in their place, pride and excitement. I got my nerve back! Kind of. I'll try not to lose it again.

"Wear it proudly. You don't want to lose something like that."

"I will." Soulful conversations with Rick, who would have thought. The loudspeaker cuts in again.

"Destination, forty minutes away." Just great. One of the further ones. At least we're not going to a port on the opposite side of the planet. That'd take hours to get to. For now, the waiting game, once again, begins.

The minutes start ticking past. Rick and I don't speak; we just sit in awkward silence as we listen to the hum of the engines. It feels like a long time has passed before there's a knock on our crate. Rick puts his finger to his lips to signal silence. I nod and turn my flashlight off. We wait to see if whoever it is goes away.

"Sam?" It's John.

"John? Why are you outside?"

"I couldn't stay in there any longer, I don't know how you're doing it. My legs are killing me." Now that he mentions it, I am really sore. If John hadn't mentioned it, I would be fine.

I hear some crates fall over before a man yells, "There's one!" Not a moment later, more crates come down.

"Let go of me," John! "Let go!" I hear his kicking, and hope he gets away. "Help! Help!" I have to be such a good guy, don't I? I jump out of my crate with my backpack on, and tell Rick to stay there. The man dragging John away has his back to me. I do the only sensible thing. I scream and tackle him. He lands with a thud, but I think John took most of the blow. I punch the guy in the side, and he lets go of John. Just when I think finally, a stroke of luck, two of this guys' friends jump on top of me. I hope John isn't on the bottom of this dog pile.

Chapter Two

Oh God, we are so screwed. The two guys that tackled me stand up, but not without holding onto my arms. I can't even stand up on my own. They jerk me up. A pain shoots through my arm; I'm pretty sure they dislocated my shoulder. I don't like being man handled to begin with, but I really don't like it when I'm being man handled with a dislocated shoulder. I hope it isn't broken, that'd really suck. I groan when the goon holding me tries to pull me back. He has to notice, because he starts to twist and pull on my arm. It hurts pretty bad. He'll get his. I look down and see that John was on the bottom of the pile. Sorry buddy, I feel your pain. He is also pulled up but not as roughly as I was. Maybe they took pity on him for being at the bottom of the pile.

John shoots me a panic stricken look. This is what he's been scared about, and it just happened. I can't leave him hanging. I have to help, so I open my big mouth.

"So what now?" I address the question to the men holding us. I fix them with a cold stare as I continue, "What's going to happen to us? Are we going to be arrested then? Turn around, forced back to the Surface?" I look around at them. The one holding John almost looks sad. While I got mister insane and muscular, John got pudgy and sensitive. I guess he did get squished; it's only fair. The total opposite of John's guy's personality being that the guy holding me has an excited look on his face. He seems like the guy that would kick a cat and laugh.

"Oh you'll see. We have something special planned." Something tells me that it isn't a grand tour. "Nobody gets in without Steven wanting them to!" Wait a minute, that's not right.

"Who's Steven? I thought Nathan was in charge." The goon holding me lets out a single "HA!" as if I'm the dumbest person alive and don't know something really obvious.

"You believe in that old loon? He lost his marbles long ago. Tried to take away everything we have to fight, became obsessed with 'finding new fuel' and 'his chance to see his father.' Just up and took off nearly fifteen years ago. We've been running the show since."

"You sure it's not a carnival, because this is ridiculo—" he twists my arm again until I can hear bone rubbing against bone. Insulting your captors is a bad idea. Pain flares through my arm, and I have to choke down a scream. I'm not giving these guys any more entertainment.

"Learn your place, runt," my captor orders me.

"Right after you learn to brush your teeth." He twists my arm again and it hurts even more. Shocker. I swallow another scream. As I'm catching my breath, I'm imagining all the ways I can cause this guy pain. My personal favorite is tying him up like a piñata at a six-year-old's birthday party.

"You never answered my question." I inform him when I can breathe.

"We're taking you to our form of court."

"Oh goody, a judge," the guy holding me smiles evilly.

"And jury and executioner." Splendid.

"So who are our judge, jury, and executioner?"

"Why would I spoil the surprise? Take them to be held." He motions for his goons to take John and me. He shoves me over to a different one of the guys and walks off.

"Don't scream," the new guy says. Before I can ask what he is going to do, he pops my arm back into place. I didn't scream, but I whimper. I feel my bone scrape across some more bone up until it went back into place. After he fixes my arm, and I stand up straight again, or as straight as I can, they lead John and me off somewhere. I hope Rick and Fred are staying hidden. I don't need them on my conscience too. I have to worry about John and me right now.

"Where are you taking us?" I ask the obvious question.

"Holding room," replies my escort. While the previous goon that was holding me loved misery, this one seemed to be drowning in it, just like John's.

"Is something wrong?" I always have to be Mr. Sensitive, don't I? "You're only man handling two kids, and sending them to jail for nothing." Okay, maybe not *that* sensitive. It's true though. He gives me a shove for good measure, "Geez, only being nice." Kind of.

"We aren't permitted to speak with you." My escort says with a straight face. Can he at least smile?

"But you just did." I let myself smile. He jerks me around again. He fixes up my arm, now he's going to trash it again. Seems pretty counterproductive to me, but I don't point that out.

"Here, I'll keep an eye on them, give that one to me." the guy walking John speaks up. His voice sounds like he should be laughing, like all he does is laugh, but he sounds raspy and depressed. It's one of the most disturbing voices I've heard. Clowns might be worse, always with that fake accent and ridiculous laugh. It's annoying.

"You sure about that?" my escort responds, "This

one's trouble."

"What have I done other than try to talk to you? Ouch." He shoves me again.

"I can handle him."

"Fine, if you're sure." I'm handed over to the guy pushing John, and my old escort takes off. Now it's just John, the sad guy, and me. We walk in silence for a few minutes before someone speaks.

"I'm sorry," mumbles our new escort.

"Why are you sorry?"

"None of this should be happening," well if you guys didn't catch us, it wouldn't be, "If Nathan was still here, all would be right. I hope he gets back soon," his eyes half glaze over. So Nathan doesn't rule this way, it's just this Steven guy.

"You're not like the rest of them, are you?" I say. Our escort looks over at me.

"No, and there's many more of us. We're going to get you two out of here, but we need to ask something of you." That usually doesn't lead up to anything good. I look over at John and see how hopeless he looks. When our escort mentioned a way to get out of this, John's face lit up. I owe it to him. I dragged him into this.

"What do you need us to do?" I ask our escort.

"Three things." Is he really going to make a list? "First of all, you'll need to survive. Second—"

"Wait, what?" I cut him off.

"Second," and I'm disregarded, "you can't win, Steven would recruit you, and it'd be impossible to get you free. Third, don't get hurt and be ready. It'll be sudden." Strangely, I'm okay with that; I just want to know why I need to survive! We come up to what looks like a cell, smells like a cell, and works like a cell. My guess, it's a cell.

"Are you really going to lock us up?" I ask.

"I'm sorry, it's what they're expecting me to do. Unless I do it, you won't be tested, and we can't get you."

"Who are 'we'? Better yet, who are you?" I ask. I want to trust this guy, if not just for John's sake, but I don't even know his name. None of the people working here have said it even.

"A friend." That's descriptive. I love descriptive people. Descriptive people are amazing.

"Can I get a name?"

"No, it'll make things harder soon."

"Okay then," he is not easy to work with, "who are 'we' then?"

"Friends." Did I ever mention how much I like descriptive people? My new friend who knows friends locks me in a cell. Hello to you too. Before he locks the door, my new friend reaches for my backpack. I shy away. "Don't worry. I'm not supposed to let you keep anything. I'll make sure this gets to your pickup when we liberate you." Grudgingly, I give him my bag.

"Just make sure you don't 'liberate' any of my cash."
Not even a smile. He won't give me anything. I turn
around to go sit in a corner, but my new friend puts a
hand on my shoulder, stopping me.

"What?" I ask irritably.

"I need to take everything." I didn't get what me
meant until I saw him staring at my necklace.

"No! You can't have this!" I grab my necklace to show
him I'm not letting go. "My mom gave it to me right
before I left. It has been in my family forever. I'm not
giving it up." He looks like he is going to argue, but must
have decided against it.

"Fine," he sighs, "just keep it hidden. They might let it
slide if they see it, but I'd still keep it hidden."

"Thank you." He shuts the door to the cell and
locks it. Now it's just John, my thoughts, myself, and
everybody that happens to walk by. Oh crap, John. He
hasn't said a word since I so gracefully got us captured.
Actually, wasn't it his fault? Doesn't matter.

"Hey John," I say gently. He looks up at me, "how're
you holding up? You've been quiet for a while." Still,
he won't talk. I wait in silence for a bit. I am about to
ask again, but then I see that he is shaking. He's crying.
"John? Is everything alright?" I walk over to him and put
my hand on his shoulder.

"I'm not cut out for this. I thought I could handle it,
but I can't." John says, his head between his knees.

30

"Hey, don't worry about it. It's only day one." I say.

"That's the problem," he says, "We barely got off the Surface, and how many times have I cried?" Mentally, I'm counting, but I'm not going to tell him that. "I screwed up big time. Your plan would have worked if I just stayed put, but no. I had to get out of the stupid crate and blow it." Again, not going to tell him he's right.

"Look," I say, "it could have happened to anybody. There were no guarantees with this. We made it farther than my dad did." It's true. My dad didn't even make it to take off before he was found out.

"But we were ready; your dad wasn't. We spent months planning to avoid exactly this." His negativity might be starting to depress me.

"As a genius once said, sometimes the best laid plans fail, or something like that. Ours weren't even the best!" I only memorize the majority of quotes. I can't ever get it word for word. I think I ease John up, but then he keeps going.

"But it's my fault we were caught. My stupid foot. I messed up man."

"It's ok. Things happen. We did our best." I stop talking while one of the guys that caught us walks by. I wait until I can't hear his footsteps any more before I   continue in a whisper, "Besides, we're getting out of here soon. Our new friend is going to help us out, remember?" I force myself to smile. Really, I have no idea what the guy is going to do. John starts rubbing his neck. "Sorry about that by the way."

"What?" John asks, confused as to what I'm talking about.

"You know, knocking that guy on top of you."

"Heh, I deserved it. Probably grew six inches in the process," my turn to laugh.

"There's the John I know. Able to make anything a joke, even his own life." My snide comment is enough to turn his attitude around.

"So what's the plan?" John asks, "Trust Mr. Friendly?"

"Nice name, maybe we should call him that for now."

"Works for me, but still, what's the plan?"

"I don't know, I guess we have to trust Mr. Friendly. It's either that, or we go with the flow and see what happens. Personally, I don't want to go to prison." I say.

"Me neither." John says, "This sucks!" He hits the bars of our cell.

"Now don't go getting hysterical on me again."

"I got this. I am totally in control. Bah!" He jumps out at me acting like he lost control. Not as funny as I would've thought it'd be. I normally would've laughed at something like that, but not this time. It's probably just the stress of the situation we're in.

"Are you alright?" asks John noting my lack of laughter.

"Yeah, I'm fine. It's nothing." John looks at me

doubtfully.

"Whatever," he says and lies down with his hands behind his head. He looks much more relaxed now than he did a minute ago. "I'm tired."

"You could've slept earlier."

"That would've been smarter than getting out, wouldn't it?"

"Just a little. Your snoring might have given us away though."

"I don't snore!" John says indignantly, sitting up on his elbows.

"Sure you don't," I make some really obnoxious snoring noises. "I was even about accurate," I'm having too much fun, "and don't even get me started on the talking. Who's Linda?"

"What?" Just play right into my hands.

"Linda, Linda wh—" I start moaning like what he would sound like in his sleep.

"Shut up, now I know you're messing with me." John says, lying back down.

"Am I?" I say, "Sometimes you snore."

"But never *that* bad." True enough.

"It's funny. Even in prison, we don't stop making jokes."

"Wrong!" John corrected me, "This isn't prison. It's just to 'hold us in place.'"

"Who told you that?" I ask.

"The guy that had his paws all over me." I'm about to ask when he was told that, but he keeps explaining, "It wasn't Mr. Friendly. It was the guy before that."

"Isn't Mr. Friendly the one who landed on you?"

"Yeah, but I was handed off for a second." I don't remember seeing that. Maybe I was just looking away.

"Hey runts!" I look up, pulled away from my thoughts, to see who was yelling at us. When did I start reacting to runt? It's the guy that grabbed me before. Great. This'll be good. "Your transport will be here in a matter of minutes. Hope you're ready." Why is he just staring at me?

"What do you mean transport? Isn't that what we're on right now."

"Filth," he spits at me. Jerk, "we're not redirecting for you two. Another transport is coming for you. One not so fancy-like." What is this guy's problem?

"Where is it going to take us?" asks John.

"It's going to take you filth to what Surface trash call your trial," an evil grin spreads across his face. He must be a real hit with the ladies.

"What is our trial?" I ask.

"Now there you go again. I'm not going to spoil the surprise."

"Come on, why not?" chimes in John, "You afraid two kids can beat the big bad wolf." Big bad wolf? Really?

"Now you shut your mouth boy." Did that really

offend that guy? Being called the 'big bad wolf' will set him off. Wow.

"You scared we're going to survive?" My old escort bangs on the bars of our cage and steps up really close. That must have really set him off.

"Now you listen here," Why is he stepping up to me? John is the one who set him off. "I don't know what you know," duh, "but nobody have better told you now what your trial will be. Because if they have, well, they may just have a slip off a platform." I don't know the guy's name, barely met him, and it turns out Mr. Friendly risked his life for John and me. "So who was it?" pries my old escort. I remain silent, John does as well, "Huh!?" He bangs our cage again.

"That's not going to help," I say. "Nobody told us anything, we just heard rumors when we were planning to come up here." I hope I don't get anybody killed by saying that.

"So buzz off will ya," says John. The guy is sneering at us as the loud speaker comes on again.

"Transport craft for Arena now docking."

"Ah haha, here comes the fun!" says our escort. Why don't I think this is going to be any fun?

He, not so gently, ripps John and me from our cell. John holds onto the bars so that he is being suspended in the air, the guys holding onto his legs until he lets go. Now he's being dragged by a leg. That's not a whole lot better.

"Hey!" he yells. He is dragged over something hard so that he hit his head. He's going to complain about this for weeks! While John is being dragged, I am being pushed and shoved to the other side of the ship. One of the guys leading us opens a door on the side of the ship, and I see it.

Chapter Three

"What is that?" I ask no one in particular. In front of me I see a ship with half a dozen prisoners, children and adults, shackled and grief stricken. I couldn't see the underside of the new ship, but for the most part the top is open. This new ship isn't nearly as long as the one we snuck into, but I'm still impressed. There are occasional columns and overhangs to provide shade, but other than that, the only elevated areas are the captain's raised level, and the low rims around the main area. The entire ship is a dull gray shade bringing only misery. The only color visible on the ship is the people.

There are three guys on the ship without shackles. All three of them are wearing what look like full body leotards with breast plates, and other pieces of metal plating coving the majority of their bodies with a red stripe running down the length of the armor. Two of them stand on either side of the prisoners and have helmets on with darkly tinted visors covering their eyes so that only their mouths and part of their noses are visible. These two are also carrying what looks like a long staff slightly longer than their bodies with electric tips on both ends. I see one of the guys twist his hand making the top of his staff spark. I don't think he would appreciate a sense of humor very much. The third guy doesn't have a visor like the others, nor does he carry a staff like the others do. Instead, he has a sword belted to his hip, and is manning the flight controls. I can't tell much more about him as he is on the captain's perch elevated from where I am.

"Keep moving," orders one of the guys behind me with a shove. I step onto the new ship having lost my balance. I don't fall but John did, completely losing his balance. Sparky skulks over to me taking a pair of shackles off of his belt.

"So what's your name?" I ask the guy putting my shackles on. He looks up from what he's doing long enough to sneer and gets back to work. "Just trying to be friendly," I say, "seems like nobody wants to give me a name." I look to my right and see that John is upright again and being shackled as well. I don't make any more attempts at conversation; it wouldn't be worth it anyway. I just stand here as the guy finishes what he's doing and walks me over to stand in line with the other prisoners. Sadly, John is escorted to the other end of the line of prisoners. The goons from each ship exchange a few words. I don't bother eavesdropping. It's much more entertaining making up what they're saying. Apparently, according to my mind, the guy from this ship wears the armor to keep himself safe from his girlfriend, and Mr. Friendly is so angry because his girlfriend left him for a rock. Apparently, she thinks it has more personality than him. That discussion is much more interesting than hearing them insult me. After they said their goodbyes, I feel the ship lurch as the engine starts up. We're being propelled forward and shooting past the cargo ship in seconds. It's hard to hear because of the wind howling, but I still yell to the guy next to me.

"So what're you in for?" He turns his head to me with a sad look on his face and shouts back his response.

"I tried to save my daughter. The NP tried to take her, but I got her to the resistance first." NP? Who's the NP?

"Who's the NP?" I ask. The man looks shocked by the question.

"You're not from around here, are you?" He shouts.

"Not exactly," I respond, "I'm from the Surface." Again, he looks shocked.

"The Surface? We haven't had anyone try to come here from the Surface for nearly ten years!" Ten years? Dad? "The NP has really cracked down. I'm amazed you made it this far. Too bad it's all going to waste." I really want to ask him what he means, but first there's something I still need to know.

"Who is the NP? And do you know who the last person to try and get up here is? Where is he?" He answers to the best of his abilities.

"The NP is the New Power. They're the ones trying to take the throne from Nathan while he is away." That answers one question, "I don't know much about the guy that tried to get up here last. Only that it was one man, and that he is now in prison." And that brings me no closer to finding my dad. My face drops in disappointment. "Look, kid, I'm sorry. There were a few other rumors going around, but that's it." I perk up again.

"Really? Can I hear them?" He looks surprised that I'm interested.

"Let me see. I think that he took down twelve of them, or was it twelve of them took him down. I don't know anymore," this guy is really flustered, "wait, I think his name was Cutter. Odd name for an odd feller." Success!

"Yes! Thank you thank you thank you!" The New Power guard closest to us hears my excitement and skulks over. He stares me down, surprisingly, he is about the same height as me. I usually have to look down at everybody, literally. I know my eyes are playing tricks on me, but when I look into his visor, his eyes look like black holes. Probably just the tint from the visor, deceiving me. The guard snarls at me and returns to his post. Does he ever talk? He's talked to me twice, if you can call it that, and all he's done is snarl and growl.

After a minute or so of staring at my shoes, trying to remain quiet—shocking, I know—I get bored and start to look around. I see cloud upon cloud, not sure if anything should be visible. As repetitive as the sky may be, I find beauty in it. The way the clouds swirl, the way the wind has a slight howl to it, I think there can't be many other things that are as beautiful. How did I never notice this on the ground? The sky didn't change; I've just never been in it as I am today. I feel kind of free up here. I almost forget that I'm in chains, almost. The ship begins to ascend and I see that we are heading into the clouds.

As soon as we enter the clouds, it's a white wash. Nothing is visible anymore. I look to my left and right, but I can't even see the guys standing next to me all that well. I don't know if it's for effect or what, but the not so friendly guard next to me activated his staff sparking both ends with electricity. The guard on the opposite end of the line does the same. The electricity is all that can be seen, then they cut it off, plunging us into nothing but white. How is the pilot driving? This is really weird. I look over to where I think he should be, but again am greeted by nothing but white.

"We're all going to die." I hear someone sob farther down the line. I wonder if he is right. We've been traveling through this field of white for a while now and I can't help but wonder if we're going to crash into something. Wait, we're in the sky. We can't crash, right? A few more minutes pass before anything happens.

"Prepare to dock!" calls the man driving. He is talking to someone who isn't there. I hear him saying landing codes and other things to somebody I can't see. The guards don't move. They don't even activate their staffs. They don't do anything. I look ahead and although the clouds have not moved, I see a gigantic looming dark object. I keep looking, hoping that I'll be able to make out more details, but no such luck. As I look over at the dark mass yet another time, I see and hear what I can only assume is a door opening. As unbelievable as it is, I see a light pouring out of the mass that we are heading towards, a light marking our destination.

When we pass through the door, the cloud cover lingers, but it's not nearly as thick as before. When the entire ship enters the room, the doors shut behind us. I think our ride would be over, that we would be taken off the ship here and now, but we keep moving. As the ship continues, we break away from the lingering clouds. Even though there are still some wisps of vapor coming off of the ship, I can see the room we are in perfectly. It's more of a tunnel than a room—a smooth, black tunnel with running lights from the roof. We continue down the tunnel to our unknown destination. When we reach the apparent end of the tunnel, the ship stops and begins to rise vertically. I didn't think that a ship could be maneuvered with this much precision. The walls are only a few feet from the ends of the ship, and the ship is barely wavering.

The ship stops and I see that there is an edge across from us. A bridge is extending from the edge of the walkway to meet the ship. Two guards dressed similarly to the one standing next to me walk onto the ship and take John. As they lead John off the ship he looks back at me and I see something on his face. I don't know what it is - panic, terror, worry? As soon as John and his escorts are off the extended bridge, it begins to retract and again the ship moves upward. The ship stops on multiple floors. One for each of us held prisoner on the ship until I'm the only one left. When the ship stops on a new floor, as expected, a bridge extends to meet the ship, and two guards are present. The guards come and take me from the ship. As the bridge retracts, the ship ascends past my line of sight.

I am lead by my two escorts into yet another tunnel that's wide and relatively tall. Single bright lights run throughout the length of the ceiling illuminating the corridor in an eerie light. We soon arrive in a large circular room with a pedestal raised in the center of the room. The pedestal is maybe only three feet in diameter and one of the only things in the room. The only others are a door with no handle leading somewhere I don't know, a container of backpacks, and a rack with a bunch of odd things resting on it.

"Make your choice," says one of the guards gesturing to the rack. I start to walk over, but the other guard still bumps me forward. I guess he doesn't think I'm walking fast enough. When I look at what's on the rack they all look like handles of some sort. Maybe they go with the door.

"What're these for?" I ask the guard.

"You'll find out soon enough."

"Are all of you so helpful? Because every one of you lovely people that I have met, even on the cargo ship, have given me about the same answer. Do you practice it?" Not surprisingly, he growls at me, "Sit Fido." I say, egging him on.

"Choose." He spits out. Guess he doesn't like Fido. Maybe Bingo is better. Regardless, I look over what's on the rack many times over, but my gaze keeps sliding back to one thing. It is on the far right side of the rack. The object is cold when I pick it up. I still don't see what's so special about it. It is large enough for me to grip it with one hand and still have some room for at least half of the other. I look to the guard.

"Now what?" I ask.

"Will you take more?" he asks me skeptically. What is the big deal anyway? It's just a piece of metal with a bunch of tech on it. One of the first things I notice is something that's a cross between a button and switch. It looks kind of like the child safety on a lighter. "You may take another, or a pack if you desire. Don't see why we have to give you so much."

"You're giving me this?" I lift the metal rod. My escort smiles when I ask this. Not a happy smile, but more of a knowing smile.

"Think of it as a loan.," he says, "Don't worry, we'll get it back." Why is that such a smiley thing? I don't see what's so special about a loan. Wait, I hope these guys aren't some sort of high-tech loan sharks. I only have the money my mom gave me. Scratch that, I don't even have that anymore; they took my backpack from me. I reach for my necklace but stop myself, remembering that I can't let them know I have it. I've only been able to keep my clothes so far, and I'm not sure how long that'll last.

I don't know what it is I picked up in the first place, so I grab one of the backpacks from a bucket. I walk back over to the guards with what I am carrying.

"You are permitted to look inside the bag to inspect the supplies." I raise my eyebrow, confused as to why looking in a bag is such a big deal. I unzip the bag to look inside. I see three objects inside: medical wrap, an injection needle filled with something that I will not touch, and weirdest of them all, a small metal disk about the size of my hand.

"What is this?" I ask taking the disk out and examining it. The disk has a slight concave shape to it. I can tell from the way the disk looks that it used to be shiny, but now it's dented and dull. "And what happened to it?"

"That is one of the rarest items in the pack, and what happened to it is that it was used." I expect him to continue explaining but he remains silent.

"And?" I pry, trying to get more of an answer out of him. "Can you at least tell me how it was used?" The guard looks to me.

"For its purpose." I'm ready to hit this guy.

"Okay, then what's this needle for?" I ask pulling the syringe out of the bag.

"Injections." Duh.

"Anything else?"

"Its purpose." I throw the syringe at him. Unfortunately, he ducks. Before the syringe hits the ground, the same guard that ducked spins around striking the needle with his staff with the electricity turned on. The small glass vile explodes into many little pieces shooting all over the room. Instinctively, I put my hands up to my face, protecting myself from the glass. None gets to me.

"That item is no longer available for you." Says the guard without any emotion while standing up, "You gave it up, so it is no longer an option for you. Would you like to sacrifice anything else?" There's nothing creepy about the sentence, but the way he said it gives me the chills. I shake my head no. "Very well. Would you like battle armor?" Battle armor, what?

"Huh?" I ask stupidly.

"Would you like to change into battle armor?" the other guard says plainly. Why are they double-teaming me now? That's not fair.

"What are you talking about?" I ask, knowing full well what the answer will be.

"Armor, for the upcoming trial," or maybe I didn't know the answer. I got an actual answer. That is unexpected.

"What trial?" I ask, hoping to get more information out of them.

"Yours."

"Right, but what am I supposed to do during this 'trial' of mine?"

"You shall see." There's the answer I expected to get the first time. I'm starting to see a pattern in the way these guys talk. I sigh.

"Am I the only one you won't tell anything too? Are the others getting answers to all their questions while I'm stuck not knowing what the deal is?" I walk up to the guards to ask them. One of them smiles at me. Great, he loves other's pain. That is going to make this so much easier. I see a light scroll by on both of the guard's visors.

"Are you ready?" They ask me in monotone in perfect unison.

"Did you guys practice that?" I ask, not knowing how they, with no signal, asked me the same thing, the same way, at the same time.

"Are you ready?" They repeat.

"I guess so, ready for what?" I respond not knowing what they mean by ready.

"Please step on the pad." One of them says, gesturing to the pedestal in the center of the room. The other starts walking, passes the pedestal and waits on the other side like a statue. I zip up the backpack and throw it over my shoulder. I turn to walk to the pedestal and see that the guard who had gestured to the center of the room has remained still other than moving his head to follow me. I stop in front of the pedestal opposite from the guard waiting.

"Please step onto the pad," he says to me.

"Why?" Instead of a non-informative response, he says nothing. I don't know which I like more. "Why do I need to get on your pad?" I ask again, this time I get an answer.

"Time is almost up. Force will be permitted unless you comply." Odd, but I don't feel like getting zapped, so I step onto the pad. Nothing special happens and I wonder why I had to get on here, then I hear it. I hear some machine creaking to life and beginning to move. "Please stand still with your arms at your sides to avoid injury." What the hell is he talking about? Just then I look up and see a circle open up in the ceiling, dropping down a tube exactly the size to fit the pedestal, or disk, or whatever. I motion to take a step down, off the pad, but the guard turns on his staff. "Remain on the pedestal," he orders me.

"Or what?" I turn around, and see the other guard standing there, also with his staff activated. I could dive for the sides, but I don't think that will get me anywhere. I take the only option left before me. I wait.

As the tube lowers, I start to feel a little claustrophobic. Normally, I have no issues with something like this, but I have no idea what is going on, which might be part of my issue.

"We shall see if you are worthy." Is the last thing I hear the guard say before the glass tube locks into a rim on the platform, effectively sealing me inside. I start pounding on the glass, thinking there is some way out that I can't see. The platform then starts to rise. I gaze into the room as long as I can, watching the guards walk away, and through the odd door. I mentally note that the door opened with the use of one of the guard's staffs. After the platform enters the ceiling, I am disoriented with running lights in a long dark tunnel.

For what feels like three times as long as it should

be, I hear nothing. Then, I hear a hum. As the platform continues to rise, the hum gets louder and higher, becoming slightly more distinguishable. I can't understand what it is; it doesn't make sense. It's still not understandable enough. I strain my ears as the platform continues to rise, trying to distinguish what the noise is. After another few minutes of guessing, I figure out what it is: cheering. Why would there be cheering? As I'm wondering to myself what the event could be, a circle opens up above me, pouring light into the relatively dark tunnel. The cheering becomes clearer than ever, and as the platform continues to rise, it becomes worse. I figure out what the cheering is for. My 'trial'.

Chapter
Four

My platform rises the remainder of the way to the top of the shaft. It's so bright wherever I am that I can't see a thing. I throw my hands up to cover my eyes and hope they adjust quickly. After a few seconds of blinking and my eyes stinging, my vision begins to clear up.

I hear a voice boom around me, "Ladies and gentleman!" It feels like the voice is almost loud enough to split my head open. "I hope you're ready for today's big show! We've got eight new competitors with us here today, and this looks like it's going to be good." The roars of the crowd and cheers grow even louder. "As for their names, who cares? Let's just hope there's some bloodshed this time. What say you judges, shall there be blood?" My vision is mostly whited out. I see that I'm in a large rectangular arena, surrounded on all sides by row after row of spectators waiting to see what's going on. I feel shaky on my feet, like the ground is refusing to stay still. Another voice booms over the crowd, even louder than the first.

"There are an interesting batch of competitors with us today." The first voice cuts the speaker off.

"Oh yes we do. Joining us today are two rare specimens we have not seen in a very long time. Numbers seven and eight are Surface dwellers!" he draws out his last two words for effect. The crowd roars louder again, some with cheering, others with booing.

"Yes, well, as I was saying," the second voice continues, "today, we have an interesting batch of competitors. As such, my colleagues and I have deemed that today, there shall be no blood." A collective sigh and groupings of boos erupt from the crowd. Tough crowd. "Although," the second voice continues, "if one of our competitors, maybe even our veteran," the apparently bipolar crowd sends a positive cheer towards the unseen speaker and whoever this veteran is, "could figure a way, to make it so that blood will be drawn, so be it. In addition, two of our very own guards shall be thrown into the arena today. There shall be your blood." The crowd continues to grow more excited.

"So there you have it!" The first voice says. "Ten competitors, eight filth, and two guards that must be retested. I hope your ready for this folks!" I look around me, and count the others in the arena. I see the rest of the guys that were on the transport with me, including John. Then, two others walk in. I've never seen these two before; I'm going to assume that they're the two guards that are entering the arena.

"What shall it be?" the first speaker says again. I look around and notice an announcers box high up in the stands behind me. So that's where he is. "Will we have a tourney, or will we see a real frenzy?" The crowd chants over and over that they want a frenzy.

"It shall be as the crowd demands!" declares the second voice that was called a judge.

"Fantastic! The frenzy is on! Powering up arena grid now. Activating fields, and weapons. Are you delinquents ready to see if you are worthy to serve with the NP? Here's the first step, don't die." Why does that sound familiar? Wait a minute; the dude that never told me his name said the same thing. What were his other two rules? Right, there was don't die, don't get hurt, and don't win. Something seems oxymoronic there. "Everything is charged and ready. Contestants, you'll figure out what to do soon enough, is everybody ready for a rumble?" This guy is really into long winded speeches isn't he? "Why don't the lovely people out there count it down, and viewers from afar, be ready to catch the action. Now, everybody, from ten, because we have ten contestants, on my count." The entire arena calls out together,

"Ten!" One of the guard's gear lights up and he looks anxious.

"Nine!" The other guard's gear lights up as well.

"Eight!" I feel a vibration in my pack, and the thing in my hand starts to emit light. I push a button on it and a two and a half to three foot beam of electricity comes out. I have an urge to say 'Luke, I am your father,' but resist.

"Seven!" John jumps. Good to know which number he is.

"Six!"

"Five!" Why is the crowd so excited about this? I mean it's pretty crazy, and why the counting?

"Four!" The guy I was talking to on the transport jumps, kind of like John did.

"Three!"

"Two!"

"One!" The guy that looks like he knows what he's doing starts vibrating and turns on his gear. He has what looks similar to a scimitar and a shield. Where'd he get a shield?

"RUMBLE!" Everyone starts running. I don't know what to do, so I just stand in place like a total idiot. John does the same. The other eight competitors charge at each other with whatever they are carrying and start attacking. The majority of them brandish arcs of electricity, coming out of their weapons. The other two guys, and John, haven't been able to figure out how to turn their weapons on. The crowd moves with the   fighters, and honestly, I do too. The first clash of electrical weapons comes with a bang. The sound of electricity fighting against another current can be heard, making my hair stand on end. Even early in the fight, a subtle scent of ozone is noticeable. Not one of the arcs of electricity looks the same as another, and mine's just as different. I see crescent shapes, things that look like maces, spears, staffs like the guards—I think it is the guards using them—use, and more.

I assume that the electrical blades will pass though anything it hits, as it's just flowing currents, but they are clashing. Every curve of an arc must be followed by another; it's almost like they're solid forms. I know I should move, but I'm transfixed. I stand still, completely vulnerable, watching the ongoing battle. I stand   watching as the fighters duck and dive away from other's electrical might. It's unbelievable. I didn't know many people could move this fast. I feel a twitch in my jaw as a grin attempts to creep on my face. This is really sadistic of me. I start to run into the fight when I notice that there was a double team going on. The two guards formed an alliance and are cutting down everyone else. I look for the eighth guy in the arena, other than John and me, but don't see him. He isn't on the floor; I don't see him injured. I only ponder the abnormality a moment longer before I turn my gaze to John.

He is backing up, cowering away from the tough and rude looking guy sulking towards him, weapon drawn. His electrical weapon looks similar to a scimitar that someone took a bite out of. It's a short, curving blade with a semi-circle taken out in the top quadrant. John, on the other hand, hasn't even figured out how to turn his on. Without a second thought, I change direction, barreling towards John and his oppressor. I fear that I won't get there fast enough. Even though I'm running, the guy with the bitten sword stared in front of John, and I have half the arena to traverse.

Somehow I manage to hear the announcer call, "And the first falls, Number Five is down thanks to Number Nine!" So one of the guards took down some poor guy. Probably the one I saw getting double-teamed. I shake off any worry I have for whoever Number Five is, and again focus on running. I have left the majority of the action far behind me to try and go help John. "What is Number Eight doing?" calls the announcer. Eight, who's eight, what happened, wait; I'm number eight, duh. The new announcement distracts the guy advancing on John long enough for me to close the remaining distance. Even though I have a sword like thing in my hand, that I can see, I don't think of slicing the guy with it. I follow my instincts. I tackle him.

He hits the ground hard, but I take a boot to the gut on the way down. I let go of him, rolling over to my back holding my stomach. Lucky for me, he also is on the ground, just not moving as fast as I am. I hold back a curse as I shakily get to my feet.

"What was that?" Comes the announcer again, "That was an uncalled for, and honestly, a pretty stupid move." I know he's talking about me. Without much hesitation, I take my beam sword, and slice at the guy on the floor's back. As soon as the electricity hits him, he spasms. I finish my cut, but I worry that I've seriously hurt him. As I look down on the poor guy, he looks as if he is having a seizure. I almost want to cry when he stops moving and closes his eyes.

"No!" I yell, hoping I didn't kill him. Sadly, my cries are drowned out by the obnoxious announcer coming over the loud speaker again. Where are those things? I swear I'm going to break them.

"And three goes down! A stunning act on Number Eight's part, but it might turn out to be in vain. Let's see if he can stand a couple more fights. The relentless frenzy has not lightened up folks! With only numbers three and five down, this is still anyone's match." And with that, my interest in what he is saying again wanes. I look to John to see if he is okay. I get one of the weirdest faces he's given me yet. I've seen a bunch of them, believe me.

"Dude," he starts, "when we get back home. You are so joining the football team." Not quite the thank you I expect, but I laugh regardless.

"Ya, we'll see about that. You can be my tackle dummy." He smiles at the idol threat.

"What is that thing?" He asks me motioning to my electrical sword.

"It's my weapon I guess." I respond with a shrug, "you have one too, you're holding it." I reach forward to show him what he's holding and flip it over. "Push that button." John looks skeptical, but pushes the button anyway. Out of his tube comes a long weapon. In John's hand is a crackling electric lance. Hand guard and everything. I'm almost jealous. He gets a lance, and all I get is a beam. How did I end up with the boring one?

"Sam!" John yells looking over my shoulder, panic in his eyes. I turn around just in time to see another guy running at us with a crazed look in his eyes. He comes in screaming, swinging high. He brings his weapon over his head like he's going to throw it to the ground, but aims at my head. I drop to a knee and raise my sword overhead to deflect his blow. When our weapons clash, I feel a sense of ecstasy run the length of my arms. With a pungent scent of burning ozone permeating the air, his weapon is deflected away from mine, knocking him off balance.

I push him back while rising to my feet, ready to strike again. He drops his weapon when I push him, so he's defenseless. Instead of immediately slashing at his belly like I want to, I hesitate. I know he must feel helpless and scared. What does this cut mean for him, other than a shock that looks really painful? What am I doing to this man's life?

"Number Two goes down!" I hear. I turn around and jerk my hand, slicing at the air where the man I've been fighting is standing. Hearing someone's breath escape from next to me, I know I've hit him by mistake. I turn and see him spasm. I quickly move my weapon away, and catch the man.

"I'm sorry!" I yell to him, hoping that somehow he can hear me. Without rage in his eyes, he looks like anyone else, like any desperate man would. I place him on the ground as gently as I can. I feel a tear roll down my cheek. Hurting good people for no good reason is not my thing. If it were a person harming another, I would stop them. They are the ones that deserve to be hurt. Slowly, he closes his eyes. At least he's no longer in pain because of the shock.

"Oh a double whammy, with Number Six also falling. Newcomer Number Eight has some blood on his hands. Too bad it isn't real blood, 'ey judgey boy?"

"Oh shut up you buffoon! You are getting your blood, or haven't you noticed that Numbers One, Nine, and Ten have figured out how to switch the settings?" I have an urge to laugh at them, but something keeps it down. Probably the somber and angry mood they just put me in. I know that they're both okay, but I just cut down two people. Well, the first one deserved it; he was going after John even though John didn't even know how to turn his weapon on. This other guy, Number Six, whoever he is, didn't deserve this.

"Uh, Sam?" John asks me.

"What." I respond without turning around.

"Where did you learn to do that?"

"Forlork taught me." I respond, still looking at the man I hurt. John scrunches up his face.

"Who?"

"Do you remember big Scott?"

"Yes, why?"

"Scott's name is also Forlork." I say the next part quickly and quietly, "when he goes to renaissance fairs."

"You learned to fight at a renaissance fair?" I look around sheepishly, slightly embarrassed.

"Uh, yes. Is that a bad thing?"

"Try awesome!" I smile again. John somehow usually manages to pull me out of my funks.

"Hey! Seven, Eight, get back in the fight! What are you doing?" It's decided, if I ever see that guy in person, I am beating the crap out of him. Maybe just one good slug would do it even.

"Come on," I say to John and start running. My gut still stings from when I was kicked, but I have adrenalin working for me now. For the most part, I'm able to ignore the pain.

"Looks like everyone is being forced into teams!" Declares the announcer, "What do you say Judge, shall we mark them as teams or keep it as is?"

"It shall be as a crowd demands." Calmly responds the Judge, before muttering, "Buffon."

"You know your microphone is still on, right?"

"No, I did not, but it's good that you know!" Something tells me that they normally bicker like this. I can't tell if they're secretly friends or not. Who knows, maybe they're even lovers. With them arguing, the Judge clearly does not hear that the crowd is chanting "teams!" but quickly gives up after no good comes of it, returning to rooting for their favorite number competitor. Through all the "One's" and "Nine's" I think I heard some "Eight's" which gave me a small, sick, sense of satisfaction.

I see the remaining four battlers, other than John and me, fighting in teams of two, dancing around each other, and around fallen fighters. I notice that none of the fallen are even stirring, just frozen where they are. Perfectly still like they're dead. John comes up behind me.

"So are we jumping into that?"

"Guess so. Just remember: don't win, don't get hurt, and be ready. Or, something like that."

"Isn't that what Mr. Friendly said?"

"Yes, I guess we'll just have to trust him for now."

"Alright. Should we have a battle cry?"

"Let's go," I say, and start running again.

"That's a really bad battle cry! I hope you know that!" John calls after me and starts running as well. I go after one of the guys I know to be a guard. The one that I believe is Number Nine. He's using an electrical whip and a short sword. No wonder he's been doing so well. He is totally decked out. He's fighting the guy I talked to on the transport, who is currently Number Four. I charge in and actually lead with my weapon this time, slicing at Nine's shoulders. He must have seen me because while he lashes out with his whip in one direction, he whirls around and deflects my attack with his short sword. The same ecstasy as before passes through my arms, readying me for a fight.

I zone the rest of the world out as I square off with this guy. He has stopped his attack on the man that I befriended, and turned his whole attention to me. Now that I have his attention, I don't know if I want it.

"You want to die?" he asks me.

"Not really. What kind of question is that?" as always, cool and respectful under pressure. He slashes at me with his sword. I counter with mine. While my weapon is tied up, he brings the whip around, hoping to get my back. I duck to avoid getting hit, narrowly avoiding the whip. We find a rhythm of slicing, ducking, and countering. It almost seems musical. I struggle and stumble through most of the fight, but always managing to recover and prevent myself from getting hit.

I see out of the corner of my eye that John is fighting the other guard. John looks as if he's struggling even more than I am. I turn my focus back to my fight, getting the hang of my opponent's moves, struggling less than before. I start to make some bolder moves, in my own world, not even hearing the crowd's cries as the fight continues, their mood shifting with our footing and lunges. The announcer and judge even stopped their bickering, commenting on each of our moves, waiting on bated breaths for one of us to slip up, to make our fatal flaw.

I get more ambitious, attacking more than defending, hoping to get a slice in, and throw him off. My efforts have the opposite effect. While trying to attack my enemy, my own balance is thrown off, essentially obliterating my defenses. I throw a very unwieldy slash, leaving myself totally vulnerable. My opponent doesn't miss this opening. I pull away in time to avoid a fatal accident, instead only allowing my foe to cut my arm. As the announcer mentioned before, Number Nine figured out how to make his weapons lethal, or at least his sword.

"Number Eight is hurt! Through his push to try and get Number Nine, he left himself wide open!" I still want to hurt that guy.

With my left arm bleeding, I want to make a tactical retreat to apply some of the gauze in my pack. I know that I won't be given that opportunity though, so I turn and slash again. I throw myself back into the fight only using my left arm when necessary, not letting any more holes open up in my defenses.

"And he's right back up on that horse, not letting anything get through again! What a surprise folks, a Surface dweller that can fight!" The crowd roars again, some of it laughter. I get back in the groove. Until I hear John scream, that is. I turn my head to see what happened. John has gotten one arm cut up, and his stomach stabbed, blood pouring out.

"Oh how I love to see blood!" Calls the sadistic announcer. The crowd's energy basically blows through the roof. Panicked and angry, I turn back to Number Nine, and unleash a new fury upon him. With a few precise, deceptive stabs and slices, he goes down, twitching on the ground. I kick him in the jaw.

"Give that to your friend for me." I spit.

"What a treat folks. Number Eight doesn't need to alter his weapon. He prefers the old fashioned method!" Ignoring that, I rush over to John, determined to stop his assailant from causing further harm. The guy that I know as Number Ten, must have also made it so that his weapon can cause actual harm, as is evident with John's mangled form. He had at some point picked up a fallen fighter's weapon, because he was dual wielding, unlike I had seen before. His original weapon, that he had altered, is a small dagger, ready to penetrate and kill. At this point, he is hanging the dagger from his belt, and only wielding a large, arc of electricity. In my typical rational fashion, I charge him head on.

I duck under his sword the first time he swings at me, hoping to set him off balance, giving me a chance to strike. Sadly, he regains his cool before I can swing at him. I knock his sword to the side once more and without waiting, leap forward to strike. My beam penetrates through his shoulder, sliding to where his heart is. As my momentum continues to carry me forward, he raises his weapon sending it through my stomach.

The pain is unlike anything I have ever felt. All the air and strength immediately rushes from my body. With my eyes still open, I fall on Number Nine, knocking the weapon from his hand, and also losing mine in the process. I hit the ground with my back and head, and see stars. I thought it hurt before, but the concussion just adds to the pain. I struggle for consciousness as my body jerks around. I try to yell out, but no words come. I reach and grab my sword, and exchange its hold in Number Nine's chest with the long sword he had stolen. As an instinct, I pull the guy's sword from my stomach, which brings more pain. It stings perhaps more on the way out than it did in. Maybe it's because I had to do the deed myself the second time.

I lie on the ground jerking around in pain and think only to look for John. I see him and most of the color is gone from his face. I control my body long enough to crawl to John, wincing every time I use my left arm.

"How is he still functional?" Calls the announcer as I bandage John with any and all gauze in my pack. "That kind of cut and jolt should have Number Eight down. How is this possible?" The crowd's cheers and calls all blend into white noise. Unrecognizable noise. When I'm done bandaging up John as best I can, I turn to where the man I was talking to and Number One continued to fight. I try to stand to go help the man, but fall as soon as I put pressure on one foot, not even getting up past a knee.

I lie on the floor, watching, as a man that I had originally thought incapable of fighting holds his own against the last standing competitor. I watch as that man is cut down by Number One, twitching and jerking on the floor. Number One didn't get the final blow with the scimitar he had altered to do actual damage, but with another weapon he had stolen. I almost breathe a sigh of relief until I see Number One raise the scimitar to finish the job.

"No!" I yell as if I could do more than lie on the ground. Number One turns to me, fire in his eyes, and does not kill the man. Instead he starts walking toward me. Any fear I felt turns to dread as I realize that he could actually kill me. When he comes to stand over me, he appears much larger than he really is. I know that he is only maybe five and a half feet tall, be he looks like he's seven right now. He hacks at me with the scimitar, and I knock it away with my sword. He drops his   scimitar and takes my sword from me. I try to resist his taking it from me, clutching my part of the hilt with all my might, but find I have no strength left to do so.

He turns my sword off and hides it in my waistband—after messing with it—covering it with my shirt. His actions are hidden from the spectator by the cloud of dust we've managed to kick up.

"Don't lose this." He says right before he brings the dagger down on me and my vision fades to black.

Chapter Five

When I come to, I'm in yet another place I don't
know. Another pattern I'm starting to see. It looks like
some kind of long, narrow sickbay. There is a roof over
my head, but I still hear the subtle whining of a ship's
engines. I try to sit up because I'm lying down. When I
try to stand up, my arm pulls me back to where I was
lying down. I look and see that I am handcuffed to the
table.

"What the?" I try tugging my arm to see if I am
imagining the handcuffs. No such luck.

"Ah, you're finally awake," says a man sauntering
over. He's wearing the same uniform as I saw guards
wear before. He looks fit, handsome I guess by some
people's standards. "We thought we'd have a surprise
new recruit, but guess not." Who is this guy? "Last out
and first up. Impressive. Maybe you'll be signed up
anyway. I'll talk to them about it." He turns away from
me and calls up to the front, "What do you think boys?"

"What?" One of the unseen guards calls back at us.

"Don't you think Number Eight here should be recruited?" returns the guy I'm talking to.

"No. He lost." The guy I'm talking to shrugs it off and mumbles so that only he and I can hear.

"You're never thinking anyways." He smiles and takes a step closer. "So what's your story?" I'm weary to tell him anything, especially while I am shackled to a bed. Not even a good bed, might I add.

"Who wants to know?" I half snarl at him. He looks around as if I could be talking to someone else.

"I do. Name's Mark." He sticks out his hand as if to shake mine. Grudgingly, I shake his.

"So I get a name. Are you going to be completely silent like all of your friends after this?"

"No," he smiles, "You'll probably want me to shut up soon enough. Most flights everyone is still out cold; those two up front are never much to talk. I keep trying, but to no avail." So he's a chatterbox. I can work with that.

"Where are we going?" I ask.

"Prison, where all the losers go. Now will you answer my question?"

"If you want to hear my story, I get to hear yours."

"Don't make any deals in there," calls one of the pilots. I guess I was talking too loud. Mark makes a face.

"Deal, just talk softly so they can't hear, Eight." Maybe

I should keep him calling me Eight for now. Not let him know my name. Who knows what this guy's story is. I will in a couple minutes, but that's a couple minutes away.

"Where do you want me to begin?" I ask, accepting his offer.

Mark smiles, "Your trip up here. It has been a long time since I've heard of one of those. What happened, is everybody on the Surface part chicken now?" I smile at that.

"Not biologically, no, but essentially in every other way, yes. Security has really cracked down, down there. I don't know if we were the first to try, but everyone has been telling me that we are the first ones to make it up here in a while."

"Ten years." Mark confirms. I nod. I want to ask about my dad, but that might give away who I am. I'm not ready to let any of the guards up here know my name unless they happen to figure it out for themselves, or they give me some really good food. That would work. "And what do you mean 'we?'" Shit. I guess I have to tell him, don't I. He doesn't need to know about Rick and Fred though. I don't even know if they are safe or not.

"Number Seven. Did you see the arena match?" He shakes his head. "Number Seven is my friend." Then I think to look around for John. I stand up as tall as I can go being handcuffed and look for him.

"He's not here." Mark calmly says.

"Well where is he?" I demanded.

"He got hurt. He was sent to the hospital before all of you were rounded up." I swallow a slight sense of panic. This is exactly what Mr. Friendly told us not to let happen. I wish I had someone to kick again. On that thought, I look around for Number Ten. He's nowhere to been seen.

"Where's Ten?"

"Also sent to the hospital. He went into cardiac arrest from having one of the arcs in him so long. The electricity overloaded his heart's natural rhythm. You had perfect accuracy too. Was that a fluke?" I start to feel a little bad. I didn't mean to kill him, just make him pay for hurting John.

"I could barely see, but I knew where I was stabbing." I pause, "Is he dead?" I ask.

"No, but not for lack of effort. You did quite a number on him. The crowd ate it up!" He checked over his shoulder to make sure neither of the pilots heard him. "Their ratings are going to skyrocket for a bit, but after nobody sees you for a while, it'll drop back down." I read into what he said maybe a little too much.

"Don't tell me I'm going to have to go back in there." I basically plead.

"You're never going to leave it," he says, "the arena

will only change forms. Always following you through your life." My face drops. "On with the rest of your story now." Mark urges. I take a deep breath and recount my story. I start with sneaking onto the cargo ship, leaving out the parts about Fred and Rick, and how John and I were captured. Again, I leave out most of the details of what Mr. Friendly said to us, and why I'm more worried than ever that John isn't here with me. I left out how I talked to the man on the transport and how he told me that my dad is indeed up here, I just don't know where. I do tell him about my choice of weapons in the arena were totally random, but keep to myself that when fighting, I had a bit of a clue as to what I was doing.

"Well, I'll be damned." Mark says, emitting a low whistle, "If that isn't a story than I don't know what is. All you need is intrigue and to not leave out a bunch of parts." I catch my breath. How could he know? "Don't worry, I won't bother you for more details." He pauses a moment considering me, "Thank you for sharing." He sounds genuine enough.

"Yeah, now what's your story? Don't forget your end of the bargain." He looks at me and smiles. He checks over his shoulder to see if either of the pilots have heard us yet.

"Good memory. I'll tell you what I can now, the rest I'll tell you later. Trust me. If you're a smart kid, you'll figure it out."

"Fine, now tell me what's going on."

"Let's see, I have about," he checks his watch, "five minutes. Let's see how much I can tell you in that. Sound good?" Why five minutes?

"I guess," I say.

"Well then, let's begin." He claps his hands together then winces and checks on the pilots. "I got involved with all of this a few years ago. Maybe six or seven at this point."

"What is 'this'?" I ask.

"In due time." He shrugs my question off, "There hasn't been much to do. Only a few jobs ever. Everyday though, I have to see more and more people, mostly innocent people, hauled off to prison. Wish all of them could know what's going on. Given some of them deserve it, don't you agree?"

"What are you talking about?"

"Don't some of these guys deserve what's coming to them?" He's trying to pry an answer from me.

"I-I don't know. I don't know what is happening to them." I shrug off his question because I seriously have no idea what he is talking about.

"Forget it then." He continues, "I've been working with the NP for less time than I've been doing what I am now. I just used to be a part of a different group, same goal though. This end is much more boring. The endless days of doing what I'm told, please." I think I might be starting to like this guy, then I'm reminded by my shackles that he is working with some people that apparently don't like me, or like people in general. "Are you any good at following orders kid?"

"Depends," simple answer, it'll keep him guessing.

"What about normally?" Or he'll reword his question.

"Can't say I am. I'm not given to many orders, but when I am, following them and conforming is not exactly a strong suit of mine." I say with a tiny hint of bite in my voice.

"Fair enough. Just know that sometimes it's better to go with the flow, it might help keep you alive."

"Now where's the fun in that?" Seriously, I can't think of a single reason that that would be fun. Okay, maybe the surviving part sounds good, but that's beside the point.

Mark shrugs, "Just thought you would like a friendly tip."

"I should be fine, thanks." What is this, counseling hour?

"Man, I'm bad at telling stories," sighs Mark. He looks at his watch, "Times up anyway." What is he talking about? "One last thing," Mark walks over to me and lifts my shirt up, exposing the weapon that was hidden in my waistband, "Don't lose this." He drops my shirt so that it again conceals any hint of the weapon.

How did he know? And how do I still have that? They

74

took the backpack I had and everything in it, whatever everything is. I used all the gauze on John, and threw the syringe away. All that's left is the disk, and I don't even know what that thing is. Mark leaves to return to the front cabin, leaving me alone. Well, not exactly alone, there are five unconscious people here with me.

I tug my arm, testing my bonds, trying to see if I can somehow manage to get free. After a minute of tugging and pulling, I give up and accept that I'm stuck. Looking around in slight despair, I see on the bed across from me where Mark was sitting is a piece of paper. That wasn't there before, was it? I stand up and stretch across the narrow aisle to grab the paper. When I have it in my hand, one of the guards piloting the ship calls back at me.

"You, sit back down." I crumple the paper in my hand so that he can't see that I have it and do as I'm told. When the guards again stop paying attention to me, I unfold the note.

Check under your bed. Without finishing the note, I look under my bed and see the backpack that I had in the arena. I return to the note. *When the time comes, grab that and be ready. We will have to move fast. At that time, use your weapon to cut your bonds. You'll know when it is time to move.*

That's weird. Why would he give me back my stuff? He even told me how to get free. And what does he mean that I'll know when it's time to move? Looking down I see that there is also writing on the back of the paper. *How's your jump?* Before I have time to ponder that, the entire cabin shakes.

"We're under attack!" Yells one of the guards. So this is what he meant when he said I'd know when it was time to move.

I whip out the weapon hidden in my pants and turn it on. Carefully, I cut through the chain of my shackle so that I still have part of it and half a chain as a bracelet. When I stand up, I'm immediately knocked to the ground because of the ship being hit again. The breath is knocked out of me. I guess it's harder to recover from shocks than anyone would think.

While I'm on the floor I use the given opportunity to grab the backpack and sling it over my shoulder. When I try to push myself back up, my left arm gives out under me because of the actual cut on it.

"Come on," I mutter under my breath. I try again using only my right arm and the bed next to me as support. I think to rush to the front cabin, but see that Mark is having a cross between a fistfight and a slap off with one of the guards while the other is trying to keep the ship up and dodge out of the way of oncoming attackers. I don't think to look out the front of the ship and instead turn around. I approach the still form of the man who talked to me on the original transport. I don't know his name, I just know him as Four. With the contraband weapon, I cut him free like I did myself. I go from person to person cutting them free, stumbling as I go. Every time I am mid-cut and the ship is hit, I have a miniature panic attack that I am going to cut someone's hand off.

As I'm freeing the last of them, a large portion of the hull tears away. "Holy shit!" I say as a wind starts whipping around me. I turn the saber off and put it in my backpack.

"Time to go!" Yells Mark as he comes my way. "Thank god you read my note. I was starting to think that you wouldn't find it."

"What's going on?" I yell over the wind.

"We're getting you out of here. Come on, we have to go. Reinforcements will be here any minute now." I know it means spending more time here, but I can't go just yet.

"Not without all of them." The wind is picking up, making me need to yell louder. I look out the giant hole in the wall to see another oddly shaped ship pulling up right beside us and opening a hatch. I see a hangar bay inside of the hatch with mounted turrets with operators watching the skies and a man.

"Mark, we have to go!" Yells the man in the other ship. Mark looks at me, urging me to go.

"Not until we save all of them," I say. Defeated, he

nods and picks up one of the people, tossing them over his shoulder.

"Are you serious?" asks the man on the other ship when he sees Mark with the man draped over his shoulder.

"The kid won't come unless we save all the others." I can' hear him, but I know the man swore under his breath before consenting. While Mark passes over one guy, I go over to Four and pick him up. Even with the strain on my arm, I manage to drag him over to Mark who passes him over to the other ship. We repeat this pattern twice more until there is only one other person left on the ship. It's the guy that after I hit him in the arena, he looked like such a helpless person I wanted to cry.

I tell Mark to go across to the other ship and start to drag the last guy myself. When I get to the giant hole in the side of the ship, I pass him off to Mark and the man on the other side. As soon as they grab him, the ship starts to pull away. The man touches his ear and shouts, "What are you doing? We still need the kid." He listens for a few seconds before shouting over to me. "He's not coming back. Reinforcements have arrived. You're going to need to jump!"

"You have got to be kidding me." I say to myself. When the ship I'm in is hit a few more times, a bunch of red warning lights and sirens go off, making my decision for me. I hear the pilot desperately trying to control the ship as I back up to jump. With what little room I have, I take a running start and jump. I feel like I'm in the air for much longer than I actually am. It feels as if time has slowed down as I do whatever I can to propel myself forward.

Still, it's not enough. Instead of dramatically landing inside the other ship and rolling like I planned, I barely catch hold. I hit the lip of the edge with my chest and struggle to hang on. I feel myself slipping until my fingers catch on the end of the platforms lip. I'm jerked to a stop, which immediately saps all the remaining energy in my left arm from me. I'm dangling by one arm because I'm forced to let go with my left. My body twists so that I can see the clouds underneath me like a merciless sea wanting to swallow me whole. I see all the crafts and vehicles flying around and some sort of fire between them. It's immediately obvious that they're not using normal guns like down on the Surface. It's also obvious that all the shooters are only okay shots.

I quickly decide to ignore the pain in my arm and grab on again. I try to pull myself up and am aided by Mark and the man. They manage to drag me up and into the ship. As soon as I get my legs up onto the side, I roll so that I am further inside. I turn and watch other crafts and people buzz around outside, and watch the transport I was just on keep putting forward, but slowly sink down. I feel a little bad for the pilot, but then I see another ship grab it with some sort of gigantic clamp, and help guide it away. When the hangar door loudly closes, I sit there with my knees tucked to my chest, my heart in my ears.

"What the hell was that?" Yells the man who I don't know at Mark, "We could have been killed! I'm sure at least some of our guys out there won't be coming back!"

"What did you want me to do? The kid wouldn't come if I didn't get the others," Mark yells back. The man who I don't know runs his fingers through his hair and looks at me.

"At least we got the kid. Weren't there two? In Davis's report, he said that there were two kids." Who's Davis? Mark's face sinks.

"The other one got hurt, he is on the way to the hospital." The man I don't know looks upset.

"At least we got one." He looks at me and starts walking over to me. Instinctively I shrink back, getting to my feet.

"What do you want with me? Who are you?"

"My name is Jinn. And you just joined the resistance."

Chapter Six

"What are you talking about?" I ask the man who identified himself as Jinn.

"My name? I'm talking about my name, it's Jinn. Didn't you hear me?" I can't tell if he is being serious.

"I heard you the first time. What do you mean resistance?" He looks at me as if he thinks I'm messing with him.

"The Ravens. We're not usually called that, but every now and then when are still referred to as Ravens. "We, as a whole, are fighting the New Power. Nearly everyone up here is fighting them. We just prefer to use pointy objects instead of words. Seems slightly more effective." If I weren't still slightly terrified, I might laugh. Jinn sticks his hand out to help me up. I take it.

"Why me?" I ask, "Why am I so important?"

"An excellent question. Sadly, it is one that is yet to be determined. I'll be able to answer your question as soon as you do something important or worthwhile."

That helps.

"Then why did you go through all of that to save me?" Seriously, they just did a jailbreak for me, and now I'm being told that there is no special reason they did it. I don't believe it.

"We were told in a report that you were clever. That you were the first in a long time to try and come up here. We thought that a brain like yours could help our cause. After that, when you were in the arena, and we were able to see your skills in combat, we knew we had to have you."

"So you did all of this to force me to fight. Your as bad as slavers." I put spite into the word slavers. They've hurt too many people on the Surface.

"You must understand. After all we have seen and learned about you, there was no other option than to get you for ourselves. It was that, or face you with you aligned with the New Power." He looks over at Mark, "You trusted Mark enough to listen to what he said and read his note."

"I didn't know that would be any better! This whole thing is crazy." I sort through the few things I know about up here in my head and find myself only more confused. Then I hit what must be true. "I just stepped into the middle of a war."

"Bingo. Everyone has to pick a side. There is no neutral. You can fight, try to hold as much of them off as you can until Nathan gets back, or conform. Do as the NP says, and accept their rule." He looks at me seriously. "I know I said that you were a part of the resistance, but this is your choice. What will it be?"

I don't hesitate. There is too much to be done, too many people that I can help. I won't do a repeat performance of the Surface, "Where do I start?" I hear Mark let out a sigh of relief and Jinn's face lights up with a smile. A sincere smile, one of the only one's that I have seen since I got up here. I let myself smile as well. Jinn's eyes slip down to my neck where they catch on something.

"Well isn't that an interesting necklace." It must have fallen out of my shirt somewhere in the middle of everything. I don't know when it did. I cover my necklace with my hand. I hope not too many people saw it. Mark looks over with a curious look.

"It must have fallen out during the break out. I didn't see it before that at all." So it only fell out long ago enough for these guys to see it. I tuck my necklace back into my shirt.

"Where did you get that necklace," he awkwardly pauses, "What's your name again?" Right, I never told him my name.

"Sam. My name is Sam," I say.

Mark pipes up, "So that's his name! I have been calling him Eight because that was his number in the arena." What is his deal?

"Wait, is this what you meant when you said that you've been doing it longer than the time you were working for the NP?"

"Bingo," says Mark, "I've been working with the resistance a long time now. When they told me I had to go undercover, I didn't think it would be as bad as it was. They never talk, and when they do, it's so boring it's painful." I have to agree with him there.

"Not too friendly towards newcomers either." I say, "What about John?" I ask thinking about how he isn't here with me right now.

"What can I say," says Jinn. Well, you could say that we're going to get him right now. Or you could say that another team is getting him as we speak. There are a couple things he could say. "You were told not to get hurt." He shrugs his shoulders. That's the best he can come up with?

"We couldn't help it!" I start to get angry.

"With what we were told about how you fight, you definitely could have prevented it," says Jinn coolly.

"With all respect, the boy had his hands tied with his own fight," Mark says on my behalf.

"He is going to have to learn to do better than that if he wants to survive in a real fight. More than one person is going to be coming after him at once, all of them aiming to kill." Jinn talks about this as if it's common discussion that happens every day. Oh yes, he must fight better or someone is going to kill him. That's totally normal.

"He'll need more time then, proper training. We can't just throw him in the frontlines."

"And we won't. On official records, he'll have died during extraction. During the time we can muster, I will take the boy," I shoot a wasted glare over at him, "with me and train him. Introduce him to the world he has chosen to come to." Mark stays silent a moment in thought before responding.

"Will they buy it? Do you think that will actually work?"

"I'm positive. They pretty much believe anything, unless someone tells them the contrary. All anyone will have seen is him jumping over to us. That'll be story enough for him being injured. A couple changes to the story and he won't have made it." Again, Mark takes a moment to think.

"Alright I'm in. Are we going to take him to your place now, or later?"

"It'll have to be now, otherwise I'm afraid they will get a chance to see him and know that I'm lying."

"Works for me."

"Who is 'they'?" I ask. Wait a minute, "Who's driving?" I have a mini panic attack thinking that we are going to crash, but Jinn and Mark just look at me like I'm crazy.

"The pilot?" Jinn says. These two must think I'm an idiot now. What a wonderful starting reputation.

"Right. Well, if we're going to your place, am I staying with you, or should I look for a hotel or something?" I think about what I said for a second and come to a realization, "Shit, I don't have any of my stuff! It was taken away before I was put on the transport before I was taken to the arena." I remember how much I lost. All my clothes, things, and the money my mom gave me.

"We have you and your friend's backpacks," says Jinn calmly.

"How can you have our stuff? It was taken away from us by a guard."

"Do you remember the man that originally told you that we were going to get you out and how to act in the arena?" I nod, "He's one of ours." That explains it! That's why Mr. Friendly was so friendly. He's one of these resistance dudes and was trying to get John and me out, and into their hands. "And you will be staying with me. It isn't safe for you to do anything otherwise." I guess that settles that matter. None of us say anything for a bit, until Mark speaks up.

"I think this is the first time you have actually offered to train someone personally, isn't is Jinny?"

"Don't call me that," Jinn replies flatly.

"Well it is, isn't it?" pushes Mark.

"Yes, this is a special circumstance though."

"What's so special about it?" asks Mark.

"You'll see." Mark throws his hands in the air and begins to pace around.

"Now don't you go all mysterious and not answering questions on me. I've had enough of that to last both of our lifetimes and still have some left over from those stupid New Power guards." I wonder if they've noticed that I'm still here? Probably doesn't matter much anyway.

"Where's my bag?" I ask. I'm still wearing the shirt Fred lent me. I don't think he is going to want it back. It's bloodied and has rips all over it. The biggest is running the entire length of the shirt defeating the purpose of the buttons.

"It's over in compartment two," Jinn says, pointing me toward where I need to go. I walk over and open the compartment. Inside, I see John and my bags, as Jinn and Mark said they would be. I take mine and unzip it. Inside lie all my clothes, some of the belongings I brought from home, and the metal tin my mom gave me. Other than slightly shifting, it all looks like nothing has happened to it.

"Is there a bathroom on this thing?" I ask to whoever is willing to answer. Again, Jinn speaks.

"No, but we will be at my house soon enough."

"Come on, I really have to use the bathroom. I've

been holding it since an hour before this whole thing started." Also, I want to get cleaned up, but I need prioritize.

"Just go over the side. That's what we all do when it's desperate on a transport," Mark says.

"That would explain flash sun showers," I mutter to myself. I look to make sure neither of them heard me.

"I'll just wait until there's a real bathroom. Are we almost there?"

"Just a little bit longer," says Jinn before he walks towards the front of the ship. He passes through a metal sliding door and leaves Mark and me in the room alone with each other.

"Don't worry," Mark says walking over to me, "Give him some time and he'll warm up to you," he smiles while he says it.

"How long did it take for him to like you?" I ask.

"I'll let you know as soon as I find out," he laughs, "I'm just joking. Jinn has his own way of doing and looking at things. He always feels like he needs to trust someone greatly before he'll do anything with them. Probably a smart move, but it gets to be such a pain." He pauses, making me think he's done before adding, "probably didn't even trust his own mother at first." I stifle a small laugh.

"Who knows, anything's possible." I look to Mark, "How did you two meet? You seem to know each other well enough."

"Short story really. An attack mission we were both on went more than a little wrong and he saved my life. Been close-ish friends ever since."

"Close-*ish*?"

"Jinn is always reserved. I'm used to it at this point, but I'm always hoping that he'll get over it." I look at him inquisitively, "I think you're the first step in that direction. He hasn't ever invited anyone to stay with him before." When he finished speaking, the intercom came on overhead.

"Approximately five minutes until landing." Mark walks over to one of the tiny windows that I didn't notice before. He smiles and opens a hatch on the side of the ship that opens horizontally instead of outward like the one I had to jump to. The wind begins to howl as I know it has been doing outside the entire time and Mark yells to me.

"Come over here! I want you to see this." After trying to decipher what he said for a moment, I walk over, nervous that I am going to fall out. When I look outside the ship I only see blue sky. I look over at Mark wondering what is so special about sky. "Fantastic isn't it?" I raise my eyebrow not knowing what he's talking about. He understands my confusion and smiles, "Look down a little." Again I lean forward but this time look down. Below me is an awe-inspiring sight.

Below me, I see what is truly my first sight of the Sky Kingdom. I see platforms of all sizes with intricate buildings on them. I notice that the platforms aren't still; they sway and move. Pretty much always staying above the clouds. It looks like a floating, moving town. They're much brighter than the towns on the surface. I can't make out any of the people very well, but I can well enough to tell that it is a bustling town, full of movement and action. Buzzing all around the town in all directions, above, below, beside, on, I see other vehicles and transports.

"It's beautiful," I say.

"Isn't it amazing?" Mark says, "can't say I remember the first time I saw her, but it was and still always is a sight to behold. I almost forgot how incredible it is, but that light is your eyes. There's just something about it that fills me with hope." I don't really know how to reply, so I just smile again and return to viewing the fleeting city beneath me. We soon start descending. As we continue to dip down, the large hangar door next to the one that Mark and I are currently at drops open. Mark steps back and pushes a button, closing the smaller opening.

"Might as well," he smiles, "We've got more than a big enough door right there." Jinn walks back out from the room he went into before.

"Grab your bags. Mark, you're welcome to stay for a

while, help me introduce the boy to the situation, and get him settled."

"Are you actually inviting me into your house?" Mark feigns surprise. I have a feeling they do this often.

"Yes, and don't make me regret it," Jinn smiles, Mark laughs.

"I can't tell you how many times I've heard that line. Let me try to count." He gets through his fingers before throwing his hands up in defeat, "Too many times. I'm pretty sure I'm forgetting some anyway." They both laugh at the stupidity of the comment.

"Follow me please," Jinn says to me. Obediently, I follow him. First thing I notice is that the house looks big. I have no idea what the interior is like, but it is a huge house.

"Wait until you see the back and training grounds," Mark says.

"There's more?"

"Much," says Jinn without turning around. I let out a low whistle. I'm impressed. The house is a large, wrap around two, maybe three I can't tell, story building. I don't know where his property line is, regardless; it is still an enormous building.

"Who else lives here?" I ask. There is no way that one mostly anti-social guy lives here all on his own.

"Just me," says Jinn, "the occasional help and house keepers, but for now, just me. And now there is also you." He says it matter-of-factly, so that I'm not sure if he meant it jokingly or aggressively. I'll go with jokingly.

"I've been here so many times that Jinn just gave me a room," Mark says, "Big place, it gets a little weird at night when you really realize how empty it is." I didn't even think of that. "As you must have figured out by now, Jinn is a cozy guy. I mean, he would give, what are they called, the big furry animals that are two colors?" I take a second to realize he was talking to me.

"Pandas?" I answer.

"That's it. He would give pandas a run for their money with how cute and cuddly he can be. Just don't catch him with a sword. That won't end pretty." I have a horrible feeling he isn't joking. At least, not about the last part.

"What, I don't look like a big ball of love to you?" Jinn adds to the discussion. Mark, for some reason, laughs.

"That all depends, my friend. Are you trying to attack me?"

"Not at the moment, no," smiles Jinn.

"Then yes, you most definitely look like a big ball of love. Minus the round part, of course," Jinn laughs. Isn't this the guy that was a total deadpan a minute ago? Maybe this is more like how he really is. That'd be good to know. I'd prefer smiley, joking, deadly guy to serious deadly guy. I'm not sure if one is better than the other though. Altogether, I would prefer him on my side. Just a thought, probably a very good thought too.

We've awkwardly been standing in front of the front door for a little while now, just talking. It isn't much an issue as Jinn seems to be happier now than he was before. I don't know what happened to make his attitude change, but I'm glad that it did. It will be much easier to live with him if he's happy.

"Well then," says Jinn, "Shall we go inside?"

"Get ready for a treat kid," whispers Mark. I can't help but smile. Jinn turns and, after unlocking it, pushes open the door to his house.

Chapter Seven

Jinn opens the doors and it is like a show. Inside, there is one massive hall. The walls are lined with suits of armor and artwork. The floors are covered in carpet and stone and wood in their respective places. It's one sight to behold.

"Wow," I say. It's about all I can manage as I look at this "house;" it's more like a crazy big mansion!

"Told you," says Mark. He to is looking around, admiring the home, "You don't ever change the decorations do you?"

"When something breaks," says Jinn. Mark laughs.

"So would that be why you never invite me over anymore?" Jinn smiles. Clearly, these two are better friends than I first thought.

"That's why I don't invite much of anyone into my humble abode anymore." Humble is an understatement. I've only seen a fraction of the front hall and already my mind is blown. I didn't think houses could be this big. Unless the house happened to belong to a king, or maybe someone like a king. It would probably be rude to ask Jinn how rich he is.

The room is flooded with light from windows all over the place. I don't see anything that would provide light for when it gets dark, but I guess I'll find out more about that later today. There are no doorways in this room other than the entrance, but there are three hallways and a staircase. One hall passes next to the staircase and into what looks like an even larger room, the other two lead off to the sides. From what I can see, they are lined with doors.

"What's behind the doors?" I ask. Jinn turns and looks at me before responding.

"You'll have plenty of time to explore in a bit."

"Fair enough," I say.

"Come," Jinn says, waving his arm, "follow me to the kitchen. We have to talk about a few things." Curious, I follow him. He leads Mark and me down the center aisle past the stairways.

The kitchen is spectacular. Jinn must really take care of the place. The kitchen looks immaculate. There is not one spot that I can find that is even slightly dirty. Nothing is sitting out or misplaced. Everything is nicely put away and stored. I'm pretty sure I see a shine coming from the counter. The entire back wall is glass. Glass colors, panels, windows, you name it. It is one impressive kitchen. I don't think I will ever get to, want to, or even consider saying that again. Jinn walks over towards his refrigerator.

"Either of you want a drink?"

"I'll just take some water," Mark says.

"Same here, please," I add.

"Two waters coming up." Instead of going into the refrigerator, Jinn turns to one of the cabinets next to it and pulls out three glasses. He fills them up with water and passes two over to Mark and me. Jinn looks over at me, "Like I said, we have a lot to talk about."

"What about?"

"Plenty of things. First of all, how did you get up here? Nobody has even attempted such a feat for over a decade. No offense, but you're what, sixteen, and you managed to succeed? Don't leave out any details. Mark mentioned to me that you may have left out parts when you were telling him the first time around." I recount the story of what happened to me, from getting on the ship to being broken out of the prison transport. As was asked of me, I don't leave out any details. I tell them all about John, and I tell them about Rick and Fred. I even tell them that one of my motives for coming up here is to look for my dad.

Mark keeps interrupting me, interjecting his thoughts, but Jinn just quietly listens, waiting for me to finish. I keep wondering what he's thinking, but wondering will do me no good.

"I knew you were keeping something from me!" exclaims Mark triumphantly, "I knew you weren't telling me everything before."

"Well, duh," I retort, "that's when I thought you were trying to kill me or something." Did he seriously expect me to tell him everything in the first few seconds of knowing him? Especially given the predicament we were in? He was, and still is, dressed like one of the New Power goons. He did talk more than the others. I guess that should have been my first clue.

"So? I still knew it." He's going to go on like this forever isn't he? He's acting like an annoying fifteen year old. Wait a minute.

I shake my head and look over at Jinn. He still has a face like stone, captured in thought. "What are you thinking?" I ask him, "Do you believe me?" He takes a moment before answering, rubbing his chin, continuing to think about what I have told him.

"I believe you. It's just-" He pauses diving back into thought, "it doesn't make any sense." That's very conclusive.

"What doesn't?" He looks up at me to answer my question. Temporarily putting his thought aside.

"It's just, if you were able to get up here in such a simple manner, not just you, but four people, only discovered through arrogance. Why has no one else attempted to come up here for years. Is it that, or have they all just slipped through our defenses?" Is he really troubled by this?

"I don't know. Even in all the rings on the surface, there was no word of anyone trying to come up here." Jinn looks at me like that means nothing to him. "Where I lived, if anyone tried to make a break for it, every normal person would know—at least, after the attempt. The last ones to find out, if at all, were the ones trying to oppress us."

"Who?" Mark asks. I turn and face him.

"The King's men. They're the police of the Surface, the military, the enforcers. I just call them the bad guys. Goons, creeps, and freaks also work pretty well."

"Well that's just fantastic," says Mark. "What, is the surface some lawless hellhole?" I almost laugh.

"Lawless, no. Hellhole, if you crave more than to serve 'His Majesty,'" saying that kills me, "yes."

"No wonder we used to get so many immigrants before. Did it get better over the past ten years or so? That's when the number of people trying to get in stopped."

"Dude, I was five ten years ago! I really only remember one thing and let me tell you, I'm no fan of that memory." Mark just looks at me like I'm going to have a highly detailed answer. I sigh, "I don't know. I guess it's gotten more routine, less brutal. At least on the outside."

"What do you mean?" asks Jinn.

"The police and the others have been doing less beatings in the streets. Now they take their victims off to the side to do it. If you don't want to see it, don't go into alleys."

"That's horrible!" exclaims Mark. "We're nothing like that up here. When Nathan is around, everyone is friendly with everyone. Sure there are fights, but it's not that bad. When the New Power tries to take the throne, it's all violence. There's a shadow of Nathan's goals, but that's it."

"Sounds gruesome," I say.

"He's putting it in an ugly light. It's not great, but it's not horrible either. The NP isn't making anything easy." None of us talk for a good full minute or two. I take a sip of my water so that I at least have something to do. Finally, Mark's phone rings.

"Yes?" He asks when he answers it. I strain my ears to try and listen in on his conversation. "I can't hear you over the rotors." He says plugging his open ear. "What?" he yells. "Oh, alright, I'll be out in a minute." He hangs up his phone and looks at us, "I need to take the 'surviving' people we rescued back to base. I'll see you guys next time. Sam, good luck; Jinn, maybe next time we can get a real drink."

"Next time we will." They both smile, "Let me walk

you to the door. Sam, please, pick any room you want as your own that's empty." It takes me a few seconds to register that he just told me to pick my place to stay.

"Do you want me to walk out with you guys?" I ask not wanting to be inside on my own. It feels awkward being inside on my own. It is not my house, or mansion, after all.

"I'm perfectly alright," says Mark, "I've got big old Jinn here to protect me. Go find your room." He leans a little closer. "Just don't pick the one with a striped carpet. That one's mine." He smiles, "Come on Jinn, I best be going."

"Right. I will be right back," Jinn says to me. I nod my head and watch as they go. I stand in place until I hear the door shut. I sigh and gather the three backpacks that I currently have in my possession. My old one, John's, and my new bag from the arena. I throw two on my back, one over each shoulder, and carry the third. I would be a good laugh for some schoolyard jerks. Actually, I think I would laugh at me too if I was in a different situation. In fact, out of the blue, I start laughing. I'm glad Jinn is outside or he would probably think that I'm insane.

I walk to the entrance room where the house split into three halls and a staircase up a floor. I put the bags down by the stairs and start a tour of the first floor. For the most part I open each of the doors, half-heartedly peering inside to see what the room looks like and decide if I would like to claim it as my own. None of them are anything special. They're all nice rooms, but nothing pops out at me. Well, the one room that does, I was told not to take. About halfway down the left hall, I open a door and it's like a show. I am forced to use a lot of willpower not to fall on the floor hysterically laughing my brains out.

Before me is the room that Mark claimed as his own. As he said, the carpet is striped like a tigers fur. The coloring is almost as extreme. The two shades for the stripes are black and another dark color, yet it seems neon. The walls are plastered with furry wallpaper that is magenta. The walls nearly put me over the edge of laughter. I look at the bed and see that the wood is beautifully, intricately carved and it also has four posts that hold up a curtain to go around whoever may sleep in the bed. The bed looked like one of the only nice things in the room. The rest was enough to make the most serious of men crack up. When I notice out of the corner of my eye the cheetah print robe hanging in the closet, I admit that it's too much to handle. I laugh and laugh all the way back to my bags in the entrance hall.

I listen for a moment and come to the conclusion that Jinn went with Mark to make their report or whatever and that they had either not left yet, or they were extremely quiet. I'm guessing the first one. I shrug my thoughts aside, grab the bags and walk upstairs. The staircase spirals on the way up while still attached to the wall. It is very classy, very modern. At the top, again, it split multiple ways. There is a hall to the left, a hall to the right, and an extremely large center room. It's probably more than just one room, but I decide to look later. Circling around the staircase to the extreme right and left, there are more doors. I decide to look at the one on the right. I walk over to the door and push it open. Inside I find the room that I claim as my own.

It is simple and plain, but it's big. In the room is a limited amount of things. There's a bed with white sheets and pillows, a nightstand, a dresser with a mirror, and a cabinet. The best part is that it has its own bathroom! I don't know why, that just seems important at the moment, probably because I'll never be able to find one of the other bathrooms in this gigantic house. When I enter the room I throw all three bags on the bed and take a look around. I survey the few pieces of furniture that I'm given. I don't know what I'm looking for; I just know I feel satisfied after inspecting the furniture for a while. I notice that the walls are pretty barren other than the large window that opens and views the front yard. It's a pretty amazing view. Although there isn't much to see, I get to see the front yard and slightly beyond. The yard is majority grass, perfectly cut and displayed bordered by hedges and an iron fence. There is a winding pathway leading to the front door. I doubt many people use it, but it is a nice touch.

Beyond the fencing and hedges, the more technologically advanced side of these platforms I saw at first shines through. It's less obvious, but it is roughly the same as what I saw on the transport into the arena. I guess what I saw then was just the extreme underside that generally only prisoners saw. There was probably no reason in anyone's mind to spruce that up and make it look good. What do they care?

Something that takes me a moment of staring at the yard to realize is that the ship that brought me here is gone. That ship has got to be built by ninjas. That was freaky quiet. Maybe the walls are just super soundproof. I haven't heard too much of the outside world since I've come inside. Then again, I have only been inside for a little while. I'm given something dangerous: time to think. These times either turn out really good, or cause a huge headache. Most of the time, when I get to think, it's just confusing. I have never really had any special direction that I let my thoughts wander.

There isn't anybody in the house, so I suppose that I could take a better look around if I wanted to. Instead, I stay in the room that I've claimed as my own and decide to unpack. I start with the backpack I brought up from the surface. I unzip the main pouch and gently take out everything that's in it and place it on the bed. I put the shirts and other articles of clothing I have away in drawers. After I put my clothes away, I realize that I really don't have much with me. All that's still on the bed are some melted candy bars, my phone charger, and the chest that my mom gave me. Seeing the candy bars makes me hungry, but not desperate enough to eat them.

Seeing the phone charger, I think to take my phone out of my pocket. I hit the button to turn it on and notice that it still has some power, barely, and most importantly, that it still works. For a moment I consider calling my mom right now, if not just to tell her that I love her and made it safely—more or less. The decision is made for me when my phone dies on the spot.

"Perfect," I mumble to myself. I take my phone charger and look around on the walls to see if there is an outlet I can use to plug it into. When I find one, I immediately realize that it's not the right shape to fit my phone, and that most outlets up here are probably like that. "Even more perfect," I say. I toss my charger and now useless phone on the bed and think to unload the rest of my pockets. I'm carrying my wallet with some of my money in it. I'm going to guess that the currency up here is different as well. Still, I open my wallet and pull out the picture of my mom and me hidden inside. I probably stand there for a good ten minutes just staring at the picture. I tuck it back, safely, inside my wallet and throw that on the bed too.

In front of me is all that I own. There is not much to it, just really stupid things that I wouldn't really need to survive. I don't know what I was thinking coming up here, I'm not ready at all. If I hadn't been picked up by Mark and Jinn, I'd be dead soon if not already. What did I get John into? He's off who knows where probably being tortured or forced to fight or something horrible. I can't believe I did that to him. All he was trying to do was be a good friend and look where that got him. I wonder if I'll ever see him again, if he will ever forgive me.

"What am I doing?" I ask aloud.

"Unpacking?" replies a voice behind me. I turn and see Jinn standing in the door, leaning against the doorframe. "I can see you picked your room," he says, "I always liked this room. It'll work well." I probably read too much into his word choice.

"I can go to a different room if you like this one." I stumble over my words thinking I might have offended my host. He laughs.

"What good is a room if nobody stays in it? Can I get you any extra sheets or pillows or anything?" It's a gracious offer, I'll admit.

"You've already given me so much just by allowing me to stay with you. How can I ask for anything more?"

"Well first, you start with, 'may I please get' and you fill it in from there. 'Oh amazing Jinn, can you work your miracles and provide something for me' would also be an acceptable answer." Modest much?

"I, uh, food? Clothes?" He says nothing staring at me. "May I please get some food and clothes, I don't have much of either."

"Much better, and yes, you may. Let's get you some food first. You've been wearing the clothes from the arena this long, what's another few minutes. Come on back to the kitchen, I'll whip something up for you. Little hungry myself." He leads me to the kitchen, asking me what I want. "I have some soup. It helps when you're nervous and upset. I keep plenty stocked." He reaches into his pantry and takes out two cans. He sets them down next to his stove and pulls out a can opener and a pot. He opens one of the cans of soup and pours it out. The soup looks normal enough, but I still have no idea how it is going to taste. Right now, as long as it isn't poisonous, I think I'll eat it.

"What's so special about the soup?" I ask. He said it helps with nerves, maybe there's a special reason why.

"It tastes good," he says, pleasantly and curtly dumping the second can into the pot. Well I guess that answers that.

"What about natural gas?" I ask, "How do you get the gas up here to burn?" He looks at the stove right in front of him and looks back at me like he has a very insightful answer. He shrugs.

"We use some of the energy left over from the converters keeping this whole place aloft." That works. He cooks for a moment in silence. "Do you have any questions for me?" he asks. "I understand that this is all new for you. Not just in a thought sense, but in physical as well."

"Ya, actually. I do."

"Ask away." I swallow.

"Why are you being so nice to me?" I know it isn't a big question, but for some reason I feel uncomfortable asking it. Probably because I don't want to know what the answer is. He chuckles.

"You will be asking the exact opposite soon enough." He smiles and stirs the soup.

"What do you mean?" I ask.

"Well," he starts, "we're going to start with your fighting. You were able to hold your own in the arena, but from what I'm told that's just barely. My guess is that you're just a lucky smart-ass. Your team work is sloppy as is the rest of your style; you don't know   anything about up here, and god, you're likely to fall off an edge and plummet to your death." I wait for him to keep speaking. When he doesn't, I say the only thing that would make sense at the moment.

"Ass." He smiles.

"That's the best you can do? I've been called much worse," alright, a big ass. "You'll grow to either love or hate me. Either way, I don't care." Reiterating my previous statement, ass.

"You're not so bad. Some of the more pleasant kids on the surface are worse than you." I smile thinking I got the better of him. He turns the stove off and pours half the soup into a bowl for me, and the other half into a bowl for him. He hands me mine and gets me another glass of water.

"We'll see about that," he says. He seems really confident, and I know that he wants me to ask, so I'll take the bait.

"What is so different about you?" Jinn looks like he has this line rehearsed and that it is one of his favorite things in the world to say.

"First of all, I get to teach you to fight. That means that I get to beat you day in and day out."

"That's nothing new," I cut him off, "fights broke out all the time on the Surface. I had to have been ready or I would have been dead," and I like staying alive.

"Second," he continues as if I had said nothing, "you can't get away from me." Fantastic, "And third," his grin grew to twice its normal size. I can tell that he loves this last one, "I get to push you off a cliff."

Chapter
Eight

"No need to look like you enjoy that thought too much," I say. Push me off a cliff? What kind of sick psychopath likes that kind of thing?

"Oh don't worry you baby, you'll be just fine." He thinks for a moment, "Or I'm majorly over-estimating you and you will hit the Surface and splat like a bug on a windshield." Is that really an issue up here? I guess it would be a major concern when everything flys.

"Thanks for the pretty thoughts," Jinn laughs. Real supportive.

"Everyone gets pushed at one point or another," says Jinn, "That's why we train everyone what to do if that happens. Soldiers get even more specialized training."

"So I'm a soldier now?" I ask.

"That remains to be seen. I have a feeling that soldier isn't enough for you. That you are going to shake this whole system down to the foundation and tell it that it's inadequate." Really, I think I'd call it stupid, but I didn't correct him. I'll let Jinn think I'm smart for now. I take a bite of my soup.

"When does all this 'training' start?"

"Tomorrow," Jinn says courtly. "Today is for you to get acquainted with the house. I don't want you going outside, and if the house is contacted, or anyone comes here, go hide in your room. Technically, you're dead right now, but that's beside the point."

"Wait a minute," I cut him off, "Dead? How can I be dead? I'm right here!" I poke myself to prove that I'm tangible.

"Obviously, you're alive, but the only way that we could get you here, is by telling control that you had died or been taken."

"So why couldn't you have said that I was taken?"

"I didn't want to be forced to go on another mission to break more people out," says Jinn matter-of-factly.

"Did you even care to get me out?" I ask. Really, I don't care right now, but it would be good to know if this guy cares anything for me. I know I just met him and all, but really, I'm not sure.

"I didn't really want to go. I thought you were just going to be another idiot that was picked up off the streets." I feel the energy in my body droop with disappointment, "But, when I found out that you came from the Surface, and fought and nearly won in the arena, I became interested." I think back to Mark and

Jinn picking me up from the second, well, I guess third, transport I rode and how they worked like clockwork. The only flaws and glitches in their plan were coming from me being unwilling to leave anybody behind. I wonder if Jinn looks at that like a weakness. Mark seemed to be annoyed by it at first, but warmed up to the idea as it started flowing. Maybe he was just going along with it.

"So what about now?" I ask, "Am I still 'interesting' enough for you?" Lame, I know, but honestly, I kind of want to know.

"For now, yes. Interesting enough. We shall see how interesting you really are tomorrow, when we start your training."

"That's a pretty horrible way to look at people." I say, "Looking at them and basing if you care solely on if they can perform in your 'training' well or not." It is really stupid. Jinn leans in close, so that I can see his pores.

"You just went up in my mind," he says calmly. "Good to know you have a heart and something of a brain. Let's just see where the rest of it is, and if you can even use it." Wow, how cheesy are some of this guy's lines? I think even I can come up with better ones. Actually, maybe not. I guess I'll see over time. Maybe I don't want to know. Wait, did he say we start tomorrow?

"What time is it?" I ask, "I've been traveling and fighting for what feels like forever. I lost track of the world around me." I feel embarrassed, but it's the truth. I don't know what time it is. When I look outside, I notice that it is dark.

"Late," Jinn says, "We didn't pick you up until later on in the day, then I was gone for a couple hours filling out reports. After that, time has just been continuing to move. It tends to work that way." No duh... jerk. Really, how long have I been out and about? John and I got on the first transport from the Surface sometime at night, and now it's night again. I don't know if it's been one day or two. I'm going to have to guess one because in the arena and the rest of the time today, I think it has been light out.

"How is it still so bright inside?" It still feels like it should be the middle of the day to me.

"Lights?" He says, "Don't you have lights on the Surface?" Please tell me he's joking.

"Of course we have lights on the Surface." Just need to clarify, "These ones are just really bright." He shrugs.

"They're just normal quality lights. There are brighter ones to make things even clearer for detailed work."

"They have brighter lights for normal housing?"

"Yes. It's available as both room lighting and focused work lighting." That's weird.

"Why are there two kinds of the same light? Why wouldn't someone look for a higher power light if they wanted a 'work light' instead of one for their 'normal lighting?'"

"One is more focused than the other. Less spread out. Then there is super focus, which isn't even a light anymore, but controlled electricity. That is what is used in the arena. That is what is used as a tool to hurt and kill." In his voice, I hear what sounds like, I don't know how to describe it, pride? Like he feels important because he knows what he's talking about. Maybe it's arrogance. I don't know. It's not the first time I've heard somebody talk like that, and I'm sure it's not going to be the last.

"Alright then. How do they control the electricity to the point it can hurt someone?" He yawns. It better not be because I'm boring him. If it is, I am so going to kick his ass.

"That," he starts, "is a discussion for a different day. For today, or what's left of it, I am going to sleep." Duh, it's late. He said that all of three seconds ago. Okay, maybe I'm exaggerating just a tad. "I can't remember, did you have sheets?"

"I, uh, think so?" I answer. I don't know why I say it like a question, but still, I do. I don't even know if what I just said is true.

"Here, I'll check, then I'm off to sleep. You should try to get some rest as well. How many hours have you been up already?" Now that he mentions it, falling flat on my face sounds like a good idea.

"Thanks," I say. He takes my now empty soup bowl and throws it in what looks like a dishwasher. That's what I'm going with. Jinn walks upstairs and I follow him. He takes a right at the top of the stairs, and again, I follow. He opens the door to my room—weird to think of it that way—and takes a look inside.

"You have sheets," he says, looking back over at me, "I don't know if you want more or not. If you do, all you need is to ask." How thoughtful of the guy that smiled at the thought of pushing me off a cliff. Jinn looks back into my room, "Is that all you have?" he asks. Right, I left all my stuff on the bed.

"All but what I'm wearing." Which right now would be a totally ripped up and dirty, even bloody, t-shirt, and also ripped up and bloody jeans. Everything else is lying out for Jinn to see. He walks into my room. Well, I guess it's his room, but I'm borrowing it.

"First, this is your room now." I catch my breath. Can he read minds? If so, I am so dead. "Second, now that you have a room, we need some stuff to fill it with." I walk into the room and see him fiddling with the things on my bed. "This is great and all," he says waving his hand over my stuff, "but it's not going to do. I, for one, am all for living simply," yet you live in a mansion. Right, that makes sense. "We will have to get you more clothes, as you asked."

"Thank you," I say, but he continues talking as if he hadn't heard me at all. Maybe he's just making a list for himself.

"Also, this," he picks up my phone and charger, "will never work up here. It's really rare to find the adapter for your power, and besides, we have better ones. One that I'll be able to reach you on at any time." Please no brain chips, please no brain chips.

"How hard would it be to get one of those adapters? There's some stuff on there that I really need." Like my pictures of my dad. How else am I supposed to ask   people if they've seen him? Jinn just looks at me. "What?" Right, he said, they were really rare. My bad.

"Got it." So much for the pictures.

"There are a few other errands we must run as well, but those can wait until after I train you for a bit. As long as we stay out of overly populated areas, we should be fine. I don't see why we would even need to leave the grounds." How big is this place? "Yes, that shall do nicely," Jinn says to himself. Do I want to know what he's thinking about? Probably me screaming while falling down, down, down before I go splat on the Surface. Why do I keep thinking of that? It's not the most cheery thought I've ever had. Then one possibly less pleasant strikes me.

"When do I need to wake up tomorrow?" I know it's not the world's most pressing matter at the moment, but it is important to me. Jinn laughs.

"We'll make that a surprise." My stomach drops.

"Come on," I complain, "I've been up for at least twenty-four hours. Can I at least get one night of rest?" Jinn looks withdrawn in his thoughts. Does he really have to think about this? Maybe he is just a horrible person. A horrible person that doesn't want to let me sleep!

"Fine," I smile, "Just one day. It will give me time to set up some things for your training, and pick up some things in town. Be ready to work hard later though. Don't think you're getting off easy." He points at me as if that somehow makes me understand better.

"Deal," I say still grinning. Work hard tomorrow? Sure, that will probably suck, but at least Jinn is letting me sleep for a while.

"One of the things I'm getting for you is an alarm clock. Wonderful things, not only do they tell time, but they wake you up in the morning as well." Ah, sarcasm, my second language. I could talk back and make some brash comment, but I am still more concerned about sleep sleep. "If you had one, it would tell you that it's close to midnight. Time to sleep." He lumbers out of my room taking my phone with him. I almost call after him, but realize it doesn't matter much. The phone wouldn't work anymore. The charger's useless up here. Jinn keeps walking and closes the door behind him.

I let out a sigh as I turn back to my bed, putting my hands behind my head. I look down at my stuff. My wallet, phone charger, headphones, house key, and the box from my mom are all I have left from the Surface. That, and what ever is in John's backpack, as well as the bags themselves. Already from up here, from this new life, what do I have? I have a new backpack, I don't know why it's special, this entire room, a scuffed up metal disk, and a beamsword able to kill.

I am not sure if this is any better than life was on the Surface. Actually, I take that back, it's much better, but I've only been up here for a day and for nearly that entire time, I've been running, hiding, fighting, and I don't think it is going to stop. My life feels like it's a roller costar stuck going down hill. For some reason never slowing down. Blah. I gather my things off the bed and put them on the nightstand next to the head. I go over to the dresser I put my clothes in to check for sweats or something to sleep in.

"Damn it," I swear under my breath. I forgot to pack something to sleep in. Oh well, I guess now is as good a time as any to learn to love sleeping in my boxers. I kick off my shoes at the foot of the bed and take my socks off. I take my ripped, dirty, bloody jeans off and throw them in a corner, then I take off my even more ripped, dirty, bloody shirt I used as a disguise and throw that in the same corner. Lastly, I take off my slightly less ripped, bloody, and dirty undershirt. I'm starting to notice a common theme here.

I flick the lights off and feel my way back to the bed. I lift the sheets and climb in. Surprisingly, it feels much softer than I originally thought it would. It looks pretty soft, but feels like I don't even know what. Maybe it is made out of cloud. Anything is possible I guess. I'm still the newbie up here. It's going to take forever for me to fall asleep. I thought I was tired but I feel so wired up that I'm sure I'm not going to get any sleep. I lie in bed for a few minutes before my eyes close and I slip into a nice, much needed, slumber.

When I eventually slip back into consciousness, I don't open my eyes. In fact, I pull the covers over my head and start whining. Not annoying whining, but I do mumble something along the lines of, "No, stupid sun, go away. Give me five more minutes." Then I say something about food and can't remember much about that. I fall back half asleep. I feel like I'm home, lying in my bed about to go to school, which surprisingly, is one of the only things on the Surface that is almost exactly like it sounds: hell. Not because of over-active punishments, which did tend to happen from time to time, but because it just gets really boring. We're required to go, but I swear it's the opposite of what *The King* wants. He would prefer us all to work until we drop.

"Really, I don't want to go to school mom. Give me a few more minutes." I wave above my head while complaining. I wrap the blanket tighter around me, thinking that would somehow help me sleep longer. What was I dreaming of? Must have been a nice dream. I hear someone talking to me. I can't make out who the voice is but, maybe.

"Mom?" I ask, turning, still covered by the sheets. Prying my eyes open, using my hand to shield them from light.

"Do I look like your mom?" Right. My fictional reality shatters around me and I remember where I am. The bruises on my arms and legs start aching again. The worst being the one line straight across my chest where I hit the side of Jinn and Mark's transport. Thinking of that, my arm starts to hurt all over again from basically being ripped out of its socket every few hours. Also, the place where I was stabbed with the beam-sword begins to sting. It is a dull pain, but it still sucks. I sigh and sit up.

"Nah," I say, "you're not pretty enough." I'm still squinting, waiting for my eyes to adjust. Jinn lets out a chuckle.

"Cute, but I'm not going to raise any allowance of yours for that, and I doubt your mom will. She's on the Surface, remember?" Thanks for the reminder. "You look like a mess. Why don't you go shower and then we'll get started." On what? Oh yeah, I get to start my "training" today, whoopy for me. I swing my legs around, and start to get up before I toss the sheets over my lower half.

"Uh, would you mind leaving for a bit?" I ask. Jinn cocks his eyebrow. "I don't exactly have pants on," I smile weakly. Why I'm embarrassed, I don't know? There's just something about being with someone in nothing but your boxers that doesn't feel right. Jinn laughs.

"Fine, but you'll need to learn to be comfortable around me sooner or later." With that, he politely leaves my room and shuts the door behind him. I hop out of bed and walk over to the bathroom. I look into a large mirror mounted above the sink. Geez, I'm a mess. I give myself a once-over and notice that I'm covered in cuts and bruises. My face looks incredibly filthy. Guess this is what the shower is for. I quickly shower and throw fresh clothes on. It's not that I don't like wearing destroyed, bloody clothes, but they weren't even where I left them. I go back into the bathroom and ruffle my hair so that it falls how I like it to.

Upon leaving the bathroom a second time, I notice that there are some new additions to my room. First, there's an alarm clock. Second, there's a plant, and third, well, I actually don't have a third, but it sounds better with three prongs. I leave my room and bounce down

120

the stairs so that I end up on the first floor.

"Sam?" I hear Jinn call. It sounds like he's in the kitchen so I head that way. Look at me. Day two and I'm starting to memorize the house's layout. When I enter the kitchen I see Jinn, once again, cooking. "Finally you're up," he says. Good morning to you too, cranky. "Are you ready?" he asks me. Ready?

"Ready for what?" I ask. He looks a little irritated that I can't seem to remember why I need to be ready. Wait, I remember, "When are we going to start? You said be ready to work hard and I guess I'm ready now." Am I? I have no idea, might as well get it over with.

"Do you want to eat first?" He asks. "It might make you sick, but you look like some food will do you good." He's right. I am hungry, but I have no idea what he has planned for today.

"I'll take a break a little later and eat. We can do the really hard stuff first." Jinn almost laughs at my comment. "What?" I ask. I don't see what's so funny. I thought my statement was well thought out.

"Nothing," he starts laughing again, "It's just been a while since someone actually thought there would be an easy part. It's a nice refresher that you do." That doesn't sound so good for me. This is going to hurt. I sigh.

"Where are we going to start?" I ask.

"Oh so many choices. We will have to start with the basics. Information about the world around you." Seems easy enough.

"Why is that so hard?"

"It's not. This is about the only easy thing that will be included in your training." For some reason, I have no issues believing him.

"Alright, let's begin."

"You might want to take a seat." Jinn gestures to one of the stools at the counter in his kitchen as he speaks. I walk over and plop myself down. Maybe I will have a bite to eat. I'll decide in a minute.

"The big picture; this is not like what you're used to." That's a given, "This world of ours, the Sky Kingdom, it has a life of its own. The Surface has a specific feel, we have a specific feel, and so does the kingdom in the deep. Not one of them is alike to another. They may seem similar at parts, but that's about all there is.

"Up here in the sky, it's obviously going to be colder, yet warmer than you're used to. The wind blows harder, and there are not as many clouds to block out the sun as you're used to. On the same note, it is very bright up here. That's something you'll just have to get used to. I may be over exaggerating, but it can get pretty extreme at times." I can believe that. Jinn continues, without me interrupting, "One of our biggest fears is falling."

"What do you mean falling?" I ask. It's never great to take a tumble, but really, I don't think he can speak for everyone up here when he says their biggest fear is falling."

"Falling off the side of a platform." Okay, he can speak for everyone on that mark. I, for one, would not like to plummet to my death. I have other plans in mind. Plans that aren't even close to finished. "Other than not being an idiot, there have been developments in personal air flight technology."

"Jetpacks?" Do I sound to hopeful?

"In a way, yes. Although, it's not always on a person's back." I'll have to ask him to explain that more in depth later, but for now, Jinn keeps going, explaining. "With current battles for power being waged, it is also very important to know that it is completely acceptable and even expected for people to be armed. Swords, shields, knives, you name it."

"Guns?" I ask. I never liked guns, but I'm not a bad shot.

"No, no guns other than those mounted on crafts. The winds knock the bullets off course rendering the weapon useless." I don't like guns, and there are no guns. Excellent, "Most of the time, fights are fast and furious, but we'll talk about that later."

"Let me guess, we are going to have combat training?" Jinn nods. I should get an award or something for being right. Maybe just a good pat on the back. After all, it's hard work putting two and two together.

"Let's see. I want to sum this up so that we can really get started." Jinn stands there quietly for a bit, leaning against the counter with his arms. "Other little detains you need to know are that the money is different, but there is an exchange rate." He must have tacked the exchange rate thing on because he saw that I looked really upset. My mom gave me all that money. I've been saving for so long. I'd be pissed if all of that went to waste. "The clothes and styles are different, and the rest, you'll be able to figure out as we go along, and you live here."

"Alright then," I say standing up, "What's the first lesson? Other than this, I mean." Jinn flashes me a wicked smile.

"Something very basic, and extremely important." That can only mean trouble. I think through the short explanation of what the deal is up here that Jinn told me, and what would make him smile like that. Then it hits me. This is about when he is going to push me off one of the platforms.

Chapter Nine

"No, absolutely no way," I say. I don't feel like plummeting to my death. It might just be me, but I don't want to learn how to skydive this way.

"Relax," Jinn tries to reassure me, "you'll be perfectly safe." No, going splat is not perfectly safe. It's not safe at all!

"How do you know that, huh?"

"Because I'll be ready to save you if anything goes wrong," Jinn huffs out, "And besides, I have a feeling you're going to excel." Excel in what? Hitting the ground?

"What if you fall too? What then?"

"Then we both die and we'll deserve it. Are you ready now?" My mouth drops open. Who thinks that way? It's not normal. I try and formulate another excuse not to have to go jump off one of the massive platforms that make up the Sky Kingdom. I draw a blank. "Good, now lets go." Dammit. Jinn grabs a backpack that was hidden behind the counter and slings it onto his back.

He then grabs yet another backpack so that he has to carry it in his hands. The two bags don't look at all like normal backpacks. They are longer, and look much harder. Like if I were to knock on one, I would hear an echo. The backpacks have multiple straps that connect across the chest, under the arms, and across the waist.

"Follow me," Jinn says, and I do just that. I follow Jinn to the main room where he opens the front door. "After you," he gestures out the door. I walk through the door and he follows behind me. Jinn shuts and locks the door behind him. This is not going to end well. If he's locking me out, it means that there's no getting out of this.

"Come on," Jinn says to me as he continues to walk across his lawn. I follow him past the hedges and see that I am standing on something more mechanical than the rest of the house. What I'm standing on is like a high tech dock. I'm guessing it's for aircrafts to land on, but I don't know why they would land here. Jinn has that huge yard, and as I saw with the transport that brought me here, they can land directly on it. The dock makes no sense to me.

"Certain ships can't land on the lawn." Really? I need to look around, make sure he doesn't have something that can read my mind. Maybe he probed me. I'm kind of hoping for the first one—much less painful.

"Now what?" I ask, letting out a breath of air. Jinn smiles like that's what he was waiting for. Can I read minds now too? That'd be so cool! Jinn throws one of the heavier looking backpacks to me. I catch it with a thud, almost being knocked over. What is in this thing?

"Noted. We'll need to work on your strength." Noted? Am I just some test subject? That would be extremely bad if Jinn is about to have me jump and learn to fly. It would be pretty cool if I grew wings though. None of my shirts would fit. People would stare at me, and it would all together be a pain. Maybe wings aren't such a great idea. "Well, put it on," Jinn says, sounding slightly irritated.

I swing the bag around and put it on over both shoulders. I feel the weight of it trying to drag me to the ground, forcing me to lean forward while standing. I'm sure I look like an idiot, but Jinn doesn't give anything away as he puts on the other backpack and fastens the straps tightly and securely. Guessing that he knows what he's doing, I do the same. I clip the straps together which helps relieve some of the weight, but the bag is still a little too heavy for comfort. When I look at Jinn to make sure I attached it correctly, I notice that he is standing right at the edge of the platform.

"Come here," he says to me.

"Do you really think I'm that gullible?" I ask in response. "And what's in this thing? Rocks?"

"I assure you it's not rocks. I can also promise you that I will not be pushing you. Not yet. First you must learn how to live through the experience." Fantastic! I get to learn, and then I get to fall to what might be my death. Can this day get any better? "What you are wearing is what you might call, a jetpack." Yes, yes it can. I have a jetpack! I've wanted one of these since I was a kid! Well, a smaller kid. Point is, I've wanted one for a while now. "I'm going to teach you how to use this." I keep myself from letting a grin spread across my face so large that nothing else would be seen. Just teeth and nothing else. Those smiles hurt, but in a good way. That makes no sense.

"First," Jinn starts, "you have to engage control." He uses his elbows to smack the sides of his jetpack, backpack, thing and two handles protruding from metal bars come out. The controls look simple enough and are located just within comfortable arms reach for Jinn. Is his custom fit? Is he really lucky? Or do they all happen to be perfect for their user? I shrug and hit my backpack in roughly the same place I saw Jinn hit his. To my surprise, even though it was expected, two control handles drop out.

Now that I can see them, I can easily tell the details of the handles. The steal is bolted together so that it will hold strong and true even if it has to take a lot of punishment. Then again, I've never seen this thing in action and what it's required to endure, but I'm just guessing. The handles themselves look like intricately carved wood with metal and buttons and controls sticking out at so many parts that the wood cased the electronics more than anything.

"I'm going to have you try to touch off, hover, and land." Jinn proceeds to grab hold of his two controls. He can move the handles around in a full range of motion as if there is no hindrance. Jinn then jumps, and pushes a button on top of both of his controls. The backpack, jetpack, whatever, snaps open on the bottom and starts to hum quietly. I expected to see large tongs of smoke and fire spewing out of the bottom as I'd always imagined, but no such thing occurs. Instead, it looks like the air around the base is disturbed slightly by heat, creating waves in the air around the base of the jetpack.

"Now you try it," says Jinn, "it's quite easy, well, for an experienced flyer like myself." He starts to boast, or maybe just talk down to me. I can't tell if he's joking or what.

"Get on with it please," I say cutting him off.

"Right. You will need to keep both control rods centered. Go on, grab them and get used to how they move." I do as he says and grab onto the two control rods on either side of my body. Even though I saw Jinn manipulate them seamlessly only moments ago, I forget that the controls seem to face no resistance. I grab hold, assuming that the controls won't budge if I rest my arms on them. Contrary to what I believe, the controls swing down so that my arms are once again resting at my sides as they were before.

"That doesn't look centered to me," Jinn says, "You need to actually try to keep the controls centred. Control isn't easy." Thank you captain obvious. I raise my arms slowly feeling for any pull against my motions. When I feel none, I try moving my arms around normally, like I would any other day. Still, no resistance. I try punching the air a couple times. It doesn't seem to be an issue for the controls.

"The goal is not to look like a moron and spiral out of control. Center your controls and I'll tell you what to do from there." Jerk. I do as he says and bring my controls to center. Jinn looks at my arms and tells me a few minor things to correct before continuing. "Alright, now here's what you do," Jinn says landing. "You're going to jump, then you are going to push the two buttons on the top of your control handles." Easy enough. "Give it a try when you're ready. Watch me first, though," Again, Jinn jumps into the air, pushes the buttons on his jetpack and proceeds to hover. He looks at me expectantly.

Easy enough. I jump like Jinn did, and push the buttons. To my surprise, I hover in place.

"Wow," I gasp. I know it's not much, but I'm using a jetpack. I could almost dance. I don't know how well that would go in the air though.

"Good," Jinn says, "you can let go of the buttons.

They just engaged the left and right halves of the same engine. Now, here's the tricky part." Fantastic, "To go forward, you have to squeeze the full hand trigger on your right control stick. To stop, you have to squeeze the trigger on your left control stick." This is hard? It sounds like driving a car, but instead of pedals, there are triggers. "To change your speed, you have to use the small joystick reachable with your thumb on the right control. To change the intensity of your stop, which is a very annoying function, I don't recommend using the built-in stopper much at all. It's not pleasant. Use the joystick on the left controller. Got it?" I run through what he told me in my head to make sure I got what he said.

"How do I turn?" I ask raising my arms and flipping in place, ramming myself into the ground. The jetpack continues to drive me downward, giving me a nice tasty sample of the ground. It doesn't taste so good.

"First," Jinn says, once again landing, "kill your engine with the starters you used to begin hovering. I push the buttons on top of the two controls and my lower half falls to the floor, no longer kept up awkwardly by the jetpack. "Second, I think you just figured out how to steer."

"Ya, I guess so," I say standing up and brushing myself off.

"Do you have what I told you committed to memory?" Jinn asks me. In five minutes? That seems a little fast to memorize something, but still, it's simple enough that I think I have it down.

"Yes."

Jinn smiles. "Good." He pushes me back and suddenly I'm hurling down, down from the platform, down from Jinn watching me, down from the world I so sought after for years. I see the clouds below me coming closer. Going with instinct, and what I just learned, I grab the controls for the jetpack and activate the engine. With the engine activated, because I am falling back first, I am now falling at sort of an angle. I take firm hold of the two control bars and twist my waist to flip my body over.

I squeeze in the button on the right controller to start the propulsion. It only works minimally, pushing me forward faster, but I am still falling. I find the joystick on the right controller with my thumb and push it all the way forward.

"Ahhhhh!" I yell as I go screaming forward. I'm at a speed where the wind is ripping tears from my eyes. Too fast! TOO FAST! I ease up on the throttle so that I'm going a speed that doesn't make my eyes water. My heart continues to race from the possibly near death experience, but I don't notice it. I can't tell if it's racing because I almost died, or because of what I'm doing. I'm flying. I feel really tempted to dive lower and run my hand through the clouds, but I don't think that's such a good idea. At least not until I can easily find my way back to Jinn's house while flying. The word still sounds weird in my thoughts.

"How do I pull up?" I ask myself. If someone responded, I would probably freak out. I twist my body but that only results in an overheated rear. Right, Jinn said that the controls I'm holding control it. Isn't it funny how that works? Controls are used to control something. Who would have thought?

Instead of being as jerky as I was with the throttle, I slowly raise the control above my head. When I start to dive, I take the controls and reverse their direction, lowering them to my sides. I get impatient with the incline and lower the controls even more to fly higher. I go vertical, but keep spinning without changing the controls positions. After a complete backflip, when next I became vertical, I even out the controls to be how they were placed when Jinn had me hover. With the throttle still up, instead of hovering, I fly up.

I let go of the propulsion trigger on the right controller so that I am hovering. Where is Jinn's house? I spend a little while looking for it before I see someone standing on their platform. I can't see them that well, but it looks like they might have their arms crossed and are waiting. Yup, that's Jinn. I activate my forward momentum again and raise my arms until I am angled directly at Jinn. When I'm pointing straight at him, I put my arms so that the jetpack will hold steady while I fly the rest of the way towards him.

As I'm flying, I notice that there are not many other platforms around here. In fact, I think that there may only be one or two. For all I know, they may also be Jinn's. None of the three platforms around me, including Jinn's, have a large, deep spire below them like the arena did. Maybe it's because the arena is a bigger and heavier platform? Nah, it's probably just a special convicts' entrance. They treated me so well when I was there. I just can't wait to go back!

When I near Jinn, I ease up on the throttle until I am barely at a suspended crawl. When I'm safely over the platform, I release the throttle all together, and cut the engine. I didn't even myself out, or come to a complete stop with a hover. I land with a thud and less than graceful fall on my face. My face seems to be taking a lot of abuse here. Maybe I should buy a hockey mask and never take it off.

"Good first flight," Jinn says calmly. I grumble as I push myself up to my knees from the floor. "I didn't even have to come and save you! That was a pleasant surprise." He smiles, getting excited. "And, you screamed a lot less than I thought you would. My guess was that you would nearly hit the clouds screaming before I needed to come and save you."

"Sorry to disappoint," I say rising to my feet, "and

when you put it on full throttle, classic." He laughs, using his hands to accent his point.

"By the way," Jinn says, "you're going to want some ice." He gives me a once over to see if I'm hurt.

"Why am I going to need ice? What are you going to do to me now?" Really, if he does something like this again, I'm pulling him down with me. No hesitation, I am not falling on my own again if I can help it.

"It's nothing that I did that will make you need the ice." He looks at me like I must be crazy that I can't feel anything. Did I pull something? Sure, my arm still hurts from the arena and jumping to the transport, but other than that, I don't think that there is anything. "Here's the deal," Jinn continues changing the subject, "for safety, you're going to have to have that backpack on at all times outside."

"Are you kidding me?" I ask, "This thing is more likely to break my back than save my life!" No kidding. It's already starting to hurt. My back is driving me crazy right now.

"You didn't let me finish," Jinn says irritably, "You are going to have to wear the pack, or," I'm not sure if this is going to be good or not. "Or" can be a dangerous word, "there is another option. They are much harder to use, but they're also much more inconspicuous." It's good.

"What is it?" I ask, taking off the heavy jetpack.

"How attached are you to your footwear?" Jinn asks

me. I look down at my feet and notice that my sneakers are destroyed from everything that has happened the last few days.

"At the moment, not at all."

"Good." He says. He also takes off his jetpack and unzips it. They really work as backpacks? From the bag, he produces a pair of black boots. I hate boots. Oh *so* much.

"What are those for?" I ask.

"These," he says, "are your alternative."

"Alternative to my shoes?" What do the boots have to do with anything? I thought he was going to show me something I could use instead of a heavy jetpack backpack.

"To the jetpack," Alright then. That makes sense. Actually, no. No it doesn't make any sense at all.

"How are boots," I ask, stretching my back, "going to replace a jetpack? Am I going to fall to my death, but look classy doing it?"

"They will propel you. Two separate systems instead of one system powered by two engines. Just put them on. I'll explain it to you." I sit down on the floor to take my shoes off. As I take one of my shoes off, he throws the boots to me, letting them clatter to the floor. They must be either much more durable or much less expensive than the jetpacks. I attempt to put one of the boots on while sitting down. I have no success. I spend the next few minutes dancing around trying to get one of the boots on. After I get one on, I spend another minute or two trying to get the other one. Somewhere, while trying to figure it out, it occurs to me to do what had worked the first time.

After I get both boots on, I stand up in front of Jinn. I make sure my jeans aren't tucked into my boots or anything like that. They look different from what I'm used to, but the boots are actually kind of classy. It still feels weird wearing them though.

"Are you done?" Jinn asks me.

"Getting them on? Yes."

"Took you long enough. Don't you ever wear good shoes down on the Surface?" Harsh.

"Not really. If we do, they usually get all messed up because of all the work we have to do." Jinn nods his head.

"These are much more confusing to use than the jetpack," Jinn tells me.

"And why are they so much worse?"

"Because they were almost an aftermarket thought. An opportunity to try a new technology."

"What technology?" I ask. If it is something explosive, I am ripping these things off my feet.

"Mental connections." How he manages to say that without any emotion is a mystery to me.

"Are these shoes going to fry my brain?" Have to get

the essentials down. Most important is the flaying of my brain.

"No. The mental connections they have are to activate, deactivate, and change the speed of the propulsion system. That's all. Nothing else is their purpose and besides, it was recently discontinued."

"Okay, so how do I start it up?" I ask, "What do I need to do to use these things?"

"Actually, it's supposedly really simple," This doesn't sound too good. Actually, supposedly is never really what it is supposed to be. "You just think of what you what them to do. Start, stop, speed up, slow down, you name it." Seems simple enough.

"Can they cook breakfast?" I ask.

"Just try to turn them on," Jinn says indifferently. Lighten up dude, just trying to have some fun.

On. I look around and see that absolutely nothing has happened.

Start. Still nothing.

Go. Nada.

Up up and away! Nothing happens.

Come on, can't you help me out here?

You didn't say please. Responds a voice. I look around to see if there was a third person here.

"Did you say that?" I ask Jinn. He looks at me confused.

"No."

Yes. I look down at my feet. *Yes, hello, can you not tell who is talking to you?* I look up back at Jinn.

"Jinn, why was the mental connection technology discontinued?" He looks at me like it's one of the most random questions he's heard in a while.

"Some of the users claimed to have heard a voice. It went away after a short while, but it was enough to discourage the continuation of the technology."

Does he want me to go away?

"No, I'm sure he doesn't," I say out loud.

"He doesn't what?" asks Jinn. Oh boy.

"Nothing," I say, shrugging off his question.

Do you plan to be polite? Asks the shoes. I sound like I belong in the loony bin.

Do you always plan to be so annoying?

Manners. Bah, fine.

Would you please work with me and turn on? I think in a polite voice. I definitely belong in some mental help facility. Then suddenly, I'm lifted up into the air.

Chapter Ten

I swing my arms around trying to maintain my balance.

Simmer down will you? Says the shoes.

Oh, shut up. This is a lot harder than it looks. I hear Jinn take in a breath. I look over and he looks genuinely surprised.

"It actually works. Nobody else, even I, has been able to make those work." So he expected failure? I wobble a bit longer while Jinn debates with himself about what I can be doing differently before he comes to an epiphany. "How did you make them work?" he asks. What a concept.

"I asked nicely." He gives me this look of utter disbelief. Does that really sound so odd?

After you were told to.

Were you always an annoying pair of shoes?

No, my intelligence chip was transferred here a long time ago. I'll make you a deal. If you can find a new body for me, I'll cooperate with you and aid you. This sounds really creepy and concerning. It sounds like something comparable to someone telling me to go kill something so they can take it over.

Fine, I'll do it. I agree mentally.

Hold on tight. The boots say to me. Man, I sound insane. The boots thrust picks up and I once again find myself flying through the air. I turn and angle myself, following the boots' direction, listening to tips and tricks they give me. I find that it is much easier to fly using the boots than it is with the jetpack. As cool as the jetpack is, I think I can live without the cool factor. This is so much better. The fact that I have a copilot doesn't hurt.

"Can I ask you something?" I say out loud.

What is it?

"How fast do you want a new body? And what were you before?"

As fast as you can get me one would be nice. What I was before doesn't matter. If you can get me a humanlike body, I would be in your debt.

There's something to remember.

"Got it. Also, do you have a name?" I feel silly asking it, but I don't feel like calling this voice, this intelligence 'boots' all the time.

I don't have a name. Not one that you would be expecting. I was called Digital Alternative Core Processor.

"So your name is Dac?"

I suppose you could call me D.A.C.P.

"Dac it is. I don't care about the *P.*"

I see no reason for dropping the final letter, but if it is more appeasing to you that way.

"Yes, yes it is." I fly around a bit longer, before I say, "Let's try something fun," I smile.

Your thoughts are transferred directly to me. Are you sure you are ready for this Sam? How did it know my name? Right, linked to my thoughts, got it.

"I'm sure." I lean back until I do an entire back flip. I play around for a while doing flips and other tricks in the air. This is great! I don't know when it has felt this great just to be having fun. Best part might be that Dac isn't trying to tell me what to do. In fact, he—is Dac a he?—tries to help me out as I go along. Even though I'm not necessarily ready to stop flying, I return back to Jinn's house, and land without falling, or stumbling, or anything like that. It felt kind of cool.

Jinn applauds me. Not a good applaud, but one of those slow, yippy-for-you claps. "Look who can land," he stops clapping; "I think we'll keep you with the boots. They work for you." Then he mutters under his breath, "And not for anybody else." Way to spread the love.

"Works for me," I say. "What now?"

"Seems like you have flying down, although, I have no idea how you managed that," he says out of the side of his mouth. "But," he speaks up again, "I want to see how you fight. I could go off of what I'm told, but that will most likely end up getting somebody killed." On that cheery note, Jinn picks up both jetpacks and starts walking back towards the house. I follow him.

"My mom always told me not to run in the house. You sure you want to fight inside?"

"We're not fighting inside. I just don't want to carry these things around." He shakes the jetpacks, "and there are a few things I need to grab to test you." Really? A test? I've never been good at tests. When we get back to the house, Jinn opens the door and walks off to put the jetpacks away. I stick my hands in my pockets and stand there awkwardly, not knowing what to do. When Jinn gets back, he says to me, "Let's go," nodding with his head towards the kitchen.

We walk through the kitchen and Jinn looks at the clock. He shakes his head and keeps walking. He opens a small section of the glass wall and walks out, beckoning me to follow him. I follow behind him a short distance away. I wait for Jinn to turn around because it looks like his yard has ended, but he starts getting shorter.

"What?" It takes me a full ten seconds to realize that he is walking down a hill. Duh, good job genius. I walk to the edge of what I thought was the end of the yard and it is incredible.

Jinn's yard is huge! Not only does it extend much farther than I thought it would, but there's so much stuff! He has a circle set up like a miniature version of an arena to fight in. Placed along the side I see a couple sheds big enough that they might be small houses on the surface —I wonder what those are filled with—and along the back there is one huge structure that's very long, with what looks like multiple garage doors running along it.

Nearly the entire yard has grass covering it, the rest is stone and dirt. Not a single bit of evidence of the ingenuity that keeps this place aloft. After looking around for a short while I see that Jinn is still walking, totally oblivious to the fact that I'm not right behind him. I jog to catch up. I'll take a look at everything back here later. I reach Jinn before he gets to the center circle. He doesn't have to turn around to know I'm there because he hears the grass and dirt crunch under my feet.

"That is one of the dumber things you could've done," he says without turning around.

"What? Jogging to catch up?" I let out a sigh.

"Yes. You are going to want all your energy. First," he starts, "I want to see how your overall fighting experience is. Second, I want to see weapon mastery and what you can handle. Third, I want to test your endurance. Most fights don't last long, but when they do, you need to be ready for it."

"How long do you plan for this to take?" I ask.

"Anywhere between a couple minutes to a couple hours. We will be at this all day if we have to." We reach the circle and he turns to look at me, "Although, with how fast you were able to get flying down, you should be able to pick this up pretty fast as well, right?"

"Right," I say. How fast did I get flying down? My stomach rumbles, "Can we eat first? I'm hungry."

"No, not until we are done here, then I'll get you food." That must be why he looked at the clock. "Think of it as motivation." Nobody gets between me and my food. I let out a sigh.

"Fine," I say, "where do you want to start?" He drops a long bag with a clank, which I didn't see he had before. Hey, the guy has a mansion, why not a lot of bags?

"You choose." What's that supposed to mean? Jinn kneels down and unzips the bag. Inside are at least a dozen different weapons.

"Are those sharp?" I ask. I don't feel like becoming confetti today. Is that so bad?

"No, I don't know if you are ready enough for actual blades yet. These are essentially the same. The weighting and all will be about the same as the actual weapon. The only difference is that these bruise, not cut." So I get to be a giant purple blob. Fantastic.

I squat down and after sifting through the bag, choose one that looks similar to a sword and the electrical weapon I have. I'm guessing that it is the non-lethal equivalent of the two.

"A sword," Jinn says. No duh. "That seems to be your primary weapon of choice. You have chosen it twice now. Once in the arena and again here."

"It just looked like it would be good to fight with. I have the best idea of what I'm doing with it."

"A good reason for the choice. There's nothing wrong with a sword, just wondered if you favored a more exotic weapon."

"Nope, plain and simple." Simple enough I guess.

"Well then. Are you ready?" Jinn says, pulling out a similar weapon to the one that I selected. "This isn't my favorite, but it will do for testing you." Jinn flips the baton like weapon a couple times before turning to face me. I flip mine in response, nearly dropping it.

"Ready," I say. Without a response, Jinn rushes in, leading with his weapon. I step to the side, deflecting with my sword. I lose my footing slightly and trip over my feet. Before I can regain my balance, Jinn whirls around and attacks again. I bring my weapon up in time to deflect, but I'm thrown to the floor.

"Sloppy," he says before jumping to attack me. He brings his weapon over his head to smash down, but I roll out of the way before he can make contact. That would've hurt.

"Watch it!" I yell, "Are you trying to kill me?" Jinn responds with another flurry of blows. I finally regain my footing and stand up. This is crazy. I continue deflecting blows right before Jinn connects.

We go on like this for what feels like an eternity, dancing in and out. I'm mostly defending myself, Jinn giving little opening for attack. The few times I do lunge forward to try and hit him, I end up losing my balance and have to quickly correct myself to avoid getting clobbered.

All throughout his push, Jinn doesn't relent. He continues pressing his attack, not easing up at all. My muscles ache as I block more and more hits. Finally, when my arms can't take it anymore, I raise my sword once again to block yet another blow of Jinn's. As soon as he connects, my weapon goes spinning out of my hands. Even though I'm disarmed, Jinn still swings his weapon back around. I dive out of the way to avoid getting hit. I get out of the way this time, but his next comes before I'm even done rolling.

Luckily, I still have enough forward momentum to continue moving out of Jinn's way. Not so luckily, my sword is the opposite direction of the way I went. While I'm looking for my sword, Jinn arcs his sword back around and cracks me in the side, sending me to the ground. I grab my side where he hit me and lie on the ground.

"Good. Nice, solid base to work off of," Jinn says, swinging his weapon around, bringing it forward to rest on it like a cane.

"Are you joking?" I ask from the floor, "Were you trying to kill me just now?" I'm pretty sure he broke, or at least bruised some of my ribs. This is going to sting for a while.

"No, why would I want to kill you?" Jinn asks sarcastically, "I was supposed to be your enemy. Enemies don't go easy. The New Power's fighters will go for the kill. Don't think that anything else will happen."

"Great, people that want to kill me. Wait, why do they want to kill me again?" Seriously, what did I do?

"Because we want you. They want you for themselves, or dead," he shrugs, "Either would work." I let my head drop back down to the ground so that I stare up at the sky. Even higher in the sky than I am now anyway.

"Why are you both after me. Why am I so important?"

"That's exactly what I am trying to find out. It's also the reason that officially, you're dead right now. My hope is that it will stave off the rest of the Ravens and the New Power long enough for me to train you and find out why you are so important to everyone." Right. The resistance core Jinn is a part of are called Ravens. Weird name. Not the worst I have heard.

"Are you going to tell me how I did with your prongs?" I say still sucking in air trying to catch my breath and calm the pain in my side.

"Everything surpassed what I was expecting. I thought that you would crumble under my first attack. I'll be honest. It surprised me a little bit to face some resistance."

"I'm just full of surprises," I smile, still breathing deeply.

"I'm counting on that," says Jinn, leaning in. He looks up at the sky to estimate the time. "What do you say that we're done for the moment. You hungry?" I smile, sitting up ignoring any pain in my side.

"Always." Jinn sticks his hand out to help me up and I take it. He flips me violently so that I land facedown.

"What was that for?" I demand, pushing myself up.

"As long as I'm holding this," Jinn raises his sword so that it's obvious what he is talking about, "and we're training. Don't trust me."

"Not sure I do normally," I mumble under my breath. I gently push myself to my feet while Jinn puts both his and my weapons away in the bag he carried out here.

"Think fast," Jinn says as he swings the bag at my gut. As a reflex, I grab the bag into my stomach and recoil onto one foot. "Time to get your strength training started. Why don't you carry that for me." The bag is really heavy and cumbersome to carry. All the training weapons balanced to approximately their real counterparts' weight, taking a large toll. Jinn starts walking back towards the house leaving me to follow.

"Come on now," he says with a wave of his hand. I follow him back to the house lugging the bag with me. Strangely, my side doesn't hurt as much as it did just a moment ago. Why wouldn't it hurt? Whatever, doesn't matter, I wont complain. No pain isn't a bad thing.

"Bag please," Jinn says when we get back to the house. I give him the bag and he goes off to put it away. I sit in the same chair as I sat in last night waiting for him to get back.

"So, what do you want to eat?" he asks me when he gets back, rubbing his hands together.

"I don't know. Do you have anything special to eat up here?" I ask. Seems like it might be interesting to have something I have never eaten before.

"Maybe. I don't know what you should try. I have a few things you shouldn't have just quite yet." I don't know if that is a good or bad thing to hear. "I got it," he says before walking to the refrigerator. He pulls out something that I can't see. He gets a pot of water that he starts to boil and puts the food it in. After he gets it started, Jinn turns to me, ignoring the food.

"How much more work do you think you can do today?" Is he seriously asking me this?

"Depends," I say.

"On?"

"How much more do we need to do?" Jinn smiles.

"I'm going to show you a real treat after we eat." Jinn turns back around and returns to his cooking. When Jinn finishes, he pulls out some buns and lays them out.

"Hot dogs? You're making hot dogs? You do realize that we have those on the Surface, right?"

"You have never had one cooked like this," Jinn says, handing me my plate. It doesn't look any different.

"Why is it so different?"

"Because of how our energy is made," Jinn says matter-of-factly. I shrug and take a bite of the hot dog. It doesn't taste all that different to me. Honestly, I don't know why Jinn made such a big deal about it. Then the after taste hits me. It's hard to describe, but it tastes lighter, like there is more flavor in it. Maybe I'm crazy. How could there be more flavor?

"Pretty good right?" asks Jinn after he has eaten half of his.

"Ya," I say, "What is it that's different about these again?" Really, I don't know.

"The way we cook them up here burns off less flavor, making it more savory." I knew it!

"Alright." I say calmly while happy dancing in my head. Jinn and I finish our hot dogs quickly.

"Ready for your treat?" Jinn asks me as I'm stuffing the last bits of my fourth hot dog into my mouth. Since I can't exactly talk right now, I just nod my head and hope that no food came flying out. "Back outside we go." He takes my plate as well as his own and puts them into a dishwasher before we head back outside.

I stop in the fighting ring that Jinn and I sparred in moments ago, but Jinn keeps walking. With a shrug, I follow him.

"What is it you want to show me?" I ask, mentally noting that we are walking towards what I earlier thought is a giant garage in the back of the yard.

"You'll see," he says simply. I swallow my complaint and continue to follow him. Jinn walks me over to the two doors on the farthest right. I still think they look like garage doors.

"Close your eyes," Jinn says.

"Seriously?"

"Close your eyes." He says again. Alright. I close my eyes and stand there awkwardly. I hear Jinn open the two doors right in front of me, but I can't tell what's inside, if anything. I hear Jinn pull a tarp off of something, like it was covering it to keep it nice. I hear it again. What is he doing?

"Okay, you can open your eyes now," Jinn says. Not doing the whole stupid- open-my-eyes-slowly-so-it-builds-suspense thing, I just open my eyes. I can't tell exactly what I'm looking at. Each of the two garages has the nearly identical same two things in them. "Go on," encourages Jinn, "take a closer look." I walk into the one on the far right to take a closer look.

I first look at the larger of the two that is dominating the center of the room. It looks like a kind of motorcycle but different. It looks a little thicker, but also, it has a small set of wings. Maybe the most noticeable difference is that on the back, there is something that is comparable to a small rocket booster. The controls look a little weird. The way it is ridden looks like it's elongated to the point that the rider has to all but lie down on it. That might actually be smart if it's ridden for a long time. I don't know. It looks weird to me.

"What is this?" I ask, pointing to the thing in the middle of the room.

"That," Jinn says with a cocky spring in his step and playing with his chin, "is a Sky Bike. One of the best ways for an individual to get around up here. Ingenious invention." Jinn looks at the machine, Sky Bike, like it is one of the most beautiful things he has ever seen.

"And what's this?" I ask, pointing to the object on the wall to the right of the Sky Bike. It looks like a surfboard without the fins that has two, sleek, thrusters attached to a motor on the back end. The engine rests on the back of the board with the two propulsion systems sticking out of the side, running parallel to the board. The thrusters only stick out a little bit so that they are right along the side of the board if they were on the same level.

In front of the engine, but still at the back end, are a

bunch of buttons and an array of controls that look like they are meant to be stomped on. This looks even more confusing to operate than the Sky Bike.

"That," says Jinn, "is a Sky Rider. Generally, it's only used by crazy kids for fun, but it serves its purposes." That sounds pretty cool, I guess. It does look like it's fun to ride though.

"So can I try it?" I ask. What, it looks like fun. Jinn scratches his chin, looking from me to the two machines back to me for a bit before saying, "I'll make you a deal." Great, another deal, what now?

"What is it?"

"If you can pass a few of my tests with these bad boys, not only can you ride them, but I'll make this shed yours." This has to be a joke.

"Seriously?" I ask.

"One hundred percent."

"Well," I say nervously, "when can we start?"

"Right now."

Chapter Eleven

Jinn helps me wheel out the Sky Bike.

"So what exactly is your test before I can ride one of these?" I ask.

"You're going to ride it," Jinn says.

"What's the catch?" I ask. There's always a catch when something sounds too good to be true.

"You have to ride it on the ground before flying it." Dang it. Oh well, I still get to ride it.

"Fine," I say grudgingly, "how do I ride it?"

"First," he says when we've gotten it a little bit away from the shed, "you have to sit on it." I swing my leg over and sit on the Sky Bike. The seat is positioned a little strangely for sitting up straight. "Next, start it. There's a go button right in front of you." Exactly as he said, on the dashboard right in front of my face, is a button that starts the bike.

I push that button and the engine roars to life. Just idling here, the bike almost seems to purr in anticipation. When's the last time Jinn used this? It doesn't look like it has much power to run on at the moment.

"What kind of gas does this thing take?" I ask.

"None," Jinn says, "it gets a solar charge as well as lunar charge when necessary. It's a clean energy that will never run out." I guess that's good.

"Alright. How do I steer and such?"

"That's part of your test. You have to figure it out." Just great. I take hold of the handles and half lie down to get a feel for the bike. I've never ridden a motorcycle, but I went dirt biking once. Maybe this is similar. I turned the handles side to side and the wheel followed. Makes sense. I lean in to look at the handles because I don't feel a throttle. I notice that the handles look like they are made to be shifted down so that instead of being horizontal, they would be vertical.

Before I have a chance to try and change the handles' positions, I lean too far forward, pushing the handles forward as well. When the handles move, the bike starts to crawl. So that's how you do it. Push the handles forward for the throttle.

I test the gas for a while to see how sensitive the controls are. After I feel like I'm comfortable with how the bike works, I start driving around the entire yard. I don't know exactly how fast I'm going because I don't look down at the speedometer all that much, but I keep going and am having fun. I even do a donut, just because I can. When I start driving back to Jinn, I start to slow down. When I'm almost back, I decide to act on an impulse and go full throttle.

Jinn waves his arms shouting for me to slow down and stop. Right before I get to Jinn, I slam the handles down so that they are vertical. The energy of the bike totally changes. The ride is different. The feel of the ground below me slips away.

What the heck?

I swivel around in my seat to see that the same kind of heat waves that were coming out of the back of the jetpack are shooting out of the miniature rocket attached to the back of the bike. I look down at my feet to see that the wheels have turned sideways and slightly receded into the bike, being used for hovering.

Why aren't I flying up? I realize that I still have the handles pushed forward from driving on the ground and think about what I know about flying, which isn't much.

I remember that a lot of flying things are inverted controls. I try pulling back on the controls and like magic, I start to lift off.

I pull up, passing Jinn. I barely get high enough to clear the garage. If I stuck my feet out, I can run on top of the roof. Instead of flying far and wide like I did with both the jetpack and Dac, I stay within the perimeter of Jinn's house. No need to make him any madder than he already is. Speaking of Jinn…

I circle the backyard, piloting the Sky Bike as masterfully as a person who has never ridden it can, and scan the backyard for Jinn. He's nowhere to be seen. As I started to loop once again, the bike beeps at me like it is going to say something.

"Ground rules," it's Jinn, "no hitting the other's bike—they're expensive, no leaving this platform's property line, and don't abandon your bike. Again, they're expensive. Catch." That's when I hear it. I twist in my seat to see Jinn close behind me on the other Sky Bike.

I am so dead.

What's that in Jinn's hand? Please tell me that that is not what I think it is. As Jinn gets closer, my hopes are dashed away. It's the stand-in sword. Jinn speeds up and flips over me so that there is no machine between him and me. It feels as if time slows down while he's up there, that I get a good look at every detail even though I know it is only a second or two, if even. He drops one of the fake blades and I, by some miracle, snap it out of the air. I have this horrible feeling I'm going to end up with even more bruises.

Jinn completes his flip and is now flying in front of me with his sword in hand. Great.

"I'm going to time this," Jinn says over the intercom. "If you last five minutes, you'll pass all my initial tests for the Sky Bike."

"Works for me," I say. I wait and he doesn't respond. Alright, I guess that's his consent. I brace for the imminent onslaught.

"You have to open your com channel." Oh, "there should be a button on the dash board in front of you that you can push." I look around for a second before I find it and push it. A light comes on the dashboard that reads 'Communication Activated.'

"Can you hear me now?" I ask with my finger still on the button.

"Yes." He pauses for a moment, "You do realize you don't need to keep your finger on the button, don't you?" How does he keep doing that? I take my finger off the button feeling a little silly. "Are you ready?" Jinn asks me.

"Yes," I say simply.

"Your five minutes begin... now." And like that, Jinn swerves from in front of me, diving below where I can see. Desperate not to let him get an advantage over me, I dive down as well. He does a couple twists and turns, me always staying right behind him. The radio crackles to life again.

"I'm going to run you through a few basic maneuvers first. Don't lose hold of your weapon, and don't fall behind." Wait, we're not fighting? This is new. Is it new? I haven't known Jinn that long, but half of his "training" has consisted of fighting, the other half nearly falling to my death. Totally normal things.

Jinn starts with a few simple twists and turns, even I can follow his movements. He gets close into his house and pulls away before hitting, dodging around close to it. Jinn swoops so close to the ground that I wonder why he doesn't use the wheels. It goes on like this for a little while before he tries something more complicated.

Jinn does a couple flips and other tricks. I nearly fall the first few, but soon get the hang of it.

"Ready for something really difficult?" No.

"Yes."

Jinn turns his bike upside-down and continues to ride.

"You have to do what I'm doing," he reminds me. With a groan, I flip my bike over. I clench my knees together tightly around the seat and have to force myself to stay put. I feel my arms getting more and more exhausted. This sucks. Luckily, Jinn flips his bike back over and I could do the same. Thank god. Jinn pours on the speed. What now? I also hit the gas and follow.

"Defend yourself," Jinn calls over the intercom as he flips over and starts to fly above me. He has his sword drawn and is riding upside down with one hand. If he wasn't coming after me, I would applaud him. Jinn swings at me with what seems like it might be full strength. I bring my blade above my head to counter.

When the two collide, I nearly lose my seat being

shoved back. I quickly, for fear of falling, scramble forward and regain my balance. I circle the bike around to see Jinn coming at me once again. I toss my sword to my other hand because he is on the other side of me now. When the two blades collide, I realize how stupid of me it was to swap sword hands. I drop it because I'm not able to hang on as well with my left hand.

"Damn it." I say.

"I can still hear you," Jinn says back over the intercom.

"Fine, let's change it up a bit." I start to dive down, but somehow, Jinn manages to come behind me and nail me with his sword. I'm knocked out of my seat. I slip away from the bike. I expect Jinn to come and help me out, but instead he grabs the bike and starts to gently guide himself and the two bikes down. Jerk. I look down and see that I'm not as far from the ground as I originally thought I was. Maybe that has something to do with falling.

Are you going to let yourself die, or are you going to use your brain? I know you have one, that's how I'm communicating with you. Great, another jerk.

"Help!" I yell as I continue to fall.

What an original plea. Dac sparks to life as I right myself so that my feet face the ground. The propulsion is set just so that I can hover in place. I look up to where I last saw Jinn, but he's not there anymore. The disappearing act is getting old! I look below where he was to see that he is on the ground. He waves to me when he sees that I've noticed him. Oh, he is so going to get it.

I descend and also fly over to where Jinn is standing. When I land, I all but smack him. Smacking isn't all that manly though, so I'm glad I refrain from that. Instead, Jinn just smiles while I look like steam is about to come out of my ears.

"Do you ever listen to what other people say?" Jinn asks me. I smile in response. "Regardless, good job," he says to me. "Again, you surpass all my expectations." What was that again?

"How? I fell off. You said that if I fall off I fail."

"True, but I also said you need to stay on for five minutes. According to my timer, you stayed on for at least double that."

"There is no way that was ten minutes," I say in disbelief.

"And then some." He pauses for a moment, "Good work with the boots by the way. I saw that you wanted to come after me. They're a good fit for you." He looks from one of the bikes back to me. "The garage is yours. Let's see how good you are on a Sky Rider." We walk the bikes back to the two garages and put them away. When they both are back away as they were before, I take the Sky Rider out. I lay it on the ground and study it for a bit.

Any ideas? I think to Dac.

Haven't the slightest. Maybe you should try dancing. It looks like maybe the buttons will light up to a rhythm. Not really. Okay, let's see. I step on the board like I would ride a skateboard, with my right foot forward. Big buttons usually do something, so...

I step on the largest button in the middle of all the others. Expecting at least a little resistance, I stomp harder than I should. There is no resistance pushing down. As I half expected, the board starts to float. It's only about a foot off the ground, but a foot is still a foot. Around the large button there are slightly smaller ones that look like they may be arrows. As good a chance as any that they'll work. I push the forward arrow. I start to lurch forward, but stop when I take my foot off. Hmm. This time when I step on it, I keep my foot down.

I start zipping around the back yard about a foot off the ground, steering and controlling the board like I would on the rare occasion that I would get to skate. I wonder how to change my altitude before the obvious answer hits me. I push down on the back of the board. The board immediately starts shooting up at an angle. Damn, I'm right on target today. I would like to record this so that for all history it can be known that I, Sam Cutter, have been right at least five times today. I have no idea when this is going to happen again. *If* it ever will.

With the board flying upward, all I hear and feel is adrenaline. It comes as a shock to me when I hear Dac in my head.

Be careful not to fall. Going splat does not seem like the world's smartest idea.

What? I make the mistake of looking down and seeing how high I am. Even though it's only been a short while, and I'm not incredibly high, it looks like I'm miles in the air.

Want to try something fun? I ask Dac in my head.

Don't you dare, he says back, *I know what you're thinking and I am telling you right now that you are going to get yourself killed.* Thanks mom.

Please, please, please, please, please. I draw the last one out, begging.

No.

Yes? Alright then! I power off the board and start free falling. Flipping backwards toward the ground.

I hate you.

I smile to myself as I continue to fall. I grab the board in my hand to prevent myself from losing it. I see the ground coming up below me and reposition myself so that I am almost in a nosedive. I put the board under my feet getting ready to ride it once again. I let myself fall a little bit longer. When Jinn comes back into focus— meaning, I can tell that he is just calmly staring at me—I stomp back on the starter and move my feet so that the board starts flying again as I come just above the grass.

I gained a bunch of speed from my free fall. I circle around a part of the yard to come back in front of Jinn. I hit stop so that the board will stop, but I keep it so that it will continue to hover. The board pulls to a stop much more abruptly then I am expecting and I am thrown from the board to sample some nice, tasty grass.

Somehow, I knew that would happen. Oh shut up. If Dac had a tongue, I'm pretty sure he would be sticking it out at me right now.

As I spit a little bit of grass out of my mouth and push myself up, I see Jinn standing in front of me with a blank look on his face and his arms crossed over his chest. I pluck a piece of grass from my mouth and start brushing myself off when I hear Jinn start to clap. I look up to see Jinn clapping with a smile on his face. What? Why is he so happy? I kind of did exactly what he said not to.

"Kid, the day you stop surprising me is the day that I die."

"You do realize that you've only known me for like, two days, right?" He smiles.

"And yet, you've done more than most trainees have in years. I hate training new recruits. Always a pain to work with the babies."

"I'm sure they're not that bad." His eyes glaze over for a moment like he's having a flash back.

"You would be surprised." Alright then. "Come on, let's go inside. Imagine it must be about time to eat again anyway." Really? In response, my stomach growls. That's not much to go off of though. I'm pretty much always hungry.

"Okay, just let me put the sky board," I guess that's its name, "away." I say and take a step. As soon as my foot hits the ground I collapse. I grunt trying to dull some of the pain I feel in my back. Why my back? Did I land funny when I was flung off the sky board? My hand shoots to my back. Ouch! Bad idea. That hurt worse. I squeeze my eyes shut, still trying to block out the pain. I hear Jinn squat down next to me, not touching me though, because of how I reacted by touching myself... Don't get any ideas.

"Where does it hurt?" Jinn asks.

"My. Back," I grunt out. Jinn reaches over and gingerly raises my shirt so that he can see my back.

"Did you lean back when I had you using the jetpack?" I think about it for a second before nodding my head yes. Jinn audibly lets out a breath of air. "Can you walk?"

"I can try," I mumble. "What the hell is wrong?"

"You severely burned your back. Some of the skin is melting away. I can fix it in a jiffy." I cough.

"Did you really just say jiffy?"

"Don't make me hurt you even more."

"Truce." I push myself up onto shaky feet. I try taking a step again and trip. This time, Jinn catches me.

"I got you. Come on, at least limp a little." With Jinn's help, after awhile, we manage to get back to the house.

Jinn walks me over to the kitchen so that I could brace against the counter.

"Where is it, where is it?" Jinn mutters to himself while he shuffles through drawers. Finally, he seems to find what he's looking for and pulls it out. I don't see what it is because he quickly shoves it in his pocket. "Come on," he says, "let's get you upstairs." Jinn has to half drag me up the stairs because even slightly starting to move my legs begins to hurt. He gets me into my room and lays me on my side.

"Why does my back hurt so much again?" I ask through labored breaths. Why doesn't it hurt so freaking much?

"You're severely burned because of what is used to power the jetpack. You were exposed to it for an extended period of time, it may or may not have poisoned your blood stream and weakened your bones."

"Fantastic," I say licking my lips. It seems like all that has happened since I came up here is that I have been threatened and nearly killed. Why is this a better life? It is kind of like it is back home, just different scenery.

"I can fix you up though. Probably," right now, I hate probably, "this cream I have, it's designed and developed specifically for this. It will hurt, and you'll probably be out for awhile. Good news is that not only will you be cured, but you will become immune to all kinds of poison from the Sky Nation." This just keeps getting better and better.

"Do it," I say. Jinn nods and sets to work. He gently pulls up my shirt, and lightly applies the cream. For all of a second it feels good, like it is sapping all the pain out. Then it gets worse. All the pain is sapped out, but after the pain is gone, it keeps going, creating pain in its wake. Needles and daggers digging into me. It's like the feeling of numbness, but a million times worse, and actually hurting. I let myself slip into unconsciousness, and what I think will be a dreamless sleep.

I dream of my family. Of my mom and dad. That my dad was never captured. That I didn't have to come up here. It may not be the worst thing that has ever happened to me, but it's not the best.

Other than my life, I dream of few words said by an unseen voice I don't recognize.

"Time is running short. One is soon to return and the other is still fighting. He may break free soon. The other two still manage to escape and resist me." The voice is dark and ominous, go figure. Who is that? What is that? Is who or what the right question? Then I hear another voice.

"I understand master. We are acting as quickly as we can. There were, complications from the Surface-" A second voice? This one sounds less menacing, but still full of power, demanding respect.

"From the Surface? None have been able to come even close!" Guess I proved you wrong. Not only did I come close, but I succeeded! I swear I'm going crazy.

"Apparently not, my lord. There were two. One escaped us." Actually, there are four of us.

"And the other?" The dark voice seems to have more interest sparked in its tone.

"Not as many possibilities as the first, but may be a useful tool still." John. Where is he? I start making demands but they never escape my head. Even though the dream is in my head, my thoughts remain silent and are not heard by my two guests with no visible bodies.

"A useful tool indeed."

Chapter Twelve

I wake up with a start, sitting up fast. I'm sweating and panting. Ugh. I groan and wipe my hand down my face. I look around me to see that I am still in my room at Jinn's house. Everything around me looks exactly the same. I guess that part wasn't a dream. I throw the blankets off to see that I'm still in my dirty, grass-stained jeans. Why can't I have a dream about some awesome girl and have that dream come true? No, all I get is a new nightmare. In all honesty, it's not that bad, just not great. I swing my legs around to stand up. When I get up I wobble slightly, but am fine after just a moment.

My stomach growls loudly. I grab my stomach and realize that I am starving. With a shrug, I shower and change my clothes. I walk down the stairs but I walk really lightly, not wanting to jar myself. Food. I really, really, want food. I turn into the kitchen and see Jinn there.

"How are you feeling?" He asks plainly, drinking

something from a plain mug. What is with older people—not to call Jinn old, he would probably kill me—and coffee?

"Starving," I say with a smile, walking over to the counter.

"Other than that?" I know he means my back.

"A little sore, but other than that, no pain. How did you do that? And how long was I out?"

"About a week. It was a special serum. It was developed a long time ago, and was discontinued. There were only about two good batches. Any others would end up hurting you more than they would help." He takes another sip of his drink. "I want you to try something," he says putting down his mug.

"A week? Are you serious?" How was I out for a week? It's only felt like a day!

"Yes." Jinn says with a straight face, "Now are you ready to try something?"

"As long as it can't hurt me," I say jokingly.

"Most likely not." Seriously? "It's a kind of drink that helps heal." Jinn pulls a bottle of some electric blue drink out of the refrigerator. "It'll either help, or make you sick. Take too much of it and you'll be dead either way. Want to try it?" I seriously debate saying no. I don't feel like getting any sicker, but my curiosity gets the better of me.

"Just give it to me." Jinn gives me the drink and I take

a sip. It has to be the best tasting thing I've ever had. Maybe it's not taste... I don't know. It feels like a jolt of energy is running through my body. My pain, gone. Hunger, gone. Feeling of over all crappy-ness, lessened. "This stuff is amazing," I say to Jinn.

"Good to know it works on you. That stuff has saved my life on more than one occasion. We will have to test how much you can take, but that's an experiment for another time." Good. I don't feel like feeling crappy again. Jinn looks me up and down. What is that expression in his eyes? Concern? Worry? Admiration? Maybe it's a little of all three.

"You want to go into town?" Jinn asks me. "It looks like you may need some new clothes soon, if not already." I look down at myself. I realize that I've managed to destroy two of my pairs of jeans and that these are my last. I still have a few t-shirts, but still, from what little Jinn has said and worn, they won't help me fit in.

"Yeah, sure. When are we going?" I ask, putting the blue drink down. "By the way," I ask, "what is this called?" I don't feel like calling it glowing, electric blue drink. A real name would work much better.

"It's called Blue Elixir." That's original.

"Are there other colors?" If it's called Blue Elixir, there has to be more.

"Yes, but for now all you need is blue. The others are

for desperation and cheaters. I don't even want you to consider using the others."

"Got it," I say, taking another sip, "I don't know why anyone would want a different one anyways."

"They want an easy way out. They want cheap, easy intelligence. Some want more strength. Most just want a quick fix. Some of the elixirs are straight-up drugs." So the other colors do some crazy things. Got it.

I agree that you should stay away from them. Dac? I look down at my feet in disbelief. I left my boots upstairs before I came down, so all I see are my bare feet. If Dac is in the shoes, why can I still hear him?

"Why can I hear you?" I ask aloud. Jinn cocks his eyebrow and gives me a funny look.

"Because you have ears and enough of a brain that the rest of you functions?" Jinn says, like a question. "Who are you talking to?" Right. Dac talks inside my head.

Why can I hear you? I'm not wearing the boots you're in.

I don't know. Why don't you ask your friend there. You're the first to hear—or at least acknowledge—me.

"Jinn?"

"Oh, he speaks," Jinn says. Ignoring that.

"Is it possible to still hear an A.I. while you don't have what it's in on your person?" Jinn gives me a peculiar, worried look.

"Why? Can you hear one?" No duh. Why else would I be asking?

"Yeah. Dac and I were talking yesterday, and now again, but I'm not wearing the shoes." Jinn runs a hand through his hair.

"Dac?" He asks me.

"That's his name."

Are you a he? I ask Dac mentally.

Sure, let's go with that. How much sarcasm can A.I. manage?

Well are you?

I'm not a human. Does my voice sound more masculine or feminine to you?

Masculine.

Then yes, I'm a boy. Works for me.

"This isn't good Sam. The A.I. in those jump boots—"

D.A.C.P. But according to you, it's Dac.

Oh shut up. I think back at him, *I'm trying to listen.*

"Never bonded before," Jinn continues, "I thought they were defective which is why I gave them to you."

Who are you calling defective! Dac shouts in my head. Calm down dude.

"Why is it so bad if an A.I. 'bonds' with someone?" I ask Jinn.

"Because the bond is for life. You will be hearing, what's its name again?"

"Dac."

"You'll be hearing Dac for the rest of your life." Oh boy.

You hear that buddy. We're going to be besties. Joy.

"Guess you better start making friends with Dac." Jinn says, "It's good you even got a name out of it. Most people that bonding occurs for never even get that far. AI's never share names."

"I guess we're already buddies then," I say with a smile. It won't be so bad. I'll always have someone to talk to... I'll just look crazy half the time.

I thought you already were crazy. Dac says to me.

If I'm crazy then so are so.

Touché. I smile again. I take my victories where I can.

"Regardless. Are you ready to go?" Jinn asks me.

"Yeah, just let me grab my shoes."

"Better grab the jump boots, just in case you fall."

"I'm not going to fall," I say with a wave of my hand.

"Just in case."

"Fine," I say with a sigh. I quickly run upstairs, noting the lack of pain in my back. When I return downstairs, I see that Jinn is still waiting in the kitchen, but has shouldered a backpack. Maybe it's one of the jetpacks. Nah, it doesn't look long enough. I point to his bag with a question on my face.

"Need somewhere to put our purchases, right?" Jinn says, "We aren't bringing one of your bags because we don't want anyone to question it, as well as where you are from." How does he keep doing that? I have known this guy for three days—or according to Jinn, somewhere around nine days—and he has been able to not only predict what I'm going to ask half the time, but answers my questions before I can even vocalize them. "Come on," Jinn continues, gesturing to the front door, "Our ride is going to be here soon."

"Our ride?" I ask, "I thought we were just going to take the bikes or something."

"No. You don't have a license."

"So? Technically, I'm dead. I don't see why a license would matter." Take that! I beat Jinn to something! It's a hollow victory. I know he's going to ruin this.

"Would you prefer not to go at all?" Thought so.

"No, I want to go."

"Then let's go," he says. I start walking toward the door. Jinn meets me outside.

"So what should I be looking for?" I ask, wondering what our ride will look like. I doubt there is much air traffic around here, but it's still conversation. Before Jinn can answer me, I get my answer.

"Hey guys!" I turn around and see Mark leaning out of a medium sized ship, waving.

"Hi Mark," says Jinn with a wave. When the ship touches down, Mark hops off and walks over to us.

"You guys ready to go?" He asks us. Jinn raises his arm and gestures toward the ship.

"Lead the way." We all clamber into the ship, the hatch closing behind us. I feel a gentle lurch, signaling the ship take off, but don't care to look outside. I have seen a lot of that lately, just with more dirt at the end.

"Where did you want to go again?" Mark asks Jinn.

"Just in town. We need to pick Sam up some new clothes."

"Sam?" Mark says with a drag to Jinn, "Little more than two weeks and you two are operating on a first name basis." Mark shouts to the pilot where we wanted to go and the ship sets off. Wait a minute.

"Two weeks?" I say accusingly towards Jinn.

"Oh boy," he sighs.

"What? Do you not have a calendar at your place, Jinn?" Mark laughs, slapping Jinn's shoulder.

"I've been unconscious for close to two weeks?" I raise my voice a little, "You told me it was barely under one!"

"I didn't want you to freak out," he says calmly.

"Freak out! I wasn't out cold recovering, I was in a mini-coma!" Seriously? Who keeps this from people?

"You're fine." Jinn says with a wave, "I had no doubts that you would be able to snap out of it."

"You say that like there was a chance that I wouldn't wake up," I say through half gritted teeth. Off to the side, Mark laughs.

"Oh my friend, it seems that you just keep digging

yourself into a deeper and deeper hole." He moves to wipe a nonexistent tear from his eye, "Perhaps it's best that you just stop talking now." Jinn gives a nervous half-smile.

"Perhaps you're right." Mark smiles back.

"What did you do that put him out of the game for all that time anyway? How long was he even functioning?"

"I think I got about a day other than when we first brought him back. And as for what happened, he received a lot of poisoning from jetpack propulsion," Jinn explains to Mark. Mark winces when Jinn mentions the poisoning. It was extremely painful and all, but other than that I'm fine now. It's no big deal.

"How did you deal with the poisoning? Doesn't that stuff stay in the blood stream forever?" Mark asks.

"I have some of the old cure. The serum that makes you immune to the poison. Sam took to it, just like everything else he has been given," Jinn adds the last part as a side note.

"You still have some of that?" Mark asks in disbelief.

"Plenty. I try and use it extremely sparingly."

"As well you should. Shame they don't make it anymore," Mark says shaking his head.

"You're only saying that because it actually worked on you. You're not one of the poor saps that it did more damage than good for."

"You're the one to talk," Mark says back, "it worked

for you too."

"Who said I was complaining?" laughs Jinn.

"Would you two mind filling me in on why this is so funny?" I cut in.

"You wouldn't understand," Mark says, smiling. Okay? Odd. I let it go. Mark seems to catch onto something that Jinn said only moments ago.

"What do you mean he is taking to everything?" Mark asks Jinn suspiciously with a raised eyebrow.

"The serum works. Blue Elixir works. He can fly both a Sky Bike and Sky Rider in one day better than most that I've seen training on that alone after more than five years."

"So what's wrong with that? That's great!" Mark says enthusiastically. Jinn lowers his eyes to look at my feet. Confused, Mark follows his gaze, his eyes widening when he gets to my feet.

"Jinn. You didn't."

"I did. It did."

"You have to be joking," Mark says, hoping that Jinn really is.

"Are you talking about Dac bonding with me?" I chime in. Mark looks at me in disbelief. Then he turns his head back to Jinn.

"The AI even told him its name?" Mark asks Jinn.

"Technically, it's D.A.C.P, but I call him Dac." I correct him before Dac can start nagging at me in my head. I'm sure that if Dac had a head of his own, he would be nodding approvingly at me.

"Whatever you say," Mark says with a shrug. Jinn looks at me with a question in his eyes. I'm pretty sure he wants to ask something along the lines of 'how did you get him to be quiet?' But that's only a guess. Jinn walks over to some of the few seats in the ship and sits down. We ride the rest of the way in relative silence, making small talk that I don't even care to remember. It feels like little time, if any, has passed before I hear Mark say that we're about to land.

This time, I do look out a window. We're landing at a dock like the one that I was on at Jinn's house. I can't see much of what the town looks like because we're coming up to the dock. I could've sworn we were flying higher than this. Maybe we dipped lower at some point. Doesn't matter. The ship pulls up next to the dock and hovers in place. I take a step back and Jinn and Mark step up next to me.

The large side door of the ship swings open with a thud. Jinn and Mark calmly step off, so I follow.

"I'll call you when we are ready to be picked up!" Mark yells back into the ship. The pilot gives him a thumbs-up. The door closes, and the ship we came over in flies away. Jinn and Mark start walking the length of the dock, talking with each other. I'm just curious to see what this place looks like.

180

We turn a corner to where I can see past the giant wall erected between the shopping district and the dock. It doesn't look like anything too special. It just looks like a giant outdoor shopping mall. We have some on the Surface, but very few. The ones that we do have aren't super clean or well stocked, or really enjoyable for the matter. They're just places to go to get your supplies. Half the time, they were too difficult to get. Needless to say, I became very familiar with the five-finger discount. I feel horrible that I stole from people who needed money just as much as we did, but it was more important to me at the time that my mom and I get what we need. I only exercised the "special" discount when I had no other choice.

The shopping district up here looks like possibly the exact opposite of what I know from the Surface. Mark and Jinn keep walking, like seeing this place is nothing special. I keep pace two or three steps behind them, letting my eyes wander. Everything looks much cleaner and nicer than it does on the Surface. People here line the streets. Sidewalks? I don't see much of any kind of vehicle here. Maybe that's what the dock is for. I saw plenty of ships there. Regardless, I see a huge amount of people before me. There aren't really any walls; it's all different buildings, different shops. The streets branch off into different roads.

I look for the expected street signs, and there they

are. They're not normal street signs though. Instead of street names that sometimes make no sense, these signs point to the different sections of the shopping district. Clever. Everything around me is busy, everyone working, or on a mission to get somewhere. I hear Jinn talking in front of me. I almost miss what he says because I'm too busy looking around.

"We need to get you new clothing. What you're wearing now won't completely betray your origin, but at the rate you're destroying your very limited supply, I believe we need to purchase you more." He doesn't turn around while speaking; Mark and Jinn just keep walking. I notice that we are following the signs labeling where the bulk of clothing is sold. If Mark and Jinn are actually using the signs, I don't know.

"So what is the style up here?" I ask. Jinn gives me a shrug.

"Look around you," he says, "it's similar to what you wore on the Surface. At least, what I'm guessing you wore on the Surface based on what you have with you." I look around and see that he's right. Now that I think about it, Jinn never looked odd to me, nothing looked out of place. Guess that says how much I pay attention. "Jackets are more common up here than I'm guessing they are on the Surface." He continues.

"And why is that?" I ask, looking around. I don't see too many people in jackets, but enough that what Jinn said makes sense.

"It gets cold." Simple and easy.

Mark speaks up, "So what else did you need to get? Other than the clothes of course."

"Other than the clothes," Jinn says, "we will need to pick him up a phone, and maybe some other appliances."

"Oh, I can help with that." Mark says with a smile, rubbing his hands together eagerly. Jinn sighs.

"I know you can my friend," he turns to me, "Mark really gets into his gadgets. Doesn't know how to use half of them, but likes them all the same."

"Hey!" Mark says offended, "I know how to use it all well enough."

"I'm sure you do Mark," I say patting his shoulder, "Maybe you can show me how to use some of it." Mark's grin practically consumes his entire visible face.

"Now you've done it," Jinn says. Mark starts spouting a rapid fire of things I need, why I need them, and all sorts of other stuff. I laugh, but Jinn just shakes his head and sighs. I can get used to life up here. Just need a way to get my mom up here. And free John. I know I should be more worried about both of those, especially John, and even more so after that weird dream, but right now, I'm just enjoying the moment.

Chapter Thirteen

We shop for clothes for a little while. It's really awkward. On the Surface, it isn't normal for three guys to go shopping together, especially for clothes. The only time you usually see large groups of guys in stores is when they are going to exercise their right with five fingers. Things got weird at times.

The amount of clothes we buy fits into Jinn's bag. He has me carry it. Figures. It's my stuff, I should lug it around. Next, we head to the electronics section. Mark nearly has a heart attack maybe a hundred times over before we get to the phone store.

"So which do you want?" Jinn asks me. My mouth drops open.

"You mean I get to pick?"

"Yeah, why not? It's going to be your phone, not mine," he says with a shrug.

"But isn't that expensive?" I ask, still in disbelief.

"Don't worry about it." Jinn says with a wave of his

hand. I open my mouth to argue again, but Mark puts a hand on my shoulder.

"Kid, just say thank you and accept Jinn's generosity," Mark says.

"You just want to help pick the phone, don't you?" I ask.

"Now what would make you think that?" Mark answers, obviously guilty. "Come on, let's go look at them." While we look at phones, Mark tells me so many things about them that my head feels just about ready to explode. Finally, we find one that fits me. Mark is disappointed that it's not the newest phone out there, but it's still pretty new. It's the newest of its model any-way. We pay and are off again.

"I believe that's all we need for now?" Jinn asks.

"Can't we go look at more electronics before we go?" Mark asks. "I hear they have a new shipment in." Jinn just shakes his head.

"Maybe another time. Can you call for our ride?" Mark grumbles a muted complaint.

"Fine, I'll call them." Mark walks off a short way and makes a call.

"Do you like everything?" Jinn asks me.

"Uh, yeah," I say stupidly, "thanks for everything. You didn't need to do that for me. You don't need to do any of this for me."

"It's my pleasure." Jinn says with a genuine smile. I

better remember that, I don't know when the next time I'll see one is.

Mark hangs his phone up and walks back over to us. "It'll take him a couple minutes to get over here. Can we please go back to the electronics while we wait?" Mark begs. Jinn sighs and throws him a look.

"Stop it, get away from me!" I hear a woman scream. I don't know what's wrong, but she sounds like she's in trouble. Evidently, Jinn also heard. I take off running only moments after him. What could be going on? We don't run long, but Jinn and I follow the woman's screams down a couple of twists and turns. Jinn and I stop dead. The scene in front of me makes no sense.

A woman, I'm guessing the one that screamed, is surrounded by five men armed with swords. The men are all wearing a similar uniform to each other. They all are wearing a mismatch of pants with jackets that have some design on the front. The design is a red stripe running down one side. Some of the men wore their jackets zipped up, some didn't.

"Come on, nice and easy now. We don't want any more trouble than what's required," one of the men says to the woman. The one that spoke gives a nod to another of his partners who moves forward and grabs the girl. She screams and tries to shake him off. What is going on?

"Please," the girl pleads, "Just leave me alone."

186

"Sorry, no can do," says the one that first spoke, playing with his sword. For some reason, the other men laugh at this. I look around and see some civilians watching, some completely ignoring the situation. The man holding the girl starts to pull on her arm. She screams again.

"You heard the lady," Jinn says next to me, "leave her alone now."

"You bug off!" The one that has done all the speaking says. Taking a wild guess, he's the leader. There aren't many of them, but he looks like the brain.

"No can do," Jinn says, mocking the man. The guy's face lights up cherry red. Nobody has laughed, but he looks like the entire world just made fun of him.

"You better watch your tongue, friend," the man says, raising his sword to point it at Jinn's chest. "Be a shame to have to cut it out," he smiles wickedly. Out of nowhere, Jinn pulls a sword out. Where did he get that? It looks like an ordinary sword, but there's something weird about it. His sword has a slight light blue hue to it. What the heck?

"You sure about that?" Jinn says looking confident. The guy that seemed so confident and sure of himself only moments ago now looks about ready to crap himself! Is there something special about that sword? No duh, why else would the guy look so scared of it.

Your sense of reasoning is truly awe-inspiring.

Ah, Dac. You didn't speak up the whole time I was buying things. Are you just so overwhelmed that I didn't buy a new pair of shoes?

You caught me. I was so worried that you would replace me that I started to cry. Who knew shoes could be so sarcastic.

"I'll be taking that sword now, buddy. Just hand it over here, commoners aren't allowed to carry one." The guy in the uniform says, evidently having found his nerve. He looks around to his goons with a grin.

"I suppose the New Power lets its trainees handle something like this then? Since when did they start bringing people competent enough not to skewer themselves on board?" So this is a New Power goon. He doesn't look like anything special. I would have pinned him as an ordinary street thug. Although, like Jinn said, these are just the recruits.

"You will learn your manners!" The New Power guy barks back at Jinn. Somebody has a temper issue. "You will respect the New Power! The New Power is the only way that matters. We are the future." Hive mind much?

"They just get dumber and dumber every time," Jinn mumbles, shaking his head. How is he so calm? "Mark, would you like to go help the lady out? I don't think she appreciates being held like that."

"Alright Jinn," Mark says, "Whatever you say." Mark starts walking over to the girl.

"Wait," the New Power guy says, "Jinn? As is Jinn Grant from the resistance?" Another look of panic comes over this guy's face. Seriously, he needs to work on his mood swings. He turns to one of the guys behind him, "Call for backup. This is going to be good." He looks back at Jinn with an eager gleam in his eye.

Jinn sighs, "So I guess I can't talk you out of it?" In response, four of the New Power recruits charge at Jinn. The fifth is calling for backup.

Jinn charges right back at them. He looks much like he did when we were fighting back at his house. Only difference is that now it's for real. That, and the odds are stacked against Jinn four to one.

Scratch that, five to one. The fifth guy just finished yelling into his phone for everybody nearby to come and assist them. Is Jinn really such a big deal? Evidently, yes. Jinn has already pushed two of the New Power goons back. Surprisingly, he has only done the trainees minimal damage while fighting them off, generally using the flat of his blade.

While Jinn is busy fighting two of the recruits who seem to think flanking him on either side is a good idea, one escapes Jinn's attention. With two fighting Jinn, and two trying to catch their breath, the guy that was originally talking to Jinn creeps behind him, ready to stab him in the back. Without considering any consequences, I jump forward and tackle the guy about to gut Jinn.

As we hit the ground, the guy's sword clatters away. Jinn swipes his sword behind his head less than a second later. Guess he knew what was going on. Oh well.

"Get off me!" calls the guy I tackled, pushing me off. "You're one of them aren't you!" Them? He seems to get mad all over again with my ignorance. He starts to scramble for his sword, but I get there first and kick it away. Probably should have picked it up.

That would have been smart. Says Dac in my head.

Anger management problems grabs at my leg and pulls me down to the floor again. Luckily, I half catch myself so I don't get hurt too badly from the fall.

"Let go of me!" I call as I kick the guy's jaw. I connect. He lets go of my leg to grab his jaw long enough for me to get free and take a step back. The guy gets on his hands and knees, spiting out a wad of blood. He glares at me, hate in his eyes. He bares his teeth like a rabid dog, his teeth shine red, coated with a thin layer of fresh blood.

"Look," I say, "I don't want to hurt you. Just stay down and—" He jumps up at me before I can finish what I'm saying. This time he does his best impression of a roar. I catch his shoulders before he can connect with anything. I punch him again in the jaw. When he starts to bend over slightly, I knee him in the gut. I throw him to the side and go to retrieve his fallen sword. The two that had lost their nerve earlier seem to have found it again, advancing towards Jinn.

"Sorry," I say as I pass the guy on the floor.

They must have seen, or at least heard me coming. The two that I'm running at turn and face me. I raise my sword to attack at the same time as one of the goons do. Instead of defending, I lash out and start attacking. With both of our first strikes being an attack, the two swords clang together and fall apart. I strike again, this time he blocks.

I try and find a rhythm while fighting this guy, but the second comes and attacks. I have to break my focus in order to defend myself. I frantically skip back and forth between my two opponents. I try attacking and defending in a way similar to what I saw Jinn do. It doesn't work for me. I make careless mistakes, nearly getting cut each time. The blades feel like they are getting closer and closer every time they try to take a taste of my flesh. I make one of my better decisions all day: I stop trying to mimic Jinn and get creative.

The one on my right swings his sword like a baseball bat. I duck underneath it. The one who swung can't stop the forward momentum, already committed to the swing. Before he can reset for another attack, I hook my foot behind his ankle and pull. Unprepared for the move, the guy falls with a crack. I kick his sword away, assuming he would grab for it.

You know what they say about assuming. Dac pipes up.

Oh shut up.

I turn my attention to the other remaining fighter. He seems shocked that I was able to take down one of them. He quickly snaps out of it and tries to bring his sword down on me with a great arc. I roll out of the way as my sword clangs against the floor. While he is set off balance, I tackle him to the floor.

When we hit the floor, I bash his nose with the handle of my sword. I hear a crack when I connect. With a scream, the New Power trainee clutches his nose. He drops his sword, all thoughts of conflict forgotten.

I stand and turn in time to see Jinn hit the second of his opponents in the temple with the flat of his blade. When the second guy falls, Jinn turns, ready to face another opponent. He almost looks shocked that I'm the only one still standing. I wave. After a moment of being confused, Jinn lets up. He almost even smiles.

Jinn does something and his sword shrinks into oblivion. He sticks his hand in his pocket and drops the miniature, toothpick-like sword in. Jinn walks over to Mark and gives him some money. I catch bits of what he says. Something about "hiding" and "get one." I don't even know. Mark nods in apparent agreement and walks back off in the direction of the electronics section. Less than a second after Mark walks off, Jinn turns towards me and starts sulking.

What did I do now?

You're in trouble, mocks Dac.

You do realize that that means you're in trouble too, right?

Oh, Dac says, stumped. Got you now.

Jinn grabs my arm and starts dragging me off. I didn't even see him close the rest of the distance. Guess that's what I get for losing my train of thought to argue with Dac.

"Where are we—" I start to ask before Jinn cuts me off.

"We have to get away from this. I'll tell you more in a bit. For now, follow me." Works for me. For now anyway. I half follow, and am half dragged behind Jinn for a while. We seem to be following signs at random at first. After a little bit though, we start to follow signs leading to Crafted Goods. Finally, we get to a store. The sign says "Big Man's Metal Shop" but it looks more like an armory to me. The walls have swords and other weapons lining them. Other than that, I see little figurines, canteens, and other trivial goods. It's predominately weapons though. Definitely an armory.

"How can I help you?" asks a man coming out from a back room. The man is covered with soot and tiny burns. He has rippling muscles like tree trunks for arms. His face is blackened from soot and grime. He has crazy hair, as if something just blew up in his hands, and a scraggily beard. There's no doubt that this guy has been working hard for a long time.

His face is flecked with tiny scars and burn marks. He smiles and gives off a warm feeling. After seeing the expression on Jinn's face, the man's face also fell into a look of worry.

"What's wrong?" he asks. He has a voice slightly deeper than most. It still fits the way he looks though.

"Need a place to hide for a short while. I'll explain in a bit," Jinn says, looking around nervously.

"Come back here," the man says, opening the door to the back. Jinn walks around the counter and through the door. I hesitantly follow him, unsure if the offer was also extended to me. Evidently, it was. I file in behind Jinn. The man also joins us in the back, shutting and locking the door behind him.

The man sighs, "Oh Jinn, what did you do this time?"

"Nothing," Jinn says, "Just a little scuffle with the New Power." Sure, nothing. The man sighs again, crossing his arms.

"How many bodies?" He asks casually. How is that a normal question? That is not a normal question!

"I didn't kill any," Jinn says. He turns to me, "Did you?" I open my mouth to speak, but the guy cuts me off before I can say anything.

"Who's the kid, Jinn?"

"Technically he's a ghost."

"What do you mean by that?" asks the man, not understanding. The only reason I get it is because Jinn had to spell it out for me earlier.

"Arthur, I want you to meet Sam. He's the one that made it up here from the Surface." Arthur looks over to inspect me. I give a half smile and stupid wave. I see that the expression on his inspection is more of a double take.

He looks back at Jinn. "You're joking. The mastermind behind getting up here is in his thirties and died during extraction. Died saving all the others. It says so in the report." Arthur looks at Jinn like he just won an important argument. It's Jinn's turn to sigh like Arthur doesn't understand anything he's saying.

"Who filled out the report?" Jinn asks.

"Mark. Mark Raltz." Mark's last name is Raltz?

"Who did the verbal debriefing?" continues Jinn.

"Mark again."

"And who was on the extraction job? Just the people on the ship." Jinn adds the last part seeing that Arthur was getting ready to spurt off a giant list.

"There was Mark, Joe was flying, and you." Jinn waits a moment to see if Arthur can put it all together yet. Evidently not. "Who's Mark's closest friend?"

"That's easy," Arthur says with confidence, "You are." He smiles for a moment, thinking he has a victory. Then it smacks him in the face. "You got Mark to lie for you! Didn't you!" Jinn puts a finger to the tip of his nose.

"Ding ding ding. You got it."

"But why?" Jinn shrugs.

"I like something about the kid. Wanted to train him myself. The right way." Arthur starts to stroke his beard.

"How do you know we can trust him?" Asks Arthur, suddenly suspicious. Why is he so suspicious now?

"He has drawn New Power blood. That makes him a part of the resistance." So that's what the guy meant! I put that together when I was accused of being "one of them" that he meant a Raven, that I'm a part of the resistance. Arthur continues stroking his beard in thought, but finally lets up.

"If you trust him. Then I trust him too."

"It's great and all that everybody trusts me now, but can you please not talk like I'm not here. I hate that," I say, tired of being quiet. That might have been a new record for me. Arthur looks at me.

"Very well, boy." Nothing like a friendly, venomous "boy" to make you feel welcome.

"Arthur," Jinn says, "I didn't just pick your shop at random to hide in." Arthur looks over.

"I suppose not," he says with a sigh, "What do you need?"

"How much Sky Iron do you have?" Jinn asks, his voice sounding harder than it was before.

"Why? Do you need a second?"

"No," Jinn looks over at me, "he needs a first."

Confused, I ask, "What's Sky Iron?" Arthur looks at me like I'm the dumbest person alive before he looks back at Jinn.

"Are you sure you want to get him one? He doesn't even know what Sky Iron is!" Why is Arthur so worked up about this?

"Sam has charged headfirst into fights without a second thought. He even took on armed New Power soldiers without anything to aid him."

"Oh contraire. You told me *you* took them down." Stop being stubborn!

"I fought two. Sam handled the other three." Arthur looks Jinn in the eyes for a good long while before speaking.

"Jinn, I've known you for a while now. As far as I know you've never lied to me before." He gives Jinn a funny look. "If you say that you trust the kid here, and that he's ready for a Sky Iron blade; I'll trust ya."

"Thank you," Jinn says humbly.

"I repeat, what is Sky Iron?" Geeze, can't they even answer my question? I bet they forgot I'm here again. Arthur looks over at me, directly addressing me. Finally.

"Sky Iron is a strange type of metal that is created by an ultra rare reaction." He pauses a moment to make sure I'm following along. "Do you know about the thrusters that keep the platforms aloft?" I nod my head. "When their output product collides with some of the iron and steel on the undersides of the platforms, on rare occasion, they mix together. The iron, steel, and byproduct—which only Nathan seems to know what it is—fuse together.

"The three become one. They become virtually indestructible. I've never heard of any breaking yet. The weirdest part about the new metal created is that is will take on a certain hue of color. The color supposedly fits the user's personality. I guess that's true. Jinn here's sword has a sky blue color to it." That must be the sword he was using a little while ago. "It's always interesting to see what color they turn out to be."

"So what's next?" I ask. Arthur looks to Jinn to get a nod before looking back at me.

"Now," he says, "we make you a new blade."

Chapter Fourteen

"What do I need to do?" I ask.

"You need to help make it," says Arthur, "You especially have to do the final touches. If you don't then it will be linked to me and the color will be set to my personality."

"And what would that be?" I ask.

"I get a shade of red," Arthur says.

"What does red mean?" I ask.

"How am I supposed to know?" says Arthur. I'll bug him more about the colors later. I shrug.

"How much do I need to do for making the sword?" Arthur said I would have to do some of the work making the sword. It'd be nice to know how much.

"Just the last few hits. I can do the rest."

"I want to do more," I say. Why I want to do more work, I don't know. I just do. Arthur laughs.

"You're joking right?" He looks over to Jinn.

"Told you," Jinn says, "There's just something about

him." Arthur gives a sarcastic laugh.

"You ever done any blacksmithing, boy?" He spits the "boy" like a lesser curse. What is his deal?

"No," I answer honestly. Arthur shakes his head.

"Weapons are not the place to learn, especially with Sky Iron. You can only work with that stuff for a limited time before it hardens." I thought metal needed to be purposefully cooled. Sky Iron must just be really different.

"Just let me try," I plead, "You can do all the hard stuff, just tell me the things I need to do." That can't be too bad an offer, can it? I think it sounds fair. Arthur looks to Jinn.

"It's your money. You sure you want to risk him messing things up?" Jinn gives a fake, overacted impression of shock.

"How did you ever come to the conclusion that I'm paying?"

"The boy just got up here recently. If what you're telling me is true, then the boy doesn't have two coins to rub together."

"You can bill the Ravens. You're arming a member."

"A member they don't know they have and think is dead."

"How about this," Jinn says, "Let Sam help make the blade. I'm perfectly prepared to pay, but let's make it interesting."

"What are you getting at?" Arthur asks, suddenly interested.

"If Sam manages to impress you on how he does, the blade's free and he gets all his goods here for free."

"That's a lot that you're asking," Arthur says, his mouth dropping open from what Jinn is asking of him. "What happens if I'm not impressed 'eh? What do I get?" Jinn thinks for a moment, scratching his chin.

"On top of what the blade costs, let's say a hundred thousand." If Arthur's jaw dropped before, now it fell through the floor and kept on going. People on the Surface may even see it. Jinn has to be bluffing. I knew he was loaded, but not to the point that he can risk one hundred thousand bucks on a bet. Let alone a bet on me! He barely knows me! I guess he must have a lot of faith in me. Arthur whistles.

"That's a lot of coin." No duh! "I like when you make things interesting Jinn. I get rich at the end." Jinn smiles.

"I assure you, you're not seeing any coin from me today."

"We'll see about that," grumbles Arthur, "Come boy, let's get you properly suited up." Arthur lumbers off. I look back at Jinn.

"Just don't talk back too much," he says like he expects me to talk back, oh wait, "I'll be watching. Make sure he doesn't try to cheat you. He does that." As I'm about to say something back, I hear Arthur call for me.

"Get over here boy. Don't keep me waiting. I can almost smell your money Jinn."

"Why would you smell money?" I mumble to myself as I walk over to where Arthur is. He's wearing a large lead apron that goes below his knees. Other than the apron, he has a pair of goggles on his head. There is a cabinet open behind him that has more aprons, goggles, and gloves in it.

"Time to suit you up," he says, pulling out an apron and tossing it to me. "I know he didn't say it, but part of Jinn's deals are that I'm not allowed to kill anyone that I'm working with." What a cheery thought. I throw the apron over my head and tie it behind my back. Arthur then tosses me a pair of goggles and gloves. I catch the goggles and a glove, but I drop the other.

I quickly bend over and pick it up, not wanting to give Arthur a chance to poke fun at me. I put the goggles on so that they are resting around my neck. I move to put the gloves on and see that while they will cover my hands, there are rips and tears all throughout the part that runs up to my elbows. More than half of the glove on my right arm is gone so that it only goes up a fraction of my forearm. Arthur takes a pair of gloves out of the cabinet for himself. They're still brand new. He looks at me and shrugs.

"I just bought these the other day. The pair you have are my only others." Lies. I saw plenty of other gloves in his cabinet. I'm pretty sure Arthur would chalk pointing that out under talking back, though. I listen to Jinn's advice and keep my mouth shut. "About how long do we want the blade to be?" Arthur asks me.

"I can answer that," Jinn says coming closer. He grabs one of Arthur's measuring sticks and starts to take measurements of me. After a moment or so of that, Jinn has an answer. "Blade needs to be about three and a half feet long. Maybe a little less."

"How many hands?" Arthur asks me, "For the handle?"

"Oh, a hand and a half I guess. That's what I have been using so far."

"A man that can't make up his mind 'eh? Let me go find a handle." Arthur lumbers off into a room that's farther back. After a couple sounds of things falling to the ground followed by some good old swearing, Arthur comes back. He has a handle that actually looks like it might work well. And here I thought he is just trying to spite me. "Give me a hand with this," he says, tossing the handle onto a table. He opens another door to a supply room. This one has a much more advanced and secure lock. When Arthur opens the door, I see a liquid-like metal. "Step in quickly," he says. I do as I'm told. As soon as I pass the door, Arthur, already inside, shuts the door.

It's an eerie cold inside. I can see my breath slightly, but I don't feel that cold. There is a slight chill, but it's more like the feel of constantly blowing wind. Only problem with that idea is that the air is stagnant.

"What do you keep in here?" I ask.

"It's what's required," says Arthur.

"What do you mean?" He gestures around him.

"What you see is Sky Iron. Everything melts together on the underside of the platform. We have to find it, collect it, and bring it back quickly. We generally only make it back with a couple drops at a time." Arthur walks over to a bucket, selecting it after shaking his head at a couple of other options. "Come help me with this," he says. I walk over and help him lift the bucket off a shelf.

"Holy crap," I let out a burst of air. Even though Arthur is totally ripped and there are two of us, the bucket of liquid Sky Iron is unbelievably heavy. We waddle with it between us over to a scale in the room.

"Pour it out until I say stop," Arthur instructs me. I do as he says and tilt the bucket with him. A few short seconds later, Arthur yells to stop. We put the bucket on the floor and Arthur fetches a ladle. He takes small amounts of the liquid Sky Iron and adds it to the bucket on the scale until he is satisfied with the weight. "Let's put the leftovers away," he says. Even though we just dumped a good amount of the stuff out, the bucket is still extraordinarily heavy. We somehow manage to get it back on the shelf before Arthur addresses me again.

"Once we take the Sky Iron out there, we are on a strict, merciless timer. Are you sure you still want to be involved?" I nod my head, "I would like to say I feel nothing, but that just earned you some respect. Now let's go. You carry the bucket. Do everything I say, when I say it. Are we ready?" I nod my head. I pick up the Sky Iron we just weighed out. This load is much lighter. It's the same weight as a sword. "Goggles on," Arthur tells me. I set the bucket down for a moment to put my goggles on before I pick it up again.

"Ready," I say.

"Let's go," Arthur says opening the door. I walk out even though I feel like I should be running. "Pour it into that tube there, every last drop," Arthur orders me even as he is turning around to shut the door to the room in which he stores the liquid Sky Iron. I take a second to find what tube he means. About a millisecond later I see something that looks like a miniature version of an old irrigation canal. The tube runs through a furnace to somewhere past that.

Unlike only a few moments ago, the Sky Iron no longer runs like water, but now has some viscosity to it. I check the bucket I'm pouring from to make sure all of it has run into the canal. Out of the corner of my eye, I see that Arthur is already working on the Sky Iron on the opposite end of the canal. I don't know what he's doing, but he's working feverishly.

After I make sure that every last drop of Sky Iron has been poured out like Arthur said, I look around. Jinn is standing off to the side watching like he said he would, watching what's going on. Arthur is still working, hidden just out of my line of sight.

"Handle!" yells Arthur. He doesn't look up from his work; he just keeps going. I grab the handle Arthur dug out earlier from a nearby table and run it over to him. As soon as I get the handle to Arthur, he sends me out again to fetch other things. It goes on like this for a while before Arthur gives me a different set of instructions. "Get over here." He demands. I walk over and see that on an anvil-like thing there is something actually in the shape of a sword. How did that come from a bucket of liquid?

"Hold it here and here. Don't let these parts separate or slip apart. Don't let go no matter what." I take the place of Arthur's hands as he lifts them, holding the sword exactly as he told me. Arthur grabs a hammer that I brought him earlier and starts banging on the sword. He's not randomly banging. The Sky Iron is solidifying but still isn't as hard as usually expected. Arthur is smacking it into submission and into place.

The Sky Iron is hot under my hands, even despite the gloves. As Arthur is hammering, sparks start to fly. They aren't normal sparks; they're unusually large and look more like little spheres of fire. I don't do much blacksmithing, but I'm pretty sure that's not normal. Most of the sparks are landing on my arms where the gloves cover them. Some get through to my skin. It actually feels like specific patches of my skin are on fire. I wince and almost pull my arm away.

"Hold on just a little bit longer," Arthur says, "we're almost there." I stand there, desperately wanting to do something to ease the fire on my arm, but knowing that I can't do anything. It feels like a hole is being burned straight through my arm. Point being, it's not pleasant. I don't know how much time passes. I just try to ignore the pain in my arm. "Hurry, take the hammer and hit here, here, and here." Arthur snaps me out of my trance. I do exactly as I'm told, hitting it only as many times as instructed. After I bang on the sword as many times as I'm told, Arthur takes it and starts to sharpen it. He hands me the sword to make sure I do some of the sharpening as well. Once Arthur is satisfied that it's sharp enough, he takes it and throws the majority of it into the fire.

"Why are you doing that?" I ask, "Doesn't that destroy the metal?"

"This is Sky Iron, remember. Sky Iron is not your normal metal. The fire is what helps it to be indestructible. We'll be done here in about ten minutes." Arthur slaps my back. I wince. My back is so sore from being bent over working on the sword with unbelievable intensity and attention to detail for I don't even know how long.

"Alright," I say intelligently, "How long have we been working?"

"Maybe close to an hour," Arthur says. "Normally I might have taken longer, but Sky Iron is a totally different scenario." As I saw. I raise my arms to stretch, but as soon as I stretch, my forearm starts burning. Oh ya, I got sparks from hell on it. I pull my arms back down sucking in a breath of air. "That's right, you got sparked." He looks at Jinn. "Did you already test some Blue Elixir on him?" Jinn nods.

"He's good," Jinn says. Arthur walks off. I hear a refrigerator open and close. While Arthur is gone, I carefully take off the apron, goggles, and gloves, if they can even be called that. Arthur comes back with the same drink that Jinn had me try after I woke up from the poisoning. He hands it to me and I take a generous gulp.

"Much better," I say when I'm done. I don't understand how that stuff works, but I won't question it. With everyone standing around for a moment, Arthur walks over to the fire and pulls the sword out.

"Beautiful," he says as he examines it, and I agree. The sword looks like one of the most amazing things I have seen. It's exactly the right length, the handle complements it well, and it's just, well, beautiful. "And it's good that it hasn't lit up yet. That means that you're the one it has registered as its owner." He talks about the sword like it is a sentient being. Kind of a weird thought.

What was that about inanimate sentient objects being weird? Dac says in my head accusingly.

Sorry, it's just, I don't know. I never would have expected you to be alive, kinda, *if you never talked to me.*

I guess your excuse works. For now. I almost laugh. Arthur, ignoring the look on my face, walks over and holds out the sword.

"We'll see what color it is once you hold it," he says. I'm almost nervous to take the sword. I don't know why, I just am. If the color reflects my personality, I wonder what it will be. I hope that it's not pink or something like that. I grab the sword and it feels like my arm gets a jolt of energy. As sudden as the jolt was, it runs out of my arm again. The sword flashes a blinding light. The light's intensity lessens and it settles into a pure white aura. The soft glow wafts around the sword like a contained smoke, unwilling to leave. Other than the subtle smoke, the sword itself has a white sheen to it. That doesn't seem possible, but it does.

"Never seen that one before," Arthur says, "What about you Jinn?"

"Nope," Jinn says shaking his head, "I've seen all the shades of the rainbow, but never white. I've even seen peoples' colors change, but still, no one has had white."

"So what does it mean that mine's white?" I ask. Jinn

shakes his head, still lost in thought.

"Don't know. Could be something, could be nothing. Only Nathan knows what all the colors mean." I nod my head, thinking about what the white could mean.

"Regardless," Jinn says, "Let me show you a cool trick." He looks at Arthur, "Is the sword capable of doing this yet?"

"Sword's one of the best I've put out. It better be ready." Jinn sticks his hand in his pocket and pulls out his Sky Iron blade. I gasp.

"How'd you do that?" I ask.

"Everything with Sky Iron can do that. It's a mental thing. It took me a while to get the hang of it, but because you have some assistance and training with mental communications, you should get this in no time."

"Do you mean Dac?" I ask.

"Yes. Dac. You should really stop calling—" Jinn looks cautiously at Arthur, "it by name."

Is he calling me an "it" again? I think he is. You should kick his ass.

Oh come on, he just doesn't want Arthur to know; the guy's enough of an ass.

Forget Arthur. Your Jinn buddy keeps insulting me. I think he should pay. Dac argues back.

I think you should calm down. I am not going to kick his ass for you.

"And he's gone," I hear Jinn say in the distance.

I never said kick his ass, I just thought it. We must be getting closer than your buddy over there thinks. Besides, if I had my own body I could kick his butt for myself. Can't you hurry up and get me one?

How do you expect me to pay for one? I just got up here!

What about your deal with Arthur? Good point.

"So how'd I do?" I ask randomly.

"He's back," Jinn says sarcastically, "What do you mean 'how did you do?'"

"Did I impress Arthur? Is the sword and other stuff free?" Jinn suddenly remembers what I'm talking about.

"I don't know. How did he do Arty? You seem pretty impressed with the *best* sword you have *ever* made.'"

"I'll admit it," he says, "I'm thoroughly impressed. I guess you win the bet. The kid's stuff is free. Also, never call me Arty again."

"Good to know that my wallet is safe. Now, can I please continue with my explanation?"

"By all means," I say.

"The materials in Sky Iron were made to be able to flex. Even though it is now indestructible, it can still shrink if needed to. Just imagine it getting smaller. It can be whatever size you need. You picture it and command the sword."

"You know that sounds insane right?"

"So does talking to voices in your head."

"Fair enough," I say, ignoring Dac's complaints about being called a thing again. I picture the sword being really, really small. Small enough that I could fit it in my pocket. I try once.

Nothing. Twice.

Nothing. A third time.

The sword shrinks in my hand. I don't believe what I'm seeing. This solid mass of metal is shrinking to the size of a toothpick! I audibly gasp.

"Pretty cool, huh?" Jinn says to me. I nod.

"That's nothing." Arthur says with a wave of his hand. He reaches into his pockets and pulls out two different blades. They have a red sheen to them that looks to be begging for blood. His swords glow evil in the light. Arthur throws the two swords aside and pulls out another two. He repeats this until he has pulled out a total of ten swords and clubs in all shapes and sizes and a giant scythe.

"How?" I start to ask.

"Whenever someone purchases a Sky Iron weapon and it doesn't work to their liking, I keep it. They can't be smelted back down, so I figure why waste them. I wouldn't have minded too much if your sword worked in my favor." Of all the questions I can ask, one prominently sticks in my head.

"What if they just have a 'red personality'? How do you know those are all really yours?"

"Do you remember feeling something? When I handed you your sword? Something running through you then leaving before the sword got its color?" I nod. "That's how. That happened to me for all of these." I look down at my hand to the toothpick-sized sword. If I had to imagine it smaller to make it small, it makes sense to do the opposite to make it larger. I imagine my sword being full sized again. On the first try, the sword grows back to full length.

"Impressive," Jinn says. I play around a bit, making the sword different sizes. First the toothpick again, to full, knife-sized, dagger, ending back at full.

"Show off," Arthur says. I laugh. I stop when I hear a door open. Someone walks through the store. There's a knocking on the door that leads into this backroom.

"Hello? Jinn, you there?" It's Mark.

"We're back here." Jinn calls back, "Arthur, would you please go open the door for our friend." Arthur lumbers over to the door to let Mark in.

"Jinn?" I say. He looks over to me, "How do I get this in my pocket without cutting myself up?"

"When you shrink it, it is no longer as sharp. Even though it's normally sharper than any razorblade, it won't cut you when it's that small." He finishes his explanation as Arthur gets the door unlocked.

"Jinn!" Mark calls, throwing his arms up in the air. He has a shopping bag on his shoulder. He walks over.

"Impressive sword Sammy boy." I smile awkwardly. What do you say to that? "I got you something, Sam. Jinn had me run and go grab it for you when you guys came here."

"Did it really take you an hour to find it?" Jinn asks.

"I had to find a good one. There's the *X* processor, the four twenty-sevenm the nine eighteen." Mark lists a couple other numbers and names that I don't understand.

"Mark," Jinn says cutting him off, "Just show him." Mark looks like he has his own personal cloud of rain for his parade, but gets excited again when he pulls something out from the bag.

"A laptop?" I say.

"Yup, your own computer buddy boy. This way you can keep up to date on what's happening up here and on the Surface. I just need to hack it for you so you can do the second part. Jinn told me that you were probably worried about your ma' and asked me to go grab one of these for you." I look at Jinn. Why does he care so much? He barely knows me, yet he treats me like his own son. Other than when he pushes me off of one of the platforms.

"Th-thank you," I say.

"And that's not all," Mark says with a smile, putting the laptop back in the bag. He pulls out a small box, "I got you an adapter to charge your old phone up. It won't be any good to you up here, but you can at least get your old contacts from it." It astounds me how much they care.

"Come on," Jinn says, "Let's get out of Arthur's hair."

Chapter Fifteen

"Yes, leave me. I'm already depressed that I missed out on a small fortune. No need to rub it in," Arthur says. Mark looks over at Jinn.

"One of your infamous bets?"

"Yup," Jinn says back. Apparently, this isn't the first time that Jinn has put a lot of money on the line.

"Arty lost?"

"Stop calling me that."

"Big time."

"What were the terms?"

"If Sam impresses Arthur, then the sword and everything Sam wants from this store is free." Mark almost laughs.

"That's a fool's bet. The kid has impressed everyone that he's met so far."

"Eh, shut up. Jinn conveniently left that detail out when we made the bet," Arthur grumbles. "Now get. I have orders to fill." Mark's phone rings.

"Hello?" He listens. "Yes, we will be right there. Heading over now." He hangs up his phone. "Our ride's here. Ready to go?" Jinn and I say yes.

"Bye Arthur," I say.

"Just go. Before you can think of something you want me to make." Oh I have a good idea what I want next. I just need Jinn to not be here. We leave through the front and start walking to the docks.

"So what'd you have to do?" Mark asks me, "I know Jinn said you had to impress Arty back there, but what did you do to impress him?"

"I had to make my sword," I say.

"Really?" Mark asks, astounded. "So you're a fighter, a flyer, a Surface dweller, survived poison, are a Sky Iron blacksmith, *and* Jinn likes you. That's a more than slightly impressive track list."

"Aw, you're going to make me blush," I say.

"And now he even has spunk," Jinn says. "Want to add that to your list, Mark?" I think Jinn is saying that jokingly, but Mark pulls out his phone and types something in.

"You're seriously keeping a list?" I ask.

"Why wouldn't I?" Mark says.

"Because Sam here doesn't yet realize just how crazy you are," Jinn adds. Mark looks offended.

"I am not crazy. I'm eccentric."

"That's just a nice way to say crazy."

"Who asked you?"

"You did a few years ago."

"Oh shut up." Mark and Jinn bicker about silly things that only they understand. I try to follow along, but half of it is inside jokes that they've developed over the years. We get back to the ship and it takes off. On the ride back to Jinn's house, Mark and Jinn keep talking, this time going over all the things Arthur has done to cheat people.

"Is insulting that guy really so smart?" I ask, "He is basically a walking armory."

"Arty? He's not that bad," Mark says. "He never lifts a hand to Jinn and me." Which reminds me...

"Why were those guys so afraid of you?" Jinn gives me a look.

"Because I kill them. Lots of them," he says it so calmly. I don't understand how this isn't such a big deal.

"So does Arthur apparently, and nobody is afraid of him."

"Arthur isn't the best fighter," Mark says before shifting his eyes to Jinn and half grumbling, "Second only to Nathan." He quickly covers his mouth like he involuntarily said something bad.

"Second best?" I say, "What do you mean second best?" Jinn sighs, reluctant to tell me anything.

"Since that cat is out of the bag," he shoots an accusing glare at Mark, "I'll let you know." Jinn takes a deep breath, "As far as the Ravens go, not only am I the second best fighter, but I'm the most lethal. Killing is no issue to me, and death is no stranger."

"So, what," I ask, "somebody ticks you off and you're out to kill them. That's not cool man."

"Like anything I do is going to change because you tell me that you don't like it. I'm a killer. It's what I do," Jinn says. "I'm not totally evil. I don't randomly kill people because they 'tick me off.' I kill them because they are New Power. Before that, it was people that tried to kill me. I don't do it for the fun of it. Usually." Something tells me there is a little more to that 'usually' than Jinn wants to say. I don't know what to say. What does somebody say when the only person willing to help them drops the bomb that they kill people, sometimes for fun.

"Were you fighting your hardest against me?" Seriously? That's all I can ask? Man, I'm useless when someone catches me off-guard. I'm going to have to get better about that.

"That's the best part," Jinn says. "You were able to stand toe to toe with my best. Nobody else can do that. I hope not everybody on the Surface is as skilled as you. Given that you seemed to be bumbling around, I'm guessing that there are even better." Really? That's his biggest concern.

"Not really," I say, "nobody fights with swords down

there. It's all guns. Only us geeks from stupid fairs fight with swords."

"Well you fighting with your toy swords has kept you alive so far. You have to have *some* natural talent other than what you learned play fighting with your friends."

"Why wouldn't you tell me?" I ask.

"Tell you what?"

"That you kill so many people," Jinn sighs.

"This is a war. No matter how you spin it, this is war. It's kill or be killed. I prefer the first." I can't think of anything to say. We ride the rest of the way to Jinn's house in silence. When we land on Jinn's front lawn, Jinn and I climb out. What I don't expect is that Mark also steps off the craft.

"What are you doing?" I ask.

"I'm helping to train you," he says. "That, and I'm sure that Jinn has too much food for his own good."

"I always have food," Jinn says with a smile. Mood swing much? Jinn was telling me how killing is a part of everyday life and now he's making more food jokes. I may be different than most people, but I think that there should be a little more buffer time between those two discussions than a few minutes.

Regardless of my thoughts, life progresses. For a week I'm constantly being trained. Jinn shows me sword work and basic knowledge of how life is up here while Mark teaches me all about some tech. For awhile, I wrestle with the thought of Jinn killing. I picture him as a cold ruthless killer, slaughtering anyone and everyone, drinking their blood from a golden goblet. After a couple days of that, I realize just how stupid that image is. I ignore what Jinn told me, dismissing it as I would anything else.

Another week of training and I can fight without stumbling every two seconds. In my eyes, that's a major accomplishment. I understand half of what Mark is telling me, even though I'm pretty sure that he doesn't. When I fall asleep, sometimes I still hear voices. They're like a background in my dreams. I'll be on the Surface, free, and suddenly there will be whispers, pattering around in my head. I swear it's going to drive me crazy! It's usually the same thing, always about four people, trying to control them and how it's not exactly working in the voices favor. I'm learning to tune it out, but it's still weird.

"Sam," Jinn says to me early in the morning, "Mark and I need to make a run into town. Would you like to come with us?"

"Yeah, sure," I say. "Could I go to the market district?"

"I don't see why not," Jinn says. "What do you need there?" I offer a non-committal shrug.

"Just want to look around."

"Alright," Jinn says.

"What do you guys need to do?"

"Just a meeting we need to attend," Jinn says. With that, Mark comes into the kitchen. He is wearing a cheetah print bathrobe tied around the waist. I resist the urge to laugh—like every other time I've seen Mark wearing something ridiculous these past few weeks— with every ounce of energy I can muster.

"Mornin'," he says with a yawn, scratching his head of crazy mad scientist hair.

"Good morning Mark," Jinn says with a smile.

"Morning," I say.

"We all set to go?" Mark asks Jinn.

"As soon as you get dressed." Mark inspects himself and smiles. "I was wondering why I felt a little drafty."

"Late night?" I ask.

"You could say that. I was working on a way to speed up my processor for a little while, and after that I worked on what I'd be saying today. This isn't the right time to mess up."

"So, a late night," Jinn nods his head at my comment.

"Pretty much," Mark says.

"Why don't you go get yourself cleaned up, Mark. We'll leave in twenty minutes." Jinn says.

"Can do," Mark says walking back to his room. Jinn and I eat breakfast while Mark gets showered and changes. When Mark comes out, I don't know what to think. Fist he was in the cheetah print bathrobe, now he's wearing something maybe even stranger looking on him.

A suit.

"Mark? Why are you wearing a suit?" I ask.

"Dress to impress, right?" he says back. He brushes off one of his sleeves looking for dust.

"Who are you and what have you done with Mark," I ask. Mark never dresses nice, and he never checks himself for dirt. His hair even looks half decent!

"Shut up you little twerp," Mark says jokingly. "Is this too much?" He asks Jinn. I look over at Jinn, his mouth full of cereal, a drop of milk running down his chin.

"Mhm," he grunts, swallowing his food. Jinn's wearing normal clothes. He has on a jacket, but I don't think that counts because it looks more like a motorcycle jacket than a sport coat. "I would never wear anything that nice around those lunatics. What are you going to do when you say something that pisses them off? My bet is that they'll try to kill you, or at least give you a good beating."

"I know *you* would never wear anything like this around them, but they're all scared of you to a degree."

"They're not scared of me. They just respect the fact that I could kick their butts if I wanted to," Jinn says. "Why do we even go to these things? Gerund and I always get into an argument," Who's Gerund? "That guy can't lead a pigeon to a park bench."

"One, that's a strange analogy, you can't lead a

pigeon. Two, give me another minute. I'll go change."
Mark disappears into his room again. After a few
minutes Mark comes back out. This time he's wearing
something more appropriate. He has a jacket on that
looks almost similar to Jinn's. "Better?" He asks.

"Better," Jinn agrees, "You do know that you only
have about five minutes until the transport is here to
pick us up? I would eat breakfast quickly if I was you."
Mark looks at a clock, choosing to ignore it.

"I'm not going to eat until after. I don't want to lose
my lunch midway through," Jinn sighs.

"This isn't that big of a deal." Jinn says.

"Maybe for you. I get nervous with public speaking.
You should be glad that I didn't blow it when I had to lie
about him being alive." Mark says pointing to me. Mark
is nervous with public speaking? He's never seemed like
it, always making jokes and trying to tell people random
information.

Jinn's phone rings. He picks it up.

"Hello?" He listens to what is being said on the other
end of the line. "Okay, we will be right out." He hangs up
the phone, putting it back in his pocket, "Transport's
here. Everybody ready?" Mark and I say yes. I double-
check my pockets to make sure I have everything. I feel
my phone and the now familiar weight of my shrunken
down Sky Iron sword.

During the ride on the transport, Mark and Jinn

discuss what they're going to cover in the meeting they're having today. Well, more like Mark telling Jinn something he wants to do and Jinn saying two words about it back to Mark. I'm dropped off first. The transport pulls up to the dock like it did the last time I was here. The door to the hangar of the transport opens up before me.

"We'll be back for you in an hour or so. Sound good?" Jinn informs me.

"Perfect," I say, "Good luck with your meeting thing." With that I step off the transport and it takes off again. I look behind me to see the transport rising higher, the door closing, before flying away. Alright, looks like I have some time to myself. I walk into the market district, searching for the signs that I need. When I spot one I start following it. *Crafted Goods.*

Are we doing what I think we're going? Dac asks me in my head.

That depends. What are you thinking?

You're cashing in on your free stuff, aren't you?

Big time. I hear Dac being giddy in my head, talking about everything he wants to do once he gets his own body. With all the talking we've been doing I've gotten used to him being inside my head at all times. It's going to be weird once he's gone. Is he going to be gone? Before I can come to a conclusion, a humble yet looming store appears before me: *Big Man's Metal Shop.*

I push the door open. A bell rings that I didn't hear the first time that I was here. It was probably the blood rushing through my ears from the fight only moments before that. Arthur is sitting behind the counter, eye against a large stationary magnifying glass, tinkering with something. He looks up from his work at the sound of the bell, a hint of frustration on his face. The frustration turns to a straight up scowl when he sees that it's me. I smile and wave.

"What do you want," he grumbles.

"A favor," I say, "Actually, more like a job for you. I do get my stuff here free. Remember?" He lets out a breath of air, looking down at the something in his hands. "You can finish that," I say. "I have some time. As long as it doesn't take more than an hour."

"It shouldn't," he says.

"Need some help?" I ask.

"Sure, I know you're not completely incapable. Hold this for me. Two hands might work better." I walk behind the counter to where Arthur is. I pull up one of his spare stools, sitting down. "Hold it where I am. I have to get to everywhere else for now." I take the little device. I keep looking between the clock and the thing Arthur is building. Arthur works around it seamlessly. So many tiny, intricate pieces gently being put into the correct place. It amazes me how gentle Arthur can be with this after seeing him bang on my sword like crazy.

"Perfect," Arthur says admiring his work, "As much as you annoy me. Would you like to work here part time? You seem to be the only one competent enough to help me." The offer shocks me. What shocks me even more is the tone Arthur used. Although having his usual tone of disliking me, there was a subtle hint of something else in there. Respect? I must look like I'm thinking because Arthur gives me an odd look, "What? I've already lost the bet. I can say that I'm impressed with you. I understand that the ghost will have to ask his wrangler if he can work here, but keep it in mind. It'd be nice to be able to work with someone that's a step above buffoon." How cheery.

"Uh, I'll have to ask Jinn," I say.

"I know," Arthur says back, "I said that."

"Right. Anyway, can you help me today or what?" I ask, getting back to my original purpose for coming here.

"I have to," Arthur says with a sigh. "What is it you need?"

"I have an AI in my head," I say. I don't know what to expect from Arthur. Mark and Jinn both reacted poorly to this information, but you never know.

"I can't drill that out. Unless you're asking me to kill you, then the only issue is choosing how to do it. So many fun options."

"Not what I'm asking," I say, "I need you to make a

227

body for him."

"One, why the hell would I make a body for one of those things? And two, him?"

"Yes, his name is Dac, and he is complaining that you would question him." Arthur arches an eyebrow, "I don't know, he just complains about things like that."

I just complain now, do I? Oh you are so going to get a brain full!

Do you have any idea how odd that sounds? I think back, ignoring more of Dac's complaints.

"Please," I say, not sure what else I could do.

"Fine," he says, pulling out a pad of paper and a pen, "How's it gonna look?" Dac starts launching things he wants into my head in a flurry of information. I have to yell at him to slow down. I get him to calm down and slowly give me the list of things he wants. I translate them all to Arthur, who, without judging, writes it all down, making notes and nodding. When I get through the list Arthur has multiple pages worth of notes.

"This is going to be one hell of a challenge," he says looking at his notes. "It'll be fun though." He slaps his little notebook closed, "Can't wait to get started."

"Thank you so much buddy," I say, glad that he is going to do it "This means a lot and—" Arthur puts his hand up.

"Don't grovel, it degrades you. Would've thought Jinn would have taught that to you. About the 'buddy.' Why are you coming up with pet names now?"

"It's not a pet name," I say. "I was just calling you my buddy because you are. Kind of." I correct myself. Arthur looks back through his notes. Adding a few more as he goes.

"Give me a week," he says. "Give or take a few days, and I'll get this done."

Chapter Sixteen

"Thank you, thank you, thank you!" I say. I thought Arthur would have put up more of a challenge before saying yes.

"Yeah, yeah, yeah. Now get out of here. I need to do some preparations to get started on your project."

"Alright," I say, "see you in a week then?"

"Sure," Arthur grumbles. I take out a piece of paper and write my phone number on it.

"Here," I hand Arthur the paper, "It's my cell number incase you want my help. Or for when you finish. Whatever comes first." He takes the paper, shoving it in his pocket.

"Yeah. Now get," he says with a nod of his head. I walk outside, feeling good with myself. So far things have gone well today. Let's hope that doesn't change. I walk around the market district for a while, looking at all the random shops. I pass by one that's a Sky Rider store. I walk inside and look at all the models. They have all sorts of paint jobs. One has bubbles, one has a weird face on it, and one even has flames on it. I turn when I see a giant podium in the middle of the room. On the podium is a Sky Rider labeled as the current best model. It's the same one that Jinn gave me.

While pondering Jinn's generosity, I hear a commotion. I run outside, looking for where the sound could be coming from. I don't run, but I walk purposefully through the streets. I hear the sound of glass shattering. What is going on?

Stop. Stop right where you are. Dac says in my head.

What? Why do you want me to stop randomly? I don't feel like looking as if I'm a psycho.

Not that, Dac says, *I know what you're doing. You're looking for whatever is going on. Don't get in another fight. Please keep this as a good day. I'm getting a body in a week!*

I'm not going to get in another fight. I think back.

If you keep looking for one, you will. As Dac is finishing what he is saying, I turn the corner to where Jinn and I fought a small group of New Power trainees a while ago. This time, there are more. There are about eight New Power goons, and they don't look like trainees. Seven of them have a familiar uniform on. They wear a helmet, which is similar, but the dead giveaway is the giant taser staffs and the red stripe running down their outfits.

Also, instead of two people fighting them, there is just one. And it's a girl? The girl is wearing all black. Black t-shirt, black jeans, black studded bracelet. She picks up a dropped sword. Blood is running from her temple and she has a bloody lip. She fends off as many of the New Power creeps as she can for as long as she can, but before long she gets zapped again. The guy that zapped her whips his staff around and cracks her in the side. I wince for her.

Told you, Dac says.

Oh shut up.

You can still choose not to fight.

Where's the fun in that? I pull out my Sky Iron sword and charge forward. I smash one of the guy's helmets with the hilt of my sword. There isn't a lot of visible damage, but the guy does fall to the ground, stunned. Before the others can react to another fighter, I kick one in the stomach. Not as effective as I thought it'd be. The goon does fall to the ground, but I also hurt my foot. I forgot that they have armor plating covering a good amount of their bodies, only slivers aren't covered where they need to move. I put my weight on my foot. It hurts, but I can stand. The other six New Power members get over the fact that someone has decided to help out the girl. She's still on the floor, but I see that she's breathing heavily, so that's a good sign. Ignoring that she is in fact on the floor, not moving.

"Come on guys," I say, "Six on one hardly seems fair." Like the ones from the initial transport, they don't say anything. They give me nothing to work with. Fantastic.

They come at me without speaking, like they have a hive mind. That's weird. I duck under staffs and fists. I chop one of the guy's staffs in half. I feel a sense of victory before the now four ends of two miniature staffs light up with electricity. Note to self: Don't cut staffs in half. I fight as hard as I can, pushing the goons away, but I get shocked in the process. A lot. I start to smell like an electrical socket. Now that I think about it. Sticking a fork in an electrical socket when I was younger wasn't such a good idea either. Live and learn.

Why are you thinking about electrocuting yourself in the middle of a fight? Dac asks me mentally. *You chose to fight this time. You didn't have to, but you did. The least you can do is pay attention.* He's right. Even though most of my attention is on the fight, I let myself slip for a moment. In that moment, I get zapped. Not just once, but by three staffs. I cut them all before I fall to the ground. My body doesn't twitch or anything, I'm just lying here, temporarily stunned.

"Not good," I manage to say between gritted teeth. From my current position I can see that of the eight New Power goons that were in the fight, only three remain. When did I knock five of them flat on their asses? Their armor is cut. I remember that the Sky Iron sword cut

233

through it like butter. I guess when Arthur and Jinn said that it is sharper than any razor will ever be, they weren't kidding. The three lovely gentlemen that are still standing look like they all hate me very much.

One of them is the guy who has two miniature staffs, another looks untouched, and the third has a cracked visor and his helmet has a nice dent in it about the size of the hilt of my sword. I can only see the lower halves of their faces, but that's enough to see that they might just be willing to fight each other to see who gets to kill me. Is it some special talent of mine to piss people off, because I seem to be really good at it. The three goons that are still standing begin to advance on me. I try to stand up, but my body won't move. I try again, and still nothing. I throw everything I have into it a third time.

I'm able to move my limbs, but it's taking a lot of will power. I'm not sure if I'm even using my muscles right now. Maybe I'm using them so much I can't tell anymore. Going back to my crazy theory.

I get to my feet as the three goons surround me. I can barely stand, let alone lift my sword arm.

"Shit," I mumble to myself through grit teeth. My foot that I injured when I kicked one of the goons is really starting to hurt. I want to do something to relieve the pain or the pressure on it, but I fear that if I do that, I'll be eating pavement again. I do what all good men do at some point in their lives. I bluff like I have never bluffed before.

"Only three of you? Why don't you line up so I can kick your asses more efficiently!" Did I just use the word efficiently when talking about beating someone up? So far, not so good. "Come on," I say, "I can take you." I lift my sword, barely, and wave it at them. I should never try to bluff again. This is going horribly. "What are you, chicken?" Finally, I get a reaction. They growl at me.

NEVER BLUFF AGAIN! Dac yells in my head. Ya, ya, I know. I know. Luckily, only one of them advances. I guess my bluff worked. Kind of.

Nope. Not at all. Jerk. He's right though. To my disliking, the one advancing on me is the goon that has four ways to shock me. Baring the fact that I can barely stand, how am I going to avoid getting shocked? Better yet, how am I going to fight, period? Great day this has turned out to be.

I think it's still half decent. Dac offers.

Really? How?

Well I have a body on the way, and so far, you haven't totally, completely, one hundred percent lost yet.

Love the optimism. I guess he's right though. I'm still on my feet, and they are only coming at me one at a time. The guy advancing on me stops dead in his tracks, like something is controlling him. He still has a snarl on his face, but he's yet to try to kill me again.

"Answer required. Identify yourself." He says it like a

robot. What the hell? Is he seriously asking me what my name is in the middle of a fight? Oh well. Any time bought is good time.

"I'm the candy man, nice to meet you," I say with my usual seriousness. The guy cocks his head back as if searching for something.

"Identity does not exist. Identify yourself." Are you kidding me?

"Hey buddy, are you alright?" I ask. He looks like he's about to bust a vein. He has these flashes of intense pain and other times, he is just sneering. It's weird.

"Irrelevant. Identify yourself." This guy's a nutcase. I know that he's New Power and all, but something isn't right. "This is your final warning. Identify yourself or force will be required." Alright then. Might as well try honesty.

"The name's Sam," I say. What's the harm in telling them that?

"Samuel. Prepare to be processed. We are recommending that you preserve your strength. It will be required in your trial."

"My trial?" I ask, "What are you talking abou-" Then it hits me. "No. No way. On what grounds do you think you can put me through all that again?"

"Again?" He asks me.

Way to go big mouth. Dac says in my head. Oh this sucks. Let's see. How do I get myself out of this one?

"I had to see someone go through it." He doesn't look like he's buying it. Great.

"Records display your participation in games. Number Eight. Showed most promise, but ran when being transported. Number Eight took second place during trials."

"How do you know all of that?" I demand to know. It's been little more than a month since that. I thought that nobody would remember. All the people that are standing around watching, being useless, start talking. They're all saying things along the lines of recalling what happened. Some even bragged that they were at the match. A few of those even pretended they recognized me instantly. If I had the energy to spare, I would go over and punch some of them. Right now though, I need to focus on the guy before me as well as his two buddies.

"All fight logs are recorded in databases that we have access to," but he's not at a computer.

"Are you even human?" I ask. I know that it sounds like something out of a science fiction book, but right now, they're acting more like robots than people. It's just a little fishy to me.

"Yes." I wait for more explanation. I don't think that any more is needed. He did answer my question, but still. It's getting annoying. I thought we were past the whole not answering my questions thing weeks ago, but

I guess I thought wrong. I sigh.

"Do I know you? Under the mask." He remains silent. Whatever. Bought time is bought time. I can actually move now. I've only done small things, but it's more than I could do a minute ago. I risk a quick glance at the girl. She's still down, but still breathing. Probably shocked one too many times. Maybe it's blood loss from the wound on her head. I want to help her, but I can't back down right now. The guy with two miniature staffs takes a step forward. I involuntarily flinch.

"That is irrelevant." Committal answer, alright. He takes another step forward. This time, instead of flinching, I lift my sword.

"Sorry," I say, "But if you want to take me, I'm not going to make it really easy for you." I'm moving a little more sluggishly than normal, but it's better than a minute ago.

I have to admit, Dac says, *your bluffs are getting better.* I almost thank him, but I realize that it's an insult. Jerk. All three of the New Power goons start slowly advancing on me. Great, three on one. I guess it was eight on one not too long ago. This shouldn't be too bad.

"Any chance we can go one on one?" I ask. The three keep advancing. "Didn't think so." One of the two with a long staff jabs at me. I step to the side, knocking the staff down with my sword and trapping it under my foot. I turn to counter another attack, but the guy whose staff is under my foot finds opportunity and yanks his staff up, flipping me onto my back. My lungs empty themselves of air as I hit the ground. My head follows my back with a crack. I'm seeing double now. I concentrate enough to shrink my sword and put it into my pocket. Probably not the smartest thing to do, but I have a feeling that I'm not going to be able to win.

I try to stand back up, but fall as soon as I get to my feet. I half catch myself, half fall on top of the girl. From where I fall I am staring at her face. Even through all the blood and dried tears, there's something about her. She's beautiful. I don't think I've ever seen anyone that tops her.

It's sick that you're thinking of this now. Dac says to me, but I barely hear him. Even though we're both bleeding and I'm about to get the shit beaten out of me by New Power goons, if I could freeze the world for a moment, it would be right now. Maybe something is wrong with me. Might be the concussion for all I know.

I'm grabbed, not too gently, by two of the goons under both my arms. I try to get my footing so I could try and get away, but the third kicks my legs out. I try to lift my head, but even that small act proves nauseating. I try getting my footing again. This time, before my legs are kicked out, I get a taser to the back. I don't try to rise a third time. My mind hasn't given up, but my body sure has. I'm calculating ways to get out of this and ways to

239

beat these guys.

My plans die when the third guy picks up the mystery girl. If I was only putting myself at risk, I'd have no issue doing something unusually stupid, but I won't put someone else in danger. I let myself be roughly dragged, and the girl be carried without putting up a fight, but I don't like it.

Sam. Are you alright? Dac asks me, *I can only see from your eyes and around you when I'm lucky. You're not looking so good. Get up and fight! I can tell in your head you're not done yet.*

"I wish," I say out loud.

Come on, it's not over yet. Aren't you normally the one giving pep talks? I give a half-hearted chuckle, *I know you're not doing great, but come on! Try to do something! Move! Anything!* I try moving my fingers, by some miracle, I can. *Just ignore any resistance and try to fight back.*

Shut up and let me think, I say, getting back to my previous thoughts of escape. This is going to hurt with me having a concussion, but I decide to be more of a doer than a thinker this time. I catch my feet under me for a second so that I can get more leverage. I ram my head into the guy on my right's exposed jaw. He lets go of me to grab his jaw. I think I might have broken it. Hopefully at least cracked one of his teeth. I'd even settle for a really badly bit tongue. My head is spinning worse than it was before. Just ignore it. Just ignore it.

With my free hand, I slug the other guy holding onto me in the jaw as well. He too lets go when I connect. I whip around to hit the first guy I got again, but because of my head injury, I become dizzy and lose my balance. I punch the guy's full body armor by mistake. I hold my hand because it hurts! Instead of doing damage to him, he forces me to my knees. He punches me in the jaw. I turn my head with the blow to try and lessen the damage.

Nothing feels broken, but I do feel like throwing up. Moving fast is not a good idea right now. I spit out a wad of blood. This feels like serious déjà vu.

I'm grabbed under my arms again, jerked to my feet. Here comes the nausea again. Joy. They start dragging me, much less carefully than before. My head and arms seem to be finding every post and wall they can. It's a miracle that I'm still conscious. Or is it a punishment? I don't know. The more time I'm spending up here, the more I learn that I know little, if anything. Maybe that's just how it seems.

I'd tell you to fight again, but I think you would probably die in the process. Thanks for the support, but he's right. After the goons are done bashing me against any surface they can, one pulls out a blade and puts it to my throat. This day just gets better and better.

I notice that I'm being dragged to the docks. Jinn is

so going to kill me. That is, if these guys don't do it for him first.

You're in such a cheery mood right now. Dac says to me. I smile.

Did I do the right thing? I ask him back. He doesn't respond for a moment. I can tell he's thinking.

Yes. I think you did. If you're talking about you and how you are, then yes, you did the right thing, Sam. If you're talking self-preservation wise, you went the exact wrong direction. I smile again.

Thanks for supporting me. I think to Dac.

I keep telling you not *to do things. You do what you want to regardless of my opinion.* Oh Dac. Trying to sound smart.

Remember that we're mentally linked. I know that you secretly wanted to do the same things I did. I'd say that ninety percent of the time you agree with me. That's the truth. Looking deeper into Dac's programming or whatever, I can tell that he has been agreeing with me most of the time. *I think that somehow you're more man than program Dac.*

How do you figure? I'm still just code stuck in your stupid shoes. I'm not flesh and blood.

No. You may not have skin. But just the way you are, and how you act and talk, that's more human than a lot of people I know.

Thanks, Sam. I wish that was true.

It is. Don't worry. I'll make sure you get that body.

How? You're probably about to be killed.

I'll find a way. I think back. I can't really concentrate anymore, so communicating with Dac will be extremely difficult for the time being. When we get to the docks, there is this giant ship. It doesn't look like the small one that I was on when I was taken to the arena. This one is much bigger. It almost looks like the cargo ship I came up here in. When I'm dragged inside, I see that it's more like the cargo ship than I originally thought. It has cargo alright. Cages and cages worth.

Cages full of people. Two options; this is either a slave ship or a prison ship. As strange as it, I'm praying that I'm going to prison. Other than what seems like an over exaggerated million cages full of people, the ship is lined with dozens of New Power soldiers, fully armed.

One of the soldiers on board opens a cage on the floor next to the wall of the ship. The two that are carrying me carefully and gently ease me back then throw me in. When I hit the wall, my breath is knocked out of me. Again. Even though moving hurts, I force myself to sit up against the wall. I don't know why, but it gives me some consolation that I can do that.

The guy carrying the girl throws her in only slightly more gently than I was. I try to catch her, but fail miserably. They slam the cage door shut with a bang. One of the guards pulls out a key and locks the door. The

New Power jerks walk away soundlessly. Sure they have footsteps, but none say a word, they just walk. Creepy. Maybe they do have a hive mind. That wouldn't be good.

"We'll get out of this," I promise, not just myself, but Dac, and the girl, and everybody here that was imprisoned wrongly. I kind of did attack some New Power guys, but still, I was just defending the girl. I'm going to chalk this one up under wrongly imprisoned, no matter what others think.

Chapter Seventeen

The ship is actually a relatively smooth ride. I thought it would be bumpy like the one I first came up here in, but it's not. I sit here, in my corner, watching the girl. I feel a little creepy about the whole "watching a girl as she sleeps" thing, but I do. There isn't anything else to do. I'm being hauled off to the arena, again, and there's nothing I can do about it! It's so frustrating! In my mind I bang my fist against the wall, but in life, I just sit here slumped against the wall.

"This stinks," I say out loud.

"Sorry," comes a random voice above me. That's not what I meant, but now that I think about it, it does reek pretty badly. I ignore it. I've smelt things plenty worse—tar burning flesh in a factory on the Surface for example. Even though it's not cold, I shiver from the memory.

I wonder how that kid's doing now. Probably never stopped working, just changed factories. Maybe he was a delivery boy for a while. Poor kid. I snap myself out of my pathetic memory flashback back into my potentially even more pathetic situation in life. I look over at the girl again. The even rising and falling of her chest, the obvious wounds but lack of pain on her face. I can't just leave her lying there. I muster whatever strength I can at the moment and crawl over to her. I drag her back to the wall. I prop myself back up against the wall. After that, I try to prop the girl up too. It kind of works. I try to make it so that she can sit up on her own, but she keeps falling over and ends up with her head on my shoulder. I'm alright with that. I just don't want to get slapped. Especially right now.

When I'm done moving her around I notice something weird. Other than the guards, air, and engines, there's no sound. Nobody is talking and nobody is moving. Everything is still, not making a sound. Maybe they are all lost in their thoughts. I am. Given that this only lasted a few minutes, I was still thinking about it. I look at the girl and wonder what her history is.

You mean her history of boyfriends, Dac says.

I can hear you, I think back, *That's good. That means I can either think straighter, or I am getting better at this.*

I think it's a little of both.

Probably, I think back. I look at my shoes. It's nice to know that a friend is always going to be there.

Or just to tell you that you're an idiot. Maybe it's not so nice. Still doesn't totally suck. I wonder how long this ride is. I never made it all the way to the prison before, and I don't know how fast we're going. Jinn taught me how to get a good estimation, but I would need to be able to see outside, being outside is better. I'm not that good at figuring all that out anyways. While I'm mentally scolding myself for not paying more attention between Mark and Jinn's lessons, the girl lets out a small moan.

"Where am I?" She asks weakly, digging her head deeper into my shoulder. Nice to know I'm a good pillow. Her voice sounds like it's usually very stern, but it sounds so soft and quiet right now. Maybe the stern guess is wrong.

"Do you want the truth? Or something that sounds nice?" I offer.

"We're dead, aren't we?" She assumes the truth is that we're dead? That's a little over the top.

"No," I say, "It's not that bad. Still sucks though. We're uh, kind of, on our way to prison."

"Lovely," she says, again fluffing my shoulder. "What are you in for?" Straight forward. That's a total contrast from all the other people I've talked to at first up here.

"Kicking some New Power ass. There was this girl who didn't look like she was doing so good. I stepped in to help her out." She lets out a soft laugh.

"Doesn't look like you did so great either."

"Details," I say. She might be almost as cocky as I am. *I don't think that's possible,* Dac says, *I would know. I'm in your head all the time.* Creepy. Ignoring that.

"Why were those creeps attacking you in the first place?" I ask the girl. Really, this is something that I would like to know. What did I get myself into?

"Start insulting them and they'll do that," she says with a bit of a smile. "It feels great talking down to them, but sucks when they come after you." That answers it. She antagonized them. Could she be a part of the resistance?

"Same goes for fighting them," I say, holding my question. "It's fun until you start losing."

"Sounds about right," she says back. "Why is my head on your shoulder by the way? I was expecting either the floor or your lap." Uh.

"I figured that being slapped across the face was better than being hit other places."

"You're a first class comedian," she says to me.

"Thank you, thank you," I say mockingly, "I'll be here

as long as I'm incarcerated."

"Your second joke already? Anxious to prove that you're funny, aren't you?" She says, not moving her head much.

"Here's one that isn't as funny. What's your name?" I ask. She smiles. Why is that so interesting?

"Why do you think I'm going to tell you that?" she asks me.

"Because, I said please," I argue jokingly.

"Only issue with that is that you didn't." I make a funny face.

"Really? I want a do over then. Would you *please* tell me your name?" I emphasize the "please".

"I thought you said you're not joking for this one?"

"I couldn't resist," I say. I didn't think I was being all that funny, but alright, I'll go with that.

"Fine," she says, "Rose."

"Like the flower?" I ask.

"Yup," she says, "My dad told me he named me that because he saw a rose planted before Nathan took off. He said that other than my mom and me, it's one of the most beautiful things he has ever seen." Roses are great and all, but I never thought they were super pretty. I guess they were a small symbol for hope, in a way. A strong, red little flower standing alone. Sometimes covered with soot and ash to the point of being black. It's a resistant flower, like all of us survivors... Am I really over analyzing a flower?

And you think I'm weird, Dac says mentally. Not the time.

"And did your dad also give you a last name, or is Rose so great that none is needed?"

"Harrow. My last name is Harrow," she responds like she's about to fall asleep. She has never opened her eyes during this conversation, just had her head on my shoulder, all but whispering. Rose Harrow, huh. Not a name I think I'll be forgetting soon. "What about you?" she asks, "What's your name?"

"Sam. Sam Cutter."

"Nice to meet you Sammy." Not many people call me Sammy. I think that only my mom and people trying to insult me have. Rose doesn't sound like she's doing either of those though, "We might just end up being cell mates."

"We're not there yet," I say, "We're still flying there. The fun hasn't even begun yet."

"I thought that was when we were getting our butts handed to us," she says with a smile.

"I don't know what you're talking about," I say, "I took down five of them before they got me."

"Impressive," Rose says, "They still got you though."

"Again, details." We stop talking while a guard passes our cage. I saw him and knew to shut up, but how did she? Must be going off her ears. Or she's waiting for me to talk. Or she fell asleep. Last one seems most likely. I wait until the guard is farther away before speaking again.

"You still awake?" I ask Rose.

"Sadly," she says, "I wish I could sleep. Hurts all over, and I'm feeling really dizzy."

"The dizziness is probably from the gnarly gashes across your head, and the pain from the electrocutions and hitting the ground multiple times. Also, me falling on you." I add the last part in very quickly and extremely quietly. I hope she didn't hear it.

"Do me a favor and pick up my hand and slap yourself."

"I'm guessing you heard that last part."

"Yup. Good of you to say it though. It's better for you than if I found out later." I jokingly pick up her hand and touch it to my face before gently putting it back down.

Before you can even think about it, that doesn't count as holding hands. Dac says to me.

How did you know I was going to think that? I ask back mentally.

Just a feeling.

You're starting to know me a little too well. If Dac could shrug, I'm sure he would.

I'll be able to shrug soon enough! That is, if I'm still going to be able to get my body.

I'll get it for you. We'll get out of here. I think back to him, sounding optimistic. Trying to sound optimistic anyway. I turn my attention back to Rose.

"How did you get banged up so badly that you can't move? I'm hurting pretty bad, but at least I can still move." She nuzzles her head against my shoulder again, digging in deeper.

"Electrocution after electrocution. It wasn't fun."

"I wouldn't think so." That explains it, I guess. I was shocked a lot less than she was. That's probably why I can still move. I didn't see her entire conflict after all. We sit in silence for a moment. I imagine what her fight must have looked like. All I know for sure is that the electrocutions must have sucked, big time. I got a good amount of those, and that wasn't pleasant to begin with. More must be miserable. It was tough to move for me. Still is.

"Why did you help me?" Rose asks me out of the blue.

"Help you with what?" I ask back, confused.

"The New Power. They could have just dragged me off and bugged nobody else, but you had to involve yourself and join me. Why?" She looks at me a moment, "Are you a Raven?"

"I'm not sure what I am. There are a bunch of technicalities, but point is that I'm against the New Power. And I helped you because that's what anybody would do. I wouldn't just leave you there on your own."

"It's not what anybody would do. It's what virtually nobody would do. You saw the people lined up in a ring. They'll watch and say how horrible it is, but they won't do anything. They believe the New Power might be right. The ones that don't just don't know where their loyalties lie. There's something different about you." Does she know that I'm from the Surface? I don't know why I care. It's not like it matters right now.

"Maybe that's a good thing," I say lamely. Is that really all that I can come up with? I think I might just be getting more and more pathetic as I go. Did my brain get damaged when I was shocked? Rose lets out a soft laugh.

"It's a good thing I already smacked you. I would have to do it again for making fun of me."

"I'm not making fun of you," I defend myself. "I am just saying that maybe me being different isn't so bad. I've only been different my whole life." It's true. Even though on the Surface we were all different and had equally crappy lives, I was still the odd man out. Am I still the odd man out, even up here? Up here I'm just the kid who somehow got up here from the Surface. Some title.

"Maybe not," she says, "I'm a Raven you know. My dad isn't over-joyed about me fighting, but I do regardless."

"That's, interesting," I say, not sure what I should be saying. "I doubt I would know your dad."

"Probably not. He usually works under the radar. It's still a very important job though. He gets plenty of intel for the fighters."

"I never said it isn't an important job. I didn't even know that he gathered information until you said something about it."

"That's him alright," she says sounding proud of her dad. "He helps with plans and some of the inventing too."

"Very cool," I say, "I'd like to meet him someday."

"How about this, if we get out of here, I'll introduce you to him. Sound good?"

"Sounds good." I can feel that Rose is trying to move like I was when I was shocked, but it's not working.

"Try not using your muscles," I say, trying to help her out. "Try using your mind to order your limbs to move instead. I know it sounds weird, but I forced myself to move on will power alone when I was shocked." She lets out a breath of air, trying to concentrate. After a few seconds, her eyes open. She has the most stunning eyes I've seen. They're a penetrating brown. I know brown is a normal color, but her eyes are a special brown. Maybe it's just the person that goes with the eyes. "There you go," I say.

"I'm scared," she says back. Her voice isn't very shaky, not confirming what she's saying, but there is the hint of a miniature panic attack in there.

"Why?" I ask. Man I'm stupid. What isn't there to be scared of? She's locked in a cage with a total stranger on her way to prison. Totally normal day.

"I'm afraid that I won't be able to move anymore." That's it? That's not so bad, yet the worst at the same time. I felt the same way, and I kind of entirely gave up for a bit. A dark few moments of my day.

Because everything other than that has been absolutely perfect.

"Don't worry about it," I say. "I thought the same thing. I can move again now. I'm just unbelievably sore. That has been going away though."

"Yeah." She says, obviously not convinced. I'm not sure what I can say to make her feel better, so I go with one of my less original ideas. Being extra careful, I put my arm around her. "Am I going to need to have you slap yourself again for me?" she says.

"I don't think I feel up to that again," I say, not moving my arm. "I guess you'll just have to get me when you can move for yourself."

"Don't worry," she says, "I will." That feels more like a promise than a threat to me. We sit quietly for a bit, me not knowing how to respond to her reminding me that she wants to slap me. "Thanks," she says.

"For what?" I ask.

"For, you know, not leaving me crumpled in the corner. You're right. You being different might not be so bad." I smile.

"Told you." We revert back to silence. I actually don't mind much. When I was back on the Surface, there wasn't a lot of talking usually. We normally just had to work, and nobody wanted a mouthful of ash, so we all kept our mouths shut. I look around and notice that all the guards seem to have left our immediate area. What's going on?

I hear one guard walk our way. The ways I hear him are by the clacking of his boots and whatever he's dragging across the bars of other cages keeping a constant drum going. The guard passes my cage. I see that what he's dragging against the bars is like a baton version of the electric staffs. He—I'm guessing it's a he.

I don't think I have seen any female guards yet—stops about a cage away, passing in front of mine. He stops walking and the noise of the baton being dragged against the bars stops. The guard takes a step back so that he's directly in front of my cage.

The guard winds up and smacks the cage with his baton as hard as he can. I jump a little bit. The guard bends down so that I can see his face. Oh god.

"Here's Jonny. Remember me?" It's that stupid idiot from two weeks ago. From the looks of it, his nose it still nice and broken. It's slightly crooked. Something must still be up with his jaw. I don't see anything weird, but he has a funny slur while talking. He's wearing the same uniform as all the other New Power solders, minus the helmet anyway. I sigh. "Eh, what was 'at? I didn't hear you." He smacks the cage with his baton again. This is going to be interesting.

"Yes, I remember you. It looks like you haven't gotten any prettier since I last saw you. What do you want?" Obviously, because I'm his prisoner and the pain from moving makes me want to lie still and die, I have to be a smart ass. I'm smart.

"About that," he starts, "I wanted to repay the favor. Mess you up a bit. Sound good to you?"

"No, not really. Listen, if you want to try anything, I have to go back into the arena at some point." I look like I'm thinking very hard. At the same time, the guy with a broken nose looks shocked I know that I'm going to go into the arena. "I know," I say with mock interest. "You can come in with me. We could be buddies." He growls, "Or not. Still, it'd be an excellent opportunity for a rematch."

"I don't think so. I think handling things right now will work for me. How about you?" I don't say anything,

"Good. Now get your hands off your girlfriend there, or she'll be taking just as much punishment as you." I reluctantly take my arm from around Rose.

"Can you sit up on your own?" I ask her. I can tell she tries to, because she shakes a little bit.

"Nope."

"Alright, I'm going to gently put you on the floor." I do just that. I start to turn her head so that she won't be able to see what happens, but she stops me.

"No, I want to see." So I set her head so that she can see whatever is about to happen. Well she can see our legs anyway. The cage isn't that tall. Once I make sure she is comfortable, I start to crawl out. As soon as I crawl outside, still on my hands and knees, the prick kicks me in the gut. I fall onto my stomach. He grabs me by my armpit.

"Stand up! I want to see your face." He takes his baton and smacks me with it without turning it on. I'm not sure if that made it better or worse. Bright side: no shock. Not bright side: ow! I refuse to give him a reaction. This clearly enrages him. I expect this. The guy is a bipolar lunatic. "What's wrong?" He asks with mock sympathy, "Does it *hurt*?" He hits me again with the word "hurt." Two words. Not pleasant. Being the macho man I am, this rarely ever happens, but just this once, I let out a quiet, barely existent, whimper. The jerk laughs, "Aw, poor baby, does it hurt?" he hits me again, and again. Finally, two guards come to my rescue—yeah, I doubt that's ever going to happen again—they come and taze the idiot hitting me. Take that, loser!

"That's enough. There will be no deaths. We have to test them all to see if they're worthy. If you attack one of prisoners again, we will be forced to execute you." Sorry to say that the moron isn't conscious to hear the threat against his life. Seems a little harsh, but I won't complain.

"Get back in your cell. Before we have to force you in," says one of the guards putting a sparking baton in my face. I put my hands up in defeat and crawl back in. Needless to say, they shut and lock the door behind me. I crawl back to the wall and sit myself up. I get Rose sitting up again. Her head falls on my shoulder the first time. I don't even try to correct it. I'm over it.

"That went well," she says once I'm done situating the both of us. I give her a look. "How bad?" I lift up my shirt. There are already a few bruises forming. That'll hurt in the morning.

"I'm a little banged up, but I'll be fine." It's mostly true. The bruises are nothing.

"That's good," she says.

One of the guards cuts in on our conversation, "Quiet you two! I don't want to hear another peep." Normally I wouldn't oblige, but Rose falls quiet. I'm guessing if the jerk that just beat me up did the same to her, it'd be a lot worse in her current condition.

Chapter Eighteen

We ride the rest of the way in silence. It's one of the
more difficult things that I've done, but somehow, I
manage to do it. The ride's not all that bumpy or long,
but it's not world's best ride. I don't see the ship dock,
but I feel it twist and turn so that it can come to a
standstill. Instead of docking like I thought we would do,
the ship lands. I guess prisons have a large enough
courtyard that a ship could land there.

A voice comes over the loud speaker, "You will be
released momentarily. Do not try and take this vessel,
the captain's room is more than sufficiently guarded.
Please, remove yourselves from the ship. Follow the
instructions of the guards and there will be no
problems. I repeat, follow the guard's instructions and
there will be no problems. You will be released shortly.
Thank you, have a nice day." Seems like an odd thing to
say to people that you just dropped off at prison.

I sit with Rose waiting for the door to our cage to be

opened. She hasn't made much progress in the moving department over the entire ride. She can sit up on her own and says she can walk, but we haven't exactly been able to test the walking theory. This cage seems like it would be better fit for a dog than a person.

A loud bell rings before all the locks on the cage doors pop open. I crawl over and push the door open. No issues so far. I crawl the rest of the way out of the cage and look back to see if Rose needs any help. She looks like she's doing okay. She crawls out right after me. I stand up while she gets herself the rest of the way out. When she tries to stand, she finds more difficulty than I do. I have to hold onto her because she is so unsteady.

"Not quite ready to stand yet, are you?" I say to her.

"Not yet," she agrees. As I'm walking her out of the ship, I see dozens, maybe over a hundred other prisoners climbing out of cages and funneling out. There are guards posted at random areas to help direct us out. For total dicks that are sending us to prison, they're being relatively polite. You know, for the holding-people-against-their-will types. It takes us a minute, but we follow the masses and find our way out.

There are lines of guards along both sides of the ship all the way to the entrance of the prison. Kind of looks like a strange red carpet presentation to the receptionist of misery. The distance between where the ship landed and the front door is located looks like a football field. Somehow, that sport, between all the crap that goes down on the Surface, still gets played. Other than the entrance building, tall fences can be seen. I don't just mean tall as in nine feet or so, I mean tall like twenty feet tall.

Some inmates are wandering the grounds behind the gates. A few of them are being beaten. Also behind the gates looks like a giant apartment pavilion. I'm sure that's not it though. Cheery place they got here. Outside of the gates, other than the lines of guards guiding us in the entrance building, is pretty much nothing. Patches of grass poking out of metal chunks and dirt. I'm sure my mom would want to give their gardener a stern talking to.

My mistake—this time—is thinking of my mom. I haven't seen her in a while. I wonder how she's doing. I force my eyes not to tear up, and start walking. It's hard, but I manage to force the thoughts of my mother out of my mind. The guards creating the aisles don't flinch; they don't move a muscle. They just stand there, watching all of us walk. Creepy.

The first of the prisoners—what, might as well call it as it is—reaches the entrance of the building. Two guards on opposite sides of the double doors pull them open. How polite of them. "Here, let me open the door for you. Please step through to your world of sadness and probably a good stabbing." I can imagine them saying that to the prisoners as they walk past. To my disappointment, when I walk past them, they remain silent. They don't even comment that I have to half drag Rose along with me. Probably not the first time they've seen something like this.

Inside the building it looks kind of like I expected. It looks like a reception desk at a hospital. Maybe more specifically a mental hospital, but I'm glad to say that I've never been in one of those, so I wouldn't know. There is a check-in desk with a lady sitting behind it just like any other clinic. Instead of wearing white and gowns and such, the clerk, who is actually female, wore some of the battle armor that seems to be glued to New Power members. Damn, they have a far reach. I think I need to have a talk with Jinn when I get out of this. He forgot to mention how powerful the enemy is. Maybe I should just punch him and hope that words are transferred that way. Yeah, that'll work.

All the prisoners stop whatever commenting and moving they are doing when the lady behind the desk stands up and clears her throat loudly. "Attention all new admittances. We are not here to be your enemies. We are simply here to take you to a hierarchy better fitting to your personalities. There is no need to thank us, we are just doing our duty." She pauses to see if anybody will clap. Nobody does, but one guy does make a rude gesture at her with his hands. I almost shout in approval, but I don't because I don't want the lady to confuse the admiration for herself, "Let me explain how things work on the inside. We have deemed it appropriate to let those that we have brought over govern their way of life. There are leaders, followers, and different 'clans' if you will." This lady is too cheery for her own good. If I could, I would slug her, "You all shall find your place on the inside, I'm sure." She pauses again. Perhaps checking that we have all heard her lame speech.

She continues speaking, "You may be asking yourselves what our role is." When she says "our" she motions to herself and the other New Power guards in the room.

Probably to kick us when we're down, Dac thinks to me. Agreed.

"We will be here for you," continues the lady, "Think of us as something like the secret police. The unsung heroes that only swoop in on two conditions. One, somebody is gravely injured. Two, it's time for your trial. I know you all must be so worried about it, but let me assure you. The trial is just a way for us to find those of you ready to join our ranks. If the time is not now, you will be returned here, and tried again later." She pleasantly smiles. This lady is making the arena sound like the best thing in the world. I can personally testify, it's not.

"We would have taken you to a trial straight away, but there were so many of you this time that it just couldn't be done." She lets out a sigh of disappointment. I'm fairly sure it's genuine. Everyone that watched us essentially kill ourselves in the arena seemed so happy and excited. It's just wrong. She wipes under her eye, "Please, go inside; find your new home."

The guards start herding us forward. Some of them are pushing, but most don't need to. The majority of us "guests"—prisoners—waddle forward without a shove. At the pace we're all moving, Rose and I don't look like we're walking slowly. Two guards open a set of thick double doors. I don't understand just how thick they are until they are totally open. The doors have to be three feet thick!

Slowly but surely, the masses shuffle through the doors into yet another hallway. It's not exactly a hallway; it's more of a cross between a hall and a room. When all the prisoners have filed in, the large doors behind us shut and are locked. That's their game. This is a staging room.

"Go now," the lady from before says over a speaker. I have a feeling it's a recording this time. "Go and find your place in your new lives!" With the last word, a second set of doors ahead of us opens up. It may be because everyone is scared, or from not knowing what to do, but there is a pause before everyone shuffles forward. Once we all start moving, it's like a not-so-uniform march.

After we've all left the room, the doors shut behind us with a *thump*. A trail of lights on the floor light up and the lady comes over a loud speaker again, "Attention new admittances, please follow the trail of lights. They will lead you to your new housing arrangements. Thank you." Why does she keep trying to be so pleasant? It's not working so well for her. Everyone in the group stands around, not knowing what to do, discussing it with one another. Not feeling like talking about it, I walk forward. I make it a few steps ahead of the group before the others follows me.

Rose stumbles and I have to catch her before she falls. She smiles at me sheepishly, "Guess I'm not ready to walk that much yet."

"Not quite," I say, "here, get on my back."

"That's a little too forward. We've barely met," she says. I don't see how that could have anything to do with it.

"I just mean so that I can carry you more easily."

"I know," she says before climbing onto my back. I don't get girls. I look up and notice that the entire group has halted behind me.

"What?" I ask. Nobody responds. They just stand there waiting. Weird. I turn around and start walking again, following the lights. After I've gone a few steps, I hear everybody behind me start shuffling forward again. Maybe they're all just really scared. Regardless, I walk on, and they follow me.

The lights lead us to a building closer to the center of what I thought was a giant—kind of—city of apartment complexes. We walk inside and there are multiple elevators waiting open for us. Being my usual self and not thinking about potential danger, I walk straight into one of them. When I turn around to hit a button, I see that one is already lit. Odd. I turn and see that the masses are standing in the lobby, not entering the elevators.

"Come on," I say, "They're not going to hurt you. Everybody load into an elevator." After I say that, everybody starts to pile into elevators. After ten people enter my elevator, the doors shut and the elevator starts ascending. If there are three elevators, I'm guessing that there are about thirty of us. Nah, there have to be more. The elevator stops at floor three of five.

My elevator reaches its destination first because we loaded up first. We all step off the elevator: me, with Rose on my back, last, because I went in first. I see the light trail continuing off to the left but wait here because this group of people doesn't seem to be able to do anything without following me. When the other elevators come up, I see that my thirty people estimation is way off. There are actually closer to a hundred of us.

I start following the lights again and, as expected, the other ninety-something people, not counting Rose, follow me. The lights stop at an area with quite a few doors open. A loud speaker crackles to life overhead.

"Attention new admittances," it's the same annoying lady, "these dormitories shall serve as your housing corridors. There shall be information inside. Please, only as many people per room as there are beds. Thank you." The overhead crackles again and is silent.

This time without waiting, the group divides and splits into as many of the rooms as they possibly can. You think you know a group. I carry Rose over to the room on the left at the very end of the hall.

"Want me living with you, hu?" she says into my ear from my back.

"I'd be happy to dump you somewhere else." Lie. Big fat lie. She doesn't need to know that.

"It's okay," she says, probably seeing right through my lie, "I'll keep you company," geeze. Inside the room there are two beds in one massive area. There is a personal bathroom as well. Other than a desk and chair, that's about it. Kind of a boring place.

I walk over to a bed and set Rose down. I don't arrange her perfectly, but she is able to readjust herself. It's good that she is able to do that. I walk over to the desk. There's a piece of paper sitting on it. I pick up the paper. This has to be the "information" that stupid lady was talking about. If I have to hear her voice again it will be too soon.

The paper basically says that you are responsible for maintaining the room, lights out at ten, laundry down the hall. More false promises about how great the arena is without calling it that. All the basics. Boring. I put the paper back on the desk and plop onto the other bed. This is so stupid.

Did you expect it to make sense? You got arrested because you got into a fight. Dac says with his perfect timing.

You knew you wanted to do it. Even though you kept saying no, I knew you were thinking yes. What, it's true. *We've been through this.*

Yeah, yeah yeah, whatever.

Somebody has an attitude.

You do realize that I sound like you, right? He has a point. I think it's best that I just shut up now. I can't though; I need to talk about something. Something has been troubling me during the walk up here, and still is nagging at the back of my mind. Where were all the other people? I saw plenty before we came inside, but walking over here, none. I wonder where they all are. The room I'm in has a window. I look outside, to see if anybody is wandering the streets. As weird as it is, there

266

are. Only a minute or two ago, there was nobody, but now the streets are littered with bunches of people. It's like they were invisible a minute ago. I know that can't be true though. I push the curiosity out of my mind for now.

I lie around the room, talking to Rose for the remainder of the day. Only way that I know it's getting late is when the lights shut off. I feel my way over to a bed that doesn't have a tired girl in it. It's not that hard to find one because they are the only things in the room.

I lie in bed for what feels like forever. The whole new situation I'm in is just uncomfortable. Finally, I get to sleep, but I don't find any rest there. I have another weird dream with the voices. I've grown used to the semi-regular visitation of these dreams, but this one's different. The usual topic of discussion has changed.

"What do you think of this?" Asks one of the voices.

"Which part?" says another, "The progress with the four, or the new development?"

"Both," returns the first, "but especially the new development."

"It is truly intriguing. They seem to have taken to a leader instantaneously. That hasn't happened before as far as I know." Are they talking about me? What do they mean leader?

"No, not in our records. What is special about this

one?"

"The data is inconclusive. We could attempt a genetic analysis."

"Too risky. The boy would most likely notice."

"We could have another attack him. Collect a blood sample that way." Little direct isn't it?

"There is a chance that the boy would not be damaged. Perhaps he can fight, and fight well," says the second voice. In every one of these dreams it's always the same two voices. One of them even occasionally addresses the other as "master." I never see anything during the dreams, just a curtain of black. This time, like the topic, is different. I see pinpricks of white against the black.

"We will discuss the fate of the boy later," says the first voice, "What of the four?"

"My lord," says the second, "We may not be able to decide what to do with the boy later. The other leaders wish to seek the head of the new group tomorrow."

"And?"

"They could kill the boy!" says the second voice, shocked, "What would we do then? It's not unheard of that the leader will dispose of weaklings."

"Then we shall see if he has any worth. If he dies, he was a fluke, if he lives, then let us keep a weary eye upon him." Please don't be talking about me. As much fun as people trying to kill me is, I'm kind of over it. Besides, why would anybody want to kill me? I'm just your friendly resilient pain in the ass.

On second thought, I can totally see why someone would want to kill me. If I weren't myself, I'm sure I'd want to kill me too.

That sounds weird.

"Regardless. If he survives and is not deemed worthy, we will dispose of him ourselves."

"Yes, master," hisses the second voice. Although it agrees with the first, I hear doubt in his voice. Maybe I do have somebody on my side. I don't know for certain if they are actually talking about me though.

The white pinpricks across the field of black that is my vision have been intensifying as the conversation has been going on. It seems like soon the black will be white. It stings my eyes.

"Now, of the four?" the first voice says, already over the topic that may or may not be me.

We should probably hang up now, Dac says to me. When he speaks, the two voices halt their conversation.

"Who's there?" the second voice demands. For some reason, I shoot awake. I'm lying in the same bed as I fell asleep in at the prison. Common sense. I wish that the whole arrested thing was a bad dream.

"Be silent!" the first voice hisses, "If our security has been compromised, the intruder will know all our secrets. Prepare a search to find the intruder." How can I still hear them? Normally after I wake up, the connection is broken. This is a super weird time. Nothing regarding these dreams is normal.

They're going to search for me? I don't know how to do anything to prevent that. I take the crappiest option I have. I lie around waiting for something to happen. Genius, I know.

"Hello gentlemen," says a voice that I have never heard before, "What's the fuss about?"

"We think there has been a security breach," says the second voice.

"You idiot," snaps the first, "it was clearly Armando. You should have given us fair warning."

"I had to settle into it," says this Armando character. Why does his voice sound vaguely familiar? "The AI was just recently installed and is having issues integrating. I don't think it will take." So all this is through the AI's?

Thanks a lot Dac. I think to him. *Don't respond, it might connect us again.*

"Regardless," says Armando, "It's working for the moment. What's new gentlemen?"

"Potential candidates for joining our ranks. Also, the new of the four is practically the same," the first voice relays.

"Oh contraire," tisks Armando, "The condition of the four most certainly has changed."

"What do you mean?" asks the first voice.

"Those in the Sky are running out of time," says Armando, not being specific regarding what he's talking about. I seem to be the only eavesdropper not to understand.

"You can't possibly mean..."

"Yes, yes I can, and do. How strong is your hold?"

"Other than minor resistance, we have complete control." I suppose that is partially true. The Ravens are a strong force—or so I've heard. I've only met Mark, Arthur, and Jinn—but the New Power seems to have an endless supply of goons.

"Excellent. Now extinguish the fire of resistance. Two of the four are still missing. One's will is strong, but the last is finally weakening to us."

"How much more time for the last?" asks the first voice.

"I cannot say. It is still too soon to tell. The last may crumble, or he may strengthen..." The conversation continues like this for a time. All the while I lie awake, taking in every word despite my exhaustion. I listen to these people plot, scheme, and discuss what to do next. Never do I learn any name other than Armando's. They must always be extremely careful about that.

I stay silent. I don't even speak in fear that somehow it will give me away to the New Power consorters.

Finally, at somewhere close to four in the morning, I find sleep.

Chapter Nineteen

"Wake up sleepy head." Ugh. I swat above me in the general direction of the voice telling me to break from my sacred sleep. I stayed up long enough last night. "Watch it," the voice says after my swipes. Ah ha, I'm close! I push my feeble swats harder until I connect with something. I hear a shocked gasp, "Oh you're going to pay for that one." The voice is silent. Finally, sleep. I nuzzle my head deeper into my pillow. I get about a minute of relaxation before a large bucket of water is dumped on my head.

I sit up with a start, spitting water out and being overdramatic about choking. "What the heck?" I demand, as I see Rose laughing hysterically. I don't think it was *that* funny. Not all that funny at all.

"Sorry," Rose says coming out of her laughing fit, "I needed a way to wake you up. You slapped me, so I think we're even now."

"Fine," I say getting up, "Good to see that you're

finally up and moving. When did that happen?"

"Don't know. I just felt a lot better after I woke up." She looks perfectly cheery.

"Wait a minute. Did you shower?" Lame-slash-creepy question, but she doesn't look anywhere near how groggy and gross as I feel.

"Yup," she says, "Is that a bad thing? Should I look more like you?" That settles it. I need a shower.

"Uh, no, it's just that," I stumble over words, not knowing what to ask. "I usually wake up really early. How did you have the time to shower and everything?" She looks at me like I must be at least partially crazy.

"It's the middle of the day. That's not exactly early."

"What?" I disbelievingly ask. How could it be the middle of the day? It feels like I only slept for an hour.

"Go look outside," she says, jerking her thumb toward the window. I walk over to the window and look outside. Surprisingly, as Rose said, it's the middle of the day. Unlike yesterday there are a bunch of people walking around. None of them look all too disturbed. Why would they be? We're all just trapped in a metropolitan prison. No big deal.

Something interesting I notice about all of the people walking around is that they are all wearing normal clothes. There isn't a trend of black and white stripes or orange jumpsuits. Every now and then there is one person wearing that kind of stuff, but it's not super common.

I get the brilliant idea to look down at what I'm wearing. It's still the same stuff, although wetter than what I had on yesterday. Not sure why I thought somebody would take my clothes in the middle of the night, but I did. I reach into my pockets to see if all my stuff is still there.

Phone: check.

Mostly empty wallet: check.

Sky Iron sword: check.

I look at the battery life on my phone. It's pretty high, but I have zero reception and I'm willing to bet that I won't be able to get my hands on a charger. I shut my phone down so that when I really need it, I can use it.

The fact that I still have my sword genuinely surprises me. I thought they would've taken it for sure. My pockets were never checked though, so I guess it makes sense that I still have it. I consider telling Rose that I have the sword, but decide against it. If I'm found out, I don't want her getting in trouble as well. Besides, I don't know how big of a mouth she has.

Leaving the window, I go to shower up. After I no longer smell like old gym socks, I throw on the same clothes I was wearing yesterday. The shirt is still a little damp, and everything is crunchy from the electrocutions, but I try not to mind. When I exit the bathroom, I see Rose sitting at the window, looking out. She must have pulled the desk chair over because that's the only chair we have in here.

"Want to go look around?" she asks me, not turning away from the window.

"Why would I want to do that?" I answer, "We're stuck in prison, not at a vacation resort."

"I know, but if we're going to be here awhile, might as well get used to it." Decent argument. Before I can counter, I hear a commotion in the hall.

"What now?" I mumble to myself. I open our front door and look outside. There are three guys interrogating one of the guys that came in my group. One of the new guys looks normal. Another looks scrawny and has a bit of a hunchback. He looks like he might be suffering from malnutrition. The third guy standing between the other two is the most interesting to look at. He looks like a long lost relative of a brick wall. His face has what look like knife scars all over. He's wearing a t-shirt transformed into a sleeveless shirt by ripping the sleeves off, and shorts. He doesn't look like he has any tattoos or anything like that. One thing he does have, is the person they're talking to—a few inches off the ground by his shirt collar.

The three new dudes seem to lose interest in the guy they're harassing when the short hunchback spots me. The big guy gently puts down the person from my group. The three strangers then skulk over to me. Like an idiot, I stand here and do nothing.

That's starting to become a trend for you, isn't it? Dac says.

Dac, buddy, good to hear you and know that you're alright. Now is actually a really bad time.

It's never a good time anymore, Dac complains like a little kid.

Sorry. Just give me a moment to not get killed, then we can talk.

Deal. I'm still stuck with you for now. Love the enthusiasm. Dac goes silent right when the three strangers are standing in front of me. I open my mouth to speak, but the one that looks relatively normal cuts me off.

"Are you the leada?" He has an Australian accent that's half there. It's not super prominent, but on some words, it's easier to tell than not.

"Excuse me?" I ask. Honestly, I have no idea what he is talking about.

"Your leada? Is he here?"

"What do you mean by leader?" I ask, "I know that personally I don't like taking orders." Also the truth. The guy looks like having to answer my question is going to exhaust him. My guess is that he has had to do this a bunch of times already.

"We heard one of you took charge when you first

came in. Apparently it was just a kid. Probably close to your age." He sizes me up and down. More than likely, not good, "What was the description again?" He asks the big guy.

"Tall, dark hair, carrying a girl on his back." He stops talking and stares behind me. I turn around to see what he's staring at. Rose. Standing there, waving. I'm dead.

"That about does it for me. You're coming with us." He looks over at his big friend and nods. The big guy grabs me and tosses me over his shoulder.

"Hey, what are you doing? Put me down!"

"No can do. Boss wants to meet cha," says the Australian guy. They start to walk away with me, but Rose comes out of the door and stops them.

"Where are you taking him?" she asks. She could've at least thrown a shoe at them or something.

"Can't tell you that," says the normal looking guy again.

"Then at least let me come with you."

"No can do sweetie. Boss' rules." They turn around and continue walking. I, being slung over the brick wall's son's shoulder, see Rose take off a shoe and throw it at them. It's great that she does what I thought she should, but not so great that she hits me in the head instead of connecting with any of the guys.

I struggle for a little while, trying to get out of the big guy's grip, but give up after five or ten minutes of futile effort. "I can walk you know," I say.

"I would most certainly hope so," says the normal looking guy.

"So are you going to let me?"

"No," I sigh and fall against the big guy's back. This sucks.

"Doesn't anybody think this looks weird?" We've been walking in the streets for a bit and plenty of people have been able to see me being carried over this guy's shoulder. Not only am I these guys' hostage, but they're choosing the best route to mortify me.

"We are in a prison. What do you think?" says the hunchback. He speaks in sort of a hiss. It's as if every word pains him.

"I guess you make a good point," I say, "Why can't I walk on my own though?"

"Boss's orders. You want to know, take it up with him." The one that looks relatively normal seems to be doing most of the talking. Probably because it hurts the little guy, and I have no idea how good the big guy's English is.

"Could I at least get some names to call you guys?"

"No," says the normal guy.

"Let me guess," I say, cutting him off, "I need the okay from your boss."

"Quick learna. That's good." I'm going to punch him. Maybe not when he has a bulldozer's brother as a

278

bodyguard, but I'll get him.

My escorts carry me through the town, prison thing, until we're in front of a place called, "Peggy's Cookies."

"I wouldn't recommend the chocolate chip. Let's just say it's not always chocolate." Oh that's nasty.

"Sometimes the bugs are good," says the scrawny guy. At least it's not as bad as I thought it was.

"Cookie good?" Rumbles the one carrying me. I hope that isn't the limit of his speech capabilities. That would be sad.

"Are you guys hungry or something?" I ask, "You kidnap me, then you stop for snacks. I'm sorry, but this is just horrible form."

"We are not stopping for a snack," I can feel the big guy get sad. His body reacts to his emotions, and since he's carrying me, it's easier for me to tell. I pat him on the back.

"Sorry buddy," he nods, "I'll get you a cookie after this."

"Really?" He asks, sounding hopeful.

"For sure." Because his head is turned to see me, I can see a big smile creep onto his face. He seems noticeably happier again.

"The entrance to the hideout is through here," the normal guy talks over the big guy and my short exchange. He looks at the big feller, "Bag him."

"Wait, bag me? What? You just told me where your

hideout is. Why are you going to have a bag over my head?" I guess the answer before he even tells me.

"Boss' orders." Lame. The big guy takes me off his shoulder for a moment long enough to pull a potato sack-like thing out from one of his pockets.

"Sorry new friend," he puts the bag over my head, changing my vision to nothing more than distorted shades of brown. Without anywhere else for it to go, my breath is becoming hot on my face. The big guy picks me up and throws me over his shoulder. Again. As far as I know, they open a trap door somewhere and carry me down a ladder. After that, we start walking down a tunnel.

From what I can see, the scrawny guy is following behind me, making sure I don't take the sack off. We're walking down a long tube that might be either a sewage pipe, or a service tunnel, or something. Being in the center of a platform, there are electronics all around us. Multiple different objects have lights so that there is an odd wash of color illuminating the place. Other than the lights as parts of the electronics, there are lights hanging overhead.

After walking—or in my case being carried—for a minute or so, I decide to speak up, "It smells really bad in here."

"Deal with it," the normal guy says.

At the same time, the big guy says, "Take it off." As

a result, it sounds a little like, "Dleak wet if," but that might be over exaggerating a bit. Ignoring the fact that I think they say really weird stuff, I take the sack off my head. Cool air rushes to my face.

"Much better," I say to myself, "Now if I could only walk on my own. All the blood went to my head a while ago."

"Okay," the big guy says cheerily. He puts me down. Pins and needles run through my legs. I rub my hands on my thighs trying to bring some feeling back to them.

"What are you doing," demands the bigmouth, "Pick him back up!"

"Calm down," I say standing up straight, "It's not that big of a deal. I can walk just fine." I stick my hands in my pockets as if relaxed and waiting for him to say something. I have a different reason. In my right pocket, I feel the shrunken down form of my sword. I hope it doesn't come to that, but I have a way to fight if I must.

"Fine," the scrawny one says, still sounding pained, "But we'll keep a close eye on you." I shrug.

"Works for me," I say. The normal looking guy lets out a sigh of air and continues walking. We don't walk long. About a minute more of walking passes by with no changes of scenery. The normal, supposedly, looking guy drops back and starts whispering with the frail one.

What a group of odd balls, Dac say.

No kidding. Who put them together?

No idea. Maybe the organizer is blind and has more than a few other issues.

I bet, I think back. *The big guy seems to like me, but that can change in a second.*

He is probably alright. I don't see any reason he would betray you.

He only likes me because I said I would buy him a cookie. Dac is silent for a moment.

Are you going to buy him a cookie?

Really? I think back, *I'm shocked that you would assume that I am not going to do as I say. We have known each other for a while now, and never have you said anything so hurtful.*

So that's a no?

I only have twenty bucks okay?

Knew it. Dac says partially laughing.

Oh shut up.

Nah. This is too much fun.

Jerk.

We walk a bit further before the normal looking guy comes up behind me and shoves me to the ground.

"Get down!" he yells.

"What the hell are you doing?" I ask. It doesn't even make sense. Why is he pushing me around now?

"Making sure you submit. We wouldn't want you being disrespectful, now would we?"

"Disrespectful? You've been carrying me this whole

time, and now you're pushing me around. I ought to kick your ass for that!"

"You wouldn't be able to if you tried."

"Is that a challenge?" I ask. I snap away from his grip, setting him off balance. When he's falling forward, I spring up and punch him in the gut. I didn't wait until the big guy left, but I did hit the one I wanted to. And it feels so good!

He falls to his knees, holding his stomach. One down, two to go. I whirl around, ready to fight the others, but they're just standing there, dumbfounded.

"What," I demand, "Nobody ever fought back before?" The one I hit coughs from where he is.

"Insolent child," he mutters, rising to his feet, "I suggest you start walking again, and if you try another stunt like that, I'll cut your arms off," He pulls a knife out and points it at me. I don't think he could cut my arms off with that. I consider pulling out my sword to shut him up. This seems like a good moment to use it, but I keep it concealed. He motions with his knife the direction he wants me to start walking.

"Whatever," I mumble as I go in the direction indicated. I go first and the others follow behind me. They think I've let my guard down, but that's not even close. I surprised them once by fighting back; I don't think that'll work again. The only other way I can really surprise them is by drawing my sword. I need to save that for when they're ready to kill me.

The big guy seems to hear something, because he stops dead in his tracks, and turns his head. I almost ask him what's wrong, but before I can, he runs off in the   direction we're walking, yelling, "We're back, we're back! Party!" Strange, and random.

"What's his deal?" I ask my two remaining captors. Without warning, one of the two comes up and pushes me from behind. I catch myself so that I don't totally face-plant. I turn my head so I can see who pushed me. Figures, it's the same jerk as always. The scrawny one only stands there, wheezing.

"Start walkin, slowly," orders the guy that shoved me. He grabs my shirt and puts the knife to my back.

"I was walking," I argue, "You don't need to get rough." What crawled up his butt and died? Still not touching my sword, I do as he says, continuing to walk forward. This is a long tunnel. Not counting all the stops we've made, we have probably been walking for five, maybe ten minutes. After we take a few more steps, I start to hear what the big guy did a moment ago. People. I'm not sure how many of them there are, but it sounds like a lot. Some are talking, and others are cheering. I'm starting to hate the sound of cheering. It usually ends in bad news for me.

The one holding me picks up his pace, forcing me to walk faster so that I don't get impaled. I'm walked through a back alley. Little faces and not so little faces, poke out at me every now and then. What is this place? At the end of the alley, it opens up into a large arena stage-like thing. I'm the main attraction.

The kind man escorting me shoves me to the ground yelling, "Bow before your ruler!" The crowd cheers when I hit the ground on my hands and knees. Yeah, yeah, yeah. Whatever. I stand up and brush myself off. At least, I try to until I'm shoved down again. Trying not to think of it, I stand up again.

Expecting the shove this time, I dodge by leaning out of the way. I hoped that this would imbalance him, but instead, he redirects his weight to a huge backhand slap to my cheek. Harsh. I, as a reaction, bring my hand to my cheek.

"Are you ready to do as you are told?" says the guy, raising his voice so more people can hear him speak. I spit. He seems to get enraged. He steps forward and grabs the front of my shirt. He raises his knife so that it is lined up with my face. Now would be an excellent time to be smart and draw my sword.

I break his grip and shove him backwards. Somehow, I manage not to get nicked by the knife. I reach into my pocket and pull out my sword, elongating it as I draw it out. Handy trick I learned. I point it straight at the jerk with a knife, "You really want to keep messing with me?" I ask. The white glow emanating from my sword shines brighter than usual. It looks that way at least because it's darker down here than on the topside. Before he can say anything, a voice from the crowd speaks.

"Sam?" I know that voice. John.

Chapter Twenty

There's no way. I let my sword drop to my side and turn around, forgetting about the guy I just had my blade against. "John?" I yell out. After I get the word out, the douche tackles me. I don't drop my sword, but I am face down on the floor with a surprisingly heavy guy on my back, pinning me down. I struggle to get free, but I'm thoroughly pinned. The guy on my back reaches to take my sword, but I shrink it down so that I can keep it hidden in my fist. The guy on my back looks like he doesn't understand where my sword went. His expression says that he doubts his sanity. Serves him right.

While he's confused, I twist out of his grip, and kick him off of me. I jump to my feet, extending my sword again, ready to fight. From the floor, the guy who tackled me tries to shoot daggers through me with his eyes, but I have no care for that right now. I hear a rumbling as the crowd starts chanting, "Fight! Fight! Fight! Fight!" I have a feeling something worse than a cranky guy is coming at me. I turn in a circle, expecting something to jump out at me from every shadow.

From the corner of my eye, I see something shift. I immediately turn that way. My eyes didn't deceive me. There is definitely a person there, and he is holding something sharp. I turn my sword his way, ready to fight, when I notice another like him. And another, and another. I spot five in all. Great, just great. Wonderful way to start your first day in prison.

"Stop! Halt your assault," booms a voice above the crowd. The entire stadium falls silent. Whoever just spoke stopped the fight before the first of my enemies could even step from the shadows. I look in the direction from where the voice came. It came from about the same place as John's voice. While I'm searching for the source of the voice, my would-be attackers fade away until I can no longer see them.

"You there," the voice says again, still unbelievably loud. The nimrod on the floor behind me stands up and is at attention faster than I knew he could move, "Escort this visitor to my chambers. I must have a private word with him." Please don't be a creepy old guy. Of all the things I've asked for, this might be one of the most important. The guy next to me bows—yes, honest and truly, bows—as low as he can go. He takes me by the arm and leads me away. The crowd isn't cheering, not even talking amongst themselves. They're just sitting there, shocked silence filling the massive amphitheater.

Once I've been dragged out, my escort turns to me and tries to backhand me. I catch his wrist, "Woah, calm down. What's the big deal?" I ask. He has gotten more and more worked up since we went into the tunnel under Peggy's Cookies.

"If you ever disrespect our ruler with such a display of insolence again, I will personally make your life a living nightmare." Huh?

"Insolence? What are you talking about? Do you mean not bowing like you did?" His expression remains unchanged. Without another word, he snatches his hand away and starts walking. Not knowing what else to do, I follow him. After a short walk, we arrive before what looks like a mansion. A dilapidated, oddly shaped mansion, but a mansion nonetheless. The mansion looks as if it was added in around all the electronics and technology inside this place. How big is this platform? My escort walks up to the front door and knocks. I wait about ten seconds before walking to the door, turning the handle, and walking in. My escort looks ready to lecture me violently, but is stopped short when he sees somebody standing in the entry hall.

The person standing in the hall is turned around, so all I can see of him is his shaggy, sandy blond hair and his clothes. Hearing the commotion from the door opening, the person turns around.

"John!" I yell as I run towards him.

"Sam!" He yells back. I perform the incredibly manly act of hugging my best friend.

"I've been so worried about you," I say on the verge of tears.

"Calm down man," he says, almost as excited and relieved as I am, "You're starting to sound like your mom." I give a half-hearted smile.

"Please don't ever say that again," I say, maybe because thinking about more people I haven't seen in a while is hard at the moment.

"Aw, it's not that bad," he says, still trying to run with the horribly timed joke.

"No, it's just, bad timing," I say. I force myself to let go of John and take a step back. John looks over to where the guy that escorted me is standing.

"You may go now," he says, "And shut the door behind you." The guy does exactly as John tells him. After the door shuts, I look at John.

"When did you become such a big shot?" I ask him. He shrugs.

"Not long after I came here. I met someone who I think you'll want to meet as well."

"The head honcho that demanded I come here?" I guess.

"That's just a bonus," John explains, "There's

something even better." John is acting like a giddy schoolgirl.

I start randomly guessing, "Does he have a triple chin? Seven toes? Two left feet? Four arms? One grey eye with a knife scar running through it?" I could keep going, but John stops me.

"No, Sam. Just wait. He'll be here any second now."

"I'm no good at waiting," I say.

"I know. That's why I left the door unlocked and waited here." I guess he really knows me. Now that I think about it, I did think it was weird that the door was unlocked.

"Ugh, fine." I say. I start to force back the tears behind my eyes when somebody comes down a large flight of stairs behind John. He's tall, about as tall as me, but I'm still larger. His hairline looks like it might be starting to recede, and his hair itself is a light kind of black with grey splotches all over. He has a couple scars on his face from past fights. Or from horrible cooking accidents. Depends. He has a beard, which hides a good amount of the scars, but plenty are still visible. The ones that are visible are more like barely visible white lines. The bad ones—if there are any—are mostly hidden. As far as clothes go, he is wearing normal clothes, although slightly dirty, underneath a robe-like thing. What happens next catches me completely off guard. He hugs me. He wraps me up in his arms and gives me the biggest hug of my life.

"Sam," John says lightly, "I'd like you to meet your dad." If the random hug didn't shock me, this slaps me across the face like a baseball bat. The man who is hugging me, who also is apparently my father, starts shaking. He puts his head down on my shoulder and my shirt is instantly soaked through with tears. I can't even think of anything to say. I wrap my arms around him and return the hug. It takes a moment, but I realize that this is the man that I've been looking for—one of the reasons that I came up to the Sky Nation in the first place. He has been out of my life for ten years and now, here he is, standing before me, hugging me and sobbing.

The tears I've been fighting back from seeing John burst free when the realization hits me that I'm finally seeing my dad. I start crying into his shoulder just as he is into mine. They're not tears of sadness—quite the opposite, actually. I'm so overjoyed that I can't hold it in.

"I can't believe it's really you," says my dad, his voice softer than it was a moment ago. He still has amazing control over his own voice even though he's crying, "Ten years and all I've thought about is you and your mother." He pulls me closer, like if he lets go, I'll disappear. Like I'm a mirage or something straight out of his most secret and personal dreams. The food that he's forbidden to eat, always out of his reach. After the longest hug of my life, my dad lets go, but wearily, like he's hesitant to do so.

"Hi Dad," is all I can say. Pretty stupid, but with the shock of finding my dad like this, my mind's gone blank.

"Look at you," he says, "The last time I saw you, you were this tall," He puts his hand at knee level.

"Ya, I've kind of grown," I say. What does one say to a father they haven't seen in ten years? "How've you been Dad?" I'm epically failing at this right now.

"Nowhere near as happy as I am now," he says with a smile, wiping a tear from his eye. Oh man. I knew I wanted to find my dad, but I never thought of what I'd say. He'd probably be more than a little insulted if all I did was yell, "I found Waldo!" To my relief, I don't have to say that and John saves me.

"Don't worry," John says, "It was just as awkward when I first found him."

"It's more like when I found you," my dad says. "You looked like a frightened mouse caught in a trap." John blushes, confirming my dad's story. That sounds like John alright.

"I knew it," I say. My dad hasn't stopped smiling since he stemmed the majority of his crying.

"Come," my dad says, raising an arm to beckon me, "Let's eat." I follow John and my dad through their mansion to reach a dining room where a mother load of food is waiting on a long table. Despite the enormity of the table, only three places are set. John and my dad go and grab a plate, leaving me here, gawking at the meal. "Are you coming?" My dad asks, noticing that I'm not going for the food yet.

"Ya, coming," I say. After we all fill our plates, we sit down. My dad takes the head and John and I sit on opposite sides across from each other. We eat in silence for a time. Not having eaten breakfast or lunch, I take seconds. And thirds. And fourths. I didn't eat yesterday either. With food still in front us, my dad is the first to speak.

"I want you to stay down here, Sam." I look up from my plate, my mouth overstuffed with food. I take a couple seconds to chew and swallow.

"What are you talking about?" I ask.

"I don't want you going back up to the outside. It's far too dangerous out there." Are you kidding me?

"We're in a prison. It's dangerous everywhere. Besides, nothing has happened yet." It's mostly true. "Only thing that has happened is *your* goons kidnapping me." Maybe my claim that nothing has happened isn't exactly true at all.

"A perfect example of what can happen. You would have been killed if I hadn't intervened." My mouth indignantly drops open.

"Are you kidding me?" Great start, "You didn't even know it was me!" I say, starting to get upset.

"Precisely. You're fortunate your friend recognized

you."

"I would've been fine!" I say, my voice rising.

"No, you would've been hurt," says my dad, his voice still calm and even. "Which reminds me, you will give me your sword." I lose my temper. I stand up quickly, knocking my chair back, drawing my sword. I point it at my dad's head.

"I'd like to see you try to take it." I lock gazes with my dad, breathing hard, trying to calm down. Our eyes remain locked, contesting wills. I don't know why something as basic as my dad wanting my sword gets me this fired up, but it does.

"Sit. Down," he says, also trying to keep his temper under control. His voice is full of authority, like he will have me cut down where I stand if I don't do as he says.

"Why are you hiding down here anyway, Dad?" He breaks his gaze. I know I've won, at least for now.

"It's safe," he says, "I can't be forced to fight when they can't find me." That's it.

"So you're a coward," I say accusingly. My dad takes a sudden great interest in his shoes.

"I tried," he says, still looking down. "For two years I fought to try to be free. I lost every time. I lost hope of ever getting out. Of ever seeing you or your mother again."

"So you're not a coward," I say, "You're a quitter and a coward. My memory of you is far superior to the real thing." My dad's face sinks even deeper. All the power, all the might in his face is drained away. He looks like a shadow of a man.

"I'm sorry," he says so softly that I almost don't pick it up. "Please stay down here," he begs just as quietly, still not looking at me. "You didn't fight before you were dropped off. In a week they'll force you to fight." It sounds like he's about to cry, "You don't know how bad it hurts. You won last time. You were never hit. You were free." What? What has John been telling him?

"I didn't win," I say. My dad and John both look up at me, shock on their faces, "I know full well what the electricity feels like. I've fought against it numerous times. The only way I got free was that I was broken out. John is one of the few from our group that didn't get freed." John's expression is a mix of shock, acceptance, and understanding.

"I broke one of the rules," he says, not sounding regretful at all. He says it very matter-of-factly. I shrug, not knowing how to respond. Do you remember what they were?" He asks me. I nod.

"Don't win, don't get hurt, and don't die."

"I broke one of those," John says with a smile. "Almost broke two from what I'm told."

"Not quite," I say, "We couldn't kill you. Tried our hardest, but it didn't take. Sorry, I couldn't help with the rule breaking this time."

"Very funny," John says. I shrug and smile. My tension and anger from a moment ago are gone. I almost forget about my dad. Almost. I look over at the man who has remained silent and my anger comes back.

"A week you say? Fine, in a week I'm breaking out of here. I'll take as many with me as I can."

"And just how do you plan to do that?" My dad asks.

"I'm going to hijack one of their ships," I tell him. I have a fairly high tolerance to the electrocutions now—I hope—I can fake going down and get everyone on the transport out.

"It won't work," my dad says, "That was done before. Now the ships only have enough fuel for one way."

"I thought nothing up here burned fuel."

"They installed an inhibitor so that it can only go a little more than one trip. The way they keep running is that a new password must be entered after each trip per direction," my dad explains to me. I guess it makes sense.

"Then I'll find another way," I say, "but I'm getting out. I can't just sit here and wait. I have people counting on me out there." My dad doesn't say anything this time. "Would somebody show me how to get out of here? I don't know how to get back out of this prison within a prison." My dad nods. John stands up and walks over to me.

"I'll walk you out," John says, and with that, we take

our leave. John walks me through the strange underground city, down the tunnel to the ladder that was used when I was taken down here. While we're walking, John and I made idle chit-chat, neither of us really wanting to talk about what has been going on during our time apart.

"Here we are," says John, starting to climb the ladder when we reach our destination. I stop him.

"Wait. I need you down here," John hops off the ladder, but continues to rest his hand on one of the rungs. "Try and convince everybody down here to come topside. I understand if you can't or won't, but please try." John looks at me skeptically.

"That'll be impossible. *If* I could get anybody, only a few people would come. Most are too scared."

"Then try this," I say, "Tell all the Ravens to get topside." John gives me a confused look.

"Who are the Ravens?" Right, he has been locked up this whole time. He's missing the details on what's going on up here.

"They're this resistance group. It'll take too much time to explain right now, but it'd be best to get them out." John nods, "Even if you can't get them to come, I want you to come topside. I'm getting you out."

"Alright," John says still sounding a little skeptical, but a trace of belief is in his voice, and that's enough to give me hope. "Good luck," he says, stepping away from the ladder, letting his hands slide off and fall to his side.

"You too," I say, taking his spot by the ladder, "I guess I'll see you in a week then." Before he leaves, I give John another hug. It's nowhere near as long as the first, but just as meaningful. After we let go, John sets off back down the tunnel, and I climb up the ladder.

At the end of my short climb, I push open a trap door. It swings open over my head and hits the floor with a loud smack.

Subtle, as always, Dac says. I realize that he didn't talk while we were inside the platform. *I stayed quiet because I figured you had enough on your plate with seeing your dad and that John guy. I don't know them personally, but I've seen what's in your memory.*

I still think it's weird that you can do that, I think back to him. I climb out of the hole, ending up behind a counter at Peggy's Cookies. In front of me, also behind the counter, is who I'm going to guess is Peggy—if there's even a Peggy. Across the counter are two customers I instantly recognize. They look up from their goodies. One has a muffin stuffed in his mouth. Both are holding their own big brown paper bags full of food.

"SAM!" They yell in unison excitedly. It's Rick and Fred. Man, I'm seeing everyone today.

Chapter Twenty-One

"Guys!" I yell back. I try my best to sound excited because I am, but the disappointment of my father is still weighing heavily on me. The lady behind the counter turns around and looks shocked to see me. Oh boy. I'm in trouble, aren't I? Before anything else can happen, an older lady comes out from the back room. She looks from me to the trap door and back again.

"Hello dearie," she says sweetly, "Shut the door, won't you?" She strides over to the counter like this happens everyday. It probably does. She addresses Rick and Fred, "Have you two been helped yet?" Awkwardly, I shut the trap door and walk over to the counter, intending to go to the other side. The old lady stops me, "When will you be back, and with how many?"

"I don't plan on coming back," I say, "I'm getting out of here in a week. If you want to come, be sure you're ready to leave." Why am I telling my plan to everybody I meet?

"We want out," Fred blurts out. "Are you taking the train?"

"Train? What train?"

"There's a train connecting the prison to what some of the guards call the 'Market District.' Seems odd to me. That's how we got here though. They caught us trying to sneak off that transport, threw us on the train and shipped us off here," Rick explains to me.

"And they've been wonderful regulars ever since," chimes in the old lady, "The train makes its trip over here during the fights in the arena." Random piece of unusually helpful information.

"Then that's how I'll do it," I say, "I'm going to hijack a train. Sure, I'll also have to hijack the transport we're on, but that's a minor detail."

Can you fly those things? I ask Dac hastily.

No, but I can teach you how on the fly. You can figure out the transport, and the train will just be setting it to the destination you want. He responds.

Thanks buddy, I think to him.

As long as I'm getting my body, no thanks are necessary. We're back to that now? Alright, I guess I did promise the guy.

"Rick, Fred, do you know where the train stops here?" I ask both of them.

"Sure do," Fred says, "Don't even need to get to the other side of the wall."

"Excellent," I say, "There may or may not be a giant amount of people pouring out of here within the week. I need you to get them, as well as everyone in a group called the Ravens, to the train in I guess it's six days. That is if yesterday counted. It's whatever day that I go into the arena."

"Oh dearie," says the old lady, "That's most of us here."

"Then this'll be one hell of a jailbreak." I say, sounding confident. Surprisingly, I actually feel that way a little bit.

"Then you can count me in," says the old lady, "I can help rally the troops. I know where the train stops. It's where I get my ingredients from," She reaches down and picks up a tray of cookies, "Cookie?"

"Uh, sure," I say, caught off guard by the random question. I take a cookie and take a bite. It actually tastes really good. I guess the chocolate is real this time. "Could you do me another favor?" I ask the lady. She looks at me, wondering what it is. "A big guy with a small speech issue; if he comes through here again, would you give him a cookie for me?"

Ha! I am getting him that cookie, I brag to Dac.

I'm amazed you even care. I forgot about it a while ago.

Liar.

I get it from you, he thinks to me. Probably true. Oh

well.

"Of course," the lady says, "You are such a charming young gentleman. It's a pleasure to have you in my store." She smiles, genuinely pleased. It makes me feel good about myself. Like maybe I'm moving in the right direction right now.

"Wait," I say, drawing a conclusion, "Are you Peggy?" Silly question, but I'm curious.

"At your service," she says.

"Thank you for everything, Peggy. I have to go now. I have to figure out the first part of my plan."

"Good luck with that dearie," she says with another smile. With all these good lucks, I feel like what I'm doing may end up being the death of me. It's not a pleasant feeling. Going to a few wrong buildings first, and having some issues finding my way around, I finally found the building my room is in. By the time I get there, it's dark outside. Guess I've been out for awhile. When I get to the correct door, I realize that I don't have a key or anything like that to get in. I try the handle first, hoping that it isn't locked. It is. Next, I rely on the hope that Rose is inside. I knock on the door.

I hear a pitter patter of steps coming over. Rose opens the door. She looks like she has been upset and worried all day. Her face seems to light up a bit when she sees that it's me. She throws her arms around me, giving me a hug. It's been a really huggy day, hasn't it?

"Where've you been?" She asks me, letting go. I wish that hug lasted longer. Then unexpectedly, she slaps me. "You've been gone all day. What happened?"

"First of all, ow." She shrugs like it's nothing. "It's a long story," I say, letting my hands fall to my sides. "Are you going to let me in?"

"Oh, ya, sorry," she says, walking inside. I follow her in, shutting the door behind me, "So seriously, where have you been?" She pesters, "All I know is that three weirdos dragged you off." She sits on one of the beds. I sit on the one across from her.

"I wasn't dragged," I correct her.

"Fine, carried off," she says, obviously irritated at my pathetic attempt at a joke. I go off, telling her what happened today. I leave out that I cried, and that my dad and John are from the Surface. I haven't even told her that I am yet. Not sure I want to right now. When I finish telling my edited story, she continues to sit, silent. I hope she's silent because of shock and not disbelief. I really don't feel like defending myself about what happened. She stares at me for a moment.

"They just let you go?" she asks.

"Ya. Is that not normal?"

"From what you've told me, it doesn't sound like they normally would've even let you live. I guess it's pretty lucky that your dad's in charge." I know she means no harm, but that's a touchy subject I really don't want to get into right now.

"I don't exactly want to talk about all of that right now," I tell her.

"Oh, okay," she says, I think understanding that I don't want to talk much about my dad right now. I explained to her that he's been hiding. I also managed to explain to her that I'm planning on escaping when they force us into the arena, "So run it by me again, how you plan to get out of here."

"I'm going to steal the transport they put us on after the fight. After that, I'm going to take the train, drive it back here, pile it up with convicted Ravens, and drive it out," I explain for the second time.

"You do realize how crazy that is, right?" she says skeptically. Oh ye have little faith.

"Who ever told you I was sane?" I say, smiling. She smiles too, enjoying my lame joke. "Can I go to sleep now? What time is it anyway?" She looks over at a clock on a nightstand. When did we get one of those?

"Late enough. Sleep sounds good. We got sweats in the drawer over there," she nods her head, "Don't know who brought them, but they're here."

"Weird," I say. Rose hops off the bed and goes to grab whatever was brought for her. Once she has it, she goes into the bathroom to change. I go to grab my sweats as well. I, being my awkward self, change in the middle of the room. I pull my things out of my pockets. I don't know how somebody got in here without either of us knowing—or without Rose knowing anyway, I haven't been here all day—but if they decide to come back, I don't want them to get their hands on my gear. I try hiding everything under my pillow. It's a good idea, given that nothing will break. I'm optimistic. Sky Iron is unbelievably strong, and my phone has taken so much abuse already, this is nothing.

I'm standing next to my bed, my clothes crumpled in a corner, wearing sweatpants, shoving my stuff under my pillow when Rose comes out of the bathroom. She's wearing sweatpants and a tank top, her normal clothes folded neatly tucked under her arm. She doesn't look like she tries at all, but still, she looks amazing.

"Hiding your stuff?" She asks me. I suddenly remember that my hand is under my pillow. I quickly pull it out and hold my wrist, embarrassed.

"Yeah," I say, "I thought that if they were able to get past you to deliver clothes, they'd be able to get in and take my things."

"Good thinking," she says, kind of making fun of me. "We wouldn't want them to steal your useless phone." She still doesn't know I have my sword. Probably best to keep it that way, "Anyway, I'm going to bed. Night," she says, flicking off the lights and jumping in bed. Probably a good idea. I do only have a week to plan on how to perform my first—or I guess second, but the first one wasn't my idea—jailbreak ever.

I go under the covers of the bed that I stashed my stuff in. I lie awake for a short while because I know that what I'm going to have to do to get out is really going to suck. Eventually, I find sleep.

The now familiar dreams of people talking visits me again, but just like last night, it's different. If all this change is good or bad, I don't know. This time, instead of the usual curtain of black, I can see a room. It's an eloquent sitting room; something that someone on the Surface who has more than enough money to help the rest of us out would have. A fireplace is warmly burning with a gigantic portrait of someone above the mantle. It's an oil painting of a powerful looking man dressed in a grey suit sitting in an expensive looking chair. The guy has a haircut that screams pompous and expensive. I think this guy has too much money for his own good.

"Loser," I try to say, but no words come out of my mouth. I try to raise my hand to cover my mouth as a reaction, but as I bring my hand up, it fazes in and out of reality. *What the heck?* I play with my hands and fingers. Half the time they're there, half the time, they're not. Weird. While I'm playing with my fingers, two people walk into the room.

"The boy is alive, Sir. We must act now," says the smaller of the two. He is wearing a suit and tie. I recognize his voice. He's one of the voices that I normally hear in my dreams. That sounds weird. That must make the other, the taller of the two, the other voice. He looks almost exactly like the painting. He even has the same grey suit on. There's a flower tucked into his suit jacket pocket.

"And what is it you suggest we do?" This is starting to get interesting.

"Questions will be asked if we stray from the once a week. He will either fight and win, or have him brought here before the others return when he loses. The boy will be ours one way or another. Now, what of the four?" And there goes the interesting. Right out the figurative window. The scene suddenly freezes as the two men are midway through sitting down. Maybe it's still interesting after all.

"I thought it was you," says a voice next to me. I turn and see the guy that I fought with in the arena a month and a half ago. The guy that was assigned Number One. I jump away, fazing in and out as I move. Still not used to that. "The name's Armando," he says to me.

"Sam," I say in return, "Is this a trap?"

"No," he says simply. "I'm in my right mind for now." I give him a confused look so he explains, "Sometimes they have control over me. Being the backseat driver in your own head is not an experience I would recommend."

"What do you mean 'control over you?'" I ask, still confused.

"It's like they put thoughts in my head for me. They keep trying to install an A.I. so that they can have complete control and give the A.I. a body. Crazy, right?" I laugh nervously.

"Yeah, crazy," he shrugs.

"Anyway, that's how I can talk to you." He didn't tell me much of anything about that, but I choose not to point that out. "I have to tell you something important." He pauses and shakes his head, like he's trying to clear his thoughts. "You need to get out of here." No duh.

"What do you think I'm doing?" I ask in response, "I'll be in the arena next week and I'll get out." He puts a hand up to stop me from continuing.

"Don't tell me any more," he says, "It's most important that you get out, but if you can, try and take me with you. I'll be fighting against you in the arena once again."

"So you do remember that. You gave me one heck of a beating."

"Sorry about that," he says, actually sounding a little sorry. Shocker, telling the truth, "I was fighting for control the entire time."

"Got it," I say, "Why are they trying to control you, by the way?" I ask. He looks like he's about to say something, but before he can, he starts grunting in pain and clawing at his head.

"Not the time," he says hastily, breathing heavily all of a sudden, "Got to get you out of here. I'm going to lock you out for now. Good luck." A wall of pressure rams into me, pushing me back. As soon as I lose my footing and fly back, I disintegrate, and find blackness. Quiet sleep.

The next week feels like twenty. I try and act as "normal" as I can, but the entire time I'm figuring out exactly what I'm going to do. At the same time, I'm trying to find Ravens. I actually do find some of them. Some say that Rick and Fred already got to them. Good. I guess we're making good progress. I don't know just how big this place is though, so I might be judging way off.

I do my best to explain to my entire group what the plan is. For the most part they all listen intently, and drink it all in. Luckily, my entire group I was arrested with is all Ravens. Some of them are skeptics, but there are always a few like that in the bunch. Lameos.

Either by a random, excellent miracle, or my paranoia, I manage to keep all my things with me. That's good because the sword is more than likely going to end up an important part of this escape. The last day of the supposed week I was given starts off as any of the other days that I had to impatiently wait through. Around noon, I start to get a little discouraged that anything is going to happen today.

"So what now?" Rose asks me, "I didn't sleep all night." I give her a look that says "Why?" I know. I'm talented at looks. She just shrugs like she doesn't have a clue.

"I don't know," I say, "I guess we have to keep waiting and hope that something happens." Rose sighs and plops down onto one of the beds. She puts her hands on her stomach and closes her eyes.

"Waiting is fine," she says. I've only known her for a week, so I can't tell if she's being serious, or if she is ready to run the circumference of the building. I know I'm ready to do the latter. While I'm deciding how much of a running start I'm going to need to be able to run up the side of a building without Dac's help, there's a knock on the door.

I open the door and there are three New Power officers standing there. Electrical staffs in hand. If I get tased now, the plan might fall apart. I don't know whether to feel excited or depressed that they're here. Probably excited. It means that I'm being thrown into the arena. I hope.

Did you ever think you would say that to yourself? Dac says mentally.

Not in a million years. I admit. It's crazy how things like that can change when you're planning on using it to escape.

"It's time to come with us," says the New Power soldier at the tip of the triangle facing us says, "Your trial shall begin shortly." When this guy stops talking, the one to my right speaks up.

"We have been told to bring those with experience early. So that they may have the first selection." Uh oh. I look over my shoulder and see that Rose doesn't even look like she has heard them. Is that good or bad?

"So are we going now?" I ask.

"Yes," says the one in the front.

"When are the others coming?" I ask. I don't want to end up being the only one there. I have to get the others out.

"They will follow approximately ten minutes after the veterans have departed," the one in the front says with a monotone voice. "It is time to go now. Please, follow us." Knowing that this is what I have to do, I willingly follow them. Before I go, I turn back over my shoulder, and look at Rose.

"I'll see you soon," I say. I wait for a response, but give up shortly when I see that she has fallen asleep. I shut the door to my room—cell—behind me quietly, so that she could have ten more minutes of piece before walking into a shit storm. Given that a prison isn't exactly the most peaceful place to begin with.

I'm walked through this building, through the prison. I remain silent, trying to act like this isn't all a part of the plan, more or less. As far as the plan goes, I have point A and point B. The details are still a little fuzzy.

In some scheduled corner of the prison, there is a transport ship waiting. It looks just like the one that I was put on when I first came up here. For all I know, it's the same exact one. It's already stocked with a crew, so I guess my escorts won't be joining me.

"Please," one of them says, "board the ship." I do just that. I prepare to act shocked that I get locked in place, but what's actually shocking, is that they don't. Is this because I already fought before, or is it because since it's only me, they don't think anything will happen. Whatever the reason, I'm not restrained more than I have to be, and I'm glad for that. Without anyone saying another word to each other, the ship starts to lift off. The three guards that escorted me start walking back to the center of the prison when I'm taking off, probably to get more of my group to fight. Once the ship I'm on has enough altitude, we head off.

I'm heading back into the arena.

Chapter Twenty-Two

The ride to the arena feels longer than before. It might be because I started farther from it. I don't know if that's true though. Don't exactly remember what section of sky I started in last time. Clouds are not good reference points. It might feel longer because I know what I'm getting myself into this time. Last time when I went in, I fought to not get nailed; this time, I know that I'm going to have to. This sucks. After awhile, the ship dips down into the clouds like it did last time. I don't bother asking any of the goons any questions because I have a feeling they'll be very uninformative. I'm still ready to scream from before when nobody gave me any answers.

We travel in the clouds for a time. I can't decide if this is to make things more frightening for the fighters, or to hide us while people file into the arena. Probably the second. Eventually we spot the massive tower of an underbelly of the arena. This is the only platform I've seen, other than maybe the prison that has this huge of an underside. It was probably added on as a backdoor and prep room for the combatants. It likely doesn't serve any other purpose.

You've changed, Dac says in my head.

What do you mean by that? I may have gotten a little taller, but that's nothing, I return.

Not physically, Dac says, irritated, *emotionally. From what I've seen in your memories, you were about ready to wet yourself last time you were here. Now look at you. You're analyzing the stupid thing!* He does have a point, *It's creepy, man. Seeing these little changes in you.*

I'm still me, I think back defensively.

I know you are, he says calmly. *It's just interesting to see the change.*

I guess you do have a point, I think back, conceding the point. Now that I think about it, I have changed a lot. I'm still me, but different. It's a little scary, but also really cool.

You're still your same, crazy self though, Dac says. Of course he has to have the last word and ruin my little moment of elation. It's good to know that even though I'm a little different, I'm still me though.

The ship pulls up to one of the docks running along the height of the spike beneath the arena. Like last time, two guards stand waiting. They are both fully decked out in the New Power black armor with a red stripe.

315

Both have their helmets on with their visors down so I can't see more than half of their faces. I step off my transport without having to be shoved by anybody for once and follow behind the two new guys acting as my guards. The ship I came on flies off, like it did last time. It's probably going to go pick up more people from the prison.

The New Power may think that I'm being cooperative and submissive, but that's just not who I am. That kind of stuff gets boring after a while.

The hallway I'm walked through is dimly lit. The lights reflect off the floor as I walk, their shine only interrupted when someone passes over them. Other than the lights' soft, barely noticeable hum, the only sound permeating the hall is the clacking of footsteps. When the hall ends, I find myself in a familiar large, white circular room. Against the walls is a weapons rack with only the handles of the electrical sabers. There's also the bin full of backpacks with additional gear, and the clothing rack for lameos. Seeing the armor for a second time, it resembles the New Power armor. Slightly less padded and with no red stripe, but still, they look similar. In the center of the room is the circular platform that actually raises people up into the arena. Kind of hate that thing.

"Choose your weapon," one of my guards orders me. "Because you are a veteran you may observe what each weapon is." Easy enough. I walk over to the weapons rack and pick one up. I flick it on to see what it is. I've been playing with the one I stole long enough that I have no issue finding the 'on' switch. The one that I randomly chose is a large scythe like Arthur's. No thank you, I don't feel like following in those footsteps.

I switch off the electrical scythe and put it back on the shelf. I pull another one off and it turns out to be a spear. The spear from end to end is a little taller than I am, but being unable to move my hands from the small handle, it won't work so well. I put that back too. I keep pulling out different weapons for the fun of it. I'm tempted to take a whip I come across, but decide against. Unless I have a stool, a coat, a top hat and a lion to go with that whip, I don't need it. When I get bored of seeing the different shapes of weapons, I pull off one that looks identical to the one I have. I flick it on. The blade is about the same as my Sky Iron sword.

"There we go," I say to myself.

"Select your additional equipment," says the same guard as a moment ago. I know I'm not wearing one of those stupid jumpsuits, so I walk over to the bin of backpacks. The first one I pick up has the shield and weird needle in it again. I set it to the side in case the other one is even more useless.

The second backpack I pick up has different gear in it. It has five little electrically charged knives in it.

"Is this a lethal round?" I ask the guards.

"Yet to be determined," one says emotionlessly. I consider asking them to explain the knives, but I decide against. They could probably be very useful. I close the backpack and sling it over my shoulder.

"I'm done," I say, "Is it time to go yet?"

"No," says a guard.

"When then?"

"Soon."

"How soon?" They remain silent. So that's how it's going to be.

I want to throw something at them, but I don't want to aggravate them. If they attack me now—if they electrocute me—I don't know if I'm going to be able to get up when I need to. It's a long shot to begin with; I don't need my odds to get any worse. Fighting the urge to hurl these idiots off the side of a platform, I walk over to the wall and lean against it. After a few minutes and a few bitten-off nails later, one of the guards speaks.

"Get on the platform." Instead of waiting for them to threaten to stop my heart with electricity like last time, I step on the platform. I inspect around my feet to make sure I'm standing where it will rise up. Seconds after my inspection is complete, the platform begins to rise. Soon the white room and guards are gone, left below as I'm lifted into the arena.

The white of the previous room is replaced by a

seemingly endless tunnel of black. Around me on all four sides at specific intervals are dim lights, providing the only source of illumination in here. As the lift drags on, I feel my chest welling up. All my anxiety from when I first entered the arena returning to me. My resolve falters for an instant, the panic too much for me to handle. I really think I'm losing it when I start to hear a low thrumming. It takes me all of a second to realize that it's the crowd cheering. I straighten up and take in deep gulps of air.

I must have started down lower this time than I did before because this trip feels like it's taking longer. The cheering gets louder, more definite. A hole opens above me, pouring light into the dark tunnel.

As the platform reaches the end of its journey, I'm thrown into a realm of light. Blinding light. I throw my hands in front of my face to try and block it out. I squint and lean back as if I can shy back into shadows. My plan for getting out is seeming stupider and stupider as I go. I must have been temporarily insane when I thought it was a good idea to get electrocuted!

"And here they are!" Yells the announcer. The crowd roars with approval. It's the same announcer as the last time I was here. Too bad. I was kind of, maybe a little bit, hoping that he would fall off a platform. Sure, I let that go a while back, but I was angry for a bit. I'm over it now. Mostly.

The crowd cheers continue, clearly excited that the show is about to begin. "Thirty-three new contestants are here joining us for this week's match up," continues the announcer, "Thirty-one of them are prison filth. At least they're a new batch." The crowd's cheer increases in intensity again, like they're excited that new people are in here and about to fight each other.

Thirty-one? I guess they're not putting all of us in here at once after all.

I scan the crowd for Rose, but I don't see her anywhere. The entire group I was delivered to prison with is standing around, dazed and confused. Fear on all of their faces. Maybe it's good that she's not here, that way she won't have to get hit by one of the beam weapons. It's not pleasant. I can personally testify to that.

"One of our competitors is a long time veteran. He takes his same number, as always, Number One!" Calls the announcer to rally up the crowd, interrupting my thoughts. While scanning the arena, I spot Armando. He's glaring at me like a bull wanting nothing more than to gorge me on its horns. Guess he's not in control then, "Our final entry is a brave, valiant soldier from the New Power that specifically *asked* to be put into this fight! You hear that folks, one of our soldiers giving the filth such an honor by fighting them." Real honor alright. I have no idea who the idiot is, but I know that quite a few

320

people are going to go after him, me, primarily, being one of them. Why would I pass up an opportunity to beat up a New Power goon and not get in trouble?

You were kind of sent to prison for fighting one. You're still technically an inmate, And there goes Dac; ruining my mood. He's right though. He usually is, I just don't listen.

"What'll it be, judges?" Continues the announcer, totally inconsiderate about the fact that he interrupted my conversation with Dac. I'm insane, aren't I?

Oh most definately, Dac says. I mentally growl at him. It doesn't work so well. He laughs at me.

"We know it will have to be a battle royal, but will there be blood?" Geeze, not this again.

"Unless you plan on cleaning it up yourself, no." The entire crowd boo's the judge that says that.

"Aw, come on!" Complains the announcer, "We haven't seen blood in a long while. Make the match more *exciting*!" Please don't.

"Quiet, you pansy," Ah, I knew there was something I liked about this guy. He's the same announcer that argued with the stupid one last time I was here. This is good. I have somebody to make fun of him for me, "I don't have the time to waste on such foolishness. I have a train to catch in twenty minutes. I have to be out of here and ready in fifteen." Did he just?

"Poo. Alrightty then folks, are you ready?" Calls the

announcer, getting a loud cheer from the crowd, even though they were told no blood.

"Ten!" People start lighting up, hums of electricity chaining through the arena.

"Nine!" Gasps echo through the group waiting within the arena.

"Eight!" My old number. I wonder if it's the same again.

"Seven!" Armando glares at me, ready to kill me. I lock gazes with him, unwavering.

"Six!"

"Five!"

"Four!"

"Three!"

"Two!"

"One!" And we're off. Unlike last time, I immediately flick on my electric sword and start running. By the time the others are starting to figure out how to turn their swords on and chaos is just starting to erupt around me, Armando and I are already breathing down each other's throats and clashing swords. I'm sure of my footing, doing more than just defending, I'm pushing back. I'm attacking. Sparks are coming off of both of our electrical weapons, like they're trying to stay together after the intense impacts.

"Numbers Eight and One straight off against each other," calls the announcer with an erupting crowd behind him. How did I know I'd be eight again? Without any room for error, Armando and I fight. He'll push against me, and I'll push back just as hard. The rest of the fighters ignore us, or are too busy to pay attention to us, as they all fight their own battles. I see glimpses of Rose from time to time, but I can't afford to look away and try to help her out. I need to stay focused on Armando.

He's a tough fighter, but I'm just as good. Every now and then we need to break off from each other for a moment to defend ourselves from incoming attackers. I try to keep track of how much time has passed in my head, but I can't focus on it and keep losing track. It seems like Armando and I can go on like this forever, but something happens.

Armando loses his concentration. The look in his eyes and the determination to try to nail me vanishes for a moment. It comes back a second later, but it keeps fazing in and out. Armando is fighting for control. I use this to my advantage and push harder than before. Even though he is fighting the control, he still defends himself from my attacks. Finally, I'm able to get a hit in and slash him. One hit is all I need. The electric weapon passes through his abdomen, effectively ending his fight.

Before he blacks out, Armando smiles and says to me, "Good luck," with that, he face-plants the floor.

"Number One goes down! Number One goes down!"

Screams the announcer in disbelief. I feel like I should probably be insulted, but I'm not sure. "Never had it even crossed my mind that this would happen, but our current champion has fallen!" Instead of cheering, the crowd is silent in disbelief.

I quickly scan the arena. I don't take note of any faces, but I see that less than half of the people that we started with are still standing. Dust is kicked up everywhere and the floor is littered with stunned fighters. I feel a little sorry for them. They didn't do anything to deserve this.

While I have a moment without any peering eyes because of the dust, I take out one of the knives from my backpack and shove it in my boot. There's a little pouch on the inside designed specifically for this purpose. I straighten up when I hear someone near by.

"You!" A very angry voice calls from the dust. Someone comes charging out at me with their weapon lowered like they're trying to skewer me. I consider letting them because I need to go down, but I decide against when I realize that it's that idiot that tried to kill me on the prison transport. My heart dropped when I had to hurt Armando and all the others, but this guy, I have no issue hurting him.

I roll out of the way of his charge, slicing his legs as I go. I'm tempted to use my Sky Iron sword, but I don't think he deserves that. Even though he was willing to knock all my teeth out and make a necklace of them, he still doesn't— well, maybe he does deserve it, but it's too late now.

He curses at me, no doubt a huge pain lashing through his legs, as he falls to the ground. He tries to get up, only to fail. He tries another time, failing again, but this time he manages to slice his arm on the way down. He groans in pain.

"Dude," I say, "just give up."

"Never," he spits at me, "I will *not* be defeated by *trash* like you! You are trash! You are *trash*! YOU ARE TRA-..." I slice him with the electric blade just to shut him up. He lies silent, probably still screaming at me inside his head until he blacks out.

I straighten up, ready to keep going. I've taken down the two best fighters in here. The rest shouldn't be too hard.

"Thirty-Three is down!" Screams the announcer, noticing what I just did. "This is incredible! Number Eight is on a rampage. Let's see if he can keep it up any longer. With only seven competitors left, will Eight make it all the way?" Yes... No. Wait, maybe, I'm not allowed to win. That'll blow everything. If there are only seven of us, "Nineteen goes down!" six of us left, I'll be pushing it, but I'm going to try to take someone else down. I try and spot one of the weaker fighters, but before I can do anything, someone runs me through with their sword. I look down and see the blade sticking through my stomach. Even though I know it won't kill me, it's still not a good sight. I don't enjoy seeing a sword protruding out of any part of me. It's just a *tiny* bit nerve-wracking.

"Good luck," Rose whispers in my ear as she pulls the beam sword out of my gut. I shiver as it leaves my body.

"Eight goes down!" I hear the announcer yell with a roaring crowd behind him. I fall to the floor as a numbness spreads through my body. It doesn't hurt as bad as last time. It feels more like a familiar, dull sensation.

When I hit the ground, I'm still maintaining consciousness to a degree, and my battle with myself to stay on the edge of consciousness begins.

Chapter
Twenty-Three

It doesn't take long after I go down for the fight to reach its conclusion. It feels like forever to me. Lying here, unable to move or even open my eyes, it's torture. The only way I can hazard a guess that it's over is because I hear the announcer. I can't hear him though. It's almost like I'm listening underwater. Whatever. I'm not exactly doing normal stuff. It's not my place to judge any level of weirdness.

It feels like an out of body experience. I'm vaguely aware that a giant something lands right next to me, and that I'm being lifted onto it. That's about all I know. When I'm set down, not too gently, a waiting game begins. A miniature battle in my own head begins. I'm trying to wake up. I'm normally an early riser. Maybe that contributed. I don't know what it is, but I do know that I can't afford to stay down as long as I did the first time.

Another couple minutes pass and still, there's

nothing I can do. I'm stuck. Well, so far this isn't working. I stop pushing as hard after a while because I think I've missed the train. Somewhere, I hear someone speak.

"Crossing over tracks in approximately one minute." It takes me about half that time to figure out what's said. As soon as I do understand, I don't need to push, my eyes just pop open, and it's like waking up. I sit up and look around me. I see all thirty-two of the other fighters as well as two people flying this beast. Can't I throw just one of the fighters out the door? That would make life so much better. It would make me happy.

One of the New Power goons flying this thing turns around and sees me. "One's awake," he says, hitting the other pilot's shoulder with the back of his hand. I stand up and start walking toward the flight controls and the two pilots. I'm still dizzy, but I can limp.

"So deal with him," the driver says lazily, not turning around. The one who spotted me gets out of his chair and starts walking toward me. There's something different about his armor. It's still the same material, and he has the normal helmet on but instead of a vertical red stripe, this armor has a horizontal one. It starts mid-chest, wraps around to the left, and ends at the armpit.

"Sit back down," he commands me, poorly hiding the fear in his voice. I swear he's shaking, but that might be my eyes, still slightly out of focus.

"Or what?" I ask.

"Or I'll make you," he tries to say menacingly. I pull out my Sky Iron sword and point it at him.

"Go for it," I say calmly, sure he's not going to do anything. My cockiness is rewarded. He puts his hands up in defeat.

"Look, man, I don't even like the New Power. I just need to make a living. I have a family!" He's legitimately freaking out. I guess I'm getting better at bluffing. Maybe too good.

"Look," I say, "I'm not going to hurt you. I just need to get back out there." I'm probably going to regret telling him some of that, but right now, I'm not concerned.

"You- you're not going to hurt me?" he asks with a stutter, still clearly afraid.

"Not unless you attack me. All I'm trying to do is steal this ship," I pause, considering just how stupid I am, "And then the train."

You really need to learn to stop telling everybody your plans. Dac points out.

I know, I essentially whine back, *I'll work on it later. Right now, I'm hoping it helps us out.*

The guy I'm at a standoff with looks like he's running through thoughts and possibilities in his head.

You're about to say something stupid, aren't you? Asks Dac. I ignore him.

"You're welcome to come with us you know," I say.

Yup. Says Dac plainly in my head. It's not the dumbest thing I've ever said. The guy I'm talking to visibly relaxes a bit.

"Really?" he asks, slightly hopeful. I nod my head.

"You're different than the other goons," I say. "You haven't achieved zombie status yet." It's true. The guy laughs and turns to his friend.

"It's okay, he's not going to hurt us."

"I heard," the driver says, "he's just hijacking the ship. We're going to have to do what he says." The one that I was talking to turns back to me.

"Are we going to have to do what you say?" Is this seriously a concern right now?

"Uh, not if you don't want to. As long as you don't fight me or call for backup, I can work with it. It might help if you fly this to where I need you to though." Honesty worked a moment ago, why wouldn't it again. The one standing up looks like he can't come to a decision and is stumbling to find words, so the one that is still sitting down speaks for him.

"Whatever, we'll land on the train."

"Works for me," I say.

"Hold on," the driver says as the ship lurches to the side.

"What's going on?" I ask, putting my hand up against a wall to make sure I don't fall. The dizziness is enough. I don't need the floor being uneven to help me fall over. At least the dizziness is starting to go away. The adrenaline from the first time this happened probably prevented me from noticing it, but this time there isn't anything major going on. Yet.

"It's nothing," the pilot says. "Just a sharp turn. Nobody's shooting at us."

"Why would somebody shot us?" I ask before I can help it. I'm not so sure I want to know.

"Take a wild guess," the pilot says. "We're trying to land on the train. That's breaking more than a few rules."

"Right," I say. The guy still flying hit a button by his head. A large door on the side of the ship opens up. All I can hear primarily is the wind tearing through the transport. People's clothes start whipping around and papers go flying. Still, nobody else wakes up.

It feels like I'm reliving a memory. Like the first time I was broken out of the arena. I took everyone—*nearly* everyone—with me then, and I'm breaking out even more now. Biggest difference is that this time, I'm leading the escape. I'm not a piece in someone else's plan. I'm both the director and the man on the frontlines.

An overhead speaker crackles. I see that the pilot has something in his hand that controls the intercom, "I'm going to get you close. Jump off and disable any defenses. We'll land once it's clear." I try yelling something back at him, but because of the wind, it doesn't carry far enough. The other guy notices I'm trying to say something and comes closer.

"What?" He yells when he's right in front of me, trying to be heard over the wind.

"How can I be sure you're going to land?" I ask, also yelling to be heard.

"Trust us. We'll be down in a flash."

"Alright," I yell, "What kind of defenses are there?"

"Probably none, but you still need to clear a landing zone." Easy enough. The overhead crackles again, signaling the pilot's about to say something.

"Matching speeds with the train. Get ready to jump," The one I'm standing next to gives me a nod. I walk to the opening in the hangar. Even though a small ramp is made by the opened door, instead of climbing out on it, I stay at the main part of the hull where the door hinges are. I'm holding onto the ceiling of the transport to make sure I don't fall before I want to.

The train must be four-hundred yards long! Cargo litters the top of it, looking like it's placed strategically so that there is still a passage to walk though. There's no top on the train except for the very front car that controls this beast. I notice a few Sky Bikes along the edge. I don't see many New Power goons on it, but that doesn't mean there aren't any. The train isn't following any lain down track, but it does seem to be on a set course.

Somehow, I notice the most important part last. I'm still fifty feet in the air! "I'm insane, aren't I?" I ask myself out loud. I don't say it loud enough for either of the two people that are awake on here to hear me.

Without a doubt, Dac responds to my rhetorical question.

Gee, thanks, I'm pretty sure I knew the answer, but it never hurts to have someone else tell you as well.

No problem.

I take a deep breath before doing something relatively stupid. I let go of the transport and leap off it. I involuntarily scream on the way down. It's not a high, girly scream. It's more of a manly "what am I doing" scream. Before I hit the transport, I activate Dac to slow my fall. Even though the deceleration helps, I still manage to land on a crate pretty hard.

"Ow," I say standing up. The crate I landed on, partially broken. When I get to my feet, a sharp pain lances through my side, "That's going to hurt tomorrow." At least I finally got that adrenalin boost I needed to shake the dizziness off. All I had to do was take a short skydiving lesson. Easy. I hop off the crate, stumbling when I hit the ground.

I look around to see if there are any New Power goons around. I'm hoping my flying-with-some-style stunt went unnoticed, but I'm not feeling too optimistic. I look above me and see that the transport is still there. I guess I can trust these guys so far.

I try and signal for them to come down, but I don't have any way to communicate with them. Maybe we should've thought about this before I jumped. I start waving my arms around, doing a goofy dance, trying to tell them that this is a safe spot. I know that they're probably laughing at me, but it does the trick. The ship starts lowering to the spot where I'm standing. It occurs to me only as they get really close that I should probably get out of the way.

I scramble away from the squish zone to safety. When the transport lands, or more precisely, crash-lands, there's little wreckage to be seen. The ship itself doesn't look too bad, other than the cockpit, but I don't think it'll be flying any time soon. The landing gear is obliterated, the ramp to the interior is lying a couple feet away. Luckily, it doesn't look like anybody's hurt, but none of them have woken up yet. Oh well, they'll just be sore when they do get up. The two guys that are in the New Power but want to quit step into view. They look okay for the most part. The pilot's entire suit has cracks on it. His visor is half missing from his helmet. My guess is that he hit his head, and everything else, when they crashed. The pilot is supporting the other guy. He is missing a good chunk of the right side of his suit.

I'm tempted to hold up a large sign with a nine on it, but sadly I'm lacking the sign all together. Instead, I choose to lean against a crate, holding my side. I'm still holding something. The two ex-New Power guys practically carry each other over to me.

"Amazing," the old pilot says, "You jump out of the ship and you look no worse for wear. We protect ourselves inside, and we only manage to avoid death thanks to these suits." I give a half-laugh.

"I'm glad I'm not against you," says the one with a giant hole in his suit, "You're one tough kid to kill."

"What can I say," other than that, "I'm not complaining." The one with a hole in his armor laughs for a second, but quickly stops. I can tell his side hurts because he sucks in a breath of air between his teeth. He's grabbing his side where the hole in his armor is, "What happened?" I ask.

"We were both in the cockpit," the pilot explains, "he took the worst of it."

"He took the worst?" I ask, not totally believing it. "You look like you went through a blender." He shrugs like it's nothing.

"I got hit all over. The suit took the majority of it. Most of the damage to him was done to his side. Got through the armor like it was nothing." The one with a hole groans again.

"It's nothing. I'm okay," he says, coughing.

"Doesn't look like 'nothing.' Sit down before you end up hurting yourself even worse." Somehow, he manages to laugh at me.

"Never thought I'd be taking orders from a kid. Never thought I'd break so many rules in one day either." The one with a hole in his suit says. His friend gently sets him down at the crates while I go back to the transport to check on everyone. Luckily, even though the ramp is gone, the landing gear went with it. I don't need to climb up anything to get inside. Once inside I can assess the damage better than before. Parts of this thing are falling apart. Some of the people who were in the arena have fallen out of the beds. I pick up those who are on the floor and put them back in their beds. Some are quite a bit heavier than I expected.

After I have everyone back in their beds, I happen to find some restraints that look like they either come from a mental hospital, or one of the test facilities on the Surface. Odd, but convenient. I try not to let any repressed memories from years ago creep into my mind, but there are some I can't help. I shiver with the thought, and shake off the memories. I don't want them to haunt me any more. I strap down Armando. I don't have anything against him, but he told me that the majority of the time, he's not in control of himself. I make sure to restrain anything that he could use to try and get out.

After that, I have a little more fun. I go over to the New Power creep. I restrain him as well, but I also happen to blind fold and gag him. I don't feel like hearing him call me trash again. It's not a very nice thing to say. I punch him in the gut. He doesn't wake up. I like him this way. Can I keep it?

I turn to return to the guys outside, but before I leave the ruined transport, I see a chunk of armor crushed between two large pieces of metal in the cockpit. That would explain why the one guy is so hurt. I don't try and take it with me. I leave it there and walk back to the two guys outside. They're both sitting on the floor, one breathing harder than the other.

"How much longer until we reach the prison?" I ask. As much fun as doing nothing is, I'm getting impatient. It's not even that I've done nothing. The wrecked transport is proof of that.

"Probably ten, fifteen minutes. Why?" responds the less damaged of the two.

"I'm going to have to welcome everybody aboard. After that, the tricky part is that I've got to turn this thing around." From what I've heard, the back of this thing is what opens to the prison. I'm going to have to clear that, then sprint the length of the train to get to the engine room before anyone can stop us. Fun.

"That's not that difficult," says the one with the cracked armor, "All you do is flip a switch."

"Can you get there?" I ask. Maybe I won't have to become the world record holder for longest sprint with the most on the line.

"Probably, but I don't know about him," he nods his head towards his friend sitting next to him. I squat down so that I'm eye level with him, or visor level, whatever.

"I saw your missing armor piece," I say, "I know it hurts, but you're going to get out of this." Am I really trying to comfort someone from the New Power? I haven't seen this one do any wrong and he wants out so I guess he's an alright guy, "I've seen something like this before." I can see through the visor that he's looking into my eyes, and starting to get a little teary. I can tell that right here, right now, he's putting all the hope he has on me. He's afraid that he's going to die, "The kid didn't have any armor to help him out, but he still made it. One of the worst experiences he has had in his entire life, but he's still here." I can see that he heard exactly what he wanted to. Relief floods his eyes, but he doesn't physically relax at all. Probably because of the pain. I just gave this guy his life. Not directly, but I told him that he's not going to die. "Why don't you go hide in the transport. It's probably safer there." I'm not sure why he thought he was going to die. There were plenty of worse injuries in the factories on the Surface, and those kids didn't get any chance to stop and rest. Just a moment to scream before going back to work. He looks alright, but it might be worse than I can tell.

"Ya. You're probably right." The guy with a hole in his armor says, "Can somebody help me over there?" Both the other guy and I help him limp into the broken down transport. It probably could be better if we just left him here, but I am dead set on not leaving anybody behind. It's a part of who I am.

"Are you going to be okay if we leave you here?" I ask the guy after we lie him down in the bed I was in.

"Will you be coming back for me?" He asks us.

"Unless I'm dead, yes," I say. I know it sounds grim, but it's the truth. I don't have any plans of dying though, so I'm pretty sure I'll be back.

"Then I'll be just fine," he says. The other ex-New Power guy and I leave him there and go outside.

"If I go to the back of the train to clear it for everybody coming on, will you head to the front and be ready to turn this thing around?" I ask. He looks over at me. His eye is a crazy brown that looks like there are a few other colors mixed in to help create it. It also looks like he probably broke his nose, but he isn't complaining.

"Yes, but how will I know when it's time? I won't exactly be able to see you dancing around again." Good point. At least we're being thorough this time.

"Do you have a radio inside your helmet?" I ask, "If there are other New Power goons, I can steal one of their helmets and use the radio in one of those." He raises his visible eyebrow.

"You won't be able to do it. You don't have any of the passwords," he rubs his chin in thought, "Do you have a working cell phone?"

"Actually, I do," I say, pulling my phone out of my pocket. I turn it on and see that I still have at least a fourth of my battery, as well as some service.

"Do you have any service?" He asks me right after it turns on and I see that I do.

"Yes. Is there some number I can call to connect to your helmet?" He nods. Well, that's convenient. I see the marketing now. Helmet phone, it's a phone and a helmet; your kids will love it. Super glue it to their heads and they will be forced to answer your obsessed calls at any time. Actually, maybe it's not such a good idea.

"Give me your phone," he says. I hand it to him and he starts punching in a bunch of numbers. When he's done he saves it under my contacts. "Name it," he says so that I'll be able to find it again. I try to come up with something serious, but I can't resist. I put the number down as Helmet Phone, "Call me either when it's time to go and everybody is onboard, or if something goes horribly wrong."

"Can you at least try to be optimistic?" I ask, "I'm the only one that's allowed to have occasional pessimism." There goes all credibility I have of being serious for the moment.

"Fine, I'll leave the role of being a pessimist to you. I'm going to try and get to the head of the train, we're almost there."

"Works for me. I should probably get to the back then." I jerk my thumb over me shoulder.

"Alright, good luck," he says to me before turning and jogging toward the head of the train.

"A lot of people have been saying that," I say to myself. "I hope I don't let anyone down." With that, I too, take my leave and head toward the end of the train.

I find that unlike the odd opening in the cargo that we found, the pathway between crates is like a maze. It's not hard to get lost in, but there are a lot of twists and turns that I'm forced to take. Strangely, I don't run into any New Power on my way to the back of the train. I peer off the side of the train and see that the prison is almost literally right in front of us. The train still needs to get all the way there, and then turn around. I guess that means I better hurry. I start rushing through the crates, still careful to make as little noise as possible, and check every corner before I turn.

I come to this short alley made by crates that runs perpendicular to the train. I'm guessing this has to be the last bit before the end. From what I've seen by peering over the edge whenever I get a chance, this has to be all that's left. I creep around the last crate in this row, pushing my body up against it so that if there is someone, they won't see me. It's a good thing I did that, because there are a couple New Power goons standing there. I quickly jump back behind the crate to avoid being seen.

I only put my head around the crate to count the guys. From what I see there's only three of them. All of them are armed, but still, it's only three. I can take them. Subconsciously, while analyzing the situation, I drew my sword at full length. Well, I guess I'm ready.

I sneak out from behind the crate. I manage to get behind one of the guys without being noticed. I shrink my sword to dagger size. I cover the goon's mouth I'm behind with my hand and put the dagger to his throat. I start walking him backwards so that I can get him away from the others. Once I have him behind the crates, I hit him in the head with the dagger's hilt. I catch him before he can fall loudly, and gently place him on the floor. I go back out to get one of the others the same way. I forget to cover his mouth first, and he manages to say something before I can cover it. His outburst and friend turning around startle me and I let go. Before I know it, both of them are facing me with sharp, electrical objects drawn.

"What are you doing here?" The one I didn't grab asks me.

"Great," I mumble to myself, pissed that I'm such an

idiot. I mean really, who wouldn't have covered their mouth first. I thought I've watched enough movies to know better by now, "I'm here to do… something," I say.

At least you didn't give everything *away. You were just much lamer this time,* Dac says supportively.

Oh shut up, I say. I love our relationship. Back and forth belittling comments, it's great. Loads of fun.

"I must insist that you cease and desist from whatever it is that you are doing." The same guy says to me.

"Nah," I say, elongating my sword.

You just love fights, don't you? Dac asks. I choose not to respond.

"We don't have to do this," I say to them, even though I'm ready to kick their butts, "Just roll over and play dead. Nobody needs to get hurt."

"Coward!" One of them yells at me. Oh it's on. I rush at the one that called me a coward. He gets his baton-like object up in time so that I don't cut him in half, but he didn't have an opportunity to turn the electricity on, and he's still knocked on the floor. He flies back a good foot or two before he hits the ground. I must've hit him harder than I initially thought because he is out like a light.

By the time I have the second one in mind, he's already fully prepared and has electricity jumping up and down the length of his baton. I rush up and we lock weapons with each other. We both stand there for a moment, pushing against each other to see who's the stronger. It's a testosterone competition. It's fun. Before we can find a victor, a large door opens up to our right, revealing the prison. We look over and see an ocean of bodies standing there. I can't see an end to the masses on any end.

"Hello, son," my dad says from the front of everybody, smiling evilly.

Chapter Twenty-Four

I kick the guy I'm fighting in the shin while his concentration is broken. He drops his baton and runs off through the crowd of people. In return, the entire group runs onto the train, screaming, filling through the maze and filling in any cracks they can to fit everyone on. My dad starts shouting orders while running onto the transport himself.

"Move!" He commands the people running, "Move now or we'll be leaving you behind!" He doesn't say it kindly. He more demands what he's saying, and the leaving you behind part is more of a threat than what will actually happen. Maybe my dad is more vicious than I knew. Perfect, an even more obscure painting of the man that I've held in high regard for ten years. At this point, I should probably burn the metaphorical painting of the impression I had of him. It'd be easier that way. John eventually shows up in the sea of people. I pull him aside.

"How did you get so many people?" I ask. He shrugs, people still flooding in. I didn't know there were this many people in the entire prison.

"I got your dad involved. He pretty much ordered everybody that lived in the hollow to come."

"Is he always a total jerk?" I ask. Sounds like he's an ass nearly one hundred percent of the time.

"He's just hard. He rules with an iron fist and deals with those who don't obey in his own way," John explains.

"So he's like the New Power?" I ask.

"No, not like that's he's, uh, he's. Yes. Just like the New Power. He's a tyrant." John looks like he's struggling to say that. My dad reemerges from the crowd, having a bubble around him where no one else is. It's like he's emanating an aura of power that nobody wants to penetrate. He walks right up to me, hands clasped behind his back, somehow managing to look down at me even though I'm taller.

"Go. Before the guards can mobilize," he commands me. No. I'm waiting until everybody gets on. Not just because it's the opposite of what he's telling me to do, but because that was always my plan and maybe now it's a little bit because it's what my dad doesn't want. I'm not going to spend all my time trying to spite the man... just a good amount.

"No," I say, "We're waiting until everybody is on

board," he grumbles at me, clearly annoyed.

"You idiot," what a loving tone with which to address your son, "If you wait even a moment longer, the guards will find us."

"So we have a bit of a fight on our hands. Look at everyone we have, it'll be a piece of cake," I say in my usually cocky tone. My father, looking even more pissed off, grabs my arm, squeezing tightly.

"I will not pay for your mistakes. We are leaving now and that's final." I start to get angry. Who does this guy think he is?

"I'm not the one who has been hiding for ten years. I'm not afraid to stand up and do something. We're waiting until everybody is on board."

"Insolent child!" my dad yells at me.

"Very original, not like I haven't heard that one before." My mom might have yelled at me for "copping an attitude," but I don't see it, and regardless, she isn't here. My dad raises his hand and backhands me across the face. I turn to face him and glare daggers.

"I am a commander, you are an insubordinate soldier," my dad compares, "You shall do as I command! Now get this train moving before I must put an end to you as I must with all insubordinate men! You're my son, so I don't want to have to hurt you, but if you leave me no choice, then I must." I look around skeptically, not believing what I'm hearing.

347

"What have you done to deserve to be a leader?" I ask him, challenging his authority.

"I have survived and led these people," he gestures to the people still rushing onto the train—geez, there's a lot of them—"for a decade. I know the trials needed to survive." I roll my eyes.

"You know what, you're right," I say with a little bite in my voice. John looks at me like I'm possessed. My dad gets a small look of satisfaction, followed by my fist in his face. He crumbles to the floor. I smile, "That felt good." John looks at me like I'm back and whatever had taken my place a second ago is gone. I shake my hand out. Did hurt a bit though. A good hurt.

"One question," he says to me, "What was he right about?" I smile again, not exactly sure what I said he was right about. It just felt like something that would end the argument, but I can't tell John that. I need to come up with a better story.

"He was challenging me," I say making it up as I go along, "Men fight, it's what we do. Not like you would know or anything, but boys are very violent." He playfully punches me in the shoulder. An alarm sounds from within the prison. It took them long enough to realize this is a prison break. I can see the end of the people, but still not everybody is on board. They start pushing harder, faster. I decide to start directing them, telling some to go through the maze created by the crates and others to help each other climb over. Quickly, we get everybody on board. I whip out my phone and dial the contact "Helmet Phone." I hear him pick up after it rings twice, and yell, "Go!" so that I can be heard over the people yelling and the alarms and sirens. It's very loud out here.

I'm not sure if he heard me, but I get my answer when the train lurches forward. Finally, we're moving, just not fast enough. "Can't this thing go any faster?" I yell into my phone. I think I hear him say something along the lines of it needs to pick up speed and get farther from the prison, but I'm not sure over all the other noise out here. I guess it's accurate because as we get farther, the train moves faster. Everybody on the train gives out a loud cheer, drowning out everything else. I put my phone in my pocket, and just like that, we're on our way to freedom, or so I think. I see something at the prison, and that's generally not good. The train is still moving and we're not losing speed, but black specks start coming toward us.

"What are those?" John asks, having seen them as well. I look closer and squint.

"Shit," I say under my breath.

"What?" John asks, "What's wrong? What are those things?" I shake my head, slightly annoyed, but expecting this.

"Sky Bikes," I say to John. I turn to the masses and

349

yell so that everybody can hear. "They're giving chase. Be ready for a fight!" Not many people hear me, but those that do look a little scared all of a sudden start spreading the word along the rest of the train. I don't have anything to shoot or even throw at the incoming enemies, so I resign to being forced to stand here and wait.

Knowing you, even if there is a chance of saving this, it's going to turn ugly, Dac says to me, *What are you going to do?*

I don't know, I respond, *I'm thinking.* I stare at them for a while, willing them to fall out of the sky, but no such luck. Telepathy would be too convenient right now. Sadly, I don't have any super powers. I'm about to tell Dac that I got nothing when I come up with an idea.

Finally you use that thing you have called a brain, he says before I can even tell him what my plan is. I forgot that he knows everything that goes on in my mind. Still creepy. I wait until the guys on the Sky Bikes get closer before doing anything. As they approach, I count that there are easily more than fifty Sky Bikes and more on the way. Crap. I take my phone out of my pocket and hand it to John.

"Call the contact named Jinn Grant. Tell him I said to get a small army to the dock that the train lands at out in the market district. We're going to need it." I tell John. I know it sounds like a command, and in turn a little bit like my dad, but there isn't any way around it. I need John to do this.

"Okay?" He says like a question, "Why are you asking me to do this? What are you going to—" I don't wait for him to finish before I take a running start and jump off the back of the train, "Sam!" I hear him yell, thinking I must be suicidal. The Sky Bikes are essentially right on top of me now, but there's no way that I can jump high enough to get to one of them, especially since I'm now in the middle of the air. I have another method. I kick on Dac and shoot straight towards the closest bike. As soon as I reach the same height as the driver, I reverse so that I'm going the same direction as the bikes. The guy flying the one I'm parallel to looks over at me. He looks genuinely shocked that someone is there. I give a sarcastic smile and salute him. I then proceed to knock him off of the Sky Bike and take it for myself. It takes me a second to realize that I should probably save him from dying. I look down in time to see that the guy I kicked off started up a jetpack and is flying away to safety. That's probably for the best.

I bank the Sky Bike and crash it into another. I hop off, and see that it takes out another two or three bikes beyond the original two intended. I free fall for a bit watching the carnage before I kick my boots back on. Five down, still close to fifty to go. I go for another bike, but this guy sees me coming. He tries to roll out of my way. We go into a corkscrew for a little while, but me, being my genius self and noticing the pattern, cut the power to my boots while I'm on top so that I fall on him. It works, for the most part. I miscalculated when I need to turn off my boots. Instead of falling right on top of the bike like I had planned, I barely manage to catch onto the side. It still goes down, but not the same way as I had planned. My weight overbalances the thing, tipping it over. I didn't think they were this sensitive. Maybe this guy just can't fly. That's more likely. I start free falling again, with a heavy bike threatening to crush me. Seeing that the original pilot had fallen off and is flying away via jetpack, I don't think he'll mind much if I take it. I grab hold of the handles and flip it over. I start flying towards one of the other guys on a Sky Bike and ram him. He goes flying off and the bike is spiraling out of control.

I hear people cheering, usually a bad sign. I look down and see that the people on the train are actually cheering for me. It feels good to be loved for once, not just cheered for when you get really hurt. Eh, I won't get used to it. These guys don't really know how to fight on a Sky Bike. This'll be a lot easier than I originally thought. I go to ram another guy and take him down. I stay on the bike this time instead of jumping off. There's nobody behind this guy that I can force him into if I leave this bike so it's pointless. All the remaining guys, the number which is still in the high thirties, have broken formation, figuring out that I'm dominating them because they were like dominoes. I take out as many as I can, sending them toppling, and spiraling out of control, but still it's not enough. Some get past me and start terrorizing the people on the train. A few manage to land and start attacking the people there. I almost turn around so that I can help them, but to my surprise, they're fighting back. Alright then. I whip my bike back around and crash into another guy. He doesn't fall off. This time, I get off the Sky Bike and climb over to his. I need to catch onto the other guy's bike's handles to avoid falling because the bike I was using started plummeting right after I let go. He doesn't tip immediately like the other guy did. Apparently, this one knows how to fly. While he's trying to smash my fingers to smithereens and I'm just focusing on holding on, somebody crashes into him, sending him flying.

I let go of the Sky Bike as it rolls over me. I activate my boots to avoid falling and right myself. I'm ready to take down whoever crashed into that last guy because I assume that he was trying to hit me and missed tragically; however, the guy on the bike holds up a hand, stopping me before I can unseat him.

"We're on your side," he says. I turn and see that some of the people I broke out of jail are taking flight on some of the sky bikes on the train. The only way I know it's them is that they're not wearing New Power armor. Taking one of the bikes already on the train probably would've been a smarter way to get in the fight. Oh well, my methods work.

With the help of the ten other guys on my side riding Sky Bikes, we make short work of the New Power goons coming at us. Too bad there are so many of them that it seems like we'll never get them all. We keep ramming back and forth, me being more daring and willing to jump off of my bike because I have shoes that let me fly. Whenever one of our guys is knocked off, I have to dive to catch them, giving them the bike I'm on, or if I'm lacking a bike, getting another one for them. I'm all over the place as a result. The majority of the battle, if you can call it that, is over the train, but it is still all around it as well.

At some point, the New Power goons get smart and pull out their electrical weapons. From what I can tell, it looks like they all have electric batons; none of them have the staffs. I pull out my Sky Iron sword. I fly up behind one of the goons and cut through his bike as I go. I must manage to hit something that manages the stabilization because the bike goes out of control. By now I've seen so many of the New Power goons use their jetpacks, that I have no doubt this guy will do the same. I move onto another goon, ready to take him out. I consider trying to cut through this one's bike again, but I figure I'd try something more fun. I flip above the poor sap and kick him off of his bike. Because he wasn't expecting me, he doesn't hold on tightly and goes flying. I laugh to myself. I didn't think that would really work. Cool.

As I right myself and celebrate my random victory, I get rammed from behind. I twist around in my seat and see another goon behind me with a smug look on his face. I don't know why he's so excited. All he has accomplished is stealing my idea and executing it more like we were using bumper cars than fighting. Never send a goon to do a man's work.

You're still a kid. Dac chooses to point out.

Close enough, I say. Really, it is.

Not really, but whatever you say, I swear if I could, I would hit him. As soon as he's in a body, I'm going to punch him. *What's that going to do? You'll probably break a hand.*

Fine, I think to him, *Then I'll hit you with a lead pipe.*

Fair enough. I win. I'm bumped again from behind.

"So that's how you want to play it?" I ask the guy trying to attack me, even though I know he can't hear me. I speed up so that I catch up to the train, I check behind me to make sure that the guy following me sped up as well. He did. I smile. I slam on the breaks and jump up off of my bike. I stick my arms out under me, ready to catch something. I look behind me at the same second the guy on the bike runs right into me. I grab onto his bike. The rider freaks out and lets go of the controls. I take the opportunity to grab them for myself and flip the bike over. Without much of a grip, the poor sap goes skydiving, which is an excellent pastime, as long as you remember to activate whatever you have to not go splat. Splat is bad. Very bad. Unless a bad guy goes splat; then splat is good. Very good. After I take the bike and make it right side up, the intercom on it crackles to life.

"Attention escapees," it's a voice I don't recognize. I'm not sure if that's good. At least it's not one of the guys in my dreams. That sounds weird, "Lay down your arms now and stop resisting. If you do so, only a minimal amount of injury will be delivered. It will no longer be our intent to cause harm. Stop what you are doing, and return to the facility." Who is this guy? I see that some of the guys fighting on the same side as me start looking really weary as if they might be listening to this chump. I have to prevent it. I punch the talk button on my stolen bike. Because I heard this leader guy speak, he'll be able to hear me.

"Hey buddy," I say, "what's the big deal? So far the only ones getting hurt are you guys," I circle around on the bike, trying to see who it is I'm talking to. What I'm saying is being heard on every bike, so I can't go solely on reaction right now. I need him to talk and find out which he is. "Where are you? I think you and I can settle our little debate on our own. Let the other kids play without any supervision for a while." Not the world's manliest thing to say, but it works. My only concern is that if I leave my guys by themselves, if any fall, how will they catch themselves? By some random chance, my question is answered. The intercom crackles to life.

"Sam. Tell the boys to land on the train. We found jetpacks for them." It's the guy that's the exNew Power goon. I really should learn his name. When this is over, I'll be sure to learn it. I don't need to relay any messages. All the other escapees clearly heard over their intercoms and are turning toward the train to land momentarily.

"There we go," I say over the intercom to whomever I'm trying to reach, "Now that the boys on all sides are safe, what do you say? Is the big chicken ready to take me?" I know that I'm the only one of my side left up here, and so does everybody else. It may be my imagination, but as I talk and insult their leader, it looks like all the remaining goons in the air turn toward me.

"You want a fight?" asks the leader of the goons, the prison warden anyway. He sounds furious. I don't know what it is, but there just seems to be something about me that pisses people off really easily.

"Why yes, yes I do," I say, cutting him off. Dac audibly sighs in my head. Maybe what annoys everybody is my charming personality. Nah, why would such a sparkling personality bother somebody? It doesn't make any sense. I listen for a response, for a sign of the intercom coming to life again, but no such thing happens. I scan the sky and see a bike making a beeline for me. "Oh shit," I say to myself. I turn my bike to be running parallel to the train and slam on the accelerator. Even though I think I'm going at full speed, the bike chasing me seems to be gaining. I dip lower in hopes that I might lose the guy. I'm right above the box line on the train. I can hear the escapees cheering for me, waving me on. I don't see my dad, but I don't care. Personally, I hope he's still out cold and will have a nice shiner when he wakes up.

Could you please stop being cynical and worry about not being caught right now, Dac says in my head, *The guy that you ticked off is probably right behind us.* I swivel in my seat and see that like Dac assumed, the warden is close behind me. How is he gaining on me? It takes me a moment to notice that his bike is different than mine. So that's how. He most likely has a totally supped up engine. Great. I twist back around and lean forward, willing the bike to go faster.

Speeding along, it's no time before I notice that we pass the train. Still, he's gaining on me. This isn't good. I see in the not terribly far off distance the market district. I guess time flies when you're fighting for your freedom along with the freedom of many others. I'm flying in essentially a straight line, occasionally adding curves and corkscrews.

In no time, I'm above the market district. I'm still high up, but I can see the people below relatively detailed, and can hear them all scream, not knowing what I'm doing and why there is some loon behind me, closing in. Even though this is the Sky Nation, I'm guessing this isn't normal. If it is, I guess we're flying too low.

I twist in my seat again and see that the crazy warden is even closer yet. I can now see that his uniform has two vertical stripes instead of just one, probably because he's a higher rank. He's essentially touching my bike at this point. I also see an armada of sky bikes taking off in the opposite direction and heading toward the train. I guess Jinn got the call. Took him long enough to do anything. I twist back around so I face forward. Let's see, what can I do. I've got this guy right behind me, and I'm not sure how well any of my tricks will work. I go with something I haven't tried yet. I push the bike past its limits to gain a little distance. I go up and flip around so that I'm riding upside down toward the guy chasing me. By the look of shock on the part of his face I can see—the helmet and visor he has on as well as the rest of the typical New Power uniform block the rest—that he wasn't expecting this at all. I reach my arms out as I pass over him, holding on with my legs and grab him. We're both knocked from our bikes and begin to fall.

We're holding on to each other and punching each other as we go. Don't know why I think a punch or two will make a difference. I take a second to look below me. There's a water trough or something like it. Really weird thing to find up here, especially since there aren't any horses or anything like that. Moments later, we hit the trough sending a spray of water all around us. Needless to say, it hurts. I am now cut, bruised, and wet. It's not such a fantastic combination. The goon I was fighting somehow manages to climb out of the trough. I think he landed on me. That would explain why I hurt all over. I force myself to climb half out to keep pursuing this guy, but someone punches his lights out. I look to see who it is, but the guy is standing against the sun so all I get is a silhouette, but I can tell that he's looking at me now.

"Come with me," he says.

Chapter Twenty-Five

It's not a voice I recognize. And there aren't many people out there who can punch out a high ranking New Power goon while they still have their helmet on. I don't think I want to mess with this guy. Not yet anyway.

"Alright," I say as I try to climb the rest of the way out of the trough. The mysterious guy has to catch my arm to make sure that I don't do a face-plant as soon as I get out of the water. I'm dripping wet. I didn't think there was that much water in there, but I guess there was. Why am I hurting so much unlike the other guy? Probably because he has armor and he landed on me!

"Can you walk?" The guy asks me. His voice sounds a little raspy, but not old. More like it's ready to command and growing weary of imposing power. His voice sounds totally different than the tone my dad's has taken on. My dad sounds like he's loving every minute of the power and can't wait to get more. Maybe he's one of the bad guys. I probably should've thought about that before breaking him out of prison.

"I think so," I say. I test my legs. I'm sore from the fall, but other than that I'm alright. Nothing's broken. That's a good sign. The man turns and walks away. I guess I'm supposed to follow him. I walk as straight as I can, but I have a bit of a limp. That'll go away soon enough. He hurries me through the market district, clearly not aware, or not caring, that I'm having issues walking right now. Not the first time I've had to work quickly when in pain; this is *nothing*. When I was younger, I broke my arm in the factory on the Surface and had to keep working throughout the rest of the day. Luckily, I had the next day off, so I was able to get it looked at. I was deemed incapable of working. That got me a nice month long break.

I keep looking over my shoulder, watching the fight playing out above the district as the train pulls in. At least there are reinforcements against the New Power now. It's not a seeming endless supply of New Power against eleven people fighting back. I'm not sure how effective the others were, but I'd like to think that I did the most.

I'm lead to a section of the market district I haven't explored yet. I've only ever even been to the market district a few times. I don't see any signs leading towards where we're going; in fact, it looks like all the signs are leading away. I see a food sign pointing this way every now and then, but I thought food was in a different area. Maybe there are two food courts.

After walking for awhile, we end up in front of a building that I can't believe I'm seeing.

"No way," I say as I look at the name of the store in front of me. The large sign reads *Peggy's Cookies*.

"Quickly, come inside," says the man who has done nothing but tell me where to go so far. He leads me inside. The lady at the counter doesn't look like she's surprised at all. She lets us walk right on by, eyeballing me the entire time. My escort walks into the back room.

My view is obscured by his back until he moves. As soon as I can tell what's inside, I see that this room has a large table. People are sitting around it. It's obvious that they were just having a discussion but stopped talking as soon as the guy who picked me up from the water trough and I walked in.

"Who's the boy?" Asks one of the people at the table. My escort asks like he doesn't hear the question.

"Leave. Now," demands my escort. Just what I need, another guy trying to control me. I've noticed this pattern my entire life. I'm not a fan.

Surprisingly enough, the nine people sitting around the table get up and leave. By my count, there are eleven chairs, probably because there are eleven positions. Even I can put that together. "What's your name boy?" he asks me, turning towards me.

"Who wants to know?" I ask, "A name for a name isn't that hard." If I can get a name out of this guy, I can ask Jinn about it later. I don't know many people's names that are Ravens, but he sure does.

"The guy with your life in his hands," says the guy that apparently claims to have my life in his hands. I shrug.

"Sam," I don't say it very politely; I almost spit it at the guy. I don't like him so far. At least I still have my sword if things turn ugly.

"Hmmm," he rumbles in his throat. He pulls out his phone, punches in a few numbers and puts it to his ear. I can hear someone pick up on the other end, I can't tell who it is though. "Get over here, now," says the guy I'm standing with. I think the guy on the other end says that he's on his way, but I can't be positive. That would make sense though. He hangs up the phone and puts it back in his pocket. He starts mumbling to himself about protocol and breaking rules and disgrace, among other things. While he's pacing the room having a miniature breakdown, I find a chair and sit down. I may be on my feet, but my leg is still killing me. If I never crash land in a water trough again, it'll be too soon. After sitting around for a while, Jinn walks through the door.

"Where is he Gerund? I swear if you've hurt him..." Gerund? I guess that's mystery man's name.

"Relax, Jinn. He's right over there. Jinn turns and

looks at where I'm sitting. I wave.

"Hi. I'm guessing you got my message?" His face is a cross of relief and horror. Why would he be horrified? Was he hoping I would die or be stuck in prison? Jinn smiles at my stupid comment.

"Ya, I got it alright. I was looking for you on the train. You weren't there." He thumps himself on the head when he comes to realize something, "I should've known it was you when I saw the one Sky Bike break away from the others with a tail."

"Now here's the question," I say, "Was I leading or following?" Before Jinn can respond, that Gerund guy clears his throat loudly.

"Jinn," Gerund says, sounding like he's about to begin a long lecture about how much trouble Jinn is in, "I believe there was a discussion going on before you answered your phone earlier."

"Yes, yes there was. Unfortunately, it was less important than the call I received," Jinn says plainly.

"A call from a boy who you don't know, about a boy that was reported dead," argues Gerund.

"Oh, he knows who I am?" I ask Jinn. He nods.

"I found that potentially saving a life, especially the life of the mastermind behind getting up here from the Surface, was more important than listening to another one of your boring status reports." Jinn argues for me. It's good to have him as a friend.

"And when you found that the person who had called you wasn't the boy who stands before me, you didn't stop to think that it might have been a trap." He wasn't asking Jinn. Gerund was telling him that he's an idiot. Ouch.

"When the boy on the other end of the line told me that it was a message from Sam, I had no doubt that he meant it," Jinn says, his voice unwavering, visually unaffected by Gerund's bitterness.

"How were you so sure?" Asks Gerund.

"It sounded like people were panicking. Sam has a habit of being in the middle of trouble."

"I am not always in," Jinn looks over at me, shooting me a glare, "Okay, maybe I am."

Told you so, Dac says.

I never denied it, I respond.

You just did. I hate when he gets smart.

Except for right now, I haven't denied it.

"I should have you both tried and executed," Gerund grumbles, "Along with that bumbling idiot Mark." Wait, what? Maybe I should pay more attention to this conversation and less to Dac.

Rude, He says in my head.

"You want to do what now?" I ask.

"He wants to have us executed," Jinn says. How can he be calm right now? Someone wants to have our heads chopped off, or something like that, and Jinn is calm right now! That's weird!

"Would that make you any better than the New Power, Gerund?" Jinn asks. Normally, the calm and cool strategy works, but right now, I think something more along the lines of panicking would work much better.

"I don't care," Gerund says, "You two are traitors, and must be dealt with." That sounds strangely like my dad.

"How are we traitors?" I ask. This guy is starting to piss me off now. It might be residual anger at my dad, but right now, it's working for me.

"You have betrayed our cause," says Gerund.

"Sam be quiet," Jinn adds quickly under his breath.

"We cannot afford to have any traitors. They'll be the end of us," continues Gerund.

"How have we betrayed the Ravens?" I ask, eyeballing the guy, annoyed. He needs to get his story straight.

"Jinn has trained you as a way to take control of this operation!" Excuse me, what? Is this guy crazy? "Jinn has wanted my position for years now. This will be his final move against me!"

"Right, that's exactly why I have missed over half the meetings and the ones I do come to, I practically sleep through," Jinn says sarcastically.

"All part of your plans!" Yells Gerund. Man, I'm getting tired of nut cases. Power is not a good thing. I stand up and take a step closer to Gerund.

"Calm down man," I say, "Jinn isn't planning anything."

"Lies!" he smacks something off the table. Very manly. Not. He then proceeds to draw his sword. It's Sky Iron, glowing a faint purple. I whip mine out as well on instinct.

"Come on big boy, you want to dance?" That is a horrible line, but I have no doubt that I will be saying it again in the future.

"Now, now, we don't have to resort to violence," Jinn says, stepping between us, "Besides," he says to Gerund, "I happen to know for a fact that Sam is a much better fighter than you." Taking some nonexistent queue, I put my sword away. Gerund looks from Jinn to me and back again.

"You don't want my position?" He asks.

"No, my friend, I don't." Jinn responds calmly. Man, he's good at keeping his cool. Gerund takes a deep breath and calms down, putting his sword away.

"You must forgive me," Gerund says to both of us, "My position has made me slightly paranoid. I don't know how Nathan keeps his sanity after doing this for hundreds of years."

"Perhaps he's crazy and none of us realize it," Jinn says.

"Yes, maybe," Gerund says, "Please, go. I'm sorry for... you know."

"It's fine," I say, "I'm getting used to people wanting to *kill* me." Gerund looks away sheepishly, embarrassed about his actions, "I'll see you later," I say, and take my leave, Jinn follows me. Once we're outside, he catches me by the shoulder, and turns me around.

"Where were you all this time?" He asks.

"In prison," I say, "It's not world's most wonderful place, but it's not the worst."

"Are you hurt?" He asks.

"Just from falling into a water trough," I say, "Everything else wasn't so bad." I think about my dad. That sucked. I sigh.

"Is something wrong?" Jinn asks. I look him in the eye. Jinn is more of a father to me than my real dad.

"Just disappointments," I say, "I found my friends from the Surface though. They were on the train. Their names are John, Rick, and Fred. Oh, and my dad is probably still unconscious." He raises his eyebrow, "Don't ask. We had a little disagreement."

"Alright," Jinn says, "John is the one that I talked to on the phone?"

"Right, he's cool. They're all cool. Except for maybe my dad."

"I'm getting the feeling that he's the 'disappointments' you were talking about." Jinn says, crossing his arms. I shrug.

"Ya, but whatever. He's still my dad," I say, resigned.

Jinn nods.

"Okay, I'll go look for them." Jinn says, "Do you have a way to get back to the house?"

"I can steal another Sky Bike," Jinn gives me the evil eye, "Or I can just use my boots." He nods in approval.

"There we go. I'll see you back at the house." He leaves to go in search of my friends and loser dad. Before I head back to the house though, there's something I need to do. I work my way through the market district. The fight over the train seems to be over, and I see a spike in the number of people here, so I guess everyone is safe. I wonder where Rose, John, and that ex-New Power guy are. I hope nobody has tried attacking him. I'm sure he's alright. If Jinn's over there, it'll get sorted out. I follow the signs until I start to recognize the area. I still have to follow signs, but I can sort of find my way around. I stop when I'm outside a store called *Big Man's Metal Shop*.

What are we doing here? Dac asks. Instead of responding, I just smile to myself. I walk inside, a bell ringing when I push the door open. A man lumbers out of the back covered in his usual suit of soot.

"Ah, Sam. I was wondering when you were going to show up. Your order's been done for a week. I was about ready to start using it for target practice."

"Sorry, Arthur, I've been a little tied up," I say.

"Tied up? Right. What've you been doing, scratching

your bum for the past week?" Oh Arthur, cheery as always.

"Actually, I've been in prison," I say, "And just orchestrated and executed a massive jail break."

"Am I supposed to be impressed?" Arthur asks, crossing his arms. I shrug.

"Possibly," I say, "I don't know. It was just something to do. I figured you guys would take too long to come and get me." He lets out a subtle chuckle.

"So am I to assume that you're finally ready to pick up your order?" Arthur asks me. I nod. He waves me over while walking behind one of the counters.

"Come over here," he pulls out some weird looking device. I walk over, "Give me your boots," he says.

"Why?" I ask.

"Just give them to me," he says, his normal charming self. I shrug and take off my boots. I put them on the counter.

Sam, what are you doing? Dac asks me, apparently unable to read my mind for once.

I though you knew everything I knew, I say. For once he doesn't have a response. *Are you okay?* I ask.

Yeah, he says, *I just feel really weird right now.*
Weird how?

Like something unpleasant is about to happen. Now that he mentions it, I kind of have the same feeling. I shake it off.

371

I'm sure it's not that bad. You'll like it, trust me.

If you're sure, Dac says. Arthur takes the boots and puts them in a glass box.

"Now here's the deal. I have to take a big piece of code from your shoes. It'll only take a minute, but the installation will take longer."

"How long?" He shrugs.

"A couple hours probably," Arthur explains.

"Alright," I say, "No way around it."

"You do know that this has never been done before, right?" Arthur asks, "You're one of the only people who has bonded with an AI and not died instantly or had their body taken over by the AI."

"I don't think Dac would do that," I say aloud. *You wouldn't do that, would you?* I ask in my head.

Eh, depends, he says. I know he's joking though. I hope he's joking.

"Whatever you say," says Arthur, "You're going to be disconnected with your AI until the installation is completed and you two are in close proximity." That might be the bad feeling both Dac and I had, "You sure you're ready for this?"

"Why wouldn't I be?" I ask.

"Might be a little weird having your head all to yourself after sharing it all this time."

"Nah," I say with a wave of my hand, "It'll be a relief for a little while."

I hate you, Dac says in my head.

You know you love me. I respond.

"Ready?" Arthur asks.

"When you are," I say. Arthur puts a cover on the glass box my boots are in. The box is attached to a computer, which I personally think is weird, but whatever. Arthur hits a button on the computer. Nothing happens. I was expecting big flashy lights or the shoes to tap dance or something, but nothing. What a let down.

"There we go," Arthur says randomly, "Now it's done."

"It doesn't look like anything happened," I say, pointing to the box, "Are you sure it worked?"

"Try talking to your AI," Arthur says, retreating my boots from the box. I try talking to Dac, but he doesn't respond. I try again, still nothing, "Not there, is it?" Arthur asks. I shake my head. I feel like a part of my brain is hollow, but that's ridiculous. I didn't have Dac most of my life, why would I need him now? Arthur hands me my boots, "It's only temporary. If you two get close when I'm done installing your AI into the body, you'll bond again."

"It's still weird," I say, putting my boots on. Arthur shrugs.

"Man up," real considerate, "I'll call you in a couple of hours if nothing big is going on."

"Alright," I say, "I'll see you in a couple hours." Arthur

mumbles something and takes something out of the computer. He takes whatever it is and returns to the back room. He really does spend a lot of time in there. I wouldn't be surprised if I found a bed back there. Ignoring the temptation to go look for Arthur's living space, I leave the shop.

I look around and see a hovering limo type thing off to my right. It's elongated, but not super thick. It doesn't have tires, so I guess more time and energy was spent on developing its flight abilities. It slows down as it passes me. It actually stops in front of me so I'm looking at the back most doors. The door at the back opens like a car door on the Surface. It's one of the first ones up here I've seen do that.

Two sets of hands reach out of the car and pull me in. The door shuts behind me, and the limo sets off.

Chapter Twenty-Six

"Hey! Get off of me. What's your problem?" I bark while getting the two sets of grabby hands off of me. No respect.

"Actually, Sam, that would be you," says some guy I didn't notice before. Inside the limo there are the two guys that grabbed me sitting along the sides of the limo. I'm alone in the back. The sides are lined with four New Power goons. Directly across from me is some guy in a business suit, sipping on some red wine.

"I don't even know you," I say.

"And yet you continue to be a consistent thorn in my side." He seems just as likely to hug a puppy as to try and score a field goal with it.

"How am I a 'thorn in your side,'" I ask with a horrible, mocking recreation of his voice. He takes another sip of his wine.

"Not only have you eluded me, been a constant mockery, and destroyed much of my equipment, but you have become a major distraction to my soldiers, and most recently even turned some of them away from me." Did I just hear that right?

"Wait, your soldiers?" I ask. As far as I know, I've only fought people in the New Power.

"Yes, my soldiers. It seems that you have made the foolish mistake of allying yourself with those trash gorilla fighters. 'The Resistance' I believe they call themselves." So this guy is anti-Ravens and pro-New Power. Crazy. "For years their feeble attempts to thwart me have been inconsequential, but you. For some reason, after you joined their ranks, everything you're involved in starts succeeding. Why?"

"Because I'm special and everybody loves me," I say sarcastically. "May I ask what your name is? As much fun as talking to someone without a name is, I think I'm okay with knowing."

"You have an attitude, don't you?" Points out whatever-his-name-is. I raise my eyebrow, "Fine, if you must know, I go by Steven."

"Steven? That's not a very cool super villain name," I say without thinking that it might somehow manage to upset this guy, this "Steven." "Geez, that's a lame evil name."

"Well perhaps I might be able to prove to you that there is nothing wrong with my name," Steven says taking another sip of his wine and leaning forward.

"Break his arm," he commands the two New Power goons closest to me. They make a move on me, but I kick one in the jaw as he turns toward me. The other tries to grab at me. I scoot out of the way, catch his arm as he sticks it out, and end up dislocating his shoulder. Both the goons that came at me don't try anything again.

"Still not seeing why your name is scary," I say, sitting back in my chair, feeling smug. I see on Steven's face that he's starting to become annoyed.

"Proof yet of how you are a thorn in my side. I know no other Raven that could do what you just did." Seriously? He must've never met Jinn.

"Well I got some bad news for you," I say, "There are plenty of Ravens out there that can do that." Steven looks at me like I just told him the secret to the universe.

"You don't consider yourself one of them?" He asks. The question catches me off guard. I try and find words, but I can't come up with anything. "Let me offer you this," he continues, "Join me. You can rule as a king."

"A king?"

"The most powerful monarch there is," Steven affirms.

"Well if you put it that way," There's the wind up, "I guess I can only say," Here comes the pitch, "are you out of your mind?" I wanted to use more creative language, but it doesn't feel absolutely necessary. Steven's face goes from elated and caring and full of opportunity to disappointed and maybe even a little angry.

"You're making a mistake, boy. I shall pretend that I didn't hear how rudely you addressed my more than generous offer. I shall ask you one last time. Join me, and rule." He sticks out his hand like you would see in a cheesy movie.

"Thanks, but no thanks," I say. I expect Dac to tell me that I should sign up for the power and then have an argument with him, but there's nothing. I forgot that we're temporarily disconnected; permanently, if we never get close to each other again.

"Fine," Steven says angrily, but still keeping his composure, sitting up and retracting his hand. He takes another sip of his drink, "If you are not with us, you are our enemy," I tense up, ready to have to fight the other goons in the car, "Yet you are not with our enemies. You are a wild card. There are only two ways to deal with wild cards."

"And what would that be?" I ask.

"Dispose of them," Steven says like it's the best possible solution in the world. Simple and clean. Again, I'm ready for a fight, "or you let them grow. I think we shall try the more intriguing of the options with you. You may yet join our ranks." Earlier when he said we and our, I thought he was talking about the New Power as a whole, but now I'm not so sure. Could he know the guys in my dreams?

"So what now?" I ask, "If you plan to see this wild card develop to be able to kick your ass all the harder, what are you going to do now?" He smiles.

"Pass a message on," Steven says.

"What?" I ask.

"Scurry back to the resistance and tell them that upon nightfall, they too shall fall."

"Really? Nightfall? How cliché," I say with my usual mentality, "Do you even know where they are?" He smiles.

"Let's just say the second in command will get a surprise tonight, and that we will be ordering some cookies as well." Creepy. I don't need to know about his cookie addiction. Wait a minute, Peggy's! "Goodbye, *boy*," Steven says, setting his glass down, "We shall meet again." The door to my left pops open on its own. I look out it, losing my focus. While I'm not paying attention, one of the stupid goons pushes me out.

There's nothing below me but open sky. I involuntarily scream for a little bit before I remember to turn my boots on. I can fly. Only problem is that they won't start! It takes me falling another couple seconds before I can finally get the boots to turn on. It was a lot easier with Dac helping me out. Oh well, I guess I had to stop being lazy eventually.

I scan the area and see the market district in the distance. Knowing where that is, I head towards Jinn's house. I need to tell him about what Steven plans to do.

Luckily, nobody kidnaps, imprisons, shocks, attacks, forces me to fight, gets in my head, or even notices me on my flight to Jinn's. I have a rough landing in the front yard. It's not catastrophic, but it's not as gentle as I wanted it to be. It's probably just the learning curve of flying these things without Dac's help. I run up to the front door and barge in without knocking or anything. Maybe I should tell him to lock his door tonight. Not sure how much good that'll do against the New Power, but at least it's something.

"Jinn?" I yell throughout the house, "Are you here? Jinn, we have a problem," He walks into the main hall from the kitchen.

"I should've know you wouldn't come straight back here," he sighs, "What's the problem? By the way, your friends are sleeping upstairs." They're here? I want to go check on them, but shake off the urge. This is just a little more important. I tell Jinn about my discussion with Steven. He doesn't interrupt me; he just listens and nods when he hears something important. I tell him that I think Steven in planning to do a two-pronged attack. I'm probably just doing it so that I know he's listening. When I'm done speaking he whips out his phone, punches a number in and presses it against his ear. After a few seconds someone picks up.

"Gerund, it's Jinn. We have a problem, a big problem."
He walks off to talk with Gerund. Since I'm sitting here
awkwardly on my own, I might as well go check on my
friends. It takes a little bit of looking, but I find them
soon enough. The first group I find is the two ex-New
Power guys. The one that was crushed more is asleep on
a bed, and the one that helped me out on the train is
awake, kneeling by his side. Both sets of their armor are
shoved in the corner. Jinn must've gotten them new
clothes, or they had it on under the armor.

"Hey," I say. The one on his knees turns around.
Without the headgear on, I see that he has close-cut hair.
It almost looks like a stubbly buzz, but it's longer than
that. He turns around and looks at me.

"Hi," he says looking at me. He has brown eyes.
Wouldn't have guessed. "Thanks for getting us out. I'm
Charley."

"Sam," I say sticking my hand out awkwardly.

"I know," he says, returning the awkward hand
shake, "Your name has been said more than a couple
times since you woke up on my transport."

"So I've heard," I say, running my hand through my
hair, "How are you two doing?" I ask. Charley looks over
at his friend.

"He's hurt, but nothing a little time with his family
won't heal. Your friend Jinn said that he'd send us home
as soon as he's positive that we've disappeared. That

won't take to long, will it?"

"Knowing Jinn, it won't take long at all," I say.

"Thank you," Charley says. He looks from me to his friend, "If you'll excuse me, I want to keep an eye on him. I'll see you around, Sam. You've changed my life. Saved it even."

"Um, you're welcome?" I say, not sure exactly what to do. I leave Charley to keep an eye on his friend and do whatever he was doing. The last room I look in has the first four people I was looking for in it. Rick and Fred are lying in their beds looking around, my dad is lying in a bed out cold—I just keep getting prouder and prouder of that punch—and John is up pacing the room. When I open the door, the three that are awake look over at me.

"Sam," John says, sounding relieved. He walks on over and gives me a hug.

"This might be the most you've hugged me all year. I've never seen you want to get this close to anyone except your sister and pretty much any girl before," I say to John, partially jokingly. Rick and Fred stand up and walk over to me.

"Hey buddy," Rick says, "good to see you in one piece."

"Yeah," Fred says, cutting Rick off, "We didn't know if your 'friend' was planning to help us or hurt us. He's not exactly world's most cuddly teddy bear." I can't help but laugh. My initial impression of Jinn was similar. I think I might have been closer to soiling myself than Fred was during his first experience meeting Jinn.

"You did a real job on your dad, Sam," Rick says, "Did he really deserve it?" I mock-think about it for a minute.

"Yeah," I nod my head, "I think so. It made me feel better," I say. It's the truth. Indirectly, me punching my dad's lights out helped with the prison break. Nah, that sounds like he's getting some credit. "Could I have my phone back by the way?" John pulls it out of his pocket and tosses it to me.

"You need better games on there," he says, being his typical self. "Your dad did keep me alive all that time," John says, trying to defend my dad. I pretend to not hear him.

"So are you guys going to stay here or bunk somewhere else, or what?" I ask. When the three of them give me a confused look, I elaborate, "Are you going to be staying here at Jinn's, or find some place of your own?" Weird looks are passed around. I guess nobody has thought that far ahead. "Got it," I say, clapping my hands. I open my mouth to say something else, but before I can, I hear Jinn calling for me from downstairs.

"Sam, come down here. We need to talk." I faintly hear him saying some less than kind things about Gerund as he walks back into the kitchen. I look at my friends.

"I, uh, got to go. I'll see you guys later." They say their goodbyes and I leave them to go find Jinn. I go downstairs and head into the kitchen. I'm going to guess that's where he is.

"Jinn?" I ask, walking into the kitchen. I see him pacing the room. Man, nobody can sit still right now. He looks up at me when he hears his name.

"You're limping," he says before he can come up with anything else. I shrug. Jinn walks to the refrigerator and pulls out a thing of blue elixir. "Drink this," he says, walking over to me, handing me the drink, "if the New Power is really going to attack us tonight, we can't afford to have you hurt. Nobody will admit it, possibly because they don't know, but other than me, you're probably our best fighter." I'm really not good at answering things appropriately today. Instead of saying something that might sound stupid, I down the Blue Elixir. A warmness spreads through my body as the Blue Elixir does its trick. I don't know how it happens, but this stuff always heals me. I hand Jinn the drink and he puts it back in the fridge.

"So what's the news?" I ask, "What do we need to talk about?"

"New Power troops are moving," Jinn says, turning and facing me, dead serious, "What you told me was true. It looks like they are preparing to head here and to the base within the market district."

"So what are we going to do?" I ask.

"We are going to defend here," Jinn says, "There's no way to know how many forces are heading here compared to the base in the market district. We're going to get a small group of fighters, as much as the Ravens can spare, and the rest are going to defend Peggy's Cookies."

"How did you guys decide to use a Peggy's Cookies for your secret base by the way?" I ask. It's a mostly serious question. I want to know. Jinn shrugs.

"Peggy is a nice lady who makes us cookies for free."

"Fair enough," I say, "Now, how are we going to defend this place from an army with only a few guys?"

"It depends who those few guys are," Jinn says, "If it's the right few, we might just pull this off."

"Who've you called?" I ask, assuming that he's already got some people to say yes.

"Mark is on the way," Jinn says, "He was just with Armando. Oh, sorry, you don't know who he is."

"Yes I do," I say. Jinn looks a little surprised, but not like it was totally unexpected. "We've talked before. How's he doing?"

"You mean with the injuries?" Jinn asks. I nod my head.

"Not sure. He's still out, but we're doing our best. A few medics are staying with him."

"Alright," I say. I hope Armando gets better. He didn't

look like he is too happy with his current predicament. "Who else did you get?" Jinn sighs.

"Arthur said he's in the middle of a project, but he'll be here as soon as he can. Said you would know something about it." Jinn looks at me and raises an eyebrow questioningly.

"Yeah, I asked him to do something," Jinn shakes his head.

"He'll maybe be here then, and he said he would bring reinforcements. Jackson said he and his daughter would be here," I have no idea who that is, "and a couple other Ravens are being permitted to come by Gerund, but he wants the rest protecting Peggy's. It'll be maybe ten of us against who knows how big an army." I let Jinn wallow in his misery for a minute before a realization comes to me.

"What if we could double that?" I ask aloud. More talking to myself then to Jinn.

"Numbers would help, but there's no way. Gerund is a stubborn fool who's going to get all of us killed. He'll never allow more fighters to sacrifice Peggy's just to come here," Jinn says.

"No, not more soldiers," I say.

"Then what good would they be?" Jinn asks, cutting me off before I can finish what I'm saying.

"They're not Raven soldiers anyway."

"What are you suggesting?" Jinn asks, suddenly

interested apparently.

"We've got plenty of people I just broke out of prison. Grab the ten that fought on the bikes." A light looks like it just went on in Jinn's head.

"You're right," wow, don't hear that too often. "I'll go talk to them now. See if they're willing to fight with us." Jinn rushes off to go call everybody. He must've seen who was on the bikes when he was over there.

Instead of standing around alone downstairs, I decide I need sleep right now. I go up to my room and plug my phone in. John gave it back with no battery. I lie down and try to sleep, but I can't seem to rest. At some point I give up on sleep and start playing with my necklace, thinking about my past.

After being lost in my thoughts for a while, I start to hear transports and cruisers arrive. I get up and look outside my window. It's almost dark and the party's going to start soon. I gather up all my stuff and shove it in my pockets before heading downstairs. I see Jinn with Mark and whom I'm guessing is Jackson. Why does he look so familiar? I decide to let them do their battle strategies and head outside. I look up in the massive backyard and see the sun sinking ever lower in the sky. I sigh and start to wander the yard. Somewhere in the back corner, I find Rose. Jinn brought her back here as well as all my friends. He said he recognized her and that she would need rest. He took her away from all of

Gerund's madness. She's sitting on the edge of the platform, feet dangling off the edge.

She's staring off the edge, looking at I don't know what. I walk up behind her.

"You know if you jump, I'd have to go over after you," I say sitting down next to her. She gives a weak laugh.

"Thanks," she says, pushing a strand of hair behind her ear.

"Is something wrong?" I ask.

"It's nothing," she says, shaking her head, "it's just crazy."

"What's crazy?" I know I'm being a nudge, but I don't care.

"Everything," she says, kicking her legs dangling over the edge. "A month ago, I would've never thought that there would be an all-out fight between us and the New Power. Now in only another hour or two, here we are." She sighs, ending her thought in her head. "How long ago did you sign up to become a Raven?" The question catches me off guard.

"Uh, I don't know," I say, "I didn't exactly sign up. I was just told that I'm a part of it."

"Nobody's been unwillingly recruited," she says, "They always have an option." I shrug.

"I'm fine with it. Jinn has never really called me a Raven. I don't exactly listen to what Gerund says." We sit in silence for a bit, the topic clearly closed, before Rose speaks again.

"You know what I just realized?" she asks.

"That you should never smack your best friend with frozen chicken?" I say, half trying to make a joke, half remembering something I did to John when we were fighting over this one girl.

"Uh, no," she says with a soft laugh. It doesn't sound like she's trying to make fun of me, but like she thought it was a funny comment. I guess my plan worked then, even though I still feel stupid, "You've saved my life twice now." Why are people being so dramatic about that? I haven't saved anyone's life. "I just wanted to say thank you," she says, looking embarrassed. Before I can say anything, I hear someone yell behind me.

"Where's my little Roseypoo?" I turn around and see some guy walking towards Rose and me with his arms open. He is wearing baggy shorts. I don't know what is holding them up. He has an equally large shirt on. I don't know what it is, but something about the way he walks makes flashing signs that read "douchebag" go off in my head.

"Oh my god! Todd, you're really here!" Todd? Rose stands up from next to me and runs to this "Todd" guy. Rose gives Todd a big old hug, jumping up into his arms. I look away before I see if they do anything else. Rose takes Todd by the hand and leads him over to me.

"Todd," she says, "this is Sam. Sam, this is Todd, my

boyfriend." There's the word I didn't want to hear.

"Sup bro," Todd says, giving me the finger gun. Rose sits next to me and pulls her boyfriend who clearly didn't want to sit, down next to her.

"Sam and I were just talking, Todd," Rose says, hooking her arm in Todd's. I look away before I vomit.

"Whatever," he says, "just as long as he wasn't trying to make a move on my girl. Right buddy?" Please, somebody hit him.

"Sam?" I hear Jinn yelling from the house.

"I have to go," I say quickly, standing up.

"Alright, talk later?" Rose asks.

"Later, Player," Todd elegantly adds before I can respond to Rose.

"Todd!" She says, annoyed at his rudeness.

"What?" he says, defensively, "I'm sorry, Baby. I've missed you. I just wanted a little time alone with you. Is that so bad?" Man, he knows just how to work it.

"Aw," Rose says, completely falling for it, "I've missed you too." And just like that, I'm forgotten. I leave and give them their moment alone. I get back to the house and see Jinn with the others—Mark and Jackson.

"You," Jackson says, his eyes about ready to pop out of his head, "It's you. You saved me after we fought in the arena little more than two months ago." That's all? It feels like it's been a lifetime. Jackson steps up, and gives me a hug, "And now you've saved my daughter. I have so much to thank you for." My shoulder suddenly feels a little wet, and Jackson starts shaking. Is he crying? I see Jinn and Mark respectively quiet, just watching Jackson and me. I lift my arms and hug him back. I don't know what to say, I just stand there with a sobbing grown man in my arms. After a while, Jinn loudly clears his throat. Jackson puts a stopper on his tears as best as he can, righting himself and wiping the water from under his eyes. It's a very hug filled night apparently.

"It's almost time, Sam," Jinn says, "The New Power will make their move any moment now. All your friends have agreed. The one that abandoned the New Power, Charley, has also agreed to assist us. He said his friend would as well, but sadly, he is still asleep. Charley was down here a little while ago, giving us as much information as he could about how the New Power operates," Jinn rubs his forehead, looking overwhelmed by all of this.

"What about those guys that helped in the middle of the jail break?" I ask. Jinn shakes his head.

"They're Ravens." Jinn says, "Gerund started seeing New Power massing and got scared. He's not letting any come." Damn. I'm silent for a moment, cursing Gerund out in my head.

"We can do this," I say, "Worst case, we'll let them see Mark's pajamas and that'll scare them off." I get an empty chuckle out of all of them.

"It's good to see you again, kid," Mark says. It's a nice change to hear someone call me kid, and not use it as an insult.

"Time to suit up," Jinn says, "I'll get the others from upstairs."

A few minutes later, everyone is armed and those that know how to fly one have mounted a Sky Bike. That makes Jinn, Mark, Jackson, and me all riding bikes. Nobody else knows how to fly one. Sadly, my dad woke up, so he's in the fight too. That is if he doesn't chicken out and run and hide. We're divided evenly to cover the front and backyards. Mark and Jackson are in the back with Rose, Todd, and Charley. Jinn and I are in the front yard with John, Rick, Fred, and my Dad.

"Just like the factories," John says. Rick and Fred mumble in their agreement.

"Just like the factories," I agree. Well, not exactly. In the factories, the goal was more of a protect-yourself-just-enough-to-prevent-death-or-injury to the point you couldn't work. This time the goal's just a little different.

Night falls as we all stand discussing how crazy this is. I never thought I'd be here. I'm just a normal kid. Only special thing I've ever done is get lucky and break away from the Surface. As I'm dispelling my thoughts of misery, everybody tenses up, alert. In the distance I see the sign that the attack has begun.

I see the running lights of a New Power Sky Bike.

Chapter Twenty-Seven

My bike, along with Jinn's comes to life. I keep my running light off so as to not give away my position.

"On our side," Jinn says into the radio in the bike. Everybody that doesn't have a bike has a radio shoved in their ear, and those that have bikes are using what's right in front of them.

"Same here," Charley says over the radio, "I told you they would come at us from both sides." Everyone other than Jinn, Mark, Jackson, and I are using Jinn's spare swords. They're not Sky Iron, but they'll work. I don't know about Mark and Jackson, but Jinn and I both have our swords shrunken down, but in our hands. We have them ready, but not fully out so that the light won't give us away.

"If anyone gets in trouble, get in immediate radio contact," Jinn says over the radio, "Everybody ready?" He asks. A chorus of "yeses" and "readys" resound through the radio. Jinn turns his radio off and looks at me, "You ready?" I nod my head.

"Ya, let's go," I say.

"Sam," John says. I look over my shoulder to see him, "Good luck up there. Try not to get your ass handed to you." I smile, even though I know I probably will end up as a bloody blob of purple at the end of this.

"You too," I say. I glance at my dad, but I bring my eyes back to John, "Don't let him go running off, alright?"

"Can do," John says, almost sounding happy. Jinn starts to ride forward and I follow him. We ride the length of roughly half the front yard before we take off. Even in the air, we keep our running lights off. We don't want to give our position away to the New Power. I get a better view of how many Sky Bikes there are in the air, once we're up. It's more like an overcast day than nighttime. I don't really know why we thought that keeping our running lights off would help. It's still perfectly clear outside!

"There's no way," I say to myself when I get a rough count of how many New Power goons are in the air. There must be over a hundred Sky Bikes! Not to mention the two or three transports and whatever is on the other side of the house.

"Sam," Jinn says warningly over the radio, "Don't do anything stupid." Naturally, I do exactly what he says not to. I speed right into the front lines of the New Power's ranks. I extend my sword when it's time to cut an enemy down, or destroy their bike, and shrink it down again when I'm between enemies. After I knock half a dozen guys out of the sky, the rest of the group catches on to what's going on. They break any formation they had before. The New Power is now flying really erratically. Half of the bikes are staying in the air and are trying to pick out which ones Jinn and I are while the other half, as well as the transports, are trying to land in Jinn's front yard.

"Watch out guys," I say over the radio to everybody on the platform, "It looks like you've got some guys coming your way."

"We see them," Rick says back. I look over my shoulder to check on everybody. They're all dancing around, fighting New Power goons. I turn my attention back to my fight, relatively confident that my friends below can take care of themselves. As I'm flying around, taking out as many guys as I can, I see flashes of Jinn doing the same thing. Normally I'd try to say something to him, but now doesn't seem like the right time.

I take down a few more guys. One of them starts to give me trouble. I actually get into an extended fight with him. We ride parallel to each other, slashing at each other, hoping to hit something important, but no such luck. I'm wasting too much time here. I flip over the guy to try and get at him from above. Before I can attack, one of the New Power guy's goon friends comes up and rams me in the side. I guess they learned from me at the train. I immediately clamp down on my sword in an effort not to lose it.

I try to correct the bike before I hit anything, but before I can, I crash into another goon on a bike. My bike is jerked from my grip by the force of the collision, giving me a sense of whiplash. I see my bike hurling straight towards Jinn's roof. How do I know its trajectory? I'm flying through the air right behind it.

I involuntarily scram as I try to kick my boots on, but the stupid things won't work. I get my shoes to turn on right as I see the bike crash into Jinn's roof and tumble off, taking some shingles with it. Jinn is going to be so pissed. I hope the bike at least squished somebody on the New Power. Even though I got my boots on, I can't slow my momentum quite enough. I crash into the roof, but not hard enough to severely injure myself. I'm sure I have a few new gashes though.

I grab onto part of the roof with my free hand feeling the cracked parts of the roof cut me up, always making sure not to lose my sword. I carefully shimmy to the end of the roof, almost directly in the wake of destruction my bike caused. The destruction created a couple good handholds for me to use. Once I get to the edge of the roof, I see that sadly, the bike didn't crush any New Power goons. On the bright side, it didn't get any of us either.

A quick survey of the yard shows that all three of the transports and quite a few Sky bikes made it down. Of course, there are more than a few crashed bikes as well. Why can't this be easy? I look around to see where John, Rick, Fred, and my dad are. I see that Rick and Fred are fighting together close to one of the grounded transports, using their swords more like clubs. At least they're effective. There is a large amount of New Power bodies lying around them, unconscious or farther gone.

Rick swings at a New Power soldier. The solder deflects the blow, wrenching the sword from his grip. Not thinking about his own safety, Rick dives from the dropped weapon. The New Power goon seizes the opportunity, swinging at the defenseless Rick. Fred is close enough to see what happens. Fred blocks the New Power soldier's attack and slices into his arm. Rick gets up just in time to see the New Power soldier start to fight with Fred. Sensing opportunity, Rick takes a swing at the back of the soldiers exposed neck neck, effectively decapitating him. Blood splatters both Rick and Fred staining them red.

I see that John and my dad are also fighting together. They're closer to the house. John looks like he's tired and stumbling a lot, but that might just be because no one has taught him how to fight in these kinds of conditions like Jinn taught me. I knew how to fight, but not this style of fighting. Fists and whatever I could get my hands on was more my style. All John has been taught is how to take orders and hide by my dad. My dad looks terrified and ready to drop, but I guess that's what he gets. At least he's fighting. I don't know how many times anybody has been socked or cut, so I can't properly gauge how badly hurt anyone is.

I see Jinn still up in the sky, so that's a good sign. I want to know how the others are doing, so I take a second to activate my boots. I fly over to the backyard and hover at the same height as the house's roof. Both Mark and Jackson are still in the air, but they're letting more people through than Jinn and I did. There aren't any transports over here, so that at least decreases the enemy count on the platform.

Charley is obviously giving it his all. He's using some of the training he received in the New Power against these goons. It's interesting to see the almost mirror-like moves pitted against each other. I don't watch him long, but long enough to see Charley and his opponent try and cut up on each other from the same side, dodging the same way.

I look away from Charley because I see Rose being overwhelmed. I almost go to help, but Todd comes and attacks some of the goons, drawing their attention. I guess the loser has some uses. Once more than half the goons approaching Rose turn on Todd, the guy gets so scared that he drops his sword and makes a run for the house, screaming. Coward. At least he's New Power bait.

I get ready to go back to my side to keep fighting, but before I do, my phone rings. I don't know what compels me to do so, but I hover over the house and answer it.

"Hello?" I answer, pushing the phone to my ear, trying to yell over the chaos going on around me.

"Hey Sam. Your order's finished," responds the caller.

"Arthur?" I ask, knowing full well that it's him, "Where are you?" I yell, angry that he's not here helping.

"Relax," he says, "Tell Jinn I'm sorry that I couldn't get any more guys to come, but we're on our way." I stop listening about halfway through because I notice that some of the crashed bikes have caught on fire.

"Oh that is so not good," I say aloud.

"Fine, we'll just turn around then." It takes me a second to realize that Arthur thought I was talking about him.

"No, no, no," I say, trying to keep him on the line, "Please come. We need you," I hate begging. It puts a sour taste in my mouth.

"Damn right you do," Arthur says, being his normal lovely self, "We'll be there in thirty seconds." He hangs up before I can ask my next question. Who is 'we'? I wait around on the roof for the thirty seconds. I know it's thirty seconds that might've been better spent fighting, but I want to be able to direct Arthur and whoever he's bringing.

Suddenly, two swords came flying out of darkness into the front yard. The fires are totally ruining my night vision. The running lights of the Sky Bikes did a pretty good job of ruining it already, but the fire finishes the job. Another sword and a spear shoot out of the darkness next; both find a home in the chest of a New Power goon. One lands relatively close to the house so I can get a good look at it. The blade is glowing red. Arthur? Another set of weapons comes flying out, and another, and another. I don't know if he can see me, but I start waving my arms frantically, telling him to go to the other side of the house. Apparently he gets the message.

A barrage of sharp objects comes flying out of the darkness, each one meeting its target, never coming close to getting any of our guys. Next thing I see is the sooty sunshine himself flying out of the shadows with a jetpack on. He's got his giant scythe in hand. There's a chain attaching the weapon to Arthur. That's new. I look back to the front yard to go fight, and right after I jump down, a giant mass of silver comes out of the darkness and crushes one of the New Power goons in front of me. The fire is reflecting off of the metallic figure, making it look like a creature straight from a nightmare. The metallic figure stands up slowly, almost like it's stiff. Kind of a weird thought.

When it's upright I see that the body looks like a man's, and the face is relatively close, but the face is more a cross between humanoid and robot. It's about the same height that I am, potentially slightly taller, but I'm sure I'll be able to grow taller. The way the body is built, it looks like a clothed person almost.

"Miss me?" Asks the robot. A chill runs down my spine because of the voice.

"Dac?" I ask, disbelieving. The voice that came out of the robot is exactly the same as Dac's voice in my head, no odd inflections or tin sound or anything. My friend has a body of his own.

Yeah, it's me, He says in my head. Good to know that we can still do that, *Pretty good looking, huh?*

"You kidding me?" I say aloud, "It's awesome!"

"Thank you," he says. I look at his face, or electronic equivalent, "You kept your word and got me this body. I can never thank you enough."

"Let's just stay close for a real long time," I say with a smile, even though I'm bleeding all over the place and a massive fight is going on around me.

"A long time for you, or a long time for me?" Dac asks, trying to be funny, "I'm going to last much longer than you," he says.

"Let's worry about that later," I say, "For now, we have a fight on our hands."

"Oh goody," he says, "Somehow, I knew that you would be in a fight of some sort when I found you."

"And why would you ever think that?" I ask. Dac

gives me the most "are you kidding me" look I think is possible for a robot to give.

"Just a hunch," he says, "Oh well. At least it gives me a chance to try these out." Dac flicks his right arm and a blade the size of a sword shoots out.

"Wow," I say without thinking about it. The sword is clearly Arthur's craft. It doesn't look as good as mine though. Wait a minute, "Is that Sky Iron?"

"Yup," he says, inspecting it, "Too bad it doesn't have a color. I would've liked to know what mine is."

"We'll work on that later," I say, "For now, let's not die."

"I just got this body," Dac says, "I don't plan on losing it yet." With that, we charge back into the fight. Jinn in still in the sky, Rick and Fred are around the transports, John and my dad are by the house. Even though my dad looks worse than before, he's still fighting.

Dac and I, well, we're kind of all over the place. We stick together half the time, kicking ass. The other half, we split up, still kicking ass. At some point we decide to stick together because of the sheer number of guys coming at us. I don't know how many goons the others are fighting, but it has to be less than before with how many Dac and I are handling.

"For just getting a body, you're not bad at using it," I say to Dac between attacking oncoming New Power soldiers.

"I'm an artificial intelligence, what do you expect," he says like this should be obvious.

"That's cheating," I say, "You're more person to me than machine or program or whatever." This is a very weird discussion to be having in the middle of a fight.

Yes, yes it is. Let's talk about it later then. Dac says in my head, having read my thoughts. I was kind of hoping the part where he gets one hundred percent access was over.

Agreed. I think back to him, slicing a goon simultaneously. I feel really bad that I have to hurt all these guys. It's not right. If they weren't trying to kill me, I'm sure I could never do something like this. Even though I know it's them or me right now.

Between attackers, I take a moment to throw up because of how many people I've killed. I hate this.

You'll be alright, Dac says. He doesn't say it aggressively, or angrily. He says it more like a caring best friend or brother that genuinely wants to make sure that I'm alright. I wipe my mouth with the back of my hand and keep going. After a while, it seems like we have cleared most of the people. I start to relax a bit thinking we've won. I'm exhausted. We just held off a couple hundred guys all by ourselves. I look around the yard and see that everybody has collapsed. Rick and Fred are lying on top of each other, trying to stay up. My dad is flat on the floor. I don't see a lot of blood, so I guess he was just shocked. John is leaning against the wall, his sword fallen to the floor. I see Jinn landing his bike. He hops off and looks shaky on his feet. He uses his bike as support and looks up at me.

"Is it over?" I shout across the yard to him, still unwilling to put my sword down. I wouldn't be surprised if my hand has been glued around the handle.

"Yes," he calls back, nodding his head. I almost feel happy, but about two seconds after he says yes, Dac speaks up.

"No," Dac says. Right now, that is by far my least favorite word. Another few seconds later, Dac's answer is confirmed.

"Attention remaining Ravens," it's that idiot Steven. He's talking over some giant megaphone, "Give up now or be destroyed. Your forces in the market district are tied up at the moment and may never come to save you." Steven is trying to sound pleasant the entire time he's threatening to destroy us. Classy, "I know you're down there, Sam Cutter." I stiffen up. How does he specifically know I'm here? Has he been looking for me? "Come up now, and nobody will be hurt. That is, if you do as I say." Come up where? As I'm asking myself that question, a giant airship turns on its running lights. I have to shield my face from the light. I'm sure everyone else caught in the light has to do the same. Dac doesn't. He just keeps looking at it.

"It's big," is all he says.

"Thanks, Sherlock," I say back, squinting, trying to get a look at the hulking beast for myself. I can't see much about it, but it looks like a giant ship. It's not a transport, it's more heavily armed than a transport. This is more like a flying battleship. It's elongated, but not super thin.

"Those are forbidden," I hear Jinn yell from across the yard. I doubt he was trying to yell to me, but I still hear it.

"Fly inside, Sam Cutter," Steven orders again, "Escorts will be waiting for you inside. Don't try to fight. Much less messy that way."

"Don't do it Sam!" Jinn yells. He hops on his bike and starts to drive it towards me. He must be ready to drop by now. Everyone looks like if they need to even lift their arms they'll be ready to lay down and die. I can't ask that of them.

Even if I know it's not going to end up well for me, I have to go. It'll give us a way to know what's going on.

Keep me posted on what's going on down here, and keep us in touch. I tell Dac in my head. I doubt Steven can hear me from inside his battleship, but better safe than sorry.

Can do. I won't even tell them some of the really embarrassing stuff. He's inspiring as always. I shrink my sword down and shove it in my pocket. I prepare to fight

405

to turn my boots on, but they kick on instantly. While hovering I turn around and look at Dac.

"Did you do that?" I ask.

"No," he says, "If you've been having issues with them, perhaps they simply function better when we're closer to each other." Sure, or maybe I'm just so over it right now, that the shoes do not want to piss me off.

An interesting theory, but I don't think your shoes are sentient. I almost bring up that he was in the shoes until pretty much just now, but I decide to drop it for the moment. I turn around and fly up towards the warship, flying away before Jinn gets to me. As I get closer, I see and hear a giant hatch open as well as hear my friends yelling for me to come back, and stop what I'm doing. I'm guessing the hole's where I'm supposed to go. I fly into the hole.

Once I'm inside the ship, lights are on and I can see at least ten goons waiting in this room for me. They all have their electrical staffs pointed right at me.

"Hello boys," I say, hovering, "Have you been waiting for me?" As usual, I get nothing out of them.

"Follow us," one of them says. The hatch closes below me with an echoing thud. I land on top of it. Without another word, the New Power troops start walking. They keep in a bubble like formation, keeping me in the middle. We pass through a bunch of halls and a couple rooms with more than a few twists and turns. I try to keep track of where I've been, but lose track very quickly. While we're walking, we pass a lot of New Power goons. This does not look good. There might be more people in here than there were attacking Jinn's house a minute ago. After I'm thoroughly paraded around by my ten escorts, we end in a large chamber.

There are a couple goons at different stations. I'm guessing they're controlling the ship. It makes sense that more than one person is required to pilot this beast. Close to the back, in the center of the room, sits Steven. What he's sitting on looks almost like a throne. There are a few steps leading up to the chair, and the chair itself looks ridiculous, in my opinion anyway. Steven is wearing a suit like he was before. Why is he wearing a suit while he's attacking us? Who cares if he looks like a sharp dressed nutcase?

"Samuel," of course he opens with the full name, "good to see that you have decided to join me today."

"I'm not joining you," I say. My escorts step apart and take positions along the walls of the room. At least I have a little breathing room now.

"Maybe not yet," Steven says, "But you are here with me now." I guess he has me there.

"What do you want?" I ask impatiently.

"I have decided to be generous," Steven says, sitting back in his seat and crossing his legs, "I have decided to offer you a place in my rule. Think hard." This again? I pretend to think hard for a minute before I say anything.

"I think I'm still going to have to turn you down. Can I go now?" I say arrogantly. I should probably be nicer to the guy that's holding me captive.

You never use your brain though, Dac says in my head.

What's the news down there. What's going on?

Everybody is banged up, but your dad is the only one that's out. One boy is inside crying, but Rose said she would go talk to him. She hasn't left though. Everybody wants to see what the New Power wants with you. So my dad is out cold and Todd is inside crying like a baby. That sounds about right.

Keep them posted, but don't give all the details. I tell Dac, *What do you know about this ship?* I ask him as an after thought. Maybe I can take it down. I am in the command room.

"I wasn't asking you a question, boy," spits Steven, bringing me back to were I am, "You will join me with undying loyalty, and I can assure that it will be. I have my ways," he adds the last part like he can read my mind. I don't want to end up like Armando. Mind control doesn't seem so fun. "Or I will destroy all you hold dear. I will unleash my forces on this location, and those that are cleaning up the mess in the market district will join us shortly after."

Jinn just got a call saying otherwise, Dac says in my

head, *Gerund just called him to say that they won and after a little damage control, they'll be over here as soon as they possibly can.* That's still not fast enough to help.

"Really," I say to Steven, "*You're* on clean up duty? Last I heard you lost that fight." A scowl comes across Steven's face like he's ready to jump at me. Guess his little ruse has been spoiled. Steven pushes himself up from his chair, trembling with rage. I'm really good at making friends, aren't I? He takes off his suit jacket, carefully placing it on his chair. He starts rolling his sleeves up as he walks down the steps leading to his chair to stand before me.

"Hold him!" Steven barks halfway down the steps. Immediately two of the larger goons in the room surge forward and grab my arms. I try jerking myself free, but they have a really firm grip. It almost feels like they're bruising my arms just by holding them. Steven ends directly in front of me. He looks me straight in the eyes, and I don't look away. I jerk on the two goons holding me a couple more times, but I can't get loose.

"You don't know when to shut up do you, boy?" The last word is cut short because Steven decided it's a good time to punch me in the stomach. My lungs let out all their air when Steven hits me. I bend over, but the guys holding me don't let me fall to my knees. It takes a second, but I get my feet back under me.

"Ouch," I say, not willing to give him anything.

"Are you prepared to die for your cause?" Steven asks me, putting his face close to mine. Not really, but my answer may send mixed messages. Instead of speaking, I head-butt Steven. Nobody wins with head-butts. I want to try and hold my head where I hit him, but I don't want to show Steven that what I did hurt me as well. At least it had the intended effect. Steven backs up a few steps, holding his head.

"Insolent child!" Steven yells when he stops complaining that his head hurts, "On his knees," he orders his guards. I'm forced down on to my knees and held there. I try and shake free again, but the guards still have a freakishly good grip. Steven looks at me, fuming, but knowing better than to get close again, "You just don't know when to quit, do you boy?" Steven spits at me. I open my mouth for a response, but before I can say anything, Steven slugs me in the side of the head. When he connects, his lackeys let go of me, letting me fall to my side. I want to cry, but I don't. Steven kicks me in the side for good measure and my tear resistance is really put to the test.

"Pilot," Steven yells, turning his back on me, "Angle the ship so that that entire pathetic platform is in view of forward cannons." I look to see who it is that's controlling this entire hulk, "Gunman, arm forward cannons. The rest of you, get to battle stations." I'm no expert, but I would say that's very bad news.

Do you want me to evacuate everyone, Sam? I know it'll take a few minutes to arm those cannons. It'll be enough time to get everyone out. Dac asks me mentally.

No, not yet, I respond, *I have an idea. If it starts to go wrong, then get everybody out of there.*

I know what your idea is. Are you sure it's going to work? Dac asks. I knew he would read my mind.

I have no idea, but I have to try. I get up off the floor, bringing my focus back to where I am. I have no doubt that this will suck either way. Steven's back is turned and he's walking back to his seat, so mister alert has no idea that I'm up. I come up behind the pilot of the ship while he's working. I pull out my Sky Iron sword, extending it to full length and drive it into the control consol. I see an electrical current jumping along the length of the blade, but it never makes it to the hilt.

"Are you insane?" The pilot screams, jumping away from the controls.

"Probably," I say, twisting my sword around and dragging it through the machinery.

"Stop!" The same guy screams again, trying to pull me away from the console, "Stop, you'll sink the whole ship."

"That's the plan."

Chapter Twenty-Eight

Someone else comes up behind me and grabs my shoulder, spinning me around, "You never learn, do you?" Impatiently and angrily asks Steven.

"You know, my parents and the factory drivers both told me that for the longest time." Steven's eyes become huge, like I told him another big secret.

"You," he says, "you're the boy from the Surface." I'm not sure if his tone more says it like a fact, or if he's accusing me. "Is that why you're special? Do the Ravens know?" He starts spitting out questions like he just can't ask enough, "Tell me!" he demands. I don't get a chance to answer before someone yells something in the room.

"Sir, the ship's going down," it distracts Steven for a bit, he gets away from me to bark commands.

"Can it be saved?" he asks.

"With the guns charging, no. I'm afraid it's too late," Steven swears under his breath.

"Abandon ship," he yells, "Sound the alarm, get

everyone to abandon ship!" Someone hits a button and an alarm starts ringing. A message comes over a loud speaker telling everyone to abandon ship and head to the transport bay for immediate evacuation. Nearly everyone in this room sprints out as fast as they can. The only people left in here are Steven and me. Steven is still facing away from me and breathing heavily. His breaths are shaky and a little uneven, but I get the point. He's mad.

Steven unexpectedly whirls around at me, screaming. He catches me by the shirt and looks me dead in the eyes, pulling me close even though I might head-butt him again. I won't though because I might actually be scared of this guy right now, "You cost me much, *child*. Unfortunately, we cannot finish our business today, but I assure you, one day soon, we will. It is fortunate for you that my masters have an interest in you. I warn you, do not make an enemy of me." When he's done speaking, he throws me to the floor. I land right where he kicked me so I stay down for a bit.

I see, through squinted eyes, Steven take off running. I don't get back up until he's long gone. When I get back on my feet, one thought goes through my head, "Masters?" I ask aloud. My thoughts and wondering are interrupted when I hear footsteps rushing towards me. It's only one set so I've got that going for me at least. I draw my sword out of the control panel and aim it at the passageway that I hear the footsteps coming from. A lone New Power grunt comes running out of the corridor into the room I'm in.

"What are you still doing here boy?" he asks me, "The ship's falling out of the sky!" I didn't think about that when I decided this was a good idea.

"I know," I half lie, "I'm the one who did it." I hope what I said will intimidate the guy, but it doesn't even come close to working.

"I know," he says, "I saw you do it."

"So what do you plan to do?" I ask, expecting that we're going to have to fight.

"Save the ship," he says simply.

"And how are you going to do that?" I ask, "I destroyed the controls with the canons charging; there's no hope."

"So you bought that lie?" The mystery goon says, "Good, that means the idiots did too." Wait, what?

"Wait, who are you?" I ask. He talks about the New Power like he's against them, but he sure looks like one of them.

"I don't blame you for not recognizing me," he says, "You only knew me for a few minutes. Maybe this'll jog your memory; do you remember the three rules?" No way.

"Mr. Friendly?" I ask. It can't be the same guy that told John and me what to do to be rescued from the arena when we first came up here.

"My real name is Davis, but yes, I do recall you and your friend calling me that." I'm so shocked by seeing this guy again that I don't speak until the ship lurches to one side, making the fact that the ship's going down more obvious. I shrink my sword down and put it in my pocket.

"To answer your earlier question," Davis says, "I plan to turn the cannon off. The ship will stay in more or less one piece and I'll check with Kane to see if I can get it later."

"Who's Kane?" I ask. I can honestly never say I've heard that name before.

"Nathan's brother," Davis says as he starts messing with the controls for the cannon. It takes me as long as he takes to finish turning the cannons off to put two and two together.

"Kane is the king of the Water Nation," I blurt out, confident that my answer is correct.

"Bingo," Davis says. The ship lurches again, "We should probably go now," he says. I nod and we take off running. I have no idea where I'm going, so I trust Davis and follow him for a while. As we round a corner, Davis has to pass through a doorway. Before I can get through, the door slams shut. I run headlong into it. Davis is oblivious to the fact that I'm not right behind him. So much for going this way. I bang on the door in frustration and take off running in a different direction.

I run into more closed doors as I go, but I make it past some. I have no idea if I'm going the right way, but even when my body screams for air and rest, I keep pushing. I sprint through the halls, desperate to find a way out. I hear a creaking slip through the halls. I don't know what that sound means, but I have no doubt that it is not good. A few seconds later, I find out what the noise was. My feet leave the ground and I'm thrown against the ceiling. The engines have completely given out.

"Not good," I say to myself because there is nobody around. I try crawling on the ceiling, but I'm moving way too slow. I try to stand up, see if the ship flipped over, but that doesn't work so well. I get up and I fall again. I crawl again for a bit before I decide to use my brain.

I kick my boots on and they start instantly. Maybe they weren't working so well before because Dac and I weren't connected.

I fly to the center of the hall and take off. I have to slow down, grab walls, and push off when I take corners, but other than that, I'm flying as fast as I possibly can. I still don't know if I'm going the right way, but I have to trust that it is.

Eventually I come to a large, rectangular, open room. I'm the only one in it. Along the walls there are openings on either side. Guess this is my way out. I fly to one of the openings and get out. My exit was on the side of the ship. It feels like the thing is going to roll on top of me any second now. I push hard and fast to avoid any debris falling with the ship, and parts of it that might smack me on the way out.

Once I'm out, I twist and fly up. I look around and see that I'm not exactly in the Sky Nation anymore, nor is it dark. It's daylight. I can make out buildings and landscapes and mountains. I'm back at the Surface. I almost pause my ascent when I hear a giant splash. I look below me while still flying up to see the warship crash into the water. The splash of water is so huge that it licks at my heels. I watch the water sink back down to the earth before I turn again and put everything into flying.

I fly into clouds. My vision is a total whitewash until I burst out of the clouds. I see the bottom of some platforms. I keep flying. I'm almost there, no stopping now. I fly up to Jinn's platform and land in the front yard. I see that the fires have either been put out or burned themselves out.

"Sam!" I hear almost everyone yell simultaneously. I'm pretty sure I hear Arthur yell, "Boy!" but I know that that's about as affectionate as he gets. Everyone runs over to me and I'm tackled by a few of them with a giant group hug. I try to stay standing, but it doesn't work so well. Jinn, Mark, Arthur, Dac, Charley, and Jackson are the ones still standing. I don't see Todd anywhere. Can't say I mind. I don't see my dad either. I guess he must still be out.

"We thought you bit the bullet," Rick says.

"Ya, we saw you go up into that ship and then it started going down." Fred adds.

"Good to see you still in one piece," John says. Rose doesn't say anything; she just tightens her grip.

"I knew he'd be fine," Jinn says.

"Is that why you ran to the edge of the platform over there," Mark asks, slapping Jinn on the back. "We had to hold him down to prevent him from flying off to try and save you." Thanks? Dac gives me a stern robot look.

I didn't mention anything about the end of your conversation with Steven. It didn't seem like an appropriate thing to do. Dac says in my head.

Thanks, I say back, *I don't know what to make of any of it yet. I just need some time to think it through.* Dac gives me a nod.

"So you made it," says someone walking up so that I can see them.

"Mr. Friendly!" I say. Everyone standing turns and looks at Davis, trying not to laugh.

"I thought you were toast, kid," Davis says, "I didn't realize I'd lost you until I found a Sky Bike to get away on."

"It's okay," I say, "I'm still here, aren't I?"

418

"Does this mean you still get free supplies at my shop?" Arthur says. How caring of him.

"What, Sam gets free goods?" Mark asks.

"I made a bet with Arthur," Jinn tells him.

"Unbelievable," Mark says. Jinn launches into the whole story with Arthur grumbling and adding his own details as Jinn goes. I like how easily everything returns to normal. The fight's over, so we talk about how I get free stuff from Arthur.

Now that I've slowed down, the adrenaline is starting to wear off. When I was fighting, I knew when I got hurt, but I didn't feel anything. I'm sure feeling it now. I'm more than a little sore, and if the entirety of my skin doesn't turn purple tomorrow, I will be genuinely surprised. I wince from the pain. Either nobody notices, or nobody cares. After lying there for a while in pain but happy, I grudgingly decide that it's time to get up.

"Hey, can someone help me up," I ask. Everyone climbs off me and Jinn helps me up. As soon as I'm on my feet, I stumble and Jinn needs to catch me. I give an embarrassed smile.

"Alright, we got you," Mark says, he and Jinn putting my arms over their shoulders, "Let's go inside." Everyone starts to shuffle towards Jinn's house, which, other than a couple scars, still stands.

Before we reach the front door, I hear something. I stop in my tracks and look where I hear the sound

419

coming from. Staring me square in the face is something I really don't want to see. A transport. It's a normal size one, but still, not good.

"What now," I say aloud.

Chapter Twenty-Nine

Hearing what I said, everybody else also stops and looks. I can tell that everyone is too tired to keep fighting, but it looks like we don't have much of a choice. We get ready to stand our ground. Jinn and Mark step back so that I'm supporting myself again. It isn't as bad as I initially thought it was. Still isn't pleasant though. Those of us that haven't dropped our swords are preparing to draw them. The more I look at the transport, the more confused I get. It looks less and less like a New Power transport, and more like a luxury cruiser. What's the deal here? The ship directly approaches our platform, but doesn't start attacking. I can tell I'm not the only one confused because everyone that has been a Raven longer than I have starts acting like something is up.

I don't know how there is still room with all the wreckage, but somehow, the transport finds space to land in Jinn's front yard. I guess nobody likes using the dock. Now that the ship is close, I get a better look at it. The ship is parked so that the side is facing us. It's actually not huge. It's a seemingly standard sized ship, but it looks like it's built better for comfort. Its outside is similar to the ship that Mark and Jinn picked me up in when I first came up here.

A hatch on the side opens up and becomes a ramp. Three people walk out of the transport. A man who looks like he's in his early twenties, a woman in her late twenties or thirties, and a more elderly looking man. Even though the elderly looking man is old, he doesn't truly look *that* old. He still stands up tall, is muscular, and has an aura of poise and self-confidence around him. The older man has a short, almost stubble-like, grey-black beard. The three of them walk towards us. They stop a short distance away and give me a weird look. The younger guy raises his eyebrows at me. I stare them down, not willing to back down.

"Sam, get down," Jinn says hushed behind me. I turn around to talk to him, but what I see surprises me. Because everyone was behind me, I didn't see them, but they're all kneeling. Everyone is on one knee with their right fist over their heart and their heads bowed. Even John, Rick, and Fred are bowing. They probably just went along with what everyone else did. Even Arthur shut up and bowed. Dac is also on his knee. He could've told me. Oh well. I turn back around and act like my typical self. I refuse to kneel. No way I'm giving these guys a victory. I can't be sure that they're not New Power.

"Sam, what are you doing," Jinn pesters. The youngest of the three, the younger boy, walks right up to me. He's wearing a semi-scowl on his face that doesn't look like it belongs anywhere near it. He looks like he's normally a happy person.

"Do you know who you're dealing with?" he asks.

"Some guy that showed up late to the party," I say back. I lock eyes with him and see something familiar there. What is it?

"Are you trying to take the throne?" He asks me. Throne, what? Isn't that what he's trying to do?

"Oh give it a rest," the girl says to him, "You're not going to be able to stop yourself from laughing much longer. I see you shaking." Now that she says that, I look at his face. What I thought was a scowl is really the look of someone trying to keep from laughing. I look at the guy, confused. Without warning, he starts cracking up.

Who is this guy? I think to Dac.

I don't know, he says back. It's the answer I expected, but it was good to bounce the question off of somebody who's just as clueless as I am. The guy quickly regains control of himself and stands up straight, for the most part, serious again.

"I'm sorry," he says, "But I wanted to see the look on

Jinn here's face." The weird guy's companions just sigh and shake their heads. "I don't believe we've met, have we?" I shake my head. Is this guy insane? "Well in that case," he says, "my name's Nathan."

"Wait a minute," I say, "Nathan like Nathan, king of the Sky Nation?" This is him? He's so goofy. I thought he would be really serious and straitlaced, and he's not.

"That's me," he says. The two people Nathan came with look like they're used to him acting this way.

"My Lord," Jinn says from his knee, "I have been faithfully defending your throne since you left." Nathan sighs.

"Jinn, how many times do I have to tell you? You don't have to use any title. Just call me by my name," Nathan says to Jinn.

"Have you two known each other for a while?" I ask. I've only seen the way one king rules first hand, and let me say, it wasn't pleasant. Nathan just seems so carefree.

"We've known each other for a while now," Nathan says, "Jinn is one of my captains of the guard." I look at Jinn, expecting him to look proud, but he is like a statue. That would explain why Jinn is so good at what he does and has such a big house. "I don't even know why I have a guard. There isn't much violence at all up here." I look at him like he's insane. Does he not see the wreckage around this platform? "Until recently, it seems," he says, correcting himself. "What happened here? And get off your knees everybody, it's ridiculous." As everybody stands up, Jinn starts to launch into an explanation of what happened last night. I'm guessing that Nathan will need a full explanation, but Jinn's thankfully not giving that right now. After Jinn finishes his description, Nathan finally says something.

"So it sounds like you were pretty important," he says to me. I shrug modestly, "What's your name?" He asks me.

"Sam," I say, "Sam Cutter." I stick out my hand. I don't know how you're really supposed to introduce yourself to a monarch, but this seems like a good start. He smiles and shakes my hand. He looks me in the eye at first, but his eyes slide down to my neck. I wonder what he's looking at because I don't have anything interesting right there.

"Well, would you look at that," Nathan says, releasing my hand. "Hey sis, it looks like I found your necklace." Sis? I grab at my neck and feel that my necklace fell out of my shirt at some point. I can't say I'm surprised after everything that happened. The fact that I still have it is kind of a shock.

"That's impossible," the girl who came with Nathan says. She walks over and also looks at my neck, "Or maybe not."

"What is or apparently isn't impossible?" I ask them,

confused by what they're talking about.

"You have my sister's old necklace," Nathan tells me. The girl reaches into her shirt and pulls something out. Dangling from her hand, still around her neck is a necklace. The same one around my neck. Pause, rewind. Sister?

"You're the fourth child!" I say. I haven't read those stories about the kings in forever, how do I remember them so well? It's been close to ten years. I guess because it's such a common topic, at least on the Surface, it's hard to ever forget. She laughs innocently at my random comment.

"Yes, that would be me," she says, "My name's Sarah. It never goes in any books, so I need to remind people all the time."

"Nice to meet you," I say. I'm meeting people I've only read about and dreamed of. This is insane. "How- how do I have your necklace? You can have it back if you want," I say while going for the clasp on the back of my neck.

"No, no, no, don't worry about it," Sarah says, touching my arm, "Keep it. It was passed down to you, wasn't it?"

"Y- yeah. My mom gave it to me." That's so embarrassing. Why would I say that to a super legend like this?

"Then it's rightfully yours. Do you know the story

behind it?" Sarah asks me. I shake my head. "It's a short story really. I gave it to my daughter when she was about your age. It's been passed down ever since then as soon as the current holder's child is about fifteen."

"What does that mean about me?" I ask. She said she gave it to her daughter and that it's been passed down. What's that suggesting?

"It means that I'm your some number of greats grandmother, but don't you dare call me grandma." I about want to faint. How is this possible? I'm just a kid from the Surface, nothing special about me. There's never been anything special about me. Well, I did win a hotdog-eating contest once, but that's it.

"Are you sure?" I ask, disbelief hanging heavy in my heart.

"When I designed those necklaces for my children," the older man says, stepping forward, arms behind his back, "I made it so that only they or someone from their direct family could wear it. They couldn't steal each other's. It would fall off. The fact that it is around your neck is proof that you are family." Family?

"Dad has a way with tools," Nathan says. Dad? Man I am slow today. It takes a minute, but I put it together. My eyes bulge wide with realization, "Hey, look who gets it!" Nathan says, throwing his arms out wide. "Your grandkid is kind of stupid." Nathan says to Sarah.

"Y-you-you're-" I start stuttering. The man puts a

gentle smile on his face, amused by my inability to speak.

"I have had many names," he says, "I have been called Man, Mutant, Conqueror, King, Savior, Destroyer, Uniter, and many others, but perhaps my favorite is father. Because I feel old enough," he continues with a chuckle to himself, "I don't want you calling me anything of the such. You are family, but I would prefer you call me by my name, Gabriel."

"Y-yes sir," I stutter. Gabriel gives me a funny look, "Gabriel," I say, correcting myself. "Yes Gabriel."

"There we go," he says with a smile, "How long have you had that stutter?" He asks.

"I don't have a stutter," I say.

"Oh? You've had one for the majority of our discussion," Gabriel says.

"It's just that you guys are some of my idols. I've only read about you in story books, and now you're standing right in front of me," I explain. It's embarrassing, but I don't want to look like a total idiot to these guys. Gabriel looks back at his children.

"That might be one of the nicest things anyone has ever said about us," Nathan says. The three of them smile and turn back to me.

"Wait, you said you have a necklace too?" I ask Nathan, changing the subject.

"Sure do," he says, digging in his shirt. He pulls out

a necklace similar to mine, but different. His is a round yellow crystal surrounded by a gear.

"Why is it different?" I ask.

"I made a different one for each of my children," Gabriel explains. I nod in understanding. So all four children have different necklaces. It would be interesting if I ever got to see all of them. I realize that I've been quiet probably too long and clear my throat awkwardly loud.

"Here's what I don't understand," Sarah says, thankfully filling the silence, "How are you up here? Last I knew, that necklace and my decedents were on the Surface."

"I kind of came up here against the rules," I say.

"So you're the boy from the Surface," Rose says behind me. I turn around so I can see her, "You saved my dad before." I shrug.

"That was me. I guess Mark and Jinn did most of the work, but I refused to leave without everyone," I say, "I'm not the only one from the Surface you know." I get confused looks all around.

"Have you not been telling people about us Sammy?" Fred says, standing up. George and John also rise and walk over to me.

"We may be up here," John says, "but it was all Sam's doing." I suddenly find my feet very interesting. Not many people try to say nice things about me. John looks at me with a grin on his face, "So I guess you're kind of like a prince now, huh?" I didn't think of that. I turn around and look back to Nathan, Sarah, and Gabriel. Gabriel nods.

"What the boy says is true. Even though my children and I may never die, so you will not be a full king. As a descendent of my daughter, you are a prince." I take a step back to prevent myself from falling. John, Rick, and Fred all need to grab onto me as well. Me? A prince? That's really impossible. I subtly pinch myself. Nope, I'm really awake.

"Oh Jinn, what are you doing that for," Nathan asks. I turn around and look at Jinn. He's again bowed, and I assume that he's bowed for Gabriel or someone.

"My Prince," he says from his knee. Well there's something you don't hear everyday. I squat down so that my face is level with Jinn's while he's on his knee.

"Jinn?" I say.

"Yes, my Lord?" This is awkward.

"Don't ever call me that again," I say, "And please don't bow to me. In all the time you've known me you've never done that. No need to start now."

"Well I'm not starting ever," Arthur says, "You were snot nosed then and you're snot nosed now." Charming. Will nothing change him?

"That goes for all of you," I say to everyone, standing up, "If any of you call me 'prince,' we're going to have a problem on our hands. Sam works just fine." Everyone nods, and grumbles their agreement. Nathan's phone rings. Kings have phones? I guess that makes sense.

"Excuse me," he says, walking a short distance away to answer his phone. Sarah and her father join Nathan. I wonder what's going on. As I'm making up reasons for Nathan's call, John interrupts my not-so-deep process of making things up.

"Dude," he whispers to me only loud enough that he, Rick, Fred, and I can hear it, "Punk rock chic, punk rock chic." It's obvious that he's staring at Rose. John always did have an obsession with girls. He even made up classifications and taught them to me, "Go after her," he says, "I've had the last twenty or so, it's your turn." I smile.

"Twenty isn't even close," I whisper back to John. Rick and Fred laugh. I'm not as close to them as I am John, but they do know about his love of women.

"Hey, baby," says Todd, coming out of Jinn's house. It looks like he even fixed his hair while he was hiding, "We were one hell of a team, weren't we? Now I know that I did most of the work, but I'll let you say that you did half." He drapes his arm over her shoulders and taps her on the nose. Please tell me that she isn't buying this. She was even there.

"Oh Todd, you're so sweet," Rose says giving him a hug and kiss. I'm not sure my mouth could drop any lower unless it had a drill to go to the center of the earth.

"Ouch, sorry buddy," John says, patting me on the shoulder, "Better luck next time." I smile, even though I don't feel like smiling.

He's kind of a dick, Dac says in my head. I smile for real. John's my friend, but I have to agree with the one stuck inside my head. I look over all my friends, and Todd, and see that they're all starting to be happy. Kind of a weird feeling after last night. I look to Nathan and see that he's off the phone and walking back over.

"Nathan," Jinn starts, "Where have you been for the past ten years?" There's the golden question.

"Visiting my dad," he says. Who visits their parents for ten years and treats it like a casual visit? I guess Nathan isn't dying any time soon, so anything seems like a casual visit. "By pure chance Sarah here happened to be there." Jinn looks satisfied with the answer. I still find it confusing, but I guess it works. "That was Kane that just called me," Nathan continues explaining, "Something's going on down there. I should probably check it out. Would you be okay if I disappeared for a little longer?" Seriously? He's been gone for ten years and he plans to disappear again after one day?

"What's another few days," Jinn says. He's handling this much better than I would. I would probably be screaming at Nathan and be totally pissed off.

"What about you, kid?" Nathan asks, turning to me, "How're you feeling? This too much for you?" I shake my head.

"I'm actually doing alright," I say, "As different as this all is, somehow it seems totally normal." He smiles, and it's true. When I first decided to come up here I wasn't expecting any of this at all. I expected to maybe find my dad and get my mom up here. Instead, I found myself a whole new family. Only a few of them are by blood, and everyone isn't exactly loving towards each other, but it's still good. I smile to myself. I couldn't have pictured anything better happening.

"Oh shit," I say, coming to a realization, "We have to go get mom."

End Book One

Keep reading to check out the first chapter of the second book of the Three Kingdoms Trilogy, *Water Tower*!

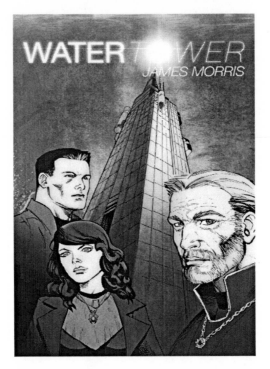

Available *now!*

www.JamesMorrisBooks.com

Prologue

Ten years. That's how long it has been since anyone has journeyed to the Sky Nation. For these ten long years life on the Surface has been deteriorating with death rates increasing, tyranny strengthening, and depression blanketing the broken land. It became so bad that a boy of only fifteen years old was driven to do anything to escape this harsh reality.

About two months ago the boy escaped the Surface. Boarding a transport along with his best friend and two others he successfully traveled to the Sky Nation. In spite of being separated temporarily early in their journey, the four managed to reunite later, only to learn that the Sky Nation was in the midst of a revolution. All of them were recruited to help protect the land from being taken over by evil forces.

The same young boy who had rebelled on the Surface fought with uncommon valor against those threatening the Sky Nation. He is the reason it still stands. The forces trying to overtake the Sky Nation are dumbfounded and terrified by this boy's defiance and willingness to fight. And now, the battle is only getting bigger.

"How is it that one boy can thwart all our plans?" grumbles a man from his seat upon a throne.

"I'm sorry, Master," a man standing before the throne apologizes weakly, bowing so low he nearly kisses the floor. "The boy was an unforeseen obstacle. I didn't know what to do."

"Of course you didn't," snaps the man on the throne. He sounds more than slightly disgusted. His tone exudes power and demands control. "Regardless of the fact, you should have been able to outsmart a simple schoolboy."

"My deepest apologies, Master," says the man on the floor, bowing even lower. "I won't let it happen again. I will go back and dispose of the boy immediately."

"And what makes you think you can?" asks the other, pushing himself up from his seat. He walks methodically towards the bowing man, clearly in no rush. He alone decides his pace, another demonstration that all others are subordinate to him.

Steven, the bowing man, begins to feel a force which grows stronger as his master draws nearer. An aura of raw power that exudes from him, creeping along the walls and floors seeking to dominate and consume. In the dimness of the throne room, Steven can almost see black tendrils reaching out to him.

"I will repeat myself only once," says the master, now standing above Steven. "What makes you think that you can take down the Surface boy, or even stand against him?" His voice mocks and antagonizes.

Steven, without looking up, starts to fabricate an answer in his mind, but the words catch in his throat making him sound as if he's choking out half-formed thoughts.

"Sir," he finally manages to say, "how could you presume that I would be incapable of being a match for a mere schoolboy?" His voice cracks.

"I have no evidence to think otherwise," retorts the other. "You have yet to answer my question, Steven."

"My deepest apologies, Master," repeats Steven. As the blanket of malevolent power creeps ever closer to him, Steven suddenly feels his skin becoming itchy. So much so that scratching it off seems the only relief. "I can handle the boy *because* he is just a boy. Because he is just a babbling little fool. Because..."

"You had legions," the master breaks in, raising his voice, "and yet, he was able to defeat you. The boy is more than just a 'babbling little fool'. If he is, then your incompetence must truly be boundless."

"My apologies, my Master," Steven utters yet again, making a motion to get down on his knees. But as he is dropping, his dominator speaks again.

"Stop your groveling. You have failed me thus far, and no amount of whimpering will change that."

Steven stands up straight. The master walks closer to him, forcefully grabs his jaw in his hand, and jerks Steven's head to look directly into his eyes. "You assured me that the Sky Nation was within your grasp, and that there was only a small, broken resistance."

"They were. There was!" Steven exclaims as best he can with his jaw in the iron grasp of his master. He starts to panic. "The boy must have revitalized them. He broke soldiers out of the rehabilitation center. That must have increased their numbers." For an instant, Steven knows he has said the right thing, and some relief crosses his face. Yet a deep scowl remains on his master's face.

"How can I forget?" his dominator spits out. Pulling Steven's face closer to his own, he hisses, "You lost nearly all our prisoners."

A realization of the magnitude of his failure shows in Steven's expression. But still, he *must* make his master understand.

"It was the boy," he says. "We had him, and he seemed to be submitting, but it turned out to be a trick."

"So a simple boy defies me and outsmarts you." The master's voice has dropped to barely a whisper, sending a shiver down Steven's spine. Steven can't even produce a syllable in response and his eyes are met with a cold glare. Dark claws are reaching out to Steven, who hopes this is just his imagination. Terrified, he feels like he is about to scratch his skin off for real. Beads of cold sweat cover his forehead.

"Master," Steven pleads, holding the claws at bay. "Please, give me another chance. I will not fail you again. I will crush those who stand in your way, and take for you what you desire."

"I have nearly all I desire already," Steven's master says, glowering at his underling. "All I want now is for you to clean up your mess and stop the boy!"

"The boy is nothing but a Surface rat..."

"Which makes him all the more dangerous," the master roars as he abruptly pushes his captive away. Stumbling and falling, Steven rubs his jaw while the other continues his tirade.

"How long has the boy been unwittingly opposing me? How long has he been the thorn in my side?" Steven's master seems genuinely curious and distraught about this. It's a topic he has been thinking long and hard about.

"I don't understand," Steven says, standing up, "The boy has only just arrived." His master's face reflects that he is beyond enraged.

"Before the boy came up, we were experiencing challenges on the Surface." The master's voice is tight with frustration. "Refusals to work, manufacturing delays, lags in worker efficiency, attacks on factories. One factory in particular was the focus of all the trouble. I wonder if it was the factory where the boy was registered."

There are always minor shows of insubordination at the factories, but none were as bold, rebellious, and great in number as those at this particular one. It got so bad it appeared this factory would be shut down. The ringleader of the mayhem was never identified. Oddly, though, in the past few months the disturbances have all but disappeared.

Steven wants to ask his master more about the factory problems and offer his services, but for the moment he wisely chooses to hold his tongue. The master becomes more perturbed as he talks and his face appears to deepen in color. He pauses and takes time to compose himself, though all he needs is an instant before he has regained control.

"The boy has been a nuisance like no other. His capacity to defy and irritate me is immeasurable."

"So what do you want, Master?"

As the master returns to his throne and folds his hands over his lap, it feels to Steven as though the dark, powerful aura has filled the entire room. It is a nearly palpable atmosphere, seemingly capable of suffocating everything it envelopes. Caught up in this force, Steven senses it is draining his very will... and his ability to resist the relentless itch! Though he struggles to show no signs of his discomfort, he finally can stand it no longer and scratches his arm, instinctively fighting this malevolent energy trying to claim him.

"I want you to eliminate Samuel Cutter," the master says with an evil smile and murder in his eyes.

www.JamesMorris.com

James has long been in love with the stories told in Science Fiction and Fantasy. A self proclaimed nerd, he proudly lines his room with the books that he loves. *Sky Bound* and *Water Tower* were written while he was in high school, *Surface* was written his sophomore year of college. Along with books, James writes and performs music that he enjoys and hopes others do as well. Raised in San Diego, California, James now lives in Nashville, Tennessee attending college. He typically prioritizes reading and writing over homework.

CPSIA information can be obtained at www.ICGtesting.com
Printed in the USA
BVOW01s1930300916

463858BV00001B/1/P

9 780983 884408